Welcome to t

Welcome to the Free Zone

Nathalie and Ladislas Gara

Translated by Bill Reed

Published by Hesperus Press Limited
28 Mortimer Street, London W1W 7RD
www.hesperuspress.com

Welcome to the Free Zone first published by Hesperus Press Limited, 2013

English language translation, introduction and notes © Bill Reed, 2013

First published in French as *Saint-Boniface et ses juifs* in 1946
© Claire Meljac. All rights reserved.

Designed and typeset by Fraser Muggeridge studio
Printed and bound by CPI Group (UK) Ltd, Croydon, CR0 4YY

ISBN: 978-1-84391-466-2

Contents

Introduction

Welcome to the Free Zone is a translation of *Saint-Boniface et ses Juifs*, published in 1946, by the journalist Ladislas Gara and his wife Nathalie.

When I was introduced to the book, I took it at first for a humorous slant on French country life during the war. But it is much more than that. While the humour ranges from farcical to black (and also turns to tragedy) it soon becomes clear that the situations, characters and events are by no means pure fiction. One of the astonishing things about this work is how two writers of non-French origin – a Hungarian and a Pole – while drawing on their own backgrounds, were also able to weave so much profound French culture into it.

In following up references and allusions while carrying out the translation, I found that many of the hidden messages, despite their light treatment, have deep resonance. During the Occupation, the privations of rationing and the cruelties of bureaucracy affected the whole population, and the authors have woven these into the narrative with such wit and skill that no explanations are needed. The effect is very immediate: I even found myself asking, 'How would I have behaved in this situation?' At the same time, generalisation and stereotype are used very circumspectly, for humorous or ironic effect, and I hope I have been faithful to this in the translation.

As the contemporary political context is significant, I would like to add a few notes on the Vichy Regime, its treatment of the Jews and the implications for some of the characters and events in the book.

On 22nd June 1940, Maréchal Pétain and his Vichy government signed an armistice with Germany. Parts of France were annexed, and the rest was divided into the Occupied and Free Zones, the latter being under Pétain's control. In 1941, a Vichy decree put the whole of France on German time – two hours ahead of the sun. The rural population, however, continued to live by astronomical time. This discrepancy between 'real' and 'imposed' time, alluded to with typical quirky humour right at the beginning of the book, is the first hint that this is a satire of – amongst other institutions – the Vichy Regime.

At the outbreak of war, there were over 300,000 Jews in France, about two thirds of them French-born 'Israelites', highly integrated into French society at all levels, and they are represented in the book by characters like Wolff and Cahen (the Military Medal places Cahen in the august company of Churchill and Eisenhower). Others were 1920s immigrants from Eastern Europe and 1930s refugees from Nazism, like Bloch, Kleinhandler and the Verès family. Many, like Pinkas, had lost their original citizenship.

At first, the Germans sought merely to exclude Jews from the Occupied Zone. But the Vichy Regime became increasingly anti-Semitic. The Statute of Jews introduced on 3rd October 1940, without any German pressure, defined a Jew as someone who had three Jewish grandparents, or two Jewish grandparents and a Jewish spouse – Frank Rosenfeld's resentment of his own grandfather and his desire to marry an Aryan can be seen in this context. His conversion to another faith would be neither here nor there for the French authorities, who were concerned primarily with race, not religion. Foreign Jews could be assigned a forced residence by the Prefect of the department where they lived – a rule found, and turned to his advantage, by Bloch. Like Wolff, French Jews initially considered themselves relatively safe, but legislation deprived them of their rights, too; in 1941 a second statute aimed to remove more Jews from public and professional life: Rosenfeld, for example, has been excluded from his profession. Jew was set against Jew, just like Rosenfeld and Bloch.

Over 75,000 Jews were deported from France, of whom 2,500 returned alive. Another 4,000 died in French concentration camps. It was not until 1995 that a public apology was made, by President Jacques Chirac, for the role of the French authorities in rounding up Jews for deportation and extermination.

Welcome to the Free Zone will inevitably be compared with Irène Némirovsky's *Suite Française*. Written during the Occupation but not published until 2005, Némirovsky's dispassionate and well-crafted work illustrated what France had, by then, officially admitted about the war years, and the book deservedly found a wide and receptive audience.

Had Némirovsky survived the Holocaust, *Suite Française* might have been published in 1946 – the year *Saint-Boniface* actually was published. Appearing long before France was ready to confront the ambiguities and betrayals of the Occupation years, *Welcome to the Free Zone* is one of the earliest works to express the true spirit of the times.

– Bill Reed, 2013

Welcome to the Free Zone

Chapter 1
Round Saint-Boniface in Eighty Minutes

I

Stopping to take a vast man's handkerchief from her bag, Mme Hermelin wiped her steel-rimmed spectacles and blew her nose vigorously.

According to the cracked sundial of Rochefontaine Château, overlooking the village, it was midday. But for strategic and economic reasons quite beyond the comprehension of Saint-Boniface's inhabitants, the clocks in the village, as throughout France, indicated two o'clock in the afternoon: the time a sundial would be showing in Kiev.

Settling her glasses back on her thin sharp nose, the retired tax inspector's wife trotted off again across country as if she had to make up the two hours stolen from her by the Administration. For years now, her angular figure, permanently engaged on some distant errand, had been part of the landscape of Saint-Boniface.

Although over sixty, she retained an elastic stride, like those indestructible Englishwomen who could almost have been modelled on her. But as she picked her way between the clumps of broom and the rivulets in the fields, scrambling over heaps of stones, she looked more like one of the scrawny goats in the bleating herds which capered among the ravines and barren hillsides all year round. Even the sound of their bells was echoed by the jangling of the bunch of keys she always wore at her waist.

On this sixteenth day of May 1942, Mme Hermelin was wearing a new dress. It was made from an offcut of mattress ticking, long considered unsuitable for any other purpose,

3

following the last renewal of her bedding. But after three years of war, in a moment of creative inspiration, it struck her that the blue and grey striped cotton was actually quite attractive, and with typical decisiveness she had immediately had a dress made. The result was indeed strikingly novel, while suitably understated, as became a lady of her standing.

In spite of her new dress, the mattress lady seemed anxious and irritable. Since the previous morning she had been searching high and low for a supply of potatoes. She needed at least 200 kilos to see her season out. For Mme Hermelin, assisted by her 'poor husband' the retired tax inspector, who was partially paralysed and increasingly senile, had turned her villa, Les Tilleuls, into a guest house. She would not wish you to get the wrong idea! It wasn't the sort of establishment which took in guests indiscriminately, or one of those hotels which she had heard would let a room to any passing couple, and which Mme Hermelin could not picture without a shiver of disgust mixed with a vague prurience. No, thank the Lord, nothing like that. Over the summer, Les Tilleuls took in only respectable (that is, undemanding) guests, who made an appropriate payment to their hosts upon departure. This arrangement suited Mme Hermelin down to the ground for, as a sister and mother to church ministers, she knew that even the guardianship of Christ's own grave had been paid for.

So at the beginning of each holiday season, an advertisement was placed in the classified section of the *Nouvelliste* to attract custom to Les Tilleuls.

Over the years, a number of families – though never the same two summers running – had savoured both Mme Hermelin's improving conversation and her house speciality, nettle soup. But in 1940 the tourists had been obliged to make way for a horde of agitated and demanding refugees. Some of the houses in Saint-Boniface had even been requisitioned. The schoolmaster, M. Longeaud, had been forced to suspend lessons so that his pretty whitewashed schoolroom could accommodate a group of refugee children from Paris. The vulgar middle classes had taken over his Lordship's country seat at Rochefontaine. Les Tilleuls, for all its daintiness, had not been spared the invasion. The main rooms had been allocated to a professor from the University of Nancy. The unfortunate mistress of the house had been exiled to an attic room whose comfort she always praised when letting it to tenants. Proudly refusing to share her own kitchen, Mme Hermelin was reduced to cooking her own meals on a spirit stove in a corner of this garret. Embittered by the experience, she took advantage of it to pose as a martyr, the victim of a plot, of a base vengeful scheme by the Maire, a creature known by all to be a godless member of the Front Populaire. 'Look at me,' she told her acquaintances at the Protestant Church, 'you see before you a refugee in her own home!'

At last the professor departed, along with his wife, his five children, his assistant, his servants, and the secretary who Mme Hermelin was convinced must be his mistress. On leaving, he had handed the landlady of Les Tilleuls an envelope containing a sum of money intended to repay her for her trouble. But while everyone in Saint-Boniface, and even in the nearby town of Francheville, knew the extent of the 'pillage', this last unimportant detail remained confidential.

The following spring, Mme Hermelin's eldest son Joseph returned to the fold. Previously a professional army officer, he had been demobilised and appointed Rationing Officer in a departmental depot.

Arriving just before Easter, he found his parents busy spring cleaning. Mme Hermelin, perched on a ladder, was dusting a picture frame, and her husband, dribbling a thread of saliva while his limbs shook spasmodically, was trying to manoeuvre a heavy mattress onto a bed in the middle of the room. Mme Hermelin, in perpetual motion herself, could not bear to see the retired tax-inspector at rest, even though he was three-quarters incapacitated. Every morning, she drew up a timetable which left him not a moment to himself. It was he who had to chop the wood, fetch the water, do the watering, and sweep the rooms, shaking and dribbling as he went. Perhaps his most important mission was to pick the nettles, and chop them up small. This task was generally scheduled for about four in the afternoon, which meant he was unable to put in an appearance at his wife's little get-togethers where she generously offered tea and tisane – but not sugar – to her acquaintances: the notary's wife, the deaconess, the mother of a Francheville tobacconist, and the widow of the Justice of the Peace.

When Joseph asked why there was such a commotion, his mother told him she was putting the house back in order for paying guests. Joseph protested. Unthinkable that the mother of a Rationing Officer, treasurer of the Veterans' Legion to boot, should stoop so low as to run a soup kitchen, as if she were no better than Sarzier, the owner of the Hôtel Panorama!

In a moment of weakness, Mme Hermelin gave in. But she quickly regretted this and, as hotel prices in the Francheville area began to rise, her regrets deepened. So she undertook an intensive letter campaign, with one aim in mind. 'Les Tilleuls must reopen' became her '*Delenda est Carthago*' and she drummed this into both her children with the relentlessness of an advertising agent.

Having used up all her writing paper, she was rewarded with the satisfaction of seeing her son Jérémie, the minister, bow to her superior reasoning. Joseph found himself surrounded, and he too was forced to give way.

And now that she had overcome all resistance, here was a new difficulty, this stupid annoying business of the potatoes.

Heedless of the trees, of their fragrant blossom, and of the greening hills which flashed with golden broom, Mme Hermelin, who had other things on her mind, continued to bound along.

Suddenly she stopped, frowned, and looked around. Nobody in sight. Fifty metres further on there was a turning, but what of it, she'd have time…

On the spot, without even seeking a bush to go behind, she crouched down by the side of the road. For Mme Hermelin was a martyr to her bladder, which frequently caused her to interrupt her walks.

She was still in this position when she heard a man's footsteps behind her. Turning, she saw M. Longeaud, the primary school teacher and clerk to the Maire of Saint-Boniface.

She leapt up smartly, showing not a hint of embarrassment, and inclining her head with all the aplomb of a woman of the world, said, 'Oh I do beg your pardon, Monsieur.'

'Oh, don't mind me!' said the schoolteacher awkwardly. He was still trying to regain his composure when Mme Hermelin continued casually, 'You're just the person I wanted to see. I have something to ask you.'

'What can I do for you?' he said, grudgingly.

He guessed it would be an official matter, and had no desire to offer a roadside consultation, especially to Mme Hermelin who was one of 'the other lot'. In M. Longeaud's view of the world, there were two distinct types of people: those who agreed with him, and the others.

'It's just this,' said Mme Hermelin. 'I'm opening my house to guests again next month and I need at least two hundred kilos of potatoes for my tenants. They're from the city, so of course they'll have ration books. But where will they be accepted, since we're not allowed potato coupons in Saint-Boniface? I know you are a clever and learned man, M. Longeaud.'

7

She spoke quickly, adopting the gracious smile she bestowed on everyone except her housemaids and her 'poor husband'.

M. Longeaud, unmoved by this flattery, assumed the official look he reserved for 'the other lot' when they came to the Mairie to renew their ration books.

'I'm afraid I don't see how I can help you, Madame. Country villages aren't entitled to potato coupons. Your clients will have to go and see if they can be used in Francheville.'

'That's all I need to know. That solves the problem.'

'In order to do that,' continued M. Longeaud imperturbably, 'your clients will first have to have their name removed from their regular supplier's list, then apply for a certificate at the Mairie where they live, have it witnessed by a notary, submit an application to sign up at the Mairie in Francheville, and then put their names down at a greengrocer's there. They may still have some problems as their domicile will be in Saint-Boniface rather than Francheville. But assuming all goes well, they will be entitled to two kilos of potatoes per month. But now I come to think of it, why don't you register your guest house officially? That could be to your advantage when it comes to rations.'

'If you say so,' said Mme Hermelin uneasily, but keeping up her smile. 'I'll have to think about it. The thing is, they're not really tenants, they're more like friends who come to stay with me in the summer... I don't think it would be fair for me to have to pay taxes like a hotel.'

The schoolteacher's thoughts were already elsewhere. He wasn't used to listening to his petitioners for more than a couple of minutes at a time. He had also just been distracted by a noise in the distance.

The sound grew louder. A car was coming up the hill. It would appear at the turning any moment now.

'Excuse me,' he said suddenly.

With one bound he reached the side of the road, threw

himself into the ditch, pulled some branches down on top of himself, and lay flat on his stomach.

Mme Hermelin watched in astonishment. Had the town clerk suddenly taken leave of his senses? It wasn't impossible; he was known to be a heavy drinker as well as an atheist, and the Almighty had a way of visiting violent punishments upon these godless beings.

At that moment, the car rattled past. Its driver, the village Curé, a corpulent man whose puffy face was sweating profusely, acknowledged the retired tax inspector's wife with a courteous wave. The car continued on its way, disappearing towards the presbytery.

A cracking of branches in the ditch signalled M. Longeaud's emergence from his hiding place. He looked rather a mess. His hair was dishevelled, his cheeks were scratched by the brambles, and his clothes were muddy, as there was still water in the ditch from the last rains. Looking anxiously around him, he pointed at the light dust cloud raised by the car and asked warily, 'Who was that?'

'The Curé,' answered Mme Hermelin, gradually getting over her amazement.

'Oh, only him,' said the schoolteacher with a sigh of relief. 'You see, I'm not keen to meet the rationing inspectors. That's why I prefer to… um… make myself scarce.'

Mme Hermelin still didn't understand.

'I've just come back from a district teachers' meeting in Francheville. On the way I stopped at a friend's house and he filled my flask for me. As you know, the transport of wine is prohibited.'

Mme Hermelin realised that under his arm the schoolteacher was clutching a container which would hold about three litres.

'Do you think that would be enough to get you into trouble?'

'You never know!' said the schoolteacher darkly. 'They've

been trying to catch me for ages. And why, you may ask? Because I don't want to see a certain section of the population victimised! They know where my sympathies lie, so they'd like me out of the way. The other day I had a letter asking me if I was sure I wasn't a Jew. I felt like saying to them, I'm afraid I don't have that honour. But if it was true, I would feel very uncomfortable indeed.'

'The Jews are reaping the punishment of the Almighty because they denied the Lord,' said Mme Hermelin sententiously. 'But the day is nigh when they will come to Him. And I myself am soon going to help one of them save his soul.'

M. Longeaud wasn't listening.

'Now it is time to awake, for the day of reckoning is at hand.'

Somewhat ashamed of having overreacted in fright, he was anxious to change the subject.

'You Protestants, you should know better than anyone. The other day Jarraud from the hardware shop was saying right there in Francheville market that we'd have to have another Saint Bartholomew's to restore order. Be warned! Take the Curé. He gets a petrol ration because he covers two parishes and he's secretary to the Farmers' Corporation. As for the Minister, he doesn't get a drop of petrol, and he has to make his rounds on his bicycle.'

M. Longeaud was on home territory now. He prided himself on his diplomatic skills. He had no time for either the Protestants or the Catholics, and enjoyed setting them up against each other, which was not hard to do in a region where memories of the religious wars still ran deep.

Meanwhile Mme Hermelin paid no more attention to him than he had to her plight. One thing only was bothering her: the 200 kilos of potatoes she needed. Longeaud was obviously no use at all, so that put an end to the matter.

She pulled out the watch she carried on a silver chain and

consulted it. 'Oh! It's nearly half past two,' she said. 'I'm already late. Goodbye, M. Longeaud.'

Turning away from the schoolteacher, she took off uphill on a side track.

She had decided to pay a visit to the hamlet of La Barbarie, and she would not leave until she had wrested a few kilos of potatoes from one of the farmers.

Ten minutes later, after crossing the ocean of mud and manure which formed a moat around La Barbarie, she reached the home of the Legras family.

II

The Legras family lived in a big house on the outskirts of La Barbarie, some way from the rest of the hamlet. Legras was a farmer by birth but a carpenter by vocation, and in the good old times before the war, when petrol in France flowed like milk and honey, you could hear his machines from afar. Nowadays, that background hum of modern times was replaced by the archaic rasp of the saw and the jarring scrape of the plane.

Mme Hermelin walked past the great outbuilding where Legras had set up his workshop, and entered the house without so much as a knock on the door. Within, a respectful silence reigned. In fact the visitor had arrived at a moment of great solemnity: with the pride of a young mother bathing her first-born, Mme Legras was submerging a great slab of butter in a large bowl of cold water.

Panicking at the sound of the door, she snatched a washtub cover up from the floor and flung it on top of the bowl. Too late! In a split second, Mme Hermelin's prying little eyes had seen everything.

'Aha! So you're making butter, my dear Delphine,' she

exclaimed, greedy and malicious at the same time. She casually removed the lid, ran her index finger across the slab of butter and brought it to her lips. 'My compliments! It tastes delicious!'

Delphine Legras had turned bright red. A short, stocky woman of indeterminate age, she had the prematurely worn-out appearance of all the local farmers' wives. Her untidy hair was held in place by a black headscarf which covered her ears and finished in a knot under her chin. Her forehead was permanently dripping with sweat as she was always behind with her work and hurrying to catch up. In addition to that, any small incident was enough to throw her into confusion, be it a stranger passing through the village, or the arrival of a letter.

But this time her panic was justified. The visitor had indeed come at the wrong moment.

'Do sit down, Madame,' she said, though no available seat could be seen in the kitchen, where the bench and the two chairs were piled up with all sorts of rags and paraphernalia. 'Have you seen the postman? He's late again.'

Not deigning to respond to this clumsy attempt to change the subject, Mme Hermelin continued ruthlessly, 'I'm glad to see the milk collectors have had the kindness to leave you enough for a good slab of butter.'

'If only!' moaned Delphine Legras. 'If you think it's good butter, you're wrong. The cream was sour. I can never get enough to make fresh butter. With everything I've got to do, I can only spare an hour or two to look after the cows. They don't get enough to eat and they don't even produce a pail of milk. It's a disaster!'

She gave a deep sigh, and raised her eyes to heaven in despair. Then, as ever when she came across anyone who might listen, she took the opportunity to bemoan her fate: her husband only left his workshop for his meals, he would let the cattle starve to death rather than tend them for half an hour...

'Of course, of course,' Mme Hermelin interrupted. 'We all have our cross to bear. I hope you haven't promised to sell this butter yet.'

'If only! It's for my daughter in Saint-Etienne. It's not very good, and she's so unhappy in the city, it's dreadful! She's managed to find a few nails for her father, who doesn't even have enough for a coffin. We hate having to ask clients to bring their own nails. It's a disaster!'

For a moment, Mme Hermelin had been tempted to give up on the potatoes in order to try to deprive the daughter in Saint-Etienne of her butter. But faced with the nail argument she had to recognise she was unequal to her opponent.

'I've come to ask if you could let me have two or three potatoes.'

Although Mme Hermelin was not very familiar with the patois, she did know how to use local expressions to good effect. This was a case in point. Farmers in the Francheville area always said 'two or three' to indicate a quantity of any size.

'So you haven't seen the postman? He should have been already.'

Mme Hermelin got the message. She didn't have much of a chance. Tortuous digressions and sudden changes of subject almost always meant a refusal.

'You had a good harvest last year, didn't you?' she went on, wheedlingly. 'You can't be short of fifty kilos or so. I'm not asking too much, am I?'

'If only!' groaned Delphine Legras. 'It's hard for us, even in the country. Just take poor Brandouille, the postman. He's not a bad man, but he does like to exercise his right arm. It goes with the job. People used to give him a drink wherever he called on his rounds – a glass of wine or a drop of homemade brandy. When he got home, he was always well away. But now…'

'Oh yes,' said Mme Hermelin, as anxiety rose within her.

'Times have certainly changed. You can get by without wine; at least it doesn't bother me personally. But as for potatoes, it's quite another matter.'

Mme Hermelin was running out of patience. But Delphine continued imperturbably as she prepared feed for her animals, 'And now his wife takes his money off him. So he's started to get into debt. Still, he's a good fellow at heart. I've known him a long time. But the other day, that postal order, he couldn't resist the temptation.'

'What postal order?'

'Didn't you hear? Twelve hundred francs sent to Mme Leborgne by her nephew in Marseille. She sometimes sends him food rations: rabbits, chickens, potatoes…'

'Ah! Potatoes!' interrupted Mme Hermelin. 'That's just what I wanted to say…'

'If only he'd kept hold of it for a few days, nothing would have happened. But like a fool, he signed in the place of Mme Leborgne. Still, I tell you, he's not a bad fellow. There was a dreadful row.'

'Yes, you can't trust the bottle for advice. You start with petty theft, and then it's a slippery slope. He's bound to lose his job.'

'No, he got away with it! His wife gave the money back to the Postmaster, who's married to Brandouille's niece, so it went no further. But he had his fingers burnt, believe you me. You should have seen how much he drank that day! Completely legless! He must still be at the café, that's why he's late.'

As she spoke, she opened the cupboard and started to put crockery away.

'Oh no!' she exclaimed suddenly. 'Almost three o'clock, and I haven't let my cows out yet.'

Her black headscarf slipped forward, and she pushed it back with a movement of exasperation. 'I haven't had time to brush my hair for three days! It's a disaster!'

'I have to go,' said Mme Hermelin. 'So how many potatoes can you let me have?'

'Potatoes?' said Delphine, wide-eyed, as if this was the first she had heard of the matter. 'Don't you have any?'

'Not a single one! And I've got people staying all summer...'

'M. Vautier's expecting guests too,' Delphine went on hurriedly. 'A gentleman with his wife and two children. They've rented a cottage near La Grange. City people, Jews apparently, so they're not short of a few francs. Vautier's charging them two hundred and twenty a month, it's dreadful. They're arriving from Marseille this evening.'

'Well, well,' said Mme Hermelin, intrigued. 'This evening, you say? And will they get potatoes?'

'I'm sure they will, because Vautier said he'd sell them anything they need.'

Delphine was getting ready to go out. She opened the door leading from the kitchen into the cowshed. A stench of manure and slurry filled the room.

'So could I count on fifty kilos?' asked Mme Hermelin, determined to force the issue.

'Fifty kilos of what?'

'Of potatoes of course!'

'You want potatoes?' said Delphine in astonishment. 'Ask Vautier. He's still got two or three in his cellar.'

'Yes, I will, but what can you give me yourself? Fifty kilos?'

On the doorstep, Delphine began to moan again. 'Potatoes! Everybody comes wanting them, it's a crying shame. My daughter in Saint-Etienne asks me for them too. She hasn't even got enough for soup. And my son in Lyon, and my other son in Nîmes, and my daughter in Sorgues! It's a disaster!'

'Well give me what you can. If not fifty kilos, then forty, or thirty.'

'I'll ask my husband... he never leaves his workshop these

days. I'm the only one doing any work! It's such an uphill struggle!'

There was nothing for it. With a longing glance back at the bowl of butter, Mme Hermelin left the kitchen, shaking her bunch of keys crossly.

III

The hamlet of La Barbarie forms part of the sprawling community of Saint-Boniface, and consists of eleven dwellings, of which only five are occupied. Owners have died, and their descendants have abandoned the countryside.

After a moment's hesitation, Mme Hermelin crossed a little rubbish-strewn square and turned into the narrow lane leading to La Serre, where Lévy Seignos lived. A farmer with his own land, he had a local reputation as something of an eccentric, as much for having attempted to introduce the cultivation of apricots and asparagus as for his beige canvas hat with its downturned brim, well-known throughout the community of Saint-Boniface. His biblical first name, however, was common in this Protestant area. Lévy Seignos had something of the bravery and entrepreneurship of his forebears who, under religious persecution three centuries earlier, had embarked on a risky new life in the wide open spaces of Louisiana and Canada. He had successfully applied the same tenacity and hard grind in his own little sphere, and as they said in Saint-Boniface, 'he wasn't badly off'.

Cadet's furious barking greeted Mme Hermelin's arrival, as she passed beneath an archway inscribed *Anno Domini 1287*, pushed open the gate – no chickens allowed to leave their droppings in the kitchen here – and stopped for a second. From the terrace there was an extensive view over the rolling hills, with their green cap of chestnut and pine woods.

Ancient though it was, La Serre was well maintained and formed a striking architectural ensemble. On the sturdy front wall of the building, successive alteration works had spared the parapets, a reminder of the religious wars.

Mme Hermelin, who would walk unceremoniously straight into the homes of the small farmers, took the trouble to knock here. The Seignos family was well set up.

The kitchen was a great, high-ceilinged room with oak panelling. At the far end, a modern range stood beside a huge fireplace. On a shelf above the radio were some history books and cloak-and-dagger novels. One wall was hung with hunting gear, another with a set of copper pans.

When the visitor arrived, Lévy Seignos was just changing from his heavy hobnailed boots into a pair of clogs. Victorine, his wife, was folding bed linen on a long table standing against the wall.

'I hope I'm not disturbing you,' trilled Mme Hermelin.

Seignos politely waved these apologies away and exchanged a few pleasantries about the weather with the retired tax-inspector's wife, while Victorine, leaving her bed linen, busied herself by the hearth preparing coffee.

Mme Hermelin didn't beat about the bush. 'Do you know Vautier's got a tenant?' she asked, thrusting her nose forward.

'Yes, I heard about it,' said Seignos. 'They shouldn't be too uncomfortable in that cottage. They're from Marseille, aren't they? But Mme Hermelin, aren't you going to have guests too?'

'How do you know?' Mme Hermelin feigned surprise, though she was well aware that an event of this importance could never escape the curiosity of Saint-Boniface. 'Yes, I've let a cottage beside Les Tilleuls to a gentleman from the city. Someone very respectable who was recommended to my son Jérémie by a church minister in Lyon.'

Delighted to be listened to, she rattled on.

'He's an architect. Latvian or Polish or Serbian or something. He's tired of the city and wants to spend the rest of his life in the country. He's rented some land from Chazelas, and I'm letting him rent an outbuilding to use as a cowshed. He's getting a couple of cows, which suits me well, because my little man at the farm hardly lets me have any milk. The rationing takes it all. And as for potatoes…'

'This gentleman, does he know how to milk a cow?' Seignos interrupted, with a sceptical smile.

'Oh, he's used to getting by,' retorted Mme Hermelin. 'And he won't be working alone. He's coming with his fiancée, and it won't be long before they are married, I'll see to that. My son, the minister, will come to perform the blessing.'

'So they're Protestants!'

'She is, but he isn't yet. All in good time. He's a very respectable Israelite.'

'Well, well!' said Seignos. 'It's a hard time for Israelites at the moment. Especially in the occupied zone.'

'Oh, I'll look after him,' said Mme Hermelin. 'He needn't worry. He's already managed to get seed potatoes, and he planted them when he first came to rent the cottage.'

'He ploughed and planted single-handed?' asked Seignos incredulously.

'He's an architect, he's well educated, so it's not a problem for him. And he got some help from Chazelas who rented him the field and sold him the seed potatoes. So at least they won't be short this summer. But look at me, I haven't even got enough to make soup with. You'd sell me a hundred kilos or so, wouldn't you?'

The die was cast. Now the owners of La Serre knew the object of Mme Hermelin's visit. Old Seignos drew on his pipe in silence. Meanwhile, his wife served coffee with a little jug of cream and some biscuits on a saucer. She offered the sugar bowl to her visitor, who picked out a lump with delicacy and put it in her coffee.

'You haven't taken enough,' Victorine protested unconvincingly.

It was just a polite formula, and Mme Hermelin knew it. But she could not resist the temptation to dive into the proffered sugar bowl again.

'If have a failing, it's my sweet tooth,' she simpered. 'Your coffee is exquisite.'

'You're too kind, it's not really very good.'

It was another formula in local code. Victorine knew better than anyone that her coffee was the best in Saint-Boniface, made from skilfully roasted barley rather than rye, and always flavoured with a few real coffee beans.

'More cream?' asked Victorine.

'Oh, just a tiny drop,' said Mme Hermelin, raising her little finger elegantly. Then, in a changed tone, 'For landowners like yourselves, a hundred kilos of potatoes is neither here nor there. It's not too much to ask, is it?'

Seignos's instinct was to give in. How could he turn down a neighbour in trouble, who just needed enough for her soup? But he answered, 'Neither here nor there? A hundred kilos of potatoes? Ask your children in the city what they think.'

'Of course,' said Mme Hermelin, 'people are short of everything in the cities. And that's why I'm taking pity on them. I'm sacrificing my own peace and quiet to open my house to them.'

She was speaking of her house guests, but Seignos and his wife, knowing nothing of her commercial projects, thought she was talking about her tenants, the architect and his fiancée.

'It's already May,' said Seignos, his pipe clenched between his teeth. 'Fifty kilos should be more than enough for your soup.

For the rest, you can use the earlies, the "rattes". They'll be ready to dig in a few days.'

'New potatoes for my clients?' she exclaimed. 'What are you thinking of! Imagine what I'd have to charge for board! And anyway, my poor husband would never be able to scrape them! I'd have to get a kitchen maid!'

This time the cat was out of the bag. Lévy and Victorine understood. This wasn't about soup for the poor demented tax inspector, reduced to slavery by his wife. It was about her little business. In that case, neighbourly solidarity was no longer an obligation.

As a diplomat might, Seignos changed his tune. 'Ah! So you're expecting boarders too! So you certainly won't have enough, even with a hundred kilos. You'll need at least two or three times as much. And I certainly won't be able to supply you.'

'I'd pay a good price,' said Mme Hermelin quietly, alarmed at her own carelessness.

Seignos almost shrugged his shoulders. Why should he care about the ten extra centimes a kilo she would offer him! Wily and clever in his own way, he had understood well before the others that banknotes had ceased to confer wealth on their owners. Had he not read and reread the history of the Revolution and the worthless paper money issued then?

'No, no, Mme Hermelin,' he said firmly. 'You'll have to look elsewhere for your guest house.'

The retired tax inspector's wife turned pale. She had just understood the full extent of her blunder.

Getting up, she took leave of her hosts with a forced smile.

Even when she hopped back down onto the main road linking Saint-Boniface to Francheville, she was still nursing her anger.

'Pharisees!' she muttered furiously. 'Godless Pharisees, I always knew it!'

The descent to the road was all the steeper as Mme Hermelin had taken a shortcut.

Following a path through some high grass ready to be scythed, she stopped under a cherry tree whose bright red fruit made her mouth water. With a little jump, she grabbed a branch, pulled it towards her, and picked off some cherries. It was early in the season and the flesh was slightly sour, but as she crushed them greedily in her mouth Mme Hermelin tasted only sweet revenge. The tree belonged to Seignos.

Stepping across some little rivulets, and taking a jump across a wider stream, Mme Hermelin made her way back to the metalled road.

A crocodile of girls aged between ten and fourteen was coming her way. Bringing up the rear, a shepherdess tending her flock, was a thin bird-like woman dressed all in grey, with a shawl over her shoulders and a stick in her hand. The girls were singing a rousing marching tune at the tops of their voices. From time to time they collapsed into giggles at some witticism.

One fine summer's eve
On the bank of the Thames – oh
An Englishman in shirtsleeves
Sang dilly dilly dally oh!

Mme Hermelin frowned. What shocking behaviour! And what a song! Shirtsleeves indeed! Why not… in his underwear! And the free school claimed to provide a more respectable education than the state! No doubt all this slipshod behaviour was the fault of Mlle Martin, the madwoman who had replaced Sister Thérèse at the beginning of the year. She had ideas above her station, that one! The parents had actually complained about the innovations, so surely Mother Félicie, who at least had some principles even if she was a Catholic, could hardly let this revolutionary in a shawl stay at the convent for long.

Mme Hermelin's thoughts, as fleeting as her gait, turned back to her potatoes. In the end, her embarrassment with Seignos had not affected her morale. She was just putting together a new plan of action when she noticed a woman coming towards her. Aged about thirty, she had slightly prominent cheekbones which gave her an attractive childlike appearance.

It was the Russian woman. A complex series of circumstances had led Countess Génia Prokoff to end up in Francheville, where she devoted herself to the 'family food parcel' business. She had kept a list of wealthy, regular clients from more prosperous times on the Riviera, for whom she tirelessly scoured the neighbouring farms to find butter and sausages. Every week she sent off a number of parcels, which earned her sufficient profit to pay her bill at the Hôtel Panorama.

Mme Hermelin regarded Génia with a mixture of disdain and admiration. She was obviously not a respectable woman because she went to the cinema – Mme Hermelin had seen her one day leaving a matinée at the Eden Palace. She smoked on the hotel terrace, and she used immodest make up. Even worse, she went barefoot in her sandals, varnished her toenails and painted stocking seams on her legs!

But secretly Mme Hermelin admired her. She envied her knack, wondering how this foreign woman managed to winkle out the scarce provisions which she herself was unable to procure, despite being a native of the region and a member of the local middle classes.

These contradictory feelings put Mme Hermelin in two minds, but as their paths were about to cross, she suddenly decided to take the initiative in greeting her.

'Good morning, Madame,' the Russian woman replied in a sing-song voice, with a sideways look at Mme Hermelin's dress.

Mme Hermelin could have ignored her. Up until then, their only contact had been a short exchange of pleasantries one day in a haberdasher's. But an idea had struck the landlady of Les Tilleuls.

'Nice afternoon, isn't it?' she said, holding out her hand to the foreigner. 'Are you going for a walk?' she added, smoothly.

'Yes, Madame.'

'So am I,' said Mme Hermelin, 'but unfortunately it's not for my own pleasure.'

'Oh!' said the Russian.

'I'll tell you why. I need potatoes. I have guests arriving in a few days and… By the way, if any of your friends feel like taking a holiday in the country, do them a favour and give them my address. The rooms are lovely, you know. Why don't you call in and see me some day?'

'I'd be delighted,' said Génia distractedly.

'Yes, I'm short of potatoes. It's sad, but it's true. You don't know where I could get any?'

A distant smile hovered on the Russian woman's lips.

'Oh!' she said. 'Potatoes? I've heard they're expensive. Sarzier gets them at the Hôtel Panorama but they cost him twelve francs a kilo.'

Mme Hermelin started. Twelve francs! That really was the end of the world! That was more than three times as much as even her most pessimistic calculations.

'Are you quite sure?' she stammered.

'Well, that's what he was saying the other day. Everything's going up.'

'But it's positively alarming. How do you think we can get by with prices like that?'

Génia let her eyes wander over the fields, where the grass

23

waved in the breeze. Then she snapped out of her daydream and looked at her watch.

'Don't let me keep you!' said Mme Hermelin, though she didn't move an inch. 'By the way, what are they giving you to eat at the Panorama these days?'

'Oh, it depends!' said Génia, who didn't have the strength to extricate herself from this conversation.

'But what, for example?'

'Well, I don't know, vegetables with meat, or maybe kid, rabbit, eggs, local cheese…'

'Well I never!' said Mme Hermelin, pinching her lips. 'You don't go without, do you, at Sarzier's! He gets it all on the black market, of course. Ah!…'

She bit her tongue. She could hardly expect the Russian woman to back her in lamenting the decline in morals and the scandal of the black market.

But Génia didn't appear to take it personally. She vaguely promised to send clients to Les Tilleuls if she had the opportunity, and made off with the long strides of a seasoned walker.

Mme Hermelin was simmering with indignation. Kid, rabbit, eggs! And Sarzier's prices were hardly any higher than what she intended to ask! It was unfair competition! As for this shameless Russian woman, she had been rather naive to ask her advice. Of course she would keep her contacts to herself, for her own illicit deals, while the French wore themselves to the bone knocking in vain at every possible door. This was an intolerable scandal.

Mme Hermelin always experienced a burst of energy at critical moments, and she instantly took two decisions. First, she would go to see the Sobrevin family. Obviously, with all those ragamuffins, they never had enough to eat; but on the other hand they were always short of money. What's more, as good Christians, they would never dare to charge her the black market rates. Then she would send an anonymous letter to the Rationing Officer in Francheville to expose the shameful practices taking place in the town. For a second, she wondered which of them to denounce, Sarzier or the Russian woman. But she didn't have to think for long. The Russian might send her some clients, so she had to be treated with care. The real enemy was Sarzier. She detested this thickset man with his hoarse voice and his great mop of red hair like a lion's mane.

Yes, Sarzier was indeed the devil who, according to the Gospel, 'walketh about as a roaring lion, seeking whom he may devour'.

V

The Sobrevin family lived at Les Mottes. This farm straddled a side road which zigzagged round the hills before finishing up at La Barbarie. The next farm was a good kilometre away.

The house itself had been built about sixty years previously in defiance of common sense and the principles of elementary hygiene. The only consideration in its layout had been minimising the costs of materials and labour. The building faced north-west, in such a manner that the sun never shone through the kitchen window, which was moreover the only window. In that area, any other room was regarded as a sort of annexe, used only for sleeping in, and the one upstairs bedroom at Les Mottes had only a single skylight. In truth, the sun did actually shine into the Sobrevins' house on two or three days a year, at the summer solstice, around six o'clock in the morning. It peeked into the kitchen just to check nothing had changed since the previous year...

Noémi Sobrevin, a short, slender, dark, lantern-jawed woman whose distended belly showed she was in the last stages of pregnancy, hadn't even noticed she had a visitor. She was off on one of her tirades, which wouldn't end until her throat had dried up completely. She was haranguing the postman, Brandouille, who listened open-mouthed in bewilderment, trying to interject a word or two here and there. But it took more than that to staunch Noémi's flow.

'A rabbit?' she sneered. 'You've got a nerve. Why not a pig, while you're at it? Hey, hello Madame Hermelin, come and sit down. That's a fine dress you're wearing. I was in Francheville the other day, to get some pants for my little Elie – he had nothing to cover his behind, poor thing – and Pilon at the café told me I could bring him as many rabbits as I wanted and he'd give me twenty-five francs a kilo. No kidding! Well, how many do you think I took him? Zero rabbits! Not one more, and not one less! And you come here all sweetness and light and ask me for a rabbit! And don't think I don't know why you need it. The Postmaster in Francheville likes a good civet, doesn't he? But would you believe it? This time you're in luck. My little Abel needs some overalls. I want something made before the war, mind, d'you hear? Proper gingham, none of your rayon! It's lucky for you the children don't like meat. At New Year I made a civet. Didine was sick all night long. Meat doesn't agree with them, they're not used to it.'

With these words, uttered as she stood on the threshold of the cowshed next to the kitchen, she disappeared for a moment, still talking, and came back holding a rabbit by the ears.

'If this one wanted to breed,' she continued, 'I wouldn't swap it for the entire contents of your sister's shop. But it's not a rabbit, it's a tigress, a lioness! I've tried all the male rabbits around, I've even been as far as La Serre. Nothing. They daren't go near her. Not one of them. She scares the life out of them. I can tell you, I've had just about enough with this rabbit. You know, the other day she got out of a little hole in the hutch, heaven knows how, just for a little look round. Now she gets out every morning. You should see how many of my cabbages she's eaten! And look how she's put on weight! Just look at those thighs! He's in for a treat, your Postmaster!'

With that, she plonked the rabbit down on some scales.

'What did I tell you? Over eleven pounds. It's not a rabbit, it's a calf. And I'm letting you have it at the official price. But the overalls will be at the official price too, eh? And I don't want any trouble, d'you hear? Today's Saturday. Go and see your sister next week and bring me the overalls. Here, I'll lend you a sack to put the rabbit in. Now get away with you! You're already late, it'll be dark by the time you finish.'

During the whole of this monologue, Brandouille, a short red-haired fellow whose nose was lit up like a Chinese lantern, had said nothing. Noémi wasn't the easiest person to have a conversation with. He grunted his agreement, took his leave, and staggered off, shaking his head.

'I do beg your pardon, Mme Hermelin,' said Noémi, changing her tone. And without a break, she set about sawing up wood. Because of her belly, she couldn't bend over, but with miraculous contortions she managed to deal with even the biggest branches. 'What a time-waster Brandouille is, when he comes here! Never stops talking! Of course he needs a rabbit! It'll take more than that to make them forget. That postal order, it wasn't *poste restante*, it was straight into his pocket! What a nincompoop! If I was his wife, I'd show him what's what!'

Now that her eyes had become accustomed to the gloom of the kitchen, Mme Hermelin looked around in horror. In her own home, every object, even the tiniest trinket, had its own sacred, immutable place. In this kitchen, there reigned such complete and improbable confusion that it made her dizzy.

On the oak dresser, family photographs with cracked glass were buried under soiled children's clothes, with little piles of seeds – beans, peas, marrow – visible here and there underneath. Enthroned on the very top was a broken clog.

Strewn on the shelves, already cluttered with empty bottles, were nails, lengths of string, dirty plates, lettuce leaves and a wet nappy. The big table in the middle of the kitchen was littered with an odd collection of objects: washing-up, vegetable peelings, filthy rags, sewing materials, a headless doll, the innards of an alarm clock, a sieve, and some cheese strainers. The sill of the only window was obviously used as a dirty washing basket. A pile of wet nappies gave off an acrid smell. Mixed up with all this were some potatoes, a handful of roasted chestnuts, some exercise books and a hymn book.

'Ah! Brandouille's postal order, yes I know,' said Mme Hermelin, 'I've heard about it.'

But Noémi Sobrevin wasn't listening. She had dropped the saw to fasten the wooden-soled shoes of a child who had just come in, with tears running down his dirty face.

'Sit still, you can see the laces are too short,' Noémi shouted in exasperation. 'I'll get you some more next week when I go to the market, if I remember…'

She started to dry the dishes left to drain on the table. Suddenly she frowned, sniffed, and brought the cloth she was using to her nose.

'Just my luck! I thought so… I've got a wet nappy instead of a tea towel. My husband's always moving them around.'

Indeed, nappies were hanging up to dry above the stove where soup was simmering in an open pot. Whether they had been washed, or simply wet by the youngest Sobrevin, Mme Hermelin could not tell.

'I'd never have sold him the rabbit,' Noémi continued, 'but he offered me some child's overalls. His sister has a haberdasher's in Saint-Paul, you know… if she opened her shop, there'd be enough clothes for all the children in the village. And my eight little ones are in rags!' She fell silent, took on a solemn, mysterious air, threw her cloth away and went to open the linen cupboard.

Mme Hermelin's eyes widened. She was fascinated by linen cupboards. Left alone in a room, she could never resist the temptation to open the doors a little and peek inside.

But suddenly she closed her eyes and clasped her hand to her chest in shock. Of the many linen cupboards she had investigated in her life, she had never seen one to compare with this.

The muddle of the dresser, the table and the windowsill was nothing compared with the crazy shambles inside this cupboard, the traditional sanctuary of any respectable household, and rightly the pride and joy of housewives everywhere. Neat stacks of white sheets, pyramids of handkerchiefs, towers of tablecloths and napkins were here replaced by a dizzying, inextricable, towering muddle of scraps of coloured textile, ribbons, stockings and shoes, mostly charitable gifts to large families, which nobody had ever tried to classify. Whenever she wanted a piece of material or clothing, Noémi Sobrevin would take a lucky dip and pull out whatever might suit the need of the moment.

Already, with the confidence of a deep-sea diver, Noémi Sobrevin had retrieved from the depths an item wrapped in tissue paper. She wiped her hands and opened the packet. It was a large lawn tablecloth with fringes, an adornment fashionable in middle-class households around the turn of the century which girls would spend months embroidering for their trousseau.

Noémi Sobrevin's eyes shone with pride as she opened it out for her visitor to see.

'You know a thing or two about quality, don't you, Mme Hermelin? What do you say to this? Entirely handmade! I'd never have thought it possible to find a piece like this in wartime. And no darning anywhere, if you please! It was a real stroke of luck! They told me it came from a charity sale. And how much do you think I paid for it? Next to nothing! Seven hundred francs! A bargain!'

Mme Hermelin, unmoved by Noémi's fantasy of luxury, did some quick mental arithmetic. For that sum, Noémi Sobrevin could have equipped her whole brood with socks, and had enough left over to buy bootees for the one on the way. But to please Noémi, she told her the table covering was magnificent and the price very reasonable.

While Noémi wrapped the tablecloth up again with exaggerated care, and returned it to the cupboard where it would remain until some new visitor was to be dazzled, Mme Hermelin took advantage of a moment of silence, and went on the attack.

'I've come to see you, my dear Noémi, because I absolutely need…' She faltered a moment, then blurted out, rather like a swimmer jumping into the water, '… fifty kilos of potatoes!'

These were the last words Mme Hermelin managed to utter in the kitchen at Les Mottes during her visit. As if to make up for time lost admiring the tablecloth, Noémi started to talk again, clearly intending to brook no interruption.

'My poor Madame Hermelin, you couldn't have come at a worse time,' she said tearfully, just pausing a second to suck from the bottle she had prepared for the current junior of the family, a one-year-old baby.

'Too hot,' she said, 'I mustn't scald him, poor thing.'

She put the bottle on the table and went back to her sawing.

'My poor Madame Hermelin, you're really out of luck. I might have had potatoes this year, enough for us and for you. But the devil has had his way. In October the children were in bed with measles – they caught it one after another – and I had to sort the first chestnuts, because they were beginning to spoil.

I didn't have time to help my husband dig the potatoes. Then suddenly it turned cold, just after All Saint's, and the frost got about eight sacks. Say hello to the lady, Didine. (A little girl, dark like her mother, had just come in.) I don't think we've even got thirty kilos left in all.'

She stopped what she was doing, opened a little door, lit a paraffin lamp and beckoned to Mme Hermelin.

'Come into the cellar and see for yourself. It's a real catastrophe... I'm going to have to use flour for the soup... as long as the miller lets me have some, because I haven't got any left...'

As the house was built into the hillside, the cellar was on the same level as the kitchen, and it only took Mme Hermelin a moment to see that the lady of the house was not exaggerating.

Noémi came back to the table, sucked on the bottle again, and pursed her lips.

'Just my luck, now it's too cold...'

She put it back on to heat up.

'Of course the neighbours could lend me some... don't cry, David, your milk's warming up! Look, I'll rock your cradle. Yes, they could lend me some, and any other year they'd have done so. But now it's everyone for himself. People don't take pity on you any more. They're persecuting the Jews and they're opening more cinemas. God sent this war to punish us. But now it'll soon be over. Up on the plateau, there was a girl of fifteen, a new Joan of Arc, who left with a cartload of men. Where to? Don't ask me. All I can tell you is she borrowed two cows from her neighbour. When she left, she said the war would be over on the 26th. So that's less than six weeks to wait. It's high time, my little Abel hasn't any clogs, and at the Mairie they only give coupons to the Catholics... You know, when I asked for a coupon for a maternity dress...'

Suddenly she stopped, as if she'd had an inspiration.

'But what d'you say, Madame Hermelin, since you're looking

for fifty kilos of potatoes, why don't you ask for a hundred, and we'll share them? Listen, I'll give you a tip. Go and see Vautier at La Grange, he's got more than enough, he wouldn't dare turn you down. He's up to his neck in the black market, and since he knows your son is in rationing...'

'Yes, yes,' said Mme Hermelin, unconvinced, as she tried to edge her way towards the door.

'You'd be doing me a favour, and my little ones too.'

Mme Hermelin was already backing out of the doorway, closely followed by Noémi, still in full flow, as she dried one of the saucepans.

'I can count on you, can't I? After my Chayou calves, I'll put a good slab of butter aside for you. So goodbye Madame Hermelin, thank you so much.'

Mme Hermelin took her leave and turned back towards Saint-Boniface, her head buzzing.

'What a waste! Eight sacks of potatoes! Eight whole sacks! And look at all the nettles round here! I bet they don't even know what to do with them. If they're poor, they've only got themselves to blame! They don't deserve the blessings of the Lord...'

VI

Philibert Vautier aimed a kick at one of the two cows which, having stopped to drink at the trough halfway between Francheville and Saint-Boniface, were reluctant to get going again. Lowing, the animal moved off at a trot, and the caravan got under way.

Vautier walked ahead of them. A lean, sturdy farmer, his cheeks were covered in a dark stubble which he shaved only on Sundays. Beside him was a strapping young man of about thirty, whose pale complexion showed, even more than his clothes did, that he was from the city. His eyes were hidden behind heavy horn-rimmed sunglasses. He wore threadbare trousers and a jacket with frayed cuffs. His blue tie, in contrast, was spotless. He was speaking enthusiastically to his companion and gesturing wildly, but Vautier was obviously listening with only half an ear.

The two cows behind them were pulling a heavily laden cart. Amongst the bags, the boxes and the battered suitcases clumsily tied with string, were a newly painted stove, an artist's easel and a set of picture frames wrapped in newspaper.

Bringing up the rear were two women. The farmer's wife, dressed all in black from her straw hat right down to her stockings and shoes, as dry and inscrutable as a mummy brought back from the dead; and a tall, fair, young woman in a tweed coat, pushing a pram with a baby sitting in it. Running up and down between the men and the women was girl of five or six with a halo of dark curls.

Mme Hermelin, who had just rejoined the main road by a shortcut, had been following the rearguard of the caravan for a few moments. Who could she be, this lady in a tweed coat? At a bend, she caught sight of the man in the suit, and all became clear. 'How silly of me,' she thought, 'it's Vautier collecting his Jew from the station!'

She sped up in order to get a better view of the newcomers. When she was about twenty paces behind the cart, she took off her pince-nez, wiped it carefully with her handkerchief, and set it back on her nose.

'Well, they look respectable, at least from behind... Ah! A stove! An easel? Oh, so he must be an artist! I wonder where Vautier caught this one? He hardly knows anyone in town... a newspaper, maybe. Yes, he gets the *Petit Dauphinois* delivered.'

Satisfied with her neat explanation, Mme Hermelin turned

her mind once more to the potato question. As it happened, Vautier's talkative companion had left off, called by his wife to attend to the pram which appeared to have broken down. Taking advantage of the opportunity, Mme Hermelin bounded forward, goat-like, to join Vautier at the head of the caravan.

'Good afternoon, Monsieur Vautier, I'm so pleased to see you. I was on the way to your house. I wanted to speak to you.'

Vautier grunted indistinctly in reply, and glanced suspiciously at the retired tax inspector's wife. What did she want of him?

'I'll tell you why,' Mme Hermelin continued smoothly. 'I've got friends coming to stay in a few days.' She had learnt her lesson, and was careful not to disclose the reopening of her guest house. 'I'm also expecting my son Joseph, you know, the one who's in rationing. He's probably going to be posted to Francheville. He's missing his parents!'

This was pure invention, somewhat influenced by Noémi's advice.

'So,' she continued even more sweetly, 'I have to feed them. And I haven't any potatoes. I could count on you for a hundred kilos, couldn't I?'

Philibert Vautier didn't move a muscle. Her request plummeted into a bottomless well. Mme Hermelin returned to the attack.

'With a fine farm like yours, and the hard work you put into it, you're not short of a sack or two, are you?'

The bony, stubbled face betrayed no emotion. Mme Hermelin's advances were like water off a duck's back. But Vautier was thinking. What point was there in selling anything to Mme Hermelin when he couldn't charge her as much as he would an outsider? If her good-for-nothing son came nitpicking around the farms, it was better that he didn't know that he, Vautier, had a sack or two of potatoes to spare at this time of year.

He put on a worried look, and shook his head.

'I'd be pleased to, but I haven't got any potatoes left. The seed potatoes haven't arrived yet, and I don't know how I'm going to sow the late crop. And you're not the only one expecting visitors. I am, too,' he said, pointing to his tenant. 'I can't let them starve, can I? They're from Marseille.'

Mme Hermelin was reaching the end of her tether. Her face black with rage, she thrust her sharp nose at Vautier in defiance:

'But you'll let me have fifty kilos, won't you?'

A sort of groan came from beneath Vautier's moustache.

'Er… it's not very convenient… I'd just as soon you got them somewhere else… It's not always very easy for us, you know.'

Vautier's new tenant had returned to his side, and appeared anxious to pick up where he had left off. Suddenly he took a step towards Mme Hermelin, bowed ceremoniously, and said with a trace of a foreign accent, 'Good afternoon, Madame…'

Mme Hermelin made a face at him which was intended to be friendly enough to hide her suppressed anger.

'Good afternoon. I understand you're from Marseille. Rationing is terrible in the cities, isn't it? It's a wretched shame. At least here in the country you won't have to worry. Especially with M. Vautier, he's just told me he's put some potatoes aside for you.'

Then, turning to Vautier and putting on a cheerful, positive tone of voice, 'But you could still spare me twenty kilos, couldn't you?'

Vautier made no reply. He busied himself with his cows, wielding his stick and swearing at them in patois.

During Mme Hermelin's little speech, the newcomer bent towards her several times. Maybe he was looking for a new audience for the lecture he had broken off? But the retired tax inspector's wife had had enough.

'I have to leave you, I'm already late. I hope to see you

again one day. We can talk about Marseille, I know it well. Do bring your wife to see me at Les Tilleuls.'

She bounded off along the road without so much as a last glance at Vautier. In front of the newcomer she had more or less managed to conceal her displeasure, but now she was alone she could let herself go. Angrily, she kicked a stone out of the way, gave her bag a good shake, and muttered,

'I should have known! That's what you get for dealing with Papists! He's got plenty for his Jew, of course! But none for me! Well, he hasn't heard the last of me. I'll have to tell Joseph about this... I'll have to tell Joseph...'

She carried on her way, mumbling vague threats. All of a sudden, a new idea struck her: after all, why shouldn't she consult Joseph about the potato question? He ought to know all the regulations, and he should be able to advise her how to use them to her advantage. That was it. She'd phone him. It would cost her three francs and seventy-five centimes, but the situation required sacrifices.

And Mme Hermelin trotted on, jangling, in the direction of Saint-Boniface.

VII

Saint-Boniface stands on a broad knoll surrounded by wooded hills. The tower of the little church can be seen for some distance around. A little below, set at an angle to the hillside, in defiance of the vernacular architecture, the school's white walls and big windows face south, while the building itself turns its back on the other dwellings.

Saint-Boniface is the little head on the great body of the local community. It is the meeting point for a large number of hamlets, some of them seven or eight kilometres distant, which comprise about a thousand inhabitants in total. Saint-Boniface itself consists of about thirty houses, half of them empty, and fifty-four souls in all.

This ancient village, huddled around its church, has always been a Catholic stronghold. But on the surrounding heights, some of the farmhouses look down malevolently. Despite subsequent alterations, the massive presence of the fortress farms, with their battlements and loopholes, still recalls their original function during the religious wars.

The village is not particularly attractive, with its Mairie accommodated in a peeling building, its dilapidated houses and its muddy little streets. It has known better days: local lore insists that Saint-Boniface was once the biggest cattle market in the area.

At the entrance to the village stands an electricity sub-station, Saint-Boniface having benefited from electric power for some years now. But paraffin lamps still burn in half the houses, as despite petrol rationing and the ease of extending the electricity from one house to the next, many country people are reluctant to adopt it. Sheer habit, or parsimony? Often, it's both. All things considered, they prefer not to stay up late but go to bed at dusk. In fact, those long evenings spent storytelling and singing the old songs are but a distant memory. Nobody sings any more, unless you count a few young Protestants in the neighbouring hamlets who strike up hymns when they get together.

Local customs have vanished along with the melodies. Of a Sunday, some of the old women still wear a little white starched bonnet; but on feast days, the Paris fashion comes to the fore, albeit a few years out of date, and made respectable by the Belle Jardinière or the Samaritaine. On weekdays, even the most comfortably off men wear tattered clothes about ready to be handed down to the scarecrows. And whatever the season, the women wear black pinafores.

The post office takes the form of a letterbox in front of the school, which Brandouille empties once a day at an unspecified time, to fit with his refreshment stops. The telephone is in the grocer's shop which is the hub of social, community and political life. It serves not only as a grocer's but also as bar and tobacconist's. In the old days, during election campaigns, the back room was used for meetings.

Right at the top of the village, by the church, is a neat little house set in a pretty garden, the best in the village. This is the presbytery, and the room giving on to the garden is used as a secular confessional by the Abbé Mignart. He is the highest spiritual authority in the village, followed by Longeaud, the schoolmaster. As Secretary of the Farmers' Corporation, a respected voice in the local branch of the Veterans' Legion, and a serious competitor for Longeaud in the role of village letter-writer, the Abbé Mignart regularly makes himself available to listen to the woes of his flock, who are less troubled by their conscience than by the Chinese puzzles which the Government inflicts on them daily.

* * *

In this spring of 1942, the shelves in the grocer's were barer than in other stores of the same kind, where imitation packets were already the norm. This was because when restrictions began to bite, Hippolyte Tournier, an individualist, had refused to submit to a system he considered too complicated. As soon as an item became subject to quotas and ration cards – coffee, sugar, cooking oil, butter, soap and so on – he stopped selling it. This simple stratagem meant he didn't have to account for coupons, and he could make money almost without trying, by using the back room to stockpile valuable supplies of un-obtainable goods.

There were only three items Tournier continued to supply: wine, tobacco and paraffin. No doubt he had his reasons.

When Mme Hermelin arrived at the grocer's, she found Tournier engaged in conversation over a bottle of red wine with Grégoire Laffont, a comfortably off village landowner. The telephone cubicle was at the back of the shop. Mme Hermelin went through to make the call, but immediately came back out: there would be a fifteen-minute wait. As a result, she was able to overhear a conversation while pretending not to listen.

Tournier and Laffont were discussing, in patois, some shady matter involving tobacco. Grégoire Laffont, a non-smoker, had not put his name down on the list for tobacco, for fear of having to delve into his wallet every ten days. But he soon realised he had made a serious mistake. You don't have to smoke tobacco. You can exchange it for a bag of nails, or for wine or clogs. He wanted to go back on his decision, but it was too late, as according to Tournier the lists were now closed. The farmer, lamenting his lost opportunity, had been obliged to admit defeat.

But since then, he had made some strange discoveries. Tournier had in fact put Laffont's name down as a matter of course, along with the sixteen other non-smokers in the village, and their rations were being meticulously delivered to him, thanks to the kind assistance of M. Longeaud, who had provided the necessary numbers for entries in the list, and who was not above acquiring a little extra tobacco as a result of this ingenious stratagem.

'And I'm telling you again,' Grégoire Laffont was saying, 'I want my tobacco. Vergnon at Les Buttes got his doctor to give him a certificate that he hadn't been allowed to smoke because of his lungs, but now he's better. So they let him put his name down.'

Tournier realised that the other man had got wind of the fake entries. If that reached the state-run tobacco company, the Régie, he would be in trouble. But he wasn't the sort to give in so easily.

'You go and pay Dr Manueli sixty francs for a certificate if that suits you, but between ourselves you'd be better off waiting until the end of next month. I'll go to the Régie and sort it out with them.'

The main thing was to play for time. Obviously he would end up losing Laffont's ration but in the meantime he could still put a few packets of tobacco aside.

The other man spat on the floor, grinding it in with the sole of his shoe.

'Well, OK, I'll wait two or three days. But I want my tobacco next month.'

'At the end of next month,' Tournier corrected him. I know the director and I'll explain it to him myself. That means you won't have to take an oath on the carrot.'

'On the what?' asked Grégoire Laffont, blinking.

'On the Régie's carrot. The cigar they have on the front of every tobacconist's, in the towns. It may look like a cigar, but I tell you it's a carrot. All the people who were late putting their names down, the Régie is making them take an oath on the carrot that they really are smokers. And woe betide those who are caught! I read it in Longeaud's paper. There was even a drawing to show you how to do it: a chap with a moustache, raising his right hand in front of a carrot.'

'It was a caricature,' interrupted Mme Hermelin, 'I saw it too.'

'A carica... what?' said Tournier, warily. 'Well, maybe it was. Anyway, that's how you have to do it. But I'll write you an affidavit saying you've always bought tobacco from me, and in return you can give me a packet or two from time to time, for my father-in-law, who can never get enough.'

'I'm not going to have you make me pay for it,' said Laffont, grudgingly.

'Jewish blood in you, eh? I'm the one who's going to have to make it worth the director's while to sort out your business, and you still want to haggle? So, is it a deal?'

The other mumbled something indistinct in agreement, and emptied his glass. He wasn't overly pleased with the outcome. Tournier had tricked him, he was sure of it.

Once Grégoire Laffont had left, Tournier went round the back of the table which served as a bar, and washed the glasses. The shelves behind him were littered with the dusty remnants of what his grocery store had once been: some old tins of wax polish, a small bag of salt, unlabelled boxes of washing powder, a huge model of a battery, two or three empty jam jars, and a large jar of mixed pickles, delivered in error some years ago by a wholesaler, which had met with a wary reception from the housewives of Saint-Boniface and not moved since.

In the centre of the room, which doubled as the Tournier family's kitchen and dining room when it was not serving as a shop, was the table which Laffont had just left. It looked as if Tournier had been eating when Laffont came in, as a large loaf and a knife remained to be cleared away.

Mme Hermelin had already been transfixed by this loaf for several minutes. She could no longer ignore the hunger brought on by her lengthy walk. Her mouth watered, like Pavlov's dog in the famous experiment. She licked her lips. Her common sense wavered for a moment, and the dark forces of instinct got the better of her. Alas, the flesh is weak!

Going up to the table she took the knife, and quickly muttered an inadequate phrase prompted *in extremis* by the civilised being which had just been extinguished inside her:

'You don't mind, do you?'

Astonished, the grocer didn't move.

Mme Hermelin quickly cut herself a thick slice of bread and took a great bite out of it.

'Um… excellent, your bread. Do you bake it yourselves? My compliments…'

The telephone rang. Mme Hermelin rushed to the cubicle, her mouth still full.

'Hello, is that you, Joseph?' she shouted in a shrill voice. 'You made me wait twenty minutes!'

She launched into the account of her woes.

'My guests are coming on Monday and I don't have a single potato. I was counting on my neighbours, but their charitable spirit appears to have deserted them… Yes, that's why I'm calling you… Yes, of course it's justified… Exactly! You can do something about it!'

The reply made her jump.

'Absolutely not!' she shrieked, an octave higher. 'I've promised these people, I can't let them down… I'm counting on you, you know… well, if that's your attitude, I'll have to apply elsewhere. Maybe someone will take pity on the wife of a retired civil servant. I'll write to Vichy, to Maréchal Pétain… to the Prefect… to everybody. A scandal? No, what's scandalous is that people like us are sacrificed like this… No, I want an answer now… don't cut me off, Miss!… Yes, right, that's right … Well, if they're seed potatoes, so what? A bit more expensive? Well, I'll just have to put up with it. Yes, yes, I understand… I'll leave it at that… Goodbye, dear.'

Mme Hermelin hung up, wiped her brow, and left the cubicle, chewing the crust she still had in her hand. So many battles joined in a single day! But the final victory was all the more intoxicating.

* * *

The next day but one, as night was falling, a gas-propelled vehicle stopped in front of the retired tax collector's house. The driver checked the address, jumped down and unloaded two large sacks labelled: 'Variety: Beauvais. Seed Potatoes.'

For once, the town had come to the aid of the country.

Chapter 2
All Roads Lead to Les Tilleuls

I

Whistling cheerfully, Longeaud crosses the schoolyard to the village road. He's getting more portly now, but that doesn't stop him keeping up a brisk pace, brandishing a stout stick on which one of his pupils has spent hours carving patterns and initials.

On the road, he overtakes the schoolmistress from the Free School, Mlle Amélie Martin, whom he greets coolly. He doesn't have much time for this strange, timid spinster. To start with, he doubts whether her qualifications are worth anything, which would explain why she has ended up as a teacher in a Catholic school, after teaching French abroad. Her grey shawl makes Longeaud think of the bats which flit around the church at dusk. It is rumoured in the village that she doesn't get on with Sister Félicie, the headmistress, and that the Curé is always finding fault with her. But that's parish politics, and Longeaud is careful not to get involved. It would be beneath his dignity.

He hurries on, eager to get to Francheville. His table companions, all 'on the same side', will be expecting him at the Café de la Poste for their regular Thursday gathering. The group consists of three or four state employees, a shopkeeper, the plumber, and the bus driver, who comes from Manvin, and only returns in late afternoon to his village high up in the hills.

Thursday is also market day, and this merry band starts with a few apéritifs and then makes its way to the Hôtel Panorama. There, over a meal served with particular care by the Patron, they indulge in heady debate. Around two in the afternoon, the session draws to a close with coffee and a few liqueurs, whereupon M. Longeaud at last reaches the euphoric state which, in the drabness of his life, is the ray of sunshine without which it would not be worth living at all.

Compared with these Thursday gatherings, he finds other forms of entertainment very dull. He has hardly read anything apart from newspapers since he completed his teacher-training. He has avoided affairs of the heart, which only cause trouble, and since he has had to lay up his Citroën he hardly goes anywhere. Although he has an old wireless, he doesn't like music. As for the news, he only listens with half an ear. Longeaud knows it's all up with the Germans anyway, and he can't be bothered with the details. That just leaves fishing, as he gave up hunting a few years ago when it began to take too much out of him. But none of that can beat a Pernod, or even a glass of red wine.

Francheville, 4.2 km. Longeaud has just reached the main road. No, nothing can beat a Pernod – oh, cherished memory! Or even the rough red wine which is also becoming hard to get. M. Longeaud has no time for those Temperance skinflints, even when they are not vegetarians and Esperantists to boot, a triple curse prevalent amongst his colleagues, but to which he has never succumbed.

Francheville, 4 km. Certainly never succumbed to that, thank God. Nor to institutional sermonizing about repentance. Obviously, you have to have your wits about you if you're to get your daily wine. M. Longeaud congratulates himself on the administrative sleight of hand he indulges in as Secretary to the Maire, which earns him the gratitude of Saint-Boniface's population. Not to mention the good grace with which he carries out the duties of village letter-writer! It's a service to all those bumpkins, which allows him to keep up his merry three litres a day, summer and winter, plus the odd glass here and there.

Francheville, 3.5 km. Plus the odd glass, of course. M.

Longeaud's penchant for red wine does not mean he turns his nose up at spirits, which sear the throat deliciously, and impart a rosy outlook on life. But from there to conclude that he's an alcoholic would be a big step, a very big step. For even if he drinks liberally – he concedes this is the word for it – he can hold his liquor. Obviously, anyone can make mistakes. And you have to make exceptions for days when the threshing is finished or the pig is slaughtered, because then you're expected to get drunk.

Francheville, 3 km. It is rather a long way, though. It's not so bad going downhill, but on the way back it's no joke climbing these steep slopes when your head is overheated and your legs are weak. But the fresh air sobers him up and allows him to escape a scolding from Mme Longeaud. She's always been cantankerous, but now she's turning into a real harpy. Maybe she would have been better-tempered if she had had children. But ever since she has had to accept that she would remain childless, she has moped, fretted, got thin as a rake, and her intolerance has taken on ridiculous proportions. Better not to think about it… Even so, children… Longeaud has given up on that idea; he's seen too many of them. Not to mention the parents! Take that dunce Grandjean's parents. You keep these cretins' noses to the grindstone for two years, three years, you drive them as hard as you can, you just about manage to get them to take the exam, which they scrape through thanks to you alone, and what recognition do you get from the parents for all your trouble? A dozen eggs! Oh, if he depended only on the gratitude of his pupils, he'd always be tightening his belt. Of course the Grandjeans are a family of reactionaries, the father is a big shot in the Veterans' Legion and the mother is a church busybody. The countryside is still in the dark ages! Look what happens when you try to teach them about progress and justice!

Francheville, 2 km. M. Longeaud is a standard-bearer for

progress and justice. It has been his lifelong vocation. Yes, he's always been an idealist, and he always will be. Even in these difficult times he has remained steadfast, he has never wavered for a moment. But – and he is proud of this – he has never sold out to any party, and this has allowed him to keep the freedom of his convictions. Anyway, party membership involves all sorts of tiresome duties. But he has never hidden where his sympathies lie. Before the war he was a member of the League of Human Rights, and of the local branch of the Front Populaire, and he could often be seen at meetings, sitting on the platform along with the other eminent figures. Whenever a compromise had to be reached on the agenda, or a well-turned resolution had to be delivered, his proposals were always appreciated. Well, maybe that's all ancient history now, but M. Longeaud has still not had his last word.

Francheville, 1 km. Ah! If only it was up to him! If his wife didn't hold him back so much, it wasn't too late for him to show what he could do. But she's always moaning, mocking his opinions, and for some time now she has even been attending mass regularly. A teacher in a state school! When he married her, he never expected that. But the Curé has got round her, as he has so many others… Hardly surprising that with ideas like that, she holds him back as she does… As if he's not big enough to look after himself! He's not going to make mistakes like that hothead Galtier, who has been suspended for speaking without choosing his audience carefully enough, and now has to take any private lessons he can get. He, Camille Longeaud, would never dream of giving ration cards to people whose papers are not in order, as Serray does in Saint-Paul. It's just pure bravado, trivial stuff, not worth the risk. You have to take care, because if you're stupid enough to get locked up, you deprive the cause of a worthy defendant in its time of need.

Francheville, 0.2 km. Yes, a worthy defendant, as events will prove. But in the meantime you have to live in the present, in the real world. And the most immediate reality is the gathering of friends, at the Café de la Poste, towards which M. Longeaud now hastens, with gusto and a parched throat.

FRANCHEVILLE ...

II

Francheville: population 4,800, according to *Larousse*. Paper mills, sawmills. 'A market town which you might take for a sub-prefecture' as the local newspaper reporter likes to say. The town is served by a pathetic little local train providing connections to the mainline routes, and some twice-weekly buses, which operate according to a whimsical timetable.

Paper mills, sawmills. But that doesn't make Francheville an industrial centre. It's a sprawling town hemmed in by steep hills dotted with hamlets and villages, whose farmers make their way down to the market on Thursdays, just as a thousand springs and tributaries flow into the lively river which splits the town in two. Throughout the ages, Francheville has been a focus of local trade, so its population consists largely of shop-keepers and craftsmen. Industrial workers are something of a novelty, but hardly noticeable. As they are few in number and do not rock the boat, Francheville has always had the good fortune to elect representatives committed to the traditional order of things.

Even in this third year of war, Francheville is still a quiet place. In fact the war never got this far: it stopped about forty kilometres away. Instead of pressing on, the occupying forces actually withdrew further north after the armistice. Francheville has suffered neither damage nor shelling. Its inhabitants have got used to the sound of planes flying south in the night. In May

1942, it is one of the few towns in Europe where blackout orders have not been enforced.

So the war has spared the population of Francheville up to now. Neither life nor property has been taken. In contrast with the dreadfully long roll of dead in the previous conflict, inscribed on the base of the War Memorial, only one person born in Francheville has been killed by the enemy. Instead of bringing notification of deaths in action, the postman delivers cards and messages from prisoners. As far as this quiet town is concerned, if it was not for these messages, and if it was not for the hundred or so refugees in and around Francheville, the war would be nothing but a distant rumble of thunder, or one of those dreadful earthquakes in China you only read about in the papers. But the Veterans' Legion is there to remind the local population that their people's defeat in war is a just retribution for their laziness, inflicted from above.

'We have been defeated… You have been defeated… Defeated… Defeated…,' speakers from Lyon or Marseille keep solemnly drumming in.

Defeated! Food ration cards, textile coupons, compulsory registration, suppliers' licences. The black market, in its victorious march across Europe, has also made its appearance in Francheville, though timidly as yet. Bartering, however, already has a number of practitioners, in particular M. Chameix, the enterprising young dispensing chemist at the Croix Blanche pharmacy. He gives up his tobacco ration, for example, in exchange for coffee; then he swaps the coffee for butter; and then he exchanges the butter for a double ration of cigarettes. You have to keep up with the times, don't you?

Francheville is a fully fledged town. But for its size, it might even consider itself a city.

Like everywhere else, there is too much of some things and too little of others at the same time. What abounds in

Francheville? Watering holes, for a start. Nobody knows the exact number, because in addition to licensed premises there are cafés, hotels and, on the outskirts, grocers who serve drinks over the counter. The Francheville climate is conducive to thirst.

Thirteen, the unlucky number. What are there thirteen of, in Francheville? Grocery stores. Actual grocery stocks vanished long ago, but visitors sometimes winkle out rarities such as a coffee grinder, a scouring pad, a toothbrush, maybe even some crockery, always on condition, of course, that the shopkeeper takes a liking to them. But on the whole, business is slow. As grocers await their official charter, they have become a sort of administration. Each of them knows how many customers he has, and what they will buy. The element of surprise has gone.

Seven, the lucky number. What are there seven of in Francheville? Seven hotels. Francheville boasts a fine gastronomic tradition. The Hôtel Farémido is proud to be one of only eleven in France to be awarded three stars by the Gourmet Guide. Its dining room has seen its share of stars, political, financial and artistic. Even today, the food there is excellent. Since 1940, the Hôtel Farémido has been full. So, indeed, have the others.

What are there six of in Francheville? There are six butchers in Francheville. They only open two days a week, but make up for it by nocturnal activity. By starlight, with their lorry or cart, or simply on foot, they are out and about in the farms, slaughtering livestock for the black market.

What are there five of in Francheville? Five places of worship. The Church, of course; then the Protestant Church, the Free Evangelical Church, the Salvation Army, and the Darbyist meeting room. The Methodists meet at each other's houses. Half the population is Catholic, and the other half is split amongst the different Protestant persuasions. Religious feeling runs high, and mixed marriages are rare.

What are there four of in Francheville? Four bookshops. Four bookshops, but nothing to read. Like an invasive weed, haberdashery has taken over the shelves. But Francheville intellectuals can resort to the Public Library where, for ten centimes, they can borrow from a collection of about 200 books: works by Zenaïde Fleuriot, by Gyp, or by Georges Ohnet.

What are there three of in Francheville? Three timber merchants. But no firewood for sale, in spite of the fact that the surrounding hills are covered in chestnuts, pines and oaks. Since the taxation of firewood, the merchants have specialised in wood for cabinet makers and clog manufacturers.

A lot of things come in pairs in Francheville. Political parties, for a start: left and right, as is proper. There are two newsagents, too: the ex-reactionary and the one who sells what used to be called 'progressive' newspapers. Nowadays all these rags carry the same news and virtually identical opinions.

There are also two tobacconists. Within living memory, no one who voted on the left had ever set foot in widow Collet's shop, and no one who voted on the right had ever bought a box of matches at old Matthieu's. These days people might be more flexible, and prepared to buy tobacco from either, but it's too late.

'La Ménagère', a foodstore chain with outlets in every little town south of the Loire, also has two branches in Francheville. The window display of one consists of photographs in red, white and blue, along with historical slogans. The manager of the other sometimes makes subversive remarks. But what of it? The money goes into the same coffers.

Then there are the two chemists'. The older one, the Croix Blanche, belongs to the Maire. It's a respectable establishment with traditional values. In the window are some flasks containing coloured liquids, an advertisement for a reputable purgative, and some jars of Abbé Soury's Youth Elixir. The other chemist's, the Pharmacie Moderne, lives up to its name. It has an illuminated sign which hasn't worked for some time, and attracts passers-by with cosmetics, bottles of Eau de Cologne, support belts for sportsmen and hormone supplements.

There are also two doctors in Francheville, one Catholic and the other Protestant. The latter also treats left-wingers, regardless of their faith. Actually, no one has ever seen Dr Manueli at mass, or Dr Colin at the Protestant Church. But the former stepped into the shoes of the Catholic doctor five years ago, and at the end of the last war the latter bought out the surgery which had Protestant patients. Since then, the lines have been drawn. Dr Colin is best known in the countryside. Dr Manueli has the ear of the tradesmen. He persuades them that their best capital is their own health, that the most sacred of their investments is the one they make in looking after themselves, and that their duty as head of household is to undertake treatment in good time, as otherwise they are rashly mortgaging their future.

And finally, there are two banks in Francheville. A Banque Populaire for the little people, and a branch of the Crédit Lyonnais, where the manager's office is nothing less than a surgery for people who suffer from financial afflictions. Behind the padded door, the manager listens sympathetically to his patients' woes, takes their pulse, and prescribes for one, an injection of Suez; for another, a massive dose of Royal Dutch; and for a third, an emergency operation on his Péchiney. International securities retain their prestige. Thus, thanks to Francheville money, the area around Reykjavik has got electricity. It may happen that the Cafro-Boer Company goes bust, or that the government of Nicaragua prohibits the export of dividends. But everyone knows that capitalism entails risks.

What is unique in Francheville? A Mairie, of course, spanking new, neo-classical with pinnacles, and daubed in administration brown. A small station; and a nice new hospital run by nuns.

There is also a post office. It is never empty, and on market days the queue stretches back into the street; for the counter itself is also the only one of its kind in Francheville. Actually, on closer inspection, there are two counters, but the second one is always closed. At any time of day there are always five or six staff absorbed in mysterious tasks behind the grille; but there is only one to deal with the public. It isn't her fault if you have to queue for an hour in order to buy a stamp. It's no fun for her: she has to work without a break, and the rules require her to make lengthy, complicated calculations whenever she reaches the bottom of the page, while the customers stamp their feet in frustration.

What can you not find in Francheville? There is no dentist. The dentist from the nearest town visits once a week, on market day. Maybe the 5,000 inhabitants, plus another 10,000 in the surrounding villages, are not enough to provide a living for a full-time dentist. In fact, hardly anyone goes to the dentist except to have a painful tooth extracted. Some traveller once said that on average, any two Arabs only have three eyes between them. Similarly, you might say that any two country people around Francheville have between them thirty-two teeth, half of which are rotten.

There is no public sports stadium in Francheville. Nor are there any baths, public or otherwise. But this absence is relatively recent. On the outskirts of Francheville are the traces of Gallo-Roman baths, and one of the fortresses overlooking the town still has the remains of a steam bath built by a sybaritic knight on his return from a crusade. They say that this bath was still in use at the end of the fifteenth century. It must have been rendered obsolete by the march of progress. But it would be wrong to draw hasty conclusions. Twentieth-century knights can still take a bath in Francheville. They only need to dismount at the Hôtel Farémido, which is fully equipped with modern facilities. If they can afford it.

At the station, there is no porter, to the great consternation of M. Frank Rosenfeld, the new tenant at Les Tilleuls, who has just got off the train with all his luggage.

III

Mme Hermelin's unexpected appearance on the station platform was a great relief to Frank Rosenfeld.

'What a good idea to come on a Thursday, it's market day. My neighbour will take your luggage up in his cart,' said Mme Hermelin. Her tenant's heavy jowls spread into a smile which revealed his gold teeth, as he bowed ceremoniously over the good lady's bony hand.

Aged about forty, he was short in stature, and squeezed into a jacket which had seen better days. His grey felt hat swung in one hand, and his head looked immodestly bald, apart from two tufts of grey hair behind his ears. He spoke French fluently, with a grating, guttural accent.

'Twenty to twelve,' said Rosenfeld, once he had helped Mme Hermelin's obliging neighbour to lift his cases onto the cart. 'I will take my lunch here. Can you recommend somewhere I can eat well without breaking the bank?'

Mme Hermelin thought for a moment. Recommending a competitor is always a delicate matter.

'I'll take you to the Hôtel Panorama,' she said, with a little hesitation. 'It's not too bad, at least until your intended can prepare you some nice meals with the produce of your farm. How is she, by the way?'

'Very well, thank you. She'll be coming to join me as soon as she gets her pass.'

In 1942, foreigners living in the free zone could not in fact go anywhere at all without special permission from the Prefecture.

'Let's hope it doesn't take long,' said Mme Hermelin, sighing, and casting her eyes up to heaven. 'What joy, to be united at last before God! Believe me, there's nothing better than family life. In the meantime, if you wish, you can eat at my house. In fact this evening we're having nettle soup. You don't get that in the city, it's such a shame. It's delicious, you'll see.'

'I would be delighted to,' he said. 'Nettle soup, you say? I'll take a note of your recipe, I like cooking myself when I have the time.'

The new tenant at Les Tilleuls, something of a handyman and a dabbler, prided himself on his many talents. Listening to him, it was easy to conclude that there were hardly any realms of human activity he was completely unfamiliar with.

'Oh, really?' said Mme Hermelin. 'How interesting!'

'One day, if you will allow me, I'll cook you some dishes which are popular in my country, like carp with sweet sauce and raisins.'

Mme Hermelin gave him a puzzled look. Was he pulling her leg? Apparently not. He went on enthusiatically, 'If we can get hold of some calves' trotters from the butcher, I'll cook them with prunes for you, it's a dish fit for a king!'

Mme Hermelin began to feel rather queasy, but she smiled bravely. They were just reaching the main square, where they found Francheville's depleted market packing up. No longer did you see pigs, mounds of butter, piles of goats' cheeses. A few scrawny calves, if you were lucky. Four or five trays of seeds, straw hats, clogs, ties and knick-knacks.

'How I wish you could have seen our markets before the war!' sighed Mme Hermelin. 'But we mustn't be self-pitying, it's a sign of ingratitude towards the Almighty. Here in the country, life goes on. I'm sorry for the poor townspeople who write begging me for a room in my house. Just reading their letters is heartbreaking.'

'I imagine your guests come from Marseille?' asked Rosenfeld, pointedly. 'You already know these people, I suppose?'

'Hardly, hardly. In fact I placed an advertisement in a Lyon restaurant which is popular with intellectuals, a very good class of people.'

'Intellectuals?' asked the foreigner. He sounded worried.

'That's what they told me. So you know who you're dealing with. Whereas if I had advertised in the paper…'

'Just a minute,' her tenant pressed her anxiously. 'What about these… intellectuals?'

'From those who wrote to me, I've selected M. Fleury, who's a distinguished musician. He's coming with his wife and daughter. I think he works at the radio.'

The foreigner seemed reassured.

'He is French, isn't he?' he asked.

'Of course,' said Mme Hermelin. 'He's a state employee, so he must be. And my other guest is an excellent gentleman too, a M. Murger.'

'Murger?' repeated the other, concerned. 'I know several Bergers who are not French. Murger sounds a bit similar. So I wonder if…'

'Oh I don't think so.' Mme Hermelin sounded apologetic. 'It's a very French name. M. Murger is a young engineer who was taken prisoner for a time, and he's here for health reasons. The nettles will do him good at this time of year.'

Her tenant seemed embarrassed. 'I only ask because…'

'I understand completely.' Mme Hermelin interrupted him benevolently. 'You're afraid of being homesick here. But don't worry, you won't be lonely. A family has just arrived from Marseilles, and I think Monsieur is in a similar situation to yours. I met him the other day as he was on his way here. Very well educated.'

'In my situation?' blurted Rosenfeld, showing signs of apoplexy.

'Yes,' said Mme Hermelin, still kindly. 'Another… Israelite, as I've heard. So you won't be alone.'

'Ah! That's the limit!' cried Mme Hermelin's new tenant, his voice guttural with emotion. 'I came to this godforsaken hole because your son, the minister, promised me there was not a single Jew in the whole village. And what do I find? There's already a whole family! I have to tell you, I'm disappointed. I'm very disappointed.'

His easy-going jovial manner was gone, and his voice had taken on a harsher tone. Pushing his hat onto the back of his head, he glared defiantly at Mme Hermelin. 'When I decided to withdraw to the country,' he said, controlling himself with difficulty, 'I was looking for a refuge, a haven where I could live undisturbed. But if this Department turns out to be like the Drôme, which I hear has become a regular Jews' playground, then I'm wasting my time!'

Mme Hermelin was worried now. 'Come, come,' she said. 'I don't actually know if he's an Israelite. All I know is, he's an intellectual and he's a foreigner.'

'A foreign intellectual is always suspect.'

'I assure you,' Mme Hermelin resumed, 'that you will be very comfortable at Les Tilleuls. Nobody's going to quiz you about your faith.'

And she added, portentously: 'I do know, of course. My son, the minister, told me. A momentous event is about to occur in your life.'

'Just so, just so,' muttered the foreigner, and continued in a calmer tone, 'You must excuse me, my nerves are all on edge. Lately the slightest thing upsets me. For example, at the ticket office, when I was changing trains, I saw someone who looked distinctly Semitic, and it really depressed me. I didn't see him again, fortunately. But that cast a cloud over my whole journey. I tell you once and for all – I don't want to see any Jews here!'

'Of course, of course,' said Mme Hermelin, anxious to calm him down. 'You'll hardly come across any in Saint-Boniface. Now, here we are – the Panorama. I will wish you bon appétit, Monsieur… Monsieur Rose… forgive me, I just can't seem to grasp your name. Will you please remind me?'

'Rosenfeld,' he said modestly. 'Frank Rosenfeld.'

'Quite so, quite so… it's just that for French people it's a bit difficult…'

'I do understand,' said M. Frank Rosenfeld. 'Why don't you just call me M. Rose. M. François Rose. It's the same thing, and it's so much easier. My respects, Madame.'

IV

M. Rosenfeld was indeed a strange man, thought Mme Hermelin. But she excused his mood swings, which she put down to his exhausting city life, the lack of food supplies, and all the trouble that people of his background were having.

Thinking about this, she went back across the market square. Suddenly, she thought she overheard her name, and turned round. Two of the farmers' wives, Noémi Sobrevin from Les Mottes and Sébastienne Latière from La Barbarie, were deep in conversation. As they had their backs to her, she decided she must be mistaken and continued on her way. But they were indeed talking about her. Sébastienne was recounting to Noémi a sensational event she had heard about from Irma Laffont, who had it from Eugénie Vautier, who had it from Rosalie Tournier. Last Saturday, Mme Hermelin had rushed into the grocer's in a frenzy, snatched a loaf of bread, and run off, 'savaging it like a dog'.

Such were the successive embellishments which the collective imagination of the village had brought to the little episode of the slice of bread the good lady had unceremoniously cut for herself at Tournier's, while waiting for her call to come through.

'I don't believe it! I don't believe it!' Noémi kept saying, wide-eyed in amazement. 'Saturday, you say? Yes, I remember. She came to see me, she made me get behind with my work. But I wouldn't have thought she'd do anything like that. She was in a bit of a state though!'

By this time, Mme Hermelin had reached the Croix Blanche chemist's, where she stopped to wonder whether to go in and buy a bottle of Abbé Soury's Youth Elixir. She had been wanting it for months, after all; but she had not yet been able to decide. Aunt Annie's recommendation was a guarantee, of course, but on the other hand the Abbé Soury was obviously a Catholic, and it was open to question whether his remedy would be quite so effective for Protestants. The matter had to be weighed up carefully. Sorely tempted, she was about to give in when something unexpected happened. A stranger, a short man of about thirty with untidy tightly curled reddish hair, came up to her.

'Mme Hermelin?'

She looked at him in surprise.

'The man in the bookshop opposite told me to speak to you. He says you take in lodgers. I'm here for a few days with my wife and my son.'

He had a foreign accent, with rolled Rs and slightly diphthonged vowels, which made his French sound very different from M. Rosenfeld's.

'That's right,' said Mme Hermelin, instantly putting on her professional smile. 'I run a guest house.'

'In Saint-Boniface, isn't it?' asked the foreigner.

'Yes, Les Tilleuls in Saint-Boniface.'

Even as she spoke, a terrible thought struck her. M.

Rosenfeld's warning was still buzzing in her ears. What if this man was also an Israelite? That would mean trouble! M. Rosenfeld might get really angry, maybe even go somewhere else. That would leave her short of a client, and of the perks she hoped for: milk, butter, eggs...

'So you'd like to spend some time in Saint-Boniface?' she continued. 'For the country air? Maybe you're from abroad? I hope I'm not being indiscreet.'

'Not at all!' said the foreigner easily. 'We're Haitian.'

'What?' said Mme Hermelin, thinking she had misheard.

'Haitian. The island of Haiti, you know?'

The wife of the retired tax inspector searched her memory. Haiti... Haiti... somewhere in those islands near America... the people who lived there were black. But this man wasn't black!

Wait a minute though... tightly-curled hair... a short flared nose... thick lips... were those not features of the black race?

Suddenly, she realised. But of course! She should have known straight away! He was one of those white black men! She had read about them. And had she not just seen in the *Nouvelliste* that a Brazilian expert had developed a technique which turned black people white? If this man was not black, he must have some black blood in him. Obvious, really, since he was Haitian.

Mme Hermelin had got to this point when a child of four, one foot on his scooter, came up to the foreigner.

'Papa! Maman is looking for you!'

The little chap looked astonishingly like his father, apart from his hair which was a deep black. His tanned face was a light mahogany colour which could indeed be from one of those little 'hot countries'.

Mme Hermelin, congratulating herself on her wisdom, turned back to the foreigner.

'If you're looking for lodgings, I can offer you a twin room. You'll be very comfortable. There's a splendid view. And you're lucky because in a few days I will be fully booked.'

Excited by the prospect of business, she had forgotten all about the Abbé Soury's Youth Elixir.

'How much?' asked the foreigner, prudently.

Mme Hermelin was going to quote him the price she had given to those who had written to her. But on second thoughts, an American, even a black one, could afford more. She immediately added an extra five francs per person, per day.

V

Leaving the main road to follow the line of chestnut trees bordering the track to Les Tilleuls, Frank Rosenfeld was now in excellent spirits. Whistling to himself, he anticipated the pleasures of a quiet, healthy life in the open air, which would quickly blot out the memory of his recent disturbed months.

For the tapestry of Rosenfeld's life in Lyon since 1940 had not exactly been woven in silk. Sometimes in the night, he would wake in a cold sweat with his nightshirt clinging to him, and listen out in terror: the terror that one day he would be picked up, sent to a concentration camp, or even deported.

He consoled himself that he had earned his place. He had fought for his country, and had medals to prove it. So far, nobody had bothered him too much, apart from the occasional identity check. But others had been less fortunate, and he was deeply disturbed by the thought he might come to share their fate. He had been questioned several times in the street by police who wanted to know if he was a Jew. He had twice been taken to a triage station. Because of his past record, he had been released on both occasions; but how could he know if he would be so lucky the next time? At Saint-Boniface, he expected to be free, at last, of all these fears.

He intended to start a new life, an entirely new life. It wouldn't be the first resurrection in Frank Rosenfeld's somewhat chequered existence. Barely twenty, at the end of the last war, he had left his native Riga to join the fight against the Bolsheviks. From there he had made his way, penniless, to Germany, where he had managed to complete his studies, supporting himself with teaching work and undeclared jobs which he picked up here and there. He also benefited from the attentions of a middle-aged widow he had been introduced to in the Romanisches Café. Having obtained his degree in architecture, he worked for a few years in Germany and then, in 1931, sensing that the Berlin political climate was too hot for comfort, he had come to try his luck in Paris. It wasn't easy at first, but in the end he managed to find a fairly secure job. Oh, it wasn't the construction of great stadiums or viaducts. All he had to do was draw up estimates for a building contractor promoting the ideal two-bedroom suburban home. 'All the latest mod cons', announced the stand at the annual Paris Trade Fair, 'Grace and space in the smallest place'.

Now, a new chapter was to open in M. Rosenfeld's life. It could be called 'Return to the Land'. But actually it was a return without a corresponding departure, since what M. Rosenfeld knew of the land was limited to what he had seen from the train. For this chapter to open, it was imperative that Saint-Boniface, this refuge, this haven, should not become a ghetto. Certainly not! Two Jews might pass unnoticed, being nowhere near the official quota when outnumbered by countless hundreds of locals spread over a wide area. But he had to look to the future, and do everything he could to prevent any possible invasion. The Semitic face at the ticket office haunted him. One of the first things to do was to go and see the Maire and get him to promise not to allow any other Jews to settle in the village.

As for Mme Hermelin, her lack of discretion had to be tackled. How dare she remind him of his intention to be converted! He had of course told her son, the minister, that he had misgivings, and that he had decided to devote himself to Christ, but he had taken care not to tell him whether this was to be a Protestant Christ or a Catholic Christ. Actually, when he was in Lyon, Abbé Paroli had leaned heavily on him in favour of Catholicism, and had even given him a letter of introduction to the Curé of Saint-Boniface. So it would be better not to commit himself before he had seen the Curé.

Conversion! Wasn't it a bit late, since the authorities wouldn't recognise recent conversions? But the priests and the ministers would. When Rosenfeld talked about this with Abbé Paroli or with the minister Jérémie Hermelin, they expounded fulsomely in unctuous reassuring phrases intended to ensure the return of the lost sheep to the fold. The lost sheep, of course, had nothing against this, as long as he was protected from the wolves. If his great-grandfather had had this bright idea, he, Frank Rosenfeld, would not be in this position today. He would be like Montaigne, whom nobody, not even Maurras, ever accused of being of Jewish descent. Suddenly he felt a bitter surge of resentment against this remote ancestor who, for some obscure fanatical reason, had refused to give up his traditional houppelande and his ringlets. The stubborn old fool! Why did he have to make such a point of singling himself out! Rosenfeld, on the other hand, had but one ambition: to lose himself in the crowd. Ah! To melt anonymously into the background, to pass unnoticed, to bide his time in anticipation of a more comfortable era in which he could be born anew. It was to this end, of course, that he had come to Saint-Boniface. Here he would till a small plot of land, marry an Aryan girl, and wait for the storm to pass.

Suddenly, Les Tilleuls came into view, a rectangular building set behind a clump of shrubs. How welcoming this house looked, and how peaceful! With the trees in leaf, it looked even more attractive than on the cold, windswept April day when he had first come to visit. Yes, it was indeed the haven, the ideal refuge…

He was approaching the house when a guttural cry made him start violently.

'*Ni, Rivke, wi bist di? Di kimst?*'

Frank Rosenfeld, thunderstruck, stood rooted to the ground.

'*Also di kimst?*' repeated the guttural voice, more loudly.

As the echo died away, a whirlwind descended on Rosenfeld, wiping out the valleys, chestnut trees and broom-bordered footpaths, and summoning up the fogs of Riga, the grey walls, the grim alleys of his native ghetto, and the Talmudists with their braided hair, who would call, in this very same voice, with the very same words, to a wife who had lingered too long gossiping in the yard…

His vision faded. On the hills and woods, the sun shone brightly once more. But Rosenfeld had not imagined it. A man had called out, in Yiddish, to a woman whose biblical name, Rebecca, was mangled by the dialect of the ghetto.

He was overcome with rage. What hellhole was this? Call it a haven? More like an ambush!

Devastated, all his illusions shattered, Rosenfeld's first thought was to turn on his heel, and head back to Francheville for the first train to Lyon.

Why is it that when heroic decisions are to be acted upon, drab reality always gets in the way? Rosenfeld's luggage was already at Les Tilleuls, his hotel room in Lyon was no longer available and, to cap it all, he did not have a pass for the return journey. There was no alternative but to face this curse.

He stepped forward determinedly to the front door. At the same moment, it opened, and someone came out. At first he could not believe his eyes. It was the man from the ticket office with the unmistakable features.

Rosenfeld felt a violent urge to throw himself on the man and strangle him. It could, after all, be seen as self-defence. But he overcame this savage impulse, and simply looked him up and down disdainfully.

'Looking for Mme Hermelin?' said the foreigner. 'She's gone up to the farm. You're the new tenant, aren't you? I was to tell you she'll be back soon.'

'That's OK, I'll wait,' said Rosenfeld, chewing his lip.

He went into the sitting room and collapsed into an armchair. He was trying to put his swirling thoughts in order when the door opened. The little red-haired man came towards him.

'I was going to unpack, but my wife has gone out with the keys in her bag.'

He fell silent, looking at the other man. Suddenly, and impertinently, he put on an air of familiarity, mixed with the mysterious complicity used by conspirators when they utter a password.

'Yid?'

That was the last straw. During his long stay in France, Frank Rosenfeld had been called foreigner, *métèque*, Israelite, Jew, *youpin*, or even *youtre*; but never Yid! He took on a disdainful air.

'None of your business. What are you doing here?'

'And what are *you* doing here?' retorted the Yid, unperturbed.

'You know perfectly well, I've rented a house.'

'Ah! A house? But what's your job?'

'And what's yours?' responded Rosenfeld aggressively.

'Me? I'm a demolition expert.'

'It suits you,' growled Rosenfeld. 'What do you demolish?'

'Cars. I dismantle them for spares.'

'And of course you're out of work at the moment. You're

Polish, aren't you?'

'Is that what you think?' said the other with a sly look. 'You couldn't be more wrong.'

'Not Polish? I don't believe you!'

'It's true though. I'm Haitian.'

'What?'

'Haitian, you heard me.'

To Rosenfeld's astonishment, he proudly produced a passport, complete with photograph.

Rosenfeld took a quick glance, and recoiled in horror. That was all he needed. These counterfeit documents would have the police knocking at the door of Les Tilleuls in no time.

'Forged papers!' he said, choking.

'Not at all,' said the foreigner. 'Absolutely genuine. Real papers.'

'You're joking.'

'I'm telling you. Don't you believe me? Why are you looking like that? Genuine fakes, see!'

VI

Mme Hermelin's white black man was telling the truth. His passport was not a common forgery, even though he was far from being a native of Haiti, a country whose existence he had never even dreamt of. But it had been issued to him by the Haitian Consul in Paris, at the consular offices, in accordance with all the formalities required by Haitian law, and on top of all that the official stamp and the signature were genuine. There was, however, just one thing...

A few months before, Bernard Bloch, age: 31, nationality: Polish, domicile: Boulogne-sur-Seine, profession: scrap metal dealer, activity: vehicle dismantling and second-hand parts sales, the owner of a small workshop, was lamenting his fate in a poky hideout in a friend's flat. He was there because he had received an urgent summons to his local police station, instructing him to bring his personal possessions and a change of clothing. It wasn't hard to guess what this would lead to. Downcast and fatalistic, M. Bernard Bloch, who had a healthy respect for the power of the law, was preparing himself for the worst when his wife, a determined and energetic little woman, took violent exception and persuaded him to cut and run, although in his particular case he could only run as far as a cupboard provided for him by a friend in Noisy-le-Sec.

On the fourth day of his voluntary incarceration, he received a visit from his wife Rebecca, whom he called Renée when in company, so as not to offend French ears.

'I've got wonderful news,' she said, 'We're going to America!'

At first, Bernard thought this was a joke in bad taste. But once she had explained her plan, he jumped at it. As she worked in a chic fashion house, it had occurred to Renée Bloch to speak to one of her clients, who happened to be the wife of the Haitian consul. This lady had taken her immediately to the consul's office. Officially, the premises were closed, as most of the consulates and legations had received instructions to leave Paris some time ago; but the Haitian consul had chosen to stay, even though it meant resigning his post. He listened to Renée's story with great interest, and offered the couple a means of escape. According to him, there was a law which allowed the consul to confer Haitian nationality for a limited period on anyone who had provided services to that country and wished to settle there. Such services could, in this particular instance, be represented by the payment of one hundred thousand francs.

It was all perfectly legal. The consul added that on arrival in Haiti they would have to swear allegiance to the constitution, a necessary formality without which the document would be worthless, and Renée had no hesitation in promising to do this.

The greatest hurdle was getting out of the occupied zone. But once in Marseille they would be able to sail directly to Martinique, and from there it would be only a short hop to their newly-adopted homeland.

They still had to find the money. You don't amass such a fortune by vehicle breaking, even over a period of eleven years. But in addition to their modest savings, they owned all their furniture, a few bits of family jewellery and a small stock of spare parts and scrap metal. If they could sell everything, it looked as if they would be able to render the requisite services to the Haitian Republic.

In the meantime, Renée had not sought to hide from this accommodating official the fact that they might not be able to afford the fare for the journey. The consul was reassuring. In Marseilles, he said, there was a philanthropic organisation which could help emigrants, provided their papers were in order.

Energised by this plan, Bernard Bloch relinquished his cupboard and his dejection, promptly took care of the liquidation of his assets, and two weeks later he was crossing, unchallenged, out of the occupied zone, hidden under a load of baguettes in the back of a baker's van. His wife and son followed the next day.

Their disappointments began in Marseille. To start with, the Blochs found that the Marseille-Martinique line had just been discontinued. The only way to get to Haiti now was from a Spanish port, which raised a number of difficulties, in addition to the considerable extra expense. One of these soon proved insurmountable. The Haitian consul, no longer officially employed in Paris when he issued the passports, had devised a clever trick. From his time as consul in a Spanish city, he had kept some headed notepaper and rubber stamps. What he had done was pre-date the passports as if he had issued them when he was in office in Spain. This trivial detail seemed of no consequence as long as they didn't have to be shown to the Spanish authorities. But as the Blochs now had to travel via Spain, they could not escape the fact that the documents were not worth the paper they were printed on.

In desperation, Bloch tried a last throw of the dice. One of his uncles on his father's side had emigrated to the United States as a young man, following a pogrom. He had set up in business in New York and still wrote, once a year, to his brother in Poland. Maybe, Bloch told himself, this uncle could help him escape the Old World.

The problem was that Bernard knew neither Uncle Isidore's address nor the nature of his business. Then he had an idea. He took himself to the United States consulate, a latter-day Wailing Wall constantly besieged by thousands of would-be émigrés. After queuing from five in the morning until four in the afternoon, repeatedly barked at and bullied by the guards, Bloch finally got what he needed, which was simply an address where he might consult the New York telephone directory. In it he found three pages full of Blochs, of which twelve were called Isidore, and seven were businessmen.

Painstakingly, he noted the seven addresses, and that evening he wrote seven identical letters, as if starting a chain, and sent them off by registered post early in the morning. Stupefied, the lady at the post office looked at him as if he was off his head.

For months, Bloch holed up in furnished accommodation in Cassis, near Marseille, and watched out for the postman morning and afternoon. Nothing. The seven Isidores might as well be dead. Bernard Bloch gave himself over to bitter reflections on the fragile nature of family ties. Seeing his funds dwindling, and after a sleepless night contemplating his fate, he told Renée:

'We've got exactly eight thousand seven hundred and twenty-one francs left. If we stay here, it will last us four months at the most. If we go and live in the country, we won't need much, and we could try to grow food ourselves.'

One hour later, at the Mairie in Cassis, Bloch was applying to the obliging secretary, Marie-Ange, for a travel pass.

VII

As Bernard Bloch came to the end of his tale, Frank Rosenfeld assumed a very sceptical expression.

'If I were you,' he said in a pitying tone, 'I wouldn't even take the trouble to unpack. I know this area well, and I can tell you the land here is poorer than almost anywhere else in France. Take my advice, it's not the place to learn farming.'

'I don't need to learn,' said the other. 'I was brought up in the country in Poland. When I was fifteen, I went to agricultural school for three years, because I wanted to emigrate to Palestine. I only came to France because I couldn't get my visa. And I'm used to manual labour. I worked at the Renault factory for two years; and since then, look, my hands haven't exactly been in my pockets.'

He spread out the short thick fingers of his strong calloused hands.

'Maybe so,' said Rosenfeld doubtfully. 'But that's even more reason to go somewhere your work will earn you good money.'

'Well then,' said Bloch with a knowing wink, 'why don't you do the same yourself?'

'Me?' said Rosenfeld, vaguely. 'It's different for me. My reasons are strictly personal.'

'Me too,' responded Bloch. 'My reasons are strictly personal too.'

'Oh come on! You don't know anyone here. And anyway, how on earth did you hit on Saint-Boniface, of all places, for your agricultural experiment?'

'Ah, well now! That's a long story. But since you seem to be interested, why don't I tell you? You're right: I don't know a soul in Saint-Boniface. But then I don't know a soul anywhere else either. My wife and I have never lived outside Paris. So when we had to choose, I said let's take pot luck. I got a Michelin map of the South-East, closed my eyes, and stuck a pencil into it. When I looked, I found the pencil was on the B of Saint-Boniface. I took a liking to the name. And I like the place too. Anyway, it's too late, I can't change my mind now.'

'Why's that? You can still go somewhere else.'

'I'm afraid not. I have an assignment order.'

'An assignment order?' repeated Rosenfeld, frowning. 'That's just for foreigners who've been expelled from somewhere. You're not telling me you've been expelled from the Bouches-du-Rhône?'

'Not exactly. I had myself expelled. It's not the same. I even paid good money for it.'

'You're joking!' burst out Rosenfeld. 'What do you take me for? You might pay to stay where you are, but not to be expelled.'

'You're wrong. It happens all the time. I was recommended to a go-between in Marseille who, for a consideration of six hundred francs, will get you an assigned residence order, top-notch mind you, anywhere in France, except in town, of course. With a good assigned residence you can stay where you please, without being bounced around the country like a tennis ball. There aren't half a lot of wandering Jews in that situation, I can tell you.'

Rosenfeld gave in with a sigh. Clearly he was up against a tough nut. He still tried to make Bloch promise he would not invite any of his Jewish friends to Saint-Boniface. But the Haitian would have none of it.

'I'm just as much at home here as you are,' he finished, 'and I will do as I please. And if that doesn't suit you,' he added with his knowing wink, '*rif mich a pischer.*'

Chapter 3
Invaded by Civilisation

I

The Vautier-Verès honeymoon did not last long.

Mutual disappointment had set in on the way to Saint-Boniface. Even before the caravan reached the La Grange farm, Eugénie Vautier was shocked to hear the 'lady from Marseille' asking insistently about the cost of living locally, and to see her expression darken when the price of certain items sounded too high. Were these new tenants not so well off, then?

Her disillusionment grew when she happened to find out that the lady was not Jewish, as she had believed, but Protestant, which was another thing altogether. Because although Jews had a reputation for being excellent clients, would it be the same thing if only the husband was Jewish? And what if it was the Protestant who held the purse strings? Eugénie thought that was all very complicated, and certainly a less attractive proposition than she had at first imagined.

The Verès, for their part, felt very let down when they found that electricity had not yet been installed in their new home, despite their landlord's assurance. When Verès asked about this on the way, Vautier broke his silence to give a lengthy but incomprehensible explanation about the 'lectric' not being ready yet, with a complex tale about suitable wood not being available for the supply pole, delays in the delivery of cabling, and a mysterious undiagnosed case of boils. But 'in two or three days' it would all be done. Verès, ever the optimist, believed him. He was not familiar with the local jargon.

The 'chalet', as gloomy as most of the houses in Saint-Boniface, hardly filled Mme Ellen Verès with delight. Some housework had been done in a hurry, with all sorts of rubbish swept into a corner. Vautier had not got round to whitewashing the walls, in spite of what he had promised in his letter. In short, apart from the furniture which had been brought down from the hayloft, the chalet had hardly changed since the departure of the last tenant, the immediate successor of the late Grandma Vautier: a fine black billy goat which entertained the local nanny-goats there every autumn.

'So this is home!' said Verès, delighted to be able to sit down at last.

As Vautier and his son were setting up the stove, Zette ran to whisper in her mother's ear. Leaving the baby in its father's care, Ellen took the girl by the hand and asked Vautier where the water closet was.

'Oh, the water closet?' said Vautier, scratching his head. 'There's a whole field behind the house, and the trees aren't far away.'

She couldn't bring herself to believe her ears. She was, after all, from the city, and Scandinavian to boot.

'But don't worry,' Vautier reassured her. 'In the winter you can use the stable, it doesn't harm the manure.'

In this gloomy picture there was nevertheless a ray of sunshine. Eugénie reappeared, having changed from her dress into an old pinny so patched that it looked like a Harlequin costume. Assuming a respectful smile, she placed on the table a basket covered with a tea towel.

'This is for your supper,' she said.

With ceremonious care, she uncovered the basket and took out a number of dishes. A piece of sausage, half a dozen eggs, a little pat of butter, two goat's milk cheeses, and even a slice of bacon, though it did look a bit rancid.

At the sight of these splendid victuals, Tibor Verès rubbed

his hands. This was the life!

Then Eugénie Vautier took another basket from her daughter, who had followed her. This one held a litre of milk, a round loaf, and a few kilos of potatoes.

'This'll do you for two or three days,' she said.

By this time Vautier had got the stove set up, and a fire was already crackling in it. He was now fiddling with a mysterious-looking object.

'What's the little metal tube for?' asked Verès.

'It's a carbide lamp. So you can see a bit better.'

'Carbide?' repeated the journalist, puzzled.

'Haven't you seen carbide before?' said Vautier, shoving a box full of little grey stones under his tenant's nose.

'Oh, I see, acetylene,' said Verès, recognising the smell.

'Carbide, 'cetylene, same thing,' answered the farmer. 'But I don't have much, mind you. People are always asking me for it.'

He unscrewed the base of the metal lamp, put some of the stones inside, blew into the burner a couple of times, placed it in an old tin can, poured some water in, and lit it. A white flame sprang up.

'*Fiat lux*,' cried Verès, delightedly.

'Oh, it's hardly deluxe,' said Vautier modestly, 'but still, it gives a bit of light.'

'How very simple and practical!' enthused the newcomer.

His wife came to examine it more warily. 'Will we know how to light it?' she ventured, timidly.

'My dear, it's simplicity itself,' Verès replied, condescendingly. 'And you'd easily mistake it for electricity.'

Left to themselves, the Verès unpacked the items they needed immediately, and set a pan of water to boil on the stove. Mme Vautier came in, carrying a steaming pot.

'Here's some soup for you,' she said. 'It's too late to start cooking this evening.'

'How well looked after we are,' cried Verès as the family sat down round the table. 'I wonder what they'll bring us tomorrow. Anyway, we've seen the last of those optical-illusion meals in Marseille which leave you starving, those "Bresse terrines" which are just boiled turnips and carrots, and that stew of Jerusalem artichokes they call "Pompadour Macédoine" just to give it a fancy name.'

After dinner, Verès lit a cigarette, congratulated himself on leaving Marseille behind, and carried on singing the praises of Saint-Boniface.

'They're so kind, you know, these farmers,' he remarked. 'They'll do anything for us. You shouldn't have let them see you were so upset that there's no water closet. We are in the country, after all. I read in a reputable history book that for a long time they were the privilege of the rich, they called them "houses of ease". And I'm sure it's still the case in these villages. Who knows, maybe "a house of ease" and "a life of ease" are connected. I'll have to look into it. Anyway, just be patient a little longer. When we're in New York we'll have a bathroom with mosaic tiles!'

Ellen humoured him, in spite of her scepticism. Since they had left Paris almost two years ago, her husband, formerly a journalist, had staked everything on this obstacle course of a journey. In Marseille it was hard not to catch emigration fever. When two refugees ran into each other, they didn't say 'How are you?' but 'Have you got your visa yet?' Verès had been no exception. He had applied for a visa to the United States, and got in touch with an association which helped intellectuals to emigrate.

The formalities turned out to be unbelievably complicated. Every official document required the provision of ten more. Guarantees of soundness in finances, morals, political views and hygiene were required one after the other, along with more and more detailed curricula vitae. When the Verès dossier had achieved the required thickness, one of the senior officials of the Washington Immigration Bureau, a latter-day Torquemada beset by nightmares, spawned the ultimate 'water test' to be inflicted on applicants before crossing the great pond: henceforth they had to provide irrefutable proof of the beliefs, morals and past history of their forebears, descendants and living relatives, as well as certified copies of death certificates for those no longer living. For people separated from extended families as a consequence of war, it was like trying to square the circle.

Uncle Sam defended himself fiercely against the washed-up wrecks of the war-torn Old World, and his imposition of arbitrary rules in this battle unquestionably gave him the upper hand.

With the help of the association, Verès had managed to make his way through the hoops of this obstacle course. All he needed now was final confirmation from the Immigration Office in Washington, which the experts told him would take two or three more months. What with the emotional stress and the effects of rationing, he had lost about fifteen kilos in the last six months. The forced sale of his Paris flat and his books had left him with a small amount of cash, which he had decided to spend on a rest cure and a fattening-up diet, in preparation for the great journey.

Exhausted by the trip from Marseille to Francheville as well as by the extravagance of their meal, the Verès were soon all asleep. But around two in the morning Ellen was awoken by a strange noise. From the ceiling, which was also the floor of the loft, came the pitter-patter of fairy feet. Soon Tibor was also awoken, by the sound of mysterious objects rolling around. From then until dawn they listened together as the rats held their merry dance.

Around half past six in the morning, Ellen went down to

the kitchen to heat a bottle for the baby who, in true Verès style, was already vociferously demanding his breakfast. A few minutes later Tibor, who had just gone back to sleep, was awoken by a tickling in his throat and a suffocating smell. Opening his eyes, he found the room was thick with smoke. And what smoke! Was the house on fire? The stairs led directly from the bedroom to the kitchen, and he rushed down in alarm.

Ellen was kneeling in front of the oven, her cheeks bright red, her eyes bloodshot, and her dressing gown covered in soot and ash. She had opened the kitchen door, but as smoke was escaping from the oven twice as fast as it was going out of the door, it was filling the whole house.

'What a clumsy thing you are!' said Verès, smiling indulgently. 'Can't you see you're cutting air off from the fire? Let me do it!'

He grabbed some sticks, threw them into the hearth, took a newspaper from an open suitcase, lit it with his lighter, and waited for the result. This duly came in the shape of a new cloud of smoke, three times as thick as before. In a fit of coughing, Verès tried to clear his throat and ran upstairs to open the window.

He repeated the exercise three times with no greater success, improvised a little scientific lecture on the combined action of warm air, cold air, soot and carbon dioxide, and started all over again.

After half an hour of intense activity, a miracle occurred. Smoke stopped escaping from the oven. Gradually, the air cleared.

'You see,' he said, 'Everything's possible if you just keep trying.'

'I don't doubt it,' said Ellen, 'but if we have to go through that every time we light the fire…'

After breakfast, which somehow used up the rest of the

butter, Verès went out to fill the can with water, taking Zette with him. Vautier was already out watering his garden.

'Water?' repeated Vautier with a troubled look. 'I'm afraid my spring is almost dry, and I still have to water the beans I sowed yesterday. So you'll need to get it from the spring down at the end of your neighbour's garden.'

'I didn't know I had a neighbour,' said Verès.

'Of course you have, didn't you see La Bardette? Go past the front of your house, straight on across the garden, take the path between the peas and the beans, and you'll see the spring a bit lower down. But don't take your daughter. She's an old woman and she doesn't like children. In fact you'll have to keep them quiet because she's got a bad temper. These old girls, you know...'

Tibor Verès thanked him profusely, took Zette back to her mother, and advanced towards his neighbour's garden on tiptoe. Now he could make out a closed door at the top of some stone steps.

Holding his breath, he took the narrow path across the garden. A little further on it forked, and the journalist stopped, unsure which way to go.

'Between the peas and the beans,' he repeated to himself vaguely. Well, he could certainly tell them apart on his plate, but in the garden all these green leaves looked the same to him. Between the peas and the beans? Life was indeed strewn with enigmas!

Fortunately, the sound of running water reached his ears and he soon saw a tiny trickle emerging from under a rock. Delighted, he filled the can and turned back up the path. As he did so, he began to tot up the number of trips he would have to make each day. He had read in some magazine that the average consumption for a civilised person, including cooking and washing, was at least ten litres per day. This can held five at best. Four tens are forty, forty divided by five is eight. In other words, eight return trips a day.

He had reached this point in his calculations and had just returned across his neighbour's garden when he saw that the door was now wide open. A wrinkled old hag, dressed in rags, a cat on each shoulder, was standing on the top step. So this evil-looking apparition was La Bardette!

Seeing the intruder, La Bardette frowned, and eyed him up and down with a cold, piercing stare. Verès bowed low, spilling quite a lot of water from his can, and addressed her in words which, on the banks of the Danube at least, pass for French-style courtesy: 'My respects, Madame.'

La Bardette nodded in reply, but her lips remained fiercely closed.

Feeling apologetic not only for his trespass but indeed for his very existence, Verès tiptoed onwards, a ballet dancer hardly touching the ground.

Eight trips a day... past this old crone's house sixteen times...

He found Ellen reviewing the provisions remaining for lunch.

'Well, I've got some potatoes,' she said thoughtfully, 'and I could open a packet of the noodles we brought from Marseille. We've still got half the cheese left, and a few slices of sausage...'

'That should be more than enough! We shouldn't pester them! We must put our trust in their sensitivity,' said the former journalist. 'I bet they'll bring us something of their own accord. A chicken, a rabbit maybe...'

But when lunchtime had come and gone without any sign of the Vautiers, it looked as if he had lost his bet.

'It's Sunday,' he told his family. 'They must be at Mass. Anyway, they're too busy during the day. We can't expect them to drop everything for our sake.'

Around three in the afternoon the whole family set off for

the village, pushing the baby in its pram.

The sun was setting when they got back to the 'chalet' at La Grange, but they were exhilarated by the beauty of the countryside, and all the better for having acquired a jar of mixed pickles which Verès had spied with cries of delight in Tournier's shop, where he had gone to sign up for wine and tobacco. There wasn't much else on the shelves, but he did find a tin of polish, and he bought a packet of rat poison in the hope of a quieter night.

Verès called at Vautier's to get the bottle of milk. He managed to prolong his visit by dragging out the small talk and making a few jokes, even though they fell on deaf ears. He wanted to give Eugénie Vautier time to refill yesterday's basket. But Eugénie just went on making soup. Verès decided it was best not to ask directly, and simply requested the services of a cat for the night, to get rid of the 'mice' in the hayloft – adopting this euphemism for fear of upsetting the Vautiers. The cat was indeed made available, and Verès shut it in the hayloft as soon as he got back. The mice would have to look out for themselves. The rat poison turned out to be three years old, so of dubious effectiveness. The polish was also completely dried up, so he could only consign it to the pile of rubbish left behind the house by Vautier's daughters when they had 'done the cleaning'.

It was getting dark. It was time to light the lamp.

Verès took great care to emulate Vautier's actions of the previous evening, but when he brought the match close to the nozzle, no flame started from it. Instead he heard only a sinister gurgling from the bottom of the can of water, in which the lamp was sitting.

'The water comes up the tube to the stone, which it dissolves to make the inflammable gas,' Verès told his family with scientific precision. 'We just have to wait a minute before we strike another match.'

Which he did. But now the effect was both unexpected and terrifying. The gurgling intensified, and then the kitchen was lit up in a brief flash before a great explosion occurred, leaving them in complete darkness. The metal body of the lamp struck the ceiling and crashed into a corner, smashing the bottle of milk.

Zette screamed. Ellen rushed into the bedroom to see if the baby was alright. The perpetrator of the accident, his face pale, took some time to get over the shock.

Verès took the lamp to show Vautier. He looked at it, shaking his head.

'You didn't pack it down hard enough. Or maybe you put too much water in. And the nozzle is blocked. You always have to look after these lamps, you know.'

In his hands this rebellious device nevertheless came back to life, and the Verès family were saved from fumbling about to make dinner in the dark, at least on that night.

But the meal itself could hardly have been more frugal. Nothing like the feast of the previous evening. On top of that, Verès could not put from his mind the openly hostile glare of his neighbour when he came back from the spring with the can of water. But his natural optimism soon reasserted itself.

'We're still getting used to things,' he told his family, philosophically. 'Once we get over this awkward period, we'll be in clover. I've known more difficult times. Well, obviously that was before *Gloomy Sunday*…'

II

The *Gloomy Sunday* episode was seminal in Tibor Verès' journalistic career. The son of a bank clerk from the Hungarian town of Szombathely, he had, for two years, scratched a living on a diet of cafés-crème in the bistros of Montparnasse. There, he composed interviews and reports for a provincial newspaper in his home country. The payments he received in return, although highly unreliable, just about allowed him to pay off his most pressing debts.

One day, he came across a curious story in his paper. A Hungarian aristocrat was reported to have committed suicide in a hotel room. The reason was shrouded in mystery, but the informant added that the poor man had spent his last evening in a night club, and had asked the leader of the gypsy band to play one of the latest hits, a lament entitled *Gloomy Sunday*. The informant hinted that it could have been the depressing refrain which gave the man the idea of taking his own life.

Verès, who had a part-time job ghostwriting columns for the editor of an evening newspaper, penned a couple of paragraphs on this story and submitted it to his French colleague.

'Not bad, your commentary. Still a bit thin, though. Needs spicing up. I'll take care of that. Here, I'll give you twenty-five francs for it.'

On page three of next day's edition, Tibor Verès found an article five times as long, headed 'The Song that Kills'. To his surprise, his colleague had 'spiced up' the story by killing off, in similar circumstances to the Baron, two more people present at the performance of *Gloomy Sunday*.

A few days later, the Sunday supplement of a national evening paper devoted a whole page to the subject, with a triple headline:

Gypsy Violins Inspire Death Wish
SUICIDE EPIDEMIC IN BUDAPEST
Hungarian Government to ban *Gloomy Sunday*?

This article – copyright Tibor Verès – with supporting photographs, brought him the princely sum of 2,500 francs, and journalistic glory. It had taken him a day's work and the payment of 25 francs to a literature student, for correcting the most glaring errors in his French. The lesson he had learnt from his Parisian colleague had not been wasted. The rights to this sensational report were sold the same day to an American agency. That very evening, Verès received a telephone call from a popular singer, inviting him to her dressing room at one of the big music halls, where she asked him for the score, the lyrics and the rights to the song.

Three days later, Tibor Verès delivered to her a faithful (if rough) translation of the song, along with the musical score, sent by air from Budapest. The refrain ran:

Gloomy Sunday, Gloomy Sunday
When the sun shone and my soul was wan
Sunday of hell
Sunday of pain
Sunday of mourning!

At the piano, the singer fingered her way through the music, and then paused in thought for a moment.

'What a whinge,' she said, pursing her lips. 'Stupid lyrics. But we can do something about that.'

She was as good as her word. With an arrangement by an accomplished musician, and lyrics in which Tibor Verès could trace not a single syllable of his translation, *Gloomy Sunday* was brought to the stage by a singer who thereby earned herself the nickname 'The Eleonora Duse of the Music Hall'. The set was by no means incidental to the effect. The star, draped from head to foot in black crepe and atmospherically lit, performed the piece in lugubrious tones, standing by a catafalque.

That was Tibor Verès' entry into the journalistic world of Paris. As a result, 'The man who brought us *Gloomy Sunday*' was able to put his name to a number of articles, ranging from the private life of Greta Garbo, through Al Capone at home in slippers, to the murky background surrounding the Mayerling Incident. Periodically, weariness and disgust got the better of him. At those times he tried something different, like a warts-and-all report on the primitive life of the cod fishermen in the Lofoten Islands when, having married Ellen Myran, a young painter, he went to visit his father-in-law, who was captain of a Norwegian tramp steamer. But the newspaper editors he submitted this to thought the subject lacked 'sex appeal', and so Tibor Verès had no choice but to fall back on his Mayerling, his Garbo and his gangsters.

* * *

Verès was woken in the night by scratching and miaowing. Clearly the cat was starving in its prison. 'Hang on a bit,' thought Verès, 'the mice probably don't come out until later.' But the tomcat seemed to get more and more impatient. Then, all of a sudden, it fell quiet. Upon which Tibor Verès thought he could hear the sound of trickling water.

He jumped. A drop had fallen on his nose. Was it raining? The roof was probably in poor repair, and rain could drip down through the hayloft to the bedroom.

But there were other droplets coming down from the ceiling. They felt warm, and had a sour smell.

Verès jumped out of bed and climbed the ladder into the hayloft. He could see the cat near a small puddle which was dripping between the floorboards just above his bed.

He lunged towards the impudent beast, but it took advantage of the open trapdoor, reached the bedroom and then the kitchen in a few leaps, and escaped through the broken pane of a window.

Verès washed his face, climbed back into bed, turned his pillow over, and tried to get to sleep. Alas! No rest for him. Within a few minutes, the dance floor was busy again.

In the morning Tibor was woken by the baby crying. He got up with a headache, scratchy eyeballs and a furry tongue, as if he had spent the night in the throes of an orgy. But he had a big job to do: they had used up all the firewood which Vautier had provided, so he had to saw up and split some of the heavy branches which his landlord had dragged to the 'chalet'.

The only tool Verès was familiar with was the fountain pen. 'Each to his own!' he used to say. 'This is the age of special-isation!' But there was no getting away from it. So he grasped one of the heavy branches, placed it in front of him, and raised the axe. Venting all his pent-up fury on it, he only managed to move the log sideways a bit.

'You'll never get anywhere like that,' said Vautier, eyeing him mockingly from his garden. 'Use my sawhorse, you can come and get it, that'll make it easier.'

Perplexed, Verès made his way towards his landlord's house. How could a horse help to split logs? Why was it sore? But he was too ashamed to ask for an explanation.

When he reached the front of the house, Verès found the youngest son, a child of about nine, splitting logs on a block, and working at a brisk rate. How deft his movements were! How easy it looked! How effective!

'I say, young man,' he said, 'Can you tell me where the horse is? I have to split some logs.' He was afraid of saying any more lest he betray his ignorance.

Wide-eyed, the child looked at him in astonishment.

'Er – it's there in front of you!'

He pointed to an object which Verès had seen many times before, but without taking it in and without wondering about its purpose. So a horse was not necessarily a mammal! Relieved, he lifted it and carried it to the chalet.

'Put the log on it, and then you can saw through it,' said Vautier.

So simple. A stroke of genius. Specialists, obviously!

Just at that moment the door of the house opened. A cloud of smoke emerged.

'The stove smokes a little,' said Verès, embarrassed. 'I bet my wife didn't put Eau de Cologne on, as I told her to.'

'What?' said Vautier.

'Yes, the stove smokes quite badly in fact, and to make it draw better I advised her to put some Eau de Cologne on, as we don't have any petrol.'

'Oh! You don't need petrol, and you don't need paraffin,' said the farmer. 'You're probably forgetting to light paper in the drawing-hole.'

'Paper in the drawing-hole?'

'Of course. You must have seen the opening in the middle of the hearth, below the oven. That's what it's for.'

Verès dropped his saw and rushed into the kitchen.

'Amazing, these country people,' he exclaimed. 'Absolutely amazing!'

Assuming a mysterious air, he took a sheet of newspaper, lit it, and poked it into the orifice under the oven. The paper burst into flame and the stove miraculously stopped smoking.

'Abracadabra!' he cried, like a magician upon completion of a particularly astonishing trick. 'I must write an article about the empirical knowledge of country people.'

He went back to his sawing operations. After half an hour of strenuous effort, his back was aching, both his hands were raw, and he had lost his left thumbnail. He had even managed to nick a piece out of one of his shoes. For all this, he had scarcely managed to chop even a day's worth of wood. In shame and humiliation, he cursed his total lack of practical skills.

His education was fundamentally lacking: he remained ignorant of the essentials. 'All they do is turn us into eggheads.' What use was the ablative absolute? Or the logarithmic table? They stuff your mind full of all this nonsense and don't even bother to teach you how to wield an axe. If he'd been Robinson Crusoe on his desert island he'd have starved and frozen to death in a matter of days. Whereas Philibert Vautier…

Vautier himself nursed the deepest disdain for his tenant. How was it possible not to know how to split logs! And as for using Eau de Cologne to light the fire…!

But he saw an opportunity. 'If you don't want to chop the wood yourself,' he said, 'I'll get my son to do it. He's used to it. It won't cost you much.'

'With pleasure,' said Verès gratefully. 'Thank you. But I'd still like to help.'

'Well, you can saw the wood up small once it's chopped. The hearth isn't very big in that stove.'

In truth, according to the contract which Vautier had drawn up himself, the rental of the chalet included the provision of firewood. But Vautier had had second thoughts. He could provide the wood, but that didn't mean he had to deliver it. He had already hinted to Verès that he would find as much wood as he wanted lying on the ground in the forest, about two kilometres away from the farm.

'But if you like,' he had added, 'I could help you by picking the wood up in my cart and bringing it to your door. It won't cost you much.'

Philibert Vautier, an old hand at ratcheting up prices, had developed a canny technique. He had discovered this commercial vocation when the exodus from Paris took place. He got plenty of practice fleecing refugees, whose gratitude for his 'little favours' he accepted with apparent humility.

Then he honed his skills on an army regiment in retreat,

which was billeted in Saint-Boniface. A licence to sell wine, along with a few battered barrels, should have been enough to earn him a sizeable profit. But he was also able to employ the soldiers, who were at a loose end and not inclined to haggle, in bringing in the hay and the oats. Never had labour in Saint-Boniface been so cheap!

When the soldiers and the refugees left the area, Philibert Vautier could afford to buy a large wood and several fields which he had long coveted. Land was still so cheap in Saint-Boniface, and money so scarce!

'Just one small thing, Monsieur Vautier,' said Verès, once they had agreed about the wood. 'I wonder if you could spare us some more provisions. We've hardly got anything remaining, apart from the potatoes. You were most munificent the other evening, but I'm afraid what you so generously gave us didn't last long!'

This flowery language irritated Vautier. Half the time, he didn't even understand his tenant. But this time he grasped the fact that the Verès family had got through all the sausage, the bacon, the cheese, and who knows? Perhaps even all of the butter!

'You mean... er... you have nothing left?' he said. 'Here, you know, we eat bread with the sausage and cheese, and we keep the bacon for making soup.'

'Yes, of course,' said Verès, lowering his eyes guiltily, 'but to be honest we were dying of exhaustion when we arrived, and we indulged in a bit of gastronomic excess.'

Vautier shrugged. These city people evidently spoke double-Dutch. But no matter. As long as his tenant was the petitioner, he was free to turn him down if he felt like it.

'Maybe,' he said. 'I'll ask the wife if she can spare you a little cheese. But I can't promise every day... I've still got some kids which haven't been weaned. If you haven't anything for soup,

I've got two or three leeks in the garden. They might be a bit tough, but it's the best I can do.'

'Leeks, excellent,' said Verès, instantly relieved. 'A vegetable which is rich in vitamin B. And for calories, a morsel of butter wouldn't go amiss…'

'Butter?' said Vautier with a helpless gesture. 'Not here, I'm afraid. My wife wanted to welcome you, so she skimmed off some cream and spent all evening making that pat of butter for you. Because all our milk goes to the rationing.'

'Now you mention milk, my Verès junior drinks almost a litre a day!' Verès interjected wittily.

'Ah! So he's called Junior!' said Vautier. 'It's not a name from round here.'

He preferred to pass over the matter of milk. He supplied rationing with as little as he could get away with, and he sold the rest to the Hôtel Panorama, for their clients' breakfast. But that was none of anyone else's business.

'So I will need milk,' insisted Verès regardless.

'If only you'd come three months ago!' said Vautier, scratching his head. 'But now I've got a calf which drinks everything that rationing doesn't take.'

Verès sighed. 'I see we've arrived at a critical moment. Everyone needs to be weaned.'

'If you say so,' said Vautier warily. 'Ah well! I have to go and muck out!'

'I've won!' cried Verès as he came into the chalet a few minutes later. His wife was washing the baby. 'I told you it's important to know how to deal with these people. I've persuaded Vautier to give us another of his nice little cheeses. And some leeks. As for the butter, it's better not to press him too hard. The calf has to be weaned first. So things will get better soon, and in the meantime I'll go down to Francheville to see what I can find.'

He came back in the evening in excellent spirits, carrying a well-filled shopping bag.

'I haven't wasted my time,' he declared. 'I've signed up everywhere. Obviously we won't get as many rations as in Marseille,' he added nonchalantly. 'It's normal, we're in the country. Unfortunately, we've already missed the distribution this month. But we'll get all our rations from next month. And I've brought some vegetables.'

Delving into the bag, he triumphantly produced turnips, carrots and Jerusalem artichokes.

'And I got all that without having to queue, which was lucky. Of course, the prettiest girl in the world…'

'Since you mention girls,' said his wife sullenly, 'Vautier's daughter has just come to tell me they can't spare us more than half a litre of milk a day.'

'But that's quite understandable,' said Verès accommodatingly. 'The calf has to be weaned. Vautier already told me this morning.'

'But it's absolutely not enough. In Marseille, with our cards, we got a litre and a half a day!'

Throughout the next week, this agonising milk problem remained uppermost in the former journalist's mind. Whenever he was not engaged in the chores of fetching water, chopping wood and writing his great work *The Paradoxes of History*, he was criss-crossing the countryside in search of a farmer willing to provide him with milk on a daily basis. But they all said they had to give everything to rationing, and they all sent the foreigner packing.

Eventually he had an idea. The Vautiers were obliged to provide a litre and a half to rationing – exactly the amount the Verès family was entitled to. Maybe if he explained the situation to the rationing office, he could get his ration at source.

But he had reckoned without the regulations, and there was

no getting round them. The milk had to be taken down to the distribution centre in Francheville, and it was only distributed in town. However, in return for a small consideration, young Legras, who collected the milk, agreed to pick up the Verès' ration and bring it back up to Saint-Boniface, along with the empty churn.

In this way, the Verès family could rely on receiving, at around five o'clock in the afternoon, the milk sent down by Vautier in the morning. As the weather was warming up, the return journey in the heat of the sun did the milk no good at all. Once it was put on the stove to heat up, it inevitably curdled.

III

In the dining room the table was already laid, and the little Empire clock had just struck twelve. At Les Tilleuls, lunch was served at half past. Bernard Bloch had made himself comfortable in an armchair and was reading the *Petit Dauphinois*. From the kitchen came the clatter of crockery, sometimes rendered inaudible by Mme Hermelin's imperious voice.

Since the last few days of May, the guest house had been practically full. Mme Hermelin felt her spirits lift. With her preoccupied brow, her anxious expression and the orders she kept barking to her husband and her new housemaid, she was the image of a captain at the poop of his ship on the ocean swell. From time to time she even addressed her passengers as peremptorily as her crew, but catching herself immediately she managed to apply a more gently modulated conclusion to sentences that were begun *allegro furioso*.

It was a week since the arrival of Rosenfeld and the 'Haitian' family, and at mealtimes there were nine at table, including the amiable hostess herself. M. Hermelin, whose disabilities rendered him unfit to be seen in polite company, was relegated to the kitchen with the maid.

Raising his eyes from the paper, Bernard Bloch noticed that another of the guests had just come in: tall, stooping and alarmingly thin, with a dull olive complexion and eyes deeply set into their sockets, jutting jaw, flared nostrils, this was Mme Gloria Clips, described as 'a character out of *The Indian Tomb*' by Tibor Verès, who was responsible for recruiting her decorative figure to the guest house.

Verès had met her at *The Walrus-Eater* on the Quai des Belges in Marseille. A former film actress, she had applied for emigration, like so many others. But she had considerably better prospects than most of the regulars at the Wailing Wall, and Verès had been very attentive towards her, secretly hoping for her support once they got 'over there'. The Indian Tomb had valuable connections in the United States, most particularly a first class guarantor in the person of her own husband, Mr Clips. Born in Prague, she had starred in silent films before marrying a wealthy American impresario. Later, they had separated and Mrs Clips had begun to travel the world.

She had entered the dining room without a sound, shooting covetous glances towards Bernard Bloch, who was smoking as he read his paper. As soon as he raised his eyes, she asked him with her nostrils twitching like the wings of a wounded bird, 'Could you spare me a cigarette?'

Bloch held out his packet of Gauloises.

'You're in luck,' he said. 'Just got my ten-day ration.'

She lit the cigarette, rapturously exhaled great puffs of smoke through her nose, and enveloped herself in a cloud, like an oriental idol. She was dressed with studied simplicity in a green turban and a voluminous white tunic drawn in at the waist with a cord, and set off, close to the neckline, by a splendid little peacock feather. This was her mascot, her keepsake. She was never without it, and whatever she was wearing she always found an inventive way of displaying it.

'And when do you set off for America, Madame?' asked Bloch. 'Any time soon?'

The Indian Tomb sighed heavily. 'I'm expecting to leave France in three weeks,' she said. 'And believe me, I can already taste the pleasure of lighting up my first Chesterfield, in Lisbon, before boarding the "Clipper"!'

'Must say it beats me why you're still in Europe,' said Bloch. 'What with things being made easy for you. Verès told me you've got a "danger visa".'

It was true. As she had retained her own nationality when she got married, Mr Clips had obtained for her a special visa intended for VIPs, writers or politicians, who were sought by the Gestapo. In fact, Mrs Clips had never bothered herself with either politics or literature. Moreover, she was of Aryan stock. The only danger she ran in France was running out of cigarettes. But Mr Clips had used his influence with some senators, and his wife's name had been added to the list of those granted emigration privileges.

'Ah, yes,' sighed the Indian Tomb. 'I should have left three months ago. Unfortunately all my money was invested in gold bars. When I got to Marseille I had to sell the gold, and then transfer the money to New York. I had some left over, so I bought some jewellery. What a tedious business! Then when everything was finally ready, and I had my dollars in New York, a few hundred pesetas in Spain and some escudos in Portugal, my American visa had run out. My husband had to apply for it to be renewed in Washington. Anyway, in a few days my ordeal will be over. I've decided to stay here until the formalities are complete. It's a delightful place and I'm very glad I followed my friend Verès' advice. But it's a shame that cigarettes are so expensive!'

Bloch tried to take refuge in his newspaper, but the Indian Tomb would not let go.

'I can't imagine what you find of interest in those pages. They send me to sleep.'

'You'd be surprised. There's something interesting every day,' said Bloch. 'When I was a lad, they sent me to a school where they taught you to make sense of what you read, and to read between the lines. That was the Bible, mind you. But what counts is the method. I still do it now. Look, today I found something really interesting. It's an advertisement. Here, read this.'

He handed her the paper, with a 'Wanted – urgent' item marked in pencil.

Artists, painters, writers, intellectuals
Return to nature in Saint-Boniface (nr. Francheville)
An idyllic estate
Friendly guidance
Address your letters to M. Du Chesne,
Château de Rochefontaine
Or preferably arrange a visit.

Just then, the door opened to reveal a man in his late forties, sporting a magnificent black beard trimmed to a point. Greeting the Indian Tomb and her companion, he settled himself into an armchair. He was indeed a fine figure of a man: smouldering eyes, a great mane of hair, well defined regular features, deliberate movements. His beard brought out the graveness and masculinity of his face. A white cravat and corduroy jacket put the finishing touches to his artistic air. On his bare feet he wore sandals with leather straps. M. César Fleury, a pillar of the National Radio Music Service, was the finest star in Mme Hermelin's constellation. His wife and daughter were to join him in the second half of June.

He picked up a back issue of *Illustration* and leafed through it with a look of disdain.

The Indian Tomb, having stubbed out her cigarette end, suddenly lost interest in her recent benefactor and turned her gaze towards the newcomer. The latter, though he knew he was being watched, pretended to go on reading.

Taking up a position in the middle of the passage, Mme Hermelin struck an old saucepan with a ladle.

The passage filled with a murmur of conversation as the guests made their way into the dining room. As well as Mme Renée Bloch and her son, little Jeannot, there was M. Murger, a tall fair young man of about twenty-five, and M. Rosenfeld who had rushed from his lodge, closely followed by his fiancée, Mlle Théodora Sten.

'Is everyone here?' enquired Mme Hermelin. 'It's 12.32.'

'My guest is late,' said the Indian Tomb, looking out of the window. 'But I think I see someone coming up the road.'

And indeed, the guests had hardly had time to take their accustomed seats around the table when the door opened, and the tall angular figure of Tibor Verès appeared on the threshold.

'I do apologise for being a little late,' he said, bowing ceremoniously to Mme Hermelin. 'My morning walk took me further than usual. I went as far as La Barbarie. You can't imagine the number of tourists out this Sunday. People from the city I suppose, seeking provisions. What a turnaround! The civilised world invading Barbary!'

Relishing the effect of this prepared witticism, he sat down at the table.

'May I ask what this delicious dish is?' he asked Mme Hermelin as he tasted the first course.

'Oh,' said Mme Hermelin, smiling with satisfaction, 'it's just a little recipe I invented, cow-cabbage salad. Excellent, isn't it? Round here they let them go to waste. It's such a shame, the country people are too ignorant to make the most of our natural resources.'

Rosenfeld, who already knew Mme Hermelin's culinary theories off by heart, made no bones about interrupting her to address himself to Bloch.

'Do you know what's showing today at the cinema in Francheville? Mlle Sten and I would like to go this afternoon.'

'No idea,' said Bloch. 'Some stupid film, probably. They're not usually up to much.'

'And I know why,' said Fleury, stroking his beard. 'It's because films these days are made by imbeciles.'

'Or rather by godless men tempting our young people away from the path of spiritual duty,' Mme Hermelin cut in to correct him. 'For is it not written in Ecclesiastes, "I will make a test of pleasure, enjoy yourself. But behold, this also was vanity."'

The boarders received these words with a few moments of respectful silence, while they cast hungry looks at the steaming dish which the maid had set before the lady of the house. It was the Indian Tomb who took up the baton: 'Anyway, those young leading men nowadays don't even stand ankle-high to the heroes of the silent films,' she said, caressing the peacock feather spread across her flat chest. 'Not a single one of them knows the meaning of love. You only have to compare the cardboard Don Juans they serve up on the screen now with someone like Rudolph Valentino – you see what I mean! Or with Gunnar Tolnaes, he was a fine young man, or with Valdemar Psilander, he had all the women swooning, they called him the Romeo of the North! He was unforgettable! So many great artists consigned to oblivion! So many masterpieces lost without trace!'

'As for me,' said Fleury as he tackled his portion of offal *en civet*, 'what I'd like to see on screen is a succession of abstract images, a shimmering play of shapes, colours, light and shade.

The absolute film, in short. It's been tried in the past, but too quickly dropped in favour of canned theatre and musical comedy. It's appalling!'

'I can't bear canned produce either,' Mme Hermelin interjected absently. 'And to think that some people actually *prefer* tinned peas...'

'Well, you're an innovator, a revolutionary,' the Indian Tomb told him soothingly.

'Maybe so,' agreed César Fleury, 'but cinema isn't the only walk of life where we need radical new thinking. Whether it's our homes or our clothes, everything suffers from a lack of imagination. The way houses and furniture are designed now is an insult to common sense.'

'Hold on!' interrupted Rosenfeld, 'we architects have made huge progress in the last few years. Just before the war my company in Paris devised what I think is a remarkable model for suburban living. A home with two bedrooms and kitchen, making use of new materials, "grace and space in the smallest place". I should add,' he said, smiling modestly, 'your humble servant did make a certain contribution to drawing up the plans.'

'Two bedrooms and kitchen,' sneered Fleury, turning upon his adversary. 'Spare me the details, I can just see it. Two bedrooms? More like prison cells! And no doubt the whole thing is done in mock-Tudor or pseudo-modernist style. I'm afraid you still haven't got out of the rut. You see, I've designed a country house, a proper one, that I'm going to have built straight after the war. And first of all, there's no fixed roof! What bizarre aberration makes architects shut us into rabbit hutches, regardless of the weather? What if I feel like reading, or singing, or playing music in the comfort of my own home, but beneath a blue sky? So my roof will be movable and removable; I turn a little handle, the roof disappears, above me only the starry night...'

'I've seen concert halls with removable roofs in the United States,' said Mlle Sten. 'And in the south of Russia, if I'm not mistaken.'

'You've been to Russia?' asked Murger, suddenly interested.

'Yes, I know it quite well. I used to teach physical education and I organised courses all over the place, in girls' schools. So I had to travel about.'

Bloch stared at her in stupefaction. Only two days ago, she had told him that she had travelled the principal countries of the world as secretary to a well-known industrialist. Mlle Sten evidently had more than one string to her bow.

She was a woman of about forty, neither fair nor dark, neither pretty nor ugly, and with a somewhat contrived air of distinction. Her features were on the heavy side, her expression was inscrutable, and everything she said conveyed a vague sense of mystery.

Mme Hermelin got up, went over to the sideboard, opened it, took out an imitation crystal bowl containing a handful of cherries, and placed it solemnly in the centre of the table. As there were so few, no one dared touch them.

'Do help yourselves,' said Mme Hermelin encouragingly. 'Our cherry tree isn't very prolific at this time of year, but we must make temperate use of the first fruits. Our health is so important, isn't it? I've worked it out, there are four each.'

'What's more,' said Fleury, returning to the attack, 'you say two bedrooms and kitchen, Monsieur Rosenfeld. And what if one day I have friends to visit, and I suddenly realise I need a third bedroom? What then? You haven't thought of that either, have you? Well, in my house, there are as many rooms as I want. My walls can be moved and adapted.'

'I've seen something similar in Japan,' said Mlle Sten nonchalantly.

'Nothing like that,' countered Fleury, as the Indian Tomb

gazed at him in admiration. 'I'll have none of that Far-Eastern promiscuity. My walls are removable, but they're insulated, so not a single sound can get through. What about your floor, Monsieur Rosenfeld, I suppose it's a perfectly flat surface?'

Rosenfeld stared at him, dumbfounded.

'In my country home,' continued Fleury, 'the floors are slightly convex, with grooves cut at the base of the walls. That means you can keep them clean in a rational manner. You wash them down with buckets of water, which drains away into a cunningly concealed outlet.'

'That really is very interesting,' said Rosenfeld with a touch of irony. 'But your convex floor must jeopardise the stability of the furniture.'

'I'm afraid you're wrong! In any truly rational home, where everything is subject to rigorous discipline, each piece of furniture has its strictly determined position, and is therefore fixed. Literally screwed to the floor. But a picture is worth a thousand words...'

He took out of his pocket some photographs of an architectural model, which he proffered to M. Rosenfeld. The latter inspected them closely. However, he forbore to comment. In the absence of serious justification, it was simply not wise to contradict an Aryan of pure lineage, especially a state employee. So he assured M. Fleury that his innovative ideas were really very interesting, and passed the photographs round to the others. By now Mme Hermelin, with exaggerated delicacy, was serving the ersatz coffee.

'Do you see the shape of my seats? They conform exactly to the contours of the human body. Because furniture must be designed to serve man, and should be structured accordingly, in the same way as clothes. What we usually do is just the opposite. Tell me honestly, ladies, how comfortable do you feel when you put on a new pair of shoes?'

And before the Indian Tomb could respond, he continued: 'It's torture, isn't it, because you have to literally mould your feet into the shape of those modern little boots of yours. But that's not all! You're actually risking your health, by enclosing them in a sort of hermetic Faraday cage, which cuts them off from the beneficial action of cosmic radiation. Now a man who wishes to achieve his full physical expression must never cover his feet completely. That's why you always find me wearing sandals in the country. And what's more, whenever the weather allows, he should walk some distance barefoot, in order to feel the earth directly, to derive health and vigour from it. You only have to look at the studies made of the natives of Indonesia, their virility is quite extraordinary…'

'How exciting!' exclaimed the Indian Tomb.

'And what's true for shoes goes also for other items of men's clothing,' continued Fleury, 'for example their shirts, or their undershorts.'

Perhaps she had finished serving the meal. Or perhaps she had heard enough of the world and its vanities. Or perhaps again, she preferred not to be a party to the suggestive turn this lecture had taken. Whatever the reason, Mme Hermelin rose from the table with dignity, and withdrew to the kitchen.

'Look at the shirts worn by men who like to call themselves civilised. They're a sort of shapeless sack. When they're too short they don't stay tucked in, and when they're too long you have these great folds of material between your legs.'

'Really?' said the Indian Tomb, her nostrils twitching.

'And as for undershorts,' Fleury went on inexorably, 'it's an even worse matter. They have so many drawbacks. The gentlemen will understand me.'

'So what's to be done?' asked the Indian Tomb eagerly.

'The only solution is to adopt the shirt I have designed. A shirt which makes undershorts entirely redundant. As it buttons at thigh level, it hugs the body closely in all circumstances, but allows absolute freedom of movement.'

'How fascinating!' gushed the Indian Tomb. 'I'd like to see the pattern!'

Jeannot Bloch, thinking she had asked for the *patron*, piped up: 'He's in the kitchen, he's washing up!'

It was no use Renée Bloch scolding her son, as the little Haitian's intervention had provoked general mirth which shattered the serious atmosphere. Fleury was left with no choice but to drop the matter.

The meal over, M. Rosenfeld and Mlle Sten prepared to go down to Francheville, and the Blochs left to give Jeannot his afternoon nap. Murger went off for one of the country walks he so enjoyed, with a copy of *War and Peace* under his arm. The Indian Tomb was secretly disappointed that she could not continue the conversation with Fleury, but it had been arranged earlier that she would go to see Ellen Verès.

'My wife's expecting you up on the hill above La Barbarie,' said the journalist. 'She's got her brushes out again, and started a painting.'

He took his cigarette case out of his pocket. The Indian Tomb sighed, watching his movements anxiously. Considerately, Verès reached out his arm towards her. She took a cigarette and lit it with relish.

Only César Fleury remained at Les Tilleuls. He intended to play some music. For this aficionado of radio, philosophy, architecture, cinematic theory and hygiene, this reformer of male fashion and polymath inventor, had an avocation: the piano.

IV

As it happened, the upright piano whose keys Mme Hermelin had tickled in her youth was an instrument of quality. Fleury caressed the keyboard, fingered some scales, struck a few chords, and then, satisfied, tackled Mozart's Sonata in A Major.

Fleury's musical gift was genuine. He could have become a virtuoso, or a distinguished composer. But his combination of exceptional skill and boundless self-satisfaction had prevented him from entirely fulfilling his true potential. Deciding that his genius relieved him of the need to work, he had come to rely on inspiration alone. This had served him in the composition of some concertos and a few symphonies, which had attracted a degree of critical acclaim. Before being appointed to a relatively modest post in National Radio, he had survived on what piano teaching work he could get.

At the moment, though, performing this cheerful little work by Mozart engendered in him an almost physical pleasure. But as he threw himself into the *Alla Turca*, he sensed the presence of someone else in the room. In fact, Génia Prokoff had already been there for a few minutes. She was listening, enchanted.

Fleury turned round, stopped playing, and prepared to stand up.

'I beg your pardon, Madame. I've finished now.'

'No, no!' protested Génia. 'Please carry on, I beg you. I do so love Mozart, and you have such feeling for him!'

'How charming!' Fleury thought to himself, looking the visitor up and down. Slavonic, no doubt, to judge from her slight accent.

He had a weakness for brunettes with almond-shaped eyes and well-defined full lips.

'The maid told me Mme Hermelin will be back soon. I have to speak to her... but please, carry on, don't mind me.'

'The wish of a pretty woman is my command,' said Fleury, semi-serious. And with another glance at her, he went back to the Turkish Rondo.

Génia listened, holding her breath. Closing her eyes, she saw herself once more in the little studio flat on the rue Bréa in Montparnasse, where she had spent her honeymoon. As a wedding present, some of her friends had given her a gramophone player and some records, amongst which was the *Alla Turca*. What a long time ago that was! Alexandre Prokoff, her husband, was then a delightful companion, full of little attentions for her. Had he not given her, two months after their marriage, a foalskin coat, with the words, 'On your pretty shoulders, this humble fur looks as fine as an ermine cape.'

As the last chords died away, Fleury paused briefly, glanced furtively towards Génia to check that she was still disposed to listen, then fell silent. Whose music would appeal to this daydreaming, romantic young woman? Mendelssohn, Schubert, Chopin? Although Fleury had limited admiration for the suave melancholy of Chopin, it seemed to suit the occasion, and after hesitating briefly he chose the Nocturne in F. A little hackneyed, maybe, facile without a doubt, but this unknown lady was unlikely to be a connoisseur.

From the opening bars, Génia trembled with emotion. As Fleury's nimble fingers leapt across the keys, she huddled herself into an armchair, overcome by an unpleasant creeping of her skin. This piece also reminded her of her past. But it was a past with much less pleasant associations.

For Génia had not stayed long in the rue Bréa studio. That happy period had been all too short.

In the Hôtel des Terrasses, on the outskirts of Paris, she had heard this Nocturne hundreds of times, for the woman in the next room was a prospective virtuoso who repeated each phrase thirty times over. Génia's misery was accompanied by the sound of those clumsy fingers repeatedly running aground on the same reefs.

Carried to Paris in 1920 on the wave of Russian emigration, Génia had, from the age of fifteen, attempted a variety of occupations. She had sold Russian sandwiches at the Colonial Exhibition, modelled for artistic photographs, and undertaken a useless apprenticeship at a beauty salon, before meeting Count Prokoff. A former officer in the Tsarist army, he had miraculously escaped the usual fate of his comrades in misfortune, having been reduced to driving a taxi in Paris for only a few weeks. He had just reinvented himself as a travelling salesman for a new brand of aperitif. The wedding took place shortly afterwards, at the Orthodox Church on the rue Daru.

However this ex-cavalry officer liked the high life. He quickly spent everything he earned, and more. Génia had to sell the foalskin coat, the gramophone along with its records, the little jewellery she possessed. The couple migrated to the Hôtel des Terrasses on the rue de Casablanca, near the Porte de Versailles. This unassuming hotel did have one advantage, in that it allowed guests to do their own cooking on an electric ring.

Fleury, far from imagining the havoc which Chopin's Nocturne was wreaking on Génia's nerves, dispatched even the trickiest passages *con brio*. All he felt was a wave of admiration towards him from the beautiful woman listening to him dreamily with her eyes closed. And of the many pleasures Fleury was capable of enjoying, admiration was the sweetest.

The Hôtel des Terrasses period had been marked for Génia Prokoff by a series of anxieties, humiliations and disappointments. With the assets of youth and a perfect figure, she had found a position as a model. Her modest pay was a welcome addition to a household budget which was chronically in the red. For a time, life improved. Every evening, Génia took tram 89 to *Le Koubouk* where, perched on a stool, she nibbled *zakouskis* and *blinis*. But Alexandre, Count Prokoff, had started his sales rounds again, and sadly, in the interests of promoting his aperitif, took to drink. He drank not fortified wines, which he despised, but vodka and *zoubrowka*; and he drank them intemperately, after the Russian manner.

It was during this period that their neighbour at the hotel began to play the Nocturne, whose staccato passages were to stick for ever as a painful reminder in the young Russian woman's mind. The Hôtel des Terrasses was suffering from an invasion of bedbugs. For a model, a room thus infested is not simply a matter of discomfort, it is a disaster. Génia incurred sly remarks from her employer as a result of the bites on the pearly skin of her shoulders. The unfortunate young woman did consider finding another hotel, but the couple owed three months' rent, as well as payment for all the breakfasts brought up to their room.

Music continued to pour from Fleury's fingertips. Certainly, it was a rather superficial piece. None of Bach's great majesty, or of Schumann's restrained passion, and of course none of the brutal sincerity of certain works by César Fleury. But Chopin was so good at plucking feminine heartstrings!

Shortly afterwards, the head of the fashion house found other marks on Génia's arms, and these were evidence of something more serious. Alexandre, embittered by his difficulties, had taken to beating his wife. Each day, the off-the-shoulder garments she modelled revealed more and more bruises. She was given notice. Out of work, confined to the hotel, she had to put up with her neighbour churning out Chopin's Nocturne all day long. Every evening, without fail, Prokoff beat her. Married life no longer had any attractions; but, in her indifference and passivity, the idea of separation did not even occur to her.

At the end of the last long *ritardando*, Fleury remained motionless for a moment, allowing the last chords to hover in the air. Then he raised his eyes to Génia, ready for her congratulations.

The young woman shook herself slightly, as if emerging from a dream.

'Chopin, isn't it?' she said. 'you play it to perfection, but I definitely prefer Mozart.'

'Ah, you prefer Mozart,' said Fleury, smoothing down his beard. 'You are right. I agree with you that Chopin is a charming musician, but ultimately second-rate. Wagner, that great show-off, was quite right when he said, "I believe in God, Mozart and Beethoven." If he were alive today, he might add another idol or two. But please allow me to introduce myself: Fleury, of the National Radio Music Service.'

'Now I understand why you play so well,' said Génia, blushing slightly.

She was troubled by the bold way he looked at her. She thought she might have guessed he had the soul of an artist, even if she hadn't heard him playing. Such an aura about him! The feeling took her back fifteen years, to when, as a girl, she was just awakening to life, and responding to everything that appeared fine, noble and mysterious.

Fleury himself felt, deep down inside, an intimate stirring. It took him by surprise, as for years now, with very few exceptions, the sight of a pretty woman had hardly roused more than a feeble echo. His gaze fell upon the soft silk of the visitor's dress, where it swelled over two pointed cupolas. Her casually crossed legs revealed firm, tanned calves, and, higher up, an area of paler skin with a delicate satiny sheen. M. Fleury felt increasingly excited.

'Do you like Beethoven, Madame?' he whispered in an insinuating tone, as if inviting an intimate confession.

'Passionately,' murmured Génia, looking away.

Without a word, Fleury returned to the piano, and the chords

of the *Apassionata* rose in the drawing room, where the closed
shutters threw intimate shadows…

V

Sunday 31st May 1942 was destined to be a memorable day for
Delphine Legras. Never had she experienced so many emotions
and such terror in the space of a few hours.

It had all begun at six in the morning, when she noticed
Fricou, the Latières' dog, skulking round the barn. For some
time she had suspected he was up to no good. The previous
night, to lure her hens to lay in the barn – they would insist on
leaving their eggs in the most extraordinary places! – she had
left two eggs in the nesting box. As soon as she awoke, she
had rushed out with dire foreboding to the corner where the
chickens spent the night, but found the box empty, and the
culprit already away as fast as his legs would carry him.

She was still in a fluster when little Abel Sobrevin brought her
a letter which Brandouille had forgotten to deliver the previous
day. Seeing the official stamp, Delphine trembled as she opened
it. Her earlier foreboding had not deceived her: it was a demand
from the tax authorities to pay the sum of six francs, ninety
centimes. Delphine's chest tightened with anxiety. What did this
demand mean? She had paid all her taxes last month. It must be
a mistake. But just the prospect of having to explain it all to the
tax inspector was enough to cause a cold sweat to break out on
her forehead.

And there were further causes for anxiety. That morning,
strangers from no one knew where had called at the neighbouring farms, demanding to buy provisions. Nobody knew
who they were, but they were certainly strangers because they
spoke French. As they would not take 'no' for an answer, old

Crouzet had lost his temper in patois and ended up threatening them with his pitchfork. That was easy for Crouzet to do, for he was a big sturdy man in spite of his fifty-five years; but what could she do, a poor defenceless old woman, if they forced their way into her house?

And finally there was this business of the evangelical meeting. The minister from Saint-Paul, who sometimes came to La Barbarie to conduct prayer meetings, had let her know in the morning that he would be arriving that very evening, instead of the following Sunday as he had previously announced. He gave her the job of informing all those concerned. It was easier said than done: what would she do if her son Emile didn't get back in time for her to get round to everybody? That would be a disaster! If only her eldest, Marc, was there! But he had got work for the whole week, planting potatoes on a big farm up on the plateau. And as for her, she had to make the cheese and look after her goats and cows.

All these troubles plunged Delphine into an indescribable state of distress, and as she busied herself with the curds and the strainers, she wondered by what miracle she would extract herself from these horrible complications.

Suddenly, the door opened. Delphine cried out in fright.

A figure with an olive-skinned face, a cadaverous look, clothed in brick-red canvas trousers with a man's shirt open at the chest, and its head swathed in a sort of green rag decorated with a bird's feather, stood before her. This apparition was brandishing a riding crop.

Instinctively defensive, Delphine placed herself in front of the table to protect her cheeses and pots of curds.

'Excuse me, Madame,' said the newcomer, whose voice was that of a woman despite the man's trousers, 'I'm looking for someone who's supposed to be round here. Maybe you've seen her go past! A young blonde woman, quite tall, with an easel.'

'A woman? With a weasel?' repeated Delphine, stunned. 'No, I haven't seen anyone, I'm sure. Especially with a weasel… anyway, there aren't any weasels round here… I've only seen the Magnon girl with her goats. But she's dark, and she isn't very tall.'

As she stammered this out in a monotone, Delphine, terrified, was wondering where this infernal being could possibly have sprung from. All in all, it was more woman than man. But that didn't explain the trousers. None of the women in La Barbarie wore trousers, even under their skirt, as women in town evidently did. Her own daughter had adopted this fashion since she moved to Saint-Etienne, and the neighbours had been shocked when, on holiday at her mother's, she had done her washing. But at least she had the decency to hide her knickers under her dress! And the rooster feather, what was it doing there? And the riding-crop! And as for a weasel…!

'Well, that's not her,' said the phantom, with an air of resignation. 'Obviously you haven't seen my friend. She must have gone another way. I'll try to find her. But before I go, I have to ask you a little favour.'

'A little favour,' muttered Delphine warily. Clearly this apparition had come to demand butter, or sausages! All this business about a weasel and a young woman was only an excuse to get into the house. For a moment she wondered where her son Marc had left the pitchfork. This crop-wielding spectre might still prove aggressive.

'Yes,' said Mme Clips with a funereal smile, running her tongue round her lips, 'I'm dying of thirst. Perhaps you would sell me a glass of milk.'

Delphine sighed with relief. The colour came back to her pale cheeks, she adjusted the scarf covering her hair, and with the back of her hand she wiped the sweat from her brow. She would even be willing to give two glasses of milk to her visitor, as long as she left immediately.

'I'll go and warm it up for you in the milk-pan,' she said, her voice shaking.

She turned towards the hearth, but the Indian Tomb stopped her with a bony hand on her shoulder. Delphine jumped, as if she had received an electric shock.

'Don't trouble yourself, Madame,' said the visitor. 'I love cold milk.'

'Cold milk?' repeated Delphine, in panic. 'Completely cold? But it would make you ill. I'd be ashamed of myself.'

'I'm used to it,' said the Indian Tomb. 'It has been boiled, hasn't it?'

'Er – yes, I'm afraid so. It won't keep otherwise, in this heat… but I could go out and milk a bowlful for you, then it would be warm.'

'No, no, I prefer it cold, and boiled.'

Greedily, she drank the bowl of milk which Delphine held out to her with trembling hands. Then the Indian Tomb thanked her, waved goodbye with her peacock feather, and went out, tapping her trousers with her riding-crop and leaving a banknote on the table.

For a long time, Delphine remained motionless in the middle of the kitchen, with her mouth open. Eventually she began to recover. What a day! It was too much for her to bear alone. She put the banknote in a safe place and ran, panting, to the Crouzets' farm to tell them all about this sensational event.

Long after the Latières' dog had eaten the last egg of the day's clutch, Delphine was still recounting to her incredulous neighbour all the elements, including a rooster's feather, a green rag, the red trousers, the weasel and the cold milk – cold *and* boiled! – which tangled together to form a fantastic horror story.

* * *

Sitting in the shade of a chestnut tree, on a bank which overlooked the path to Les Tilleuls, André Murger contemplated the sky. He had found new meanings in the chapter of *War and Peace* he was reading for the second time. He had reached the great account of the battle of Borodino, famous for the stubborn resistance put up by those defending the town. 'That's how to beat an invader,' he was musing. He too had taken part in a battle, in one single battle during the whole war, but his memory of it was nothing like Borodino.

It was the middle of June 1940, somewhere in Brittany, where André, a junior infantry officer, had spent the long months of the phoney war in a state of physical and moral torpor. All of a sudden, the enemy started to advance. Panic broke out in his garrison, reaching a peak with the arrival of a wave of refugees and two bloody bombardments. In the general confusion, measures had been taken to prepare for immediate combat. André's battalion had taken up its positions. Guns had been heard, and shots had rung out, though nobody knew from where. A brief period of uncertainty ensued, and the order was given to lower arms. Treachery? No, it was not even that. The tables had been turned by an enemy superior in both arms and numbers. The Commandant had decided there was no point in further resistance. The armistice must be imminent, so why continue to fight? However, he also gave strict orders to ensure that the men didn't take flight individually. The battalion had to surrender as a single unit. Taken prisoner along with the others, Murger had heard some of his comrades congratulate themselves on having got off so lightly. They expected, at worst, to be confined to a camp for a few weeks, after which they would be allowed to go quietly home. But two years had passed, and they were still languishing in the *Stalags*. Murger owed his release to a chronic case of bronchitis, which in fact he had carefully nurtured, but which was improving steadily since his return. The memory of this aborted battle left a bitter taste in his mouth. Maybe he was no hero, but he had the strong sense that he had been tricked. He had often thought of this while decorating the urinals of Lyon with Gaullist stickers.

The sound of footsteps floated up to him from the road. A girl was approaching from Francheville, a traveller no doubt, as she had a substantial rucksack on her back, and was carrying a large shopping bag. She stopped, hesitated, looked around her, and then noticed André, who had stood up on seeing her.

'Excuse me, Monsieur,' she called out to him. 'Is this the way to Les Tilleuls?'

In two strides, André was by her side.

'Yes, Mademoiselle,' he said. 'It's about five hundred metres further on, the first house on the left.'

He looked at her closely as he spoke. About twenty? Not much older, anyway. Not exactly slightly built, but with an apparent fragility which was belied by her resolute air and the ease with which she seemed to carry the rucksack. She had a delicate, gentle face and shining hazel eyes, of a darker shade than her short, slightly wavy chestnut hair. Her slender nose was softly rounded at the nostrils. 'A witty nose,' said André to himself. No trace of make-up on her face, even though she was evidently a 'modern' girl. 'She must have dimples when she smiles,' thought André. This childish idea struck him with such force that he searched for words which might provoke such a smile. But he only found a feeble little utterance which he regretted immediately, although it was too late to retract it: 'I know Les Tilleuls. I live there, you see.'

The hazel eyes gazed at him in slight surprise, and no smile appeared on the girl's lips. Furious with himself, Murger tried to make up for his awkwardness.

'Those are heavy bags, Mademoiselle,' he said. 'Allow me to carry them up to the house for you.'

The newcomer was wearing a knee-length blue cotton skirt, and a white summer jacket. Over one arm was a light-coloured raincoat. André was surprised that he took an interest in all these details. Even after spending hours in someone else's company, he was usually at a loss to describe what they were wearing.

The corner of a book was sticking out of the raincoat pocket. From its blue dust cover, André could tell it was from a cheap edition of classic masterpieces. What book could this stranger be reading on her travels? To the mystery of her dimples was added that of her reading habits.

'No, thank you,' said the girl firmly, 'I'm not tired. And it's not very far. But I need to tighten the strap on my rucksack. Please could you hold my bag and my coat a moment…'

André took them and, stung once more by curiosity, managed to engineer matters so that the book slipped to the ground. He glanced at it. It was the third volume of *War and Peace,* the very one he was reading himself, in a different edition.

'Thank you,' said the girl distantly, as she took back her belongings.

'I… allow me…' stammered Murger, not knowing how to ask her permission to accompany her. But she was already ten metres away, walking at a steady pace, without any regard for him.

André stood in the road and watched her slender figure recede. He lost sight of her for a moment, but then her light jacket showed briefly through the bushes before disappearing for good at the turning.

André returned thoughtfully to the chestnut tree, where he had left his book. He picked it up, and turned the pages as if seeing it for the first time. 'What a strange coincidence!' What could that unsmiling girl find of interest in this work of litera-ture? Natasha's love life? The fate of Prince Andrei? The portrayal of the times? Tolstoy's view of history? Since she was going to Les Tilleuls, André hoped he would eventually penetrate this mystery.

But who was she? Mme Hermelin wasn't expecting anyone that week. Clearly she came from further afield than Francheville. As he walked slowly back to the tree, he attempted to resolve the enigmas this unsmiling young woman presented.

VI

Noémi Sobrevin was getting ready to go into the village for her new ration book. It was her fourth attempt, for every time she had decided to go, she failed to get there before Longeaud and his volunteers put the key under the door and went for a drink at Tournier's.

She was running late again, though she had already brushed her hair and put on her Sunday best – not without difficulty, as the dress had not been designed to accommodate her protruding belly. She must hurry. Hardly enough time to give the children their tea, as they were just back from school.

She took the loaf and cut slices from it. She only had two *tartines* left to prepare when she realised she had left the cupboard door open after getting the bread out.

'Botheration!' she cried. 'I bet Griffon has got at my cheeses again!'

Dropping the knife and the loaf, she hurried back to the cupboard. The cat was nowhere to be seen, but she found the potatoes left over from lunch, which she had forgotten to put out for the hens. Grabbing the dish, she ran outside.

'Hey, chickens! Tsk... Tsk... Tsk..!'

Hearing the familiar cry, the birds gathered round her, the mother hen majestically bringing up the rear with her brood. As at every feeding time, Noémi counted the chicks.

'One, two, three, four… eleven!'

Where was number twelve? Noémi searched around and it was not long before she found the yellow chick under a bush. It was in a sorry state, having evidently been mauled by either the rooster or the dog.

'Botheration!' muttered Noémi.

For it was a hen chick, and there were only three of them in the whole brood.

She picked it up and, realising it was still alive, hurried to take it back to its mother.

But as she passed the washing-trough, she noticed some dirty trousers left on the stone.

'Oh, drat it!' she exclaimed. 'I forgot all about them! If I leave them there, Lion will chew the seat out of them!'

She put the chick on the grass, and knelt down to wash the trousers. She still hadn't finished when the two children who had not yet had their tea came out, tearful and hungry.

So with the half-washed trousers abandoned beside the moribund chick, Noémi returned to the kitchen to cut the last two slices of bread. She was just spreading some jam on when she heard Lion barking furiously outside. The dratted animal had come back home again instead of helping Elie with the cows! Obviously the dog was getting past it, he was no use on the farm any more. But what was all the barking about?

Leaving the lid off the jam jar, Noémi ran outside to see what was happening in the road. Exactly as she thought. Strangers out for a walk again.

Actually, she recognised the woman, as she had seen her in Francheville. It was the Russian from the Hôtel Panorama, who apparently went round the farms buying butter. But the man with the black beard – what a fine beard – she had not seen before. A tourist, probably. Or a butter merchant?

Reassured, Noémi returned to her kitchen, where she found that the children had taken advantage of her absence to consume more than half the jam in the jar. She was about to scold them when the youngest, David, in his high chair, began coughing. 'Oh my goodness,' cried Noémi, 'I've forgotten his cough mixture again, the poor mite!'

She set about looking for the bottle of cough syrup. Where could she have put it? In the sideboard, with the crockery? She opened it and looked inside. The syrup was not there, but she found a questionnaire which had arrived in the post a few days ago, following her application for maternity benefit, which M. Longeaud had written for her. She had even given him three cheeses. Since she was going to the Mairie, she might as well fill in the questionnaire and take it with her. But she would need her marriage certificate. Now where could that be?

She was in the process of turning out all her drawers in a search for the elusive papers, when she heard Lion barking again. There were two knocks on the open door, and a moment afterwards Tibor Verès' tall figure appeared on the threshold.

'I do apologise for this intrusion, Madame,' he said ceremoniously, 'and I hope I am not disturbing you. Please do continue to attend to your domestic duties.'

Noémi stuffed things back in the drawers at random, and turned to her visitor:

'Hello, Monsieur,' she said with a broad smile. 'You're not disturbing me. Why don't you sit down.'

'I beg of you, please allow me to introduce myself, before explaining the object of my visit,' began Verès, more awkward in front of this peasant woman than when he used to interview government ministers.

'You don't need to,' protested Noémi, delighted by the visitor's good manners. 'I know you. Obviously. Everyone here knows who you are.'

'Really?' said Verès, who found it hard to believe, but was flattered by such apparent fame.

'Of course, you're Vautier's tenant. I even met your wife and your little ones on the road the other day. Nice little kids. The girl's called Zette and the boy's called Junior. And people say you're a man of letters,' she blurted out in a constant stream.

Verès could not but admire the efficiency of the village intelligence services. In Paris, not even the neighbours he shared a landing with knew him so well.

'I see that my life is an open book to the population of Saint-Boniface. As you know everything about me, I hope you are also aware that we are singularly in need of milk supplies.'

'I know Legras' son brings it up from Francheville in exchange for your ration cards,' said Noémi. 'What it is to have small children!'

Verès groaned. 'I'm afraid that what little we have presents us with a dilemma worthy of Corneille. Do we give it to Mother, who's still breastfeeding? Or to the baby himself, who needs extra bottles? Or to Zette, who's in a critical growth phase? And,' he added with a resigned smile, 'that's not to mention myself, even though I love milk, and the Medical Faculty has prescribed me a lactic diet.'

'My goodness, so that's why you left Marseille,' added Noémi. She had followed Verès' little speech with growing admiration. Now here was a man who spoke French like in the books! Noémi loved books, especially those where dukes and marchionesses engaged in elegant conversation. Unfortunately, she could only indulge this passion when she was lying in after childbirth.

'But of course, we can't let you go short,' she continued. 'I wish I could help you out every day, but unfortunately it's impossible with all my little ones. But have you brought a can? I'll fill it for you. What else can I give you? Oh, do you like eggs?

The hens have just laid.'

Verès could not believe his ears. Eggs? So the term 'human solidarity' did have some meaning after all!

'We do indeed,' he murmured, 'we're wild about them. They represent almost a complete meal, rich in nutritional elements. I am most grateful to you.'

'Wait a moment, Monsieur,' said Noémi, 'I'll go and look in the nesting box. David, don't cough like that, I'll find your cough mixture when I come back.'

She had just disappeared into the barn when a man came into the kitchen without knocking. The journalist's face lit up. It was Brandouille.

The sudden joy which filled Tibor Verès' soul at the appearance of this figure had a deep-seated cause. He was the founder, and the sole practitioner, of a new religious sect: postalism, or religion of the postman. Verès worshipped all those, wherever they were in the world, who were entrusted with the noble mission of delivering letters, parcels and telegrams. Ever since reaching the age of reason, he had lived in the anticipation of some mysterious postal message which would magically transform his humble existence. It was an irrational belief, just like any other faith – the privilege of pure souls and children – which was the result of an almost messianic optimism. What exactly was he expecting? Everything and nothing. No hypothesis, however unlikely, seemed too improbable to him.

'Good day, Monsieur,' exclaimed Verès to the postman, in a voice quivering with hope. 'Do you have anything for me? I presume you haven't been to my house yet.'

'Which house?' said Brandouille roughly.

He was drunk, as usual at this time of day, and in a bad temper to boot.

'You know, the little house beside La Grange,' stammered Verès.

'Ah! Is that you?' said Brandouille, breathing into Verès' face a heady whiff of cheap red wine. Then he went on: 'Well, if you must know, you're a nuisance.'

'Excuse me... I beg your pardon...' mumbled Verès, taken aback.

'First of all, you should have stayed where you were,' continued Brandouille, thick-tongued. 'But you're like all the Israelites, you can't sit still. Well I've got enough work already. And you're always having letters and papers sent. Even the Maire doesn't get so many. And woe betide anyone with a parched throat when they get to your place. There's never anything to drink. You don't seem to realise that I walk thirty-five kilometres every day, just to bring your post.'

Verès listened meekly to these thunderings of a wrathful god. He had thought that by frequently slipping him a coin, he had done everything necessary to get into the postman's good books. Yet here the man was behaving with a hostility which gave the lie to his smiles of the previous days. *In vino veritas*!

'Anyway, I have got a letter for you,' spluttered Brandouille. 'And what's more, it's a registered letter.'

Verès turned pale with emotion. It had come at last, the message which would instil new purpose in his life. But from whom? From the Minister of Education in Venezuela? From the Nobel Prize Committee? From the Maharaja of Ranchipur? From the American Consulate in Marseille? Yes, of course, that's what it was. At last, the confirmation of his visa!

'Would you give me it?' he panted, reaching a shaky hand out to the dispenser of miracles.

'Easy does it!' said Brandouille slyly. 'Registered letters can only be delivered to the address shown on the cover.'

'Well, allow me to come with you,' suggested Verès timidly.

'Hark at him! I've already been to your house, and as it was shut, I wrote "Absent" on the envelope. Next time, you'll have to wait in.'

Words of wisdom! That was exactly what Verès did without fail, since the arrival of the postman was the most solemn moment of the day. As this sacred event approached, he sat in meditation, facing towards the door, just as Muslims turn towards Mecca when praying. Even that very day he had not neglected the ritual wait. He had simply left home without guessing that his god had dallied for two hours drinking at Tournier's; finding he had no money left; and converting the value of a child's overalls into glasses of wine.

At this juncture, Noémi reappeared at the door of the barn, with some eggs wrapped in a cloth. Brandouille jumped, laid on the table the latest issue of *Relèvement*, a religious journal, and started to stagger out.

'You're in a hurry to leave,' Noémi called out. 'We haven't seen much of you lately. Daren't show your face, eh?'

Brandouille, his anger doused like a flame snuffed out, mumbled something indistinct and fumbled in the darkness of the kitchen for the doorknob.

'Hold on a minute,' cried Noémi, barring his way. 'We've got a score to settle. I've been waiting a week for my little Abel's overalls, and now I find that Tournier's Angèle has been wearing them for the last three days. Now the Postmaster has had his rabbit, and the postal order business is over and done with, you're in no hurry to pay.'

Brandouille muttered in patois that his sister had been away and he had been unable to carry out the errand.

'Fiddlesticks! Everybody knows you went to your sister's at Saint-Paul, and you brought back the overalls. You just left them at the wine merchant's! And speak French at least, let this gentleman know what a wineskin you are!'

Verès watched this sacrilegious scene with a sinking heart.

How dare she! What if the god did make sacrifices to Bacchus? That was only normal: the gods are thirsty.

'Yes you are!' continued Noémi. 'Just a wineskin! And not even clever with it! Didn't you just happen to lose the tools off your bicycle the other day, when you were drunk as a newt? Along with a brand new pump? Well, you can search high and low for them. You'll find them the day I get my overalls. Now get away with you, we've seen enough of you!'

Brandouille skulked away like a beaten dog. Once on the road, he began to mutter veiled threats. Maybe he had left the pump at Les Mottes the previous Saturday. He had put his bicycle in the garage down on the main road, before walking up the hill to La Barbarie. He was plastered that day, all right! But Noémi would pay for this, and so would that Jew who had come to send him on a wild goose chase with his post.

'But Madame,' said Verès, once he had pulled himself together a little, 'are you not afraid Brandouille might be offended? What if he tried to take his revenge by not delivering your post?'

'What's that to me?' said Noémi. She was evidently not much of a postalist. 'He has to bring me the child benefit, because it needs my signature. As for the rest, well … one reminder more or less from the tax inspector… Here, I'll wrap your eggs in some old newspaper. You can pay me another time. Now I have to go to the Mairie. Oh, botheration! It's half past six! It's too late again! Drat that Brandouille for holding me up!'

As Verès was paying her for the eggs and milk, little Dina Sobrevin ran into the room at top speed.

'Maman! Maman! I was in the woods with Samuel and I saw a man with a black beard kissing a lady on the hand. We couldn't stop laughing!'

'You be quiet, you little gossip,' said Noémi, repressing a smile. Then, turning towards Verès, she explained, 'I know the lady a little, she's a Russian living in Francheville. But I wonder who the gentleman is. I saw them go past earlier.'

Verès knew only one beard in Saint-Boniface, and that was the one which belonged to César Fleury. It was highly possible that this suitor was none other than the musician from Lyon. But what did that matter! He was concerned about only one thing: the registered letter which a capricious god had kept from him that day, but which, tomorrow, would surely change the course of his life.

VII

Mlle Amélie Martin, the teacher from the Catholic school, stopped to get her breath back before tackling the steps up to Tournier's shop. It was a warm June afternoon, but despite this, she had wrapped herself in the grey cape by which everyone in the village recognised her.

She felt the cold excessively, and was never without the cape, or the white cotton gloves which she washed every night before going to bed. The reason she kept the delicate skin of her hands covered was that it bore the scars of household chores. Sister Félicie, having dismissed the housekeeper, had, little by little, left them all to her. Only a year ago, her hands had been spotless, with manicured nails, and only slightly criss-crossed by blue veins.

She went into the shop. Rosalie Tournier, a big woman with a flushed face and short hair which emphasised her double chin, let the handful of peas she was shelling drop back into the basket.

'Oh, it's you, Mademoiselle Martin, hello!' she cried. 'What's your news today? I hear Sister Félicie has gone to the market.'

'Yes,' answered Amélie. 'She's gone shopping in

Francheville… I've come to make a telephone call.'

Rosalie Tournier stared at her in amazement. That was a first! To whom? And why?

'Do you want to call Francheville?' she asked insinuatingly. 'I'll get it for you. What's the number?'

'Oh, it's not for Francheville,' answered Amélie, 'it's for Lyon.'

At the sound of this prestigious word, Rosalie froze expectantly. And as the schoolteacher said nothing: 'Oh, do you have friends in Lyon? Or family, perhaps?'

'My brother,' said Amélie. 'He had an operation this morning for appendicitis. I want to call the hospital to find out how he is.'

Rosalie Tournier took note that Amélie Martin had a brother in Lyon, and that he was in hospital. But could he be something other than a brother? She would find out by eavesdropping on the telephone call.

She got up, went into the back room, and asked for the number. She was told to wait a short time, as the line was busy.

'I'll wait here,' said the schoolteacher. 'I hope it won't be too long.'

'As you wish,' said Rosalie Tournier, disappointed. She would have liked to keep the spinster in the shop to see if she could wheedle any more information out of her.

Rosalie had just gone back to shelling her peas when the door opened. Mme Hermelin, sporting her mattress dress, bounded in.

'What a long way it is to your shop,' she complained.

On seeing her, Rosalie leapt up to put away the loaf and sausage she had laid out for tea. You never know…

'I've come to order a case of mineral water. My guests have nothing to drink. And the first hot days make one terribly thirsty.'

The previous evening, she had realised that by making a small extra charge and providing mineral water for her guests instead of wine and beer, which were now unobtainable, she could make a worthwhile profit at the end of the month. Les Tilleuls had one thing in common with certain top-class hotels: the bills were padded out with extras. Charge for shoe-cleaning, charge for breakfast in room, charge for hot water, charge for changing sheets and towels, and so on.

'Certainly,' said Rosalie, 'my husband will bring it up tomorrow. Which springs would you like? Vichy? Pestrin? Vals? Moïse?'

'Moïse!' exclaimed Mme Hermelin. Her choice, quite understandable for an avid reader of the Bible, was nonetheless also motivated by the low price of the water from the source which carried the prophet's name.

'Do sit down a moment, Madame Hermelin, get your breath back. So you're still busy?' she asked as she wrote down the order.

'Well, people come and go. Monsieur and Madame Bloch are about to leave us. They're going to live in a little farm they've rented from Monsieur du Chesne at Rochefontaine Château. I will miss them, they're very respectable people. He's an important figure in the Haitian automobile industry, would you believe!'

'Oh, really? But tell me, Madame Hermelin, did you not have another client arrive on Sunday?'

'That's right, Mademoiselle Fleury. A very respectable young lady. I was expecting her only at the end of this week, but she managed to take her holidays early. Though she left again on Tuesday.'

'Well, well,' said Rosalie, more and more intrigued. 'Why was that?'

In the telephone cubicle, Amélie sat down on the stool in

resignation. It was a long wait. But she preferred to stay cooped up in the semi-darkness rather than go back into the shop where the two women were now deep into their gossip.

Mme Hermelin took on an air of mystery, and a brief silence ensued. Rosalie was bursting with curiosity.

Enjoying the hiatus she had provoked, Mme Hermelin started to play with the pods in the basket. She took one out, split it open and tasted the little green peas, nibbling them as if they were confectionery.

'Your peas are delicious! And so sweet!'

Then she continued, 'I know why her father sent her away. I happened to be in the passage sorting out my linen cupboard when they were talking about it. Believe me, I was a bit embarrassed to overhear them like that, but I did have to put my sheets away. Well, do you know, the girl – she's called Solange – has a wealthy old aunt in Tournon. At the moment, she's not very well. It would be a pity to leave her unattended, especially as Mademoiselle Fleury has great expectations from that side of the family. Monsieur Fleury had just got a letter from her.'

'So she didn't mind leaving?'

'Of course she did! She was so comfortable at Les Tilleuls that she didn't feel like going at all. But Monsieur Fleury is a very strict father. And his daughter is very well brought-up, even if she does have her rebellious side. Anyway, she had to take the bus on Tuesday. She'll be back in a few days, when Madame Fleury is there.'

Rosalie had to content herself with this information for the moment, as Mme Hermelin suddenly jumped out of her chair as if she had been bitten by a tarantula. She reminded Rosalie again not to forget her mineral water, and rushed out, just in time to avoid coming face to face with the Abbé Mignart, the Curé of Saint-Boniface, the sight of whose portly bulk outside the shop had caused her abrupt departure. Mme Hermelin had nothing particular against the Abbé Mignart, but the mere sight of a cassock was enough to upset her. She simply couldn't help it.

'So! I see I'm out of luck again, the master of the house is not here!' said the Abbé Mignart jovially. He wiped the sweat from his apoplectic jowls and sat down heavily.

'He's not far away, Monsieur le Curé,' said Rosalie. 'If you don't mind waiting a moment, I'll go and get him. He's in the garden, hoeing the beans.'

'Very good, go and call your husband. I need to speak to him.'

From the cubicle, Mlle Martin recognised the Curé's voice. The sound of drumming on the table was familiar enough to evoke the image of his plump fingers, and she knew it was a sign of bad temper or impatience. Amélie Martin had long ago found out that the Curé's jovial manner concealed a violent, authoritarian temper, and she dreaded it.

Soon this tapping was drowned out by the clatter of clogs on the wooden floor, and Amélie heard the Abbé's voice once more.

'Good afternoon, my friend. I am the bearer of good news. The Farmers' Corporation has rallied round to get you a consignment of nails. That's the second in three months, when there are other applicants still waiting for their first. You must be pleased, eh?'

Hippolyte Tournier had nothing like the Curé's perfect diction, and Mlle Martin was unable to make out a single word from the grunting sounds that passed for an answer.

'Don't thank me,' said the Curé. 'We do what we can to help our friends. Anyway, I expect more than thanks: actions, my friend, actions. First of all, I need the kilo of honey you promised me the other day. And some coffee. I'm not asking too much this time. Just a pound will suffice for the moment.'

Amélie began to feel uncomfortable. How to get out unseen?

It wasn't possible. Her only way out was through the shop, which would certainly give the Abbé Mignart a most unwelcome surprise.

'You look as if that pleases you rather less than the voucher for the nails,' joked the Curé. 'But it can't be helped. One good turn deserves another. And I'm afraid you've got more to come. Now don't look like that, I'm not asking you to give me your right arm, I just want a kilo of butter.'

'But Monsieur le Curé,' said Tournier reproachfully, 'I gave you a big piece on Monday.'

'You are right, my friend,' said the Abbé in an easy-going manner, 'and I am eternally grateful. The butter I'm asking for this time is not for myself, but for some friends. I'm leaving tomorrow at dawn for a couple of days. And you may rest assured that I'll pay you for this butter as I usually do. More, actually, because the official price went up two francs a kilo on Monday... But I want service with a smile, you understand, with a smile... There! That's better!'

'It's just that you can hardly get butter at the official price any more,' grumbled Tournier.

'I know, I know, but it's even worse for nails, my friend. You should know that. Let me give you a piece of advice: don't be too greedy. Receiving is not everything: you also have to know how to give. It's a matter of getting by. And I have great confidence in your business sense. Everyone knows that in the villages round here, iron for nails is worth more than the fullest fat dairy products. It's not butter you'll be lacking from now on. There'll be enough for me, and even for the townspeople who come to you from time to time. Come on, don't look frightened, I'm not accusing you of anything, I'm a man of the world!'

By now Amélie's discomfort had turned to nausea. She prayed that the telephone call wouldn't come before the Curé left.

'And to help you get over the shock,' said the Abbé, 'There

are some other good tidings I haven't told you. The corporation has been informed that for heavy labour, agricultural workers are to receive an additional wine ration. You won't be left out, I'll see to that. Oh, I almost forgot. I need a little tobacco for my trip. I'll send Justine over with a tin for the butter. Don't forget my little order. Goodbye, my friend, I will see you this evening.'

Mlle Amélie Martin heard the Curé's heavy steps, followed by the harsh clatter of Tournier's clogs. Then there was silence. Shivering in the darkness of the telephone cubicle, she gathered her cape up to her chin, but despite the cold she felt sweat beading on her forehead. Stealthily, like a burglar, she slipped out of the cubicle, went into the shop and stood in the open doorway to get some fresh air. The Abbé Mignart's oily voice was still going round and round in her head. She remembered her first conversation with him, on her arrival in Saint-Boniface. He had gone on for ages, in the same unctuous tones, about his ideas on the education of country children. 'Our school should form not intelligence, but character. These youngsters are disorientated by the troubled times in which their souls are awakening, and you must concentrate above all on respect for authority and self-discipline. Our duty is to nurture clear consciences, and develop in them the higher Christian virtues of humility and self-denial, which are the only means of saving our people from moral degeneration…'

'One good turn deserves another… It's a matter of getting by… I'm a man of the world…' Was this what it all boiled down to, then? The higher Christian virtues… clear consciences… humility and self-denial… butter, honey, tobacco, coffee…

'So, Mademoiselle, have Lyon not called yet?'

Amélie Martin jumped, brought suddenly back to reality by Rosalie Tournier's question.

'No, it's taking such a long time… I wonder whether we should ask for the call again.'

'Oh, no, Monsieur le Maire waited an hour for Valence. It happens sometimes... I'll leave you again for a moment, I have a job to do for Monsieur le Curé. It's the same every time he goes away. And recently, he's been away a lot,' she added with a sly smile. 'Well, you know, they're men like all the others. They have to have their little pleasures too. That's why he always takes civilian clothes in his suitcase. His maid told me. What if he wants to go to the cinema... or even other places! Anyway, I'll be back in a quarter of an hour.'

Amélie was left alone once more. She tried to imagine the Abbé's great girth belted into a summer suit. Would he also wear a brightly coloured tie? She would have laughed if she had not felt so nauseous.

And still nothing from Lyon. She prayed that the operation had been a success.

Hearing steps outside, Amélie leant forward slightly and saw the tall figure of a man, deep in thought, swinging a shopping bag. It was the stranger from La Grange.

Tibor Verès had come to Tournier's shop for a new supply of mixed pickles, that fine condiment which he was the only person in the village to appreciate. His destiny had not been changed by the registered letter which Brandouille had refused to give him yesterday, and which he had finally received an hour ago. It was not an invitation to the White House, but simply a reminder from the owner of the furnished house the Verès family had rented in Marseille, about an overlooked gas bill.

'Mme Tournier will be back soon,' Amélie told him. 'If you can wait a few minutes...'

'Very good,' said Verès, sitting down. 'I feel quite tired after coming up this steep hill.'

Amélie, who had earlier removed her gloves, put them back on under cover of her cape. Surreptitiously, for a few moments, she watched this man, whose presence reminded her, for the first time in months, of a distant world: one of foreign cities which, in her present solitude with only Sister Félicie and the Curé for company, she yearned for nostalgically. Would she ever have the opportunity to go abroad again? Several times, she opened her mouth to speak, but thought better of it. Suddenly, she asked, 'You must be Hungarian, aren't you?'

He looked at her in astonishment.

'Yes, Mademoiselle.'

'Somebody told me, but I'd have known by your accent. I only take the liberty of asking because I know your beautiful country a little. I lived there for two years. I taught French in Budapest from 1923 to 1925.'

Tibor turned towards her with interest. 'Really? I would never have thought there was anyone in this village who had seen the waters of the Danube. You do live in Saint-Boniface, don't you?'

'Yes,' she said with a slight sigh. 'I teach at the Catholic school.'

'And in Budapest? Did you teach in a school?'

'No,' she said, 'I was a governess in a family. Ménesuit, in the villa district.'

'I am doubly pleased to have the opportunity to speak to you,' said Verès. 'You see, I have a little daughter of school age. I had almost decided to send her to Longeaud's school, but now I've met you I'm not so sure, and I think she might be better in your care. We have a few weeks before the end of the school year, don't we?'

Beneath her grey cape, Amélie wrung her hands. This stranger's accent, his slightly ponderous courtesy, his whole manner bathed her in the atmosphere of the past... strolling on a hot summer's evening at the foot of Mount Sas... riverboat outings on the Danube... the skating rink at Lagymanyos where she took her little pupil and where she had met Imré, the young dentist who had courted her for months... all these memories prompted a feeling of solidarity with the Hungarian which compelled her to be sincere. In her mind's eye she saw Sister Félicie's classroom, where the pupils spent hours stupidly learning their lessons by rote, or copying down the answers to their exercises dictated by Sister Félicie, who had, definitively, extended the method of the catechism to the whole of her teaching. Strictly constrained in a state of intellectual automatism, these little country children were carefully groomed to become, one day, the docile flock of a future Abbé Mignart.

'Well, in fact,' she said, embarrassed, 'I mean, it wouldn't be me who would teach your little girl. She would be in Sister Félicie's class, and...'

'That's a pity,' said Verès.

'And actually, no, to be honest. The children don't do badly in the village school. People speak well of Longeaud, and his classes are more advanced than ours... that's between ourselves, of course.'

Verès looked at her with some surprise, sensing that he was witnessing an internal struggle.

'I would love to, believe me, but...'

Her sentence was to remain unfinished. As she hesitated, the telephone rang. Mlle Martin got up and, excusing herself, hurried to the cubicle and shut the door.

'Hello... Herriot hospital? The information desk, please?'

Chapter 4
The Hunting Achievements of
Gendarme Auzance

I

'Hey Auzance, I've got a job for you. Go and have a look round Saint-Boniface this afternoon. Those three Jewish families up there. See how much you can find out.'

The officer in charge at the Gendarmerie in Francheville was speaking to one of his subordinates, a surly, stocky young man with bushy eyebrows and the complexion of a blood-orange.

'I got a directive this morning,' he went on. 'We have to provide details of all the foreign Jews in our district. Your colleagues can deal with the others.'

Within a few minutes, Sergeant Auzance had taken note of the requirements, mounted his bicycle, and was on his way.

Not a bad task, he thought. Jews! He knew all about that rabble from the time of the Armistice. He had turned hundreds of them back when he was posted to the demarcation line. What good sport that was. A real hunting party. And plenty of game. Large numbers of Israelites were fleeing from the occupied zone, and they managed to get through the line at several points. But along the section where Auzance was on patrol, those illegals had to be really clever to find a way through. Amongst the Jews there were also criminal suspects and 'politicals'. And you couldn't let them get by either. Just because you were out to trap hares, there was no reason to let the fox get away.

He had been transferred to Francheville a few months ago, and the duties here were much less interesting. Drunken brawls, petty theft, infringements of the rationing laws – mundane stuff.

But Auzance was not short of initiative, and he was determined to make his mark. As a result, he held the Gendarmerie record for the number of summonses issued.

Reaching the post office, Auzance braked to a halt and dismounted. For just as you don't turn a blind eye to the fox when you are hunting hares, there's no reason to deny yourself the pleasure of shooting any pheasants which come your way.

It was almost mail collection time, and people were queuing to post parcels. Auzance had his own opinion of these packages. Despite official restrictions, most of them contained rationed foodstuffs. He nurtured serious suspicions of two or three individuals, and he could already savour the delight he would take in catching the Prokoff woman in flagrante with the parcels she sent several times a week to the Côte d'Azur; and a certain stateless individual, Pinkas, who was also a particularly assiduous client of the post office.

Going in, Auzance scanned the long queue which had formed in front of the counter. The Russian woman was not to be seen. For a few days now, she seemed to have stopped sending things. But the aforementioned Pinkas was there, and he had a cumbersome parcel under his arm. 'Two kilos of butter at the very least,' thought Auzance, as he cast an expert eye over the package.

Pinkas looked like Mr Punch: tall and stooping, with greying temples, and a nervous, twitchy bearing. On seeing Auzance, he became agitated and stuffed his parcel into a large shopping bag. Obviously this stateless individual did not have a clear conscience.

Auzance savoured his triumph for a few more moments. The pheasant was right there within reach, unable to take flight. Auzance enjoyed dragging out the delightful seconds immediately before a victory, and his pleasure was enhanced by the evident discomfiture of his victim.

Suddenly Pinkas panicked, left the queue and made for the exit under cover of a commotion caused by the arrival of more people with packages. Auzance, no longer in any doubt, immediately leapt forward and caught up with him at the door.

'What do you have in that parcel?' he asked, with a chilling smile.

'Some... some things,' stammered the man. 'A present for a friend.'

'Just as I thought,' said Auzance sarcastically. 'Let's have a look at this present. Open your parcel!'

Pinkas sighed heavily, placed the package on the counter, and unwillingly set about opening it. After several attempts at unfastening the knot, he cut the string, removed the wrapping paper and folded it carefully. Then he stopped.

'I'll never get this wrapped up again,' he grumbled. 'The string's too short now. I trimmed it right down to the knot.'

'Enough of that, hurry up,' said the gendarme impatiently; he had already taken his pen from his pocket and held it poised to write the summons.

Meanwhile a small group had formed around them. Auzance didn't object. He wasn't averse to a bit of publicity from time to time.

At last the parcel was open. Just one more layer of wood-shavings, and the contents were in full view. Auzance's jaw dropped. Displayed before him were two toilet rolls and a box of suppositories.

'It's for a friend in Marseille,' mumbled Pinkas pathetically. 'He's in a bad way. They just don't have enough there.'

There was a ripple of laughter. Even in 1942, the French still liked to see Mr Punch get the better of the policeman.

As for the individual known as Pinkas, beneath his air of contrite humility he was triumphant. He regularly sent food parcels to the cities, and as he sensed Auzance had his eye on him he had taken precautions. Now he was using a messenger, Kleinhandler, to send parcels from the sub-post office in Denières, and had looked out for the opportunity to get himself caught in the act with a fake package. He had rehearsed his little performance in detail, and he hoped it would get the police off his back for a while.

'That's enough,' grumbled Auzance. 'You can wrap it up. I'll let you off this time, but don't do it again.'

And without explaining exactly what it was that Pinkas should not do again, he left the post office to the sound of stifled laughter. He knew perfectly well that he had been tricked, and he was simmering with impotent anger.

This feeling of impotence, which flushed his face and made his eyes bloodshot, revived painful, deeply buried childhood memories. Taken into care at an early age, he had been brought up by a farming family near Orléans, where he had been treated little better than the dog, though not as well as the cat. Slapped or beaten on the slightest pretext, Auzance had rapidly built up a store of hatred against his foster family, which he vowed to expend freely on anyone who later crossed his path. His main reason for joining the police force was the secret hope that this profession would provide him with plenty of suitable opportunities. In this respect, his first years of service had been disappointing. Fortunately, the Armistice had brought ample compensation. Upon promotion to the rank of sergeant, Auzance began at last to feel he was Somebody. He drew intense satisfaction from the discharge of his duties, and would hum to himself a half-remembered line from the music hall: 'Ah! The policeman's lot is such a happy one!'

He mounted his bicycle and pedalled off towards Denières. Passing the last houses in Francheville he saw Brandouille, the postman, heading for a bar. For the police, a postman is often a valuable source of information.

'Hey, Brandouille, where are you off to like that?'

Hearing his name, Brandouille stopped. Auzance got off his bicycle and challenged him:

'You deliver the post to Les Tilleuls, don't you?'

Brandouille nodded.

'So you must know those foreign Jews, Rosenfeld and Bloch. Who are these people?'

'Oh,' said Brandouille, 'They get lots of post, like all the Jews. A lot of trouble, they are. But that Bloch isn't at Les Tilleuls any more. He's rented a little house with some land near the Château. Apparently he wants to start a farm.'

'Really?' said Auzance incredulously. 'A Jew? Start a farm? And you believe that, do you?'

'Oh, I don't know,' said Brandouille, who had no fixed opinion on the matter. 'But the other one, Rosen... thingy, he's rented some land too.'

Auzance smiled sarcastically.

'And the one at La Grange? I suppose he's doing the same – it seems to be all the rage.'

'Oh, no,' said Brandouille, warming to the subject. 'Not him. But he gets a lot of post. Even from abroad. And newspapers, and registered letters, and parcels. I'm just taking him one today. From Marseille, and a big heavy one it is too. I'm glad I don't have many like him.'

'Registered letters, parcels,' said Auzance, intrigued. 'Postal orders too, eh? He wouldn't be in the black market, by any chance?'

'I shouldn't be at all surprised,' said Brandouille insinuatingly. 'It's like an office at his house. He even uses a typewriter.'

'A typewriter?' Auzance appeared impressed.

'And,' Brandouille chattered on, 'he goes about visiting the farms. Just the other day I met him at Les Mottes buying eggs and milk. Butter too, I bet. The Jews can get anything they want at that house. At a price, of course.'

He was delighted to have an opportunity, at last, of getting his own back on Noémi, who was still refusing to return his toolkit while continuing to demand the overalls.

'Next time I'm off duty, I'll buy you a drink,' said Auzance with unaccustomed generosity. Then he took his leave of Brandouille with a pat on the back, as if he were a performing dog.

All this information had dispelled the sergeant's bad temper, and he now rode determinedly towards Denières. He intended to keep a close eye on all three individuals, especially that Verès. And on the Sobrevin woman, who was supplying the black market. He could tie all that up into a very neat report.

Pedalling on with renewed energy, he noticed a cart nearing Raillon's mill. The farmer driving it must be on the way to have his grain turned into flour. That required an official pass. Have to see if he's got one! Just because you're after hares, there's no reason to pass up a thrush. Especially when you've just missed a pheasant.

So Auzance stopped and approached the farmer driving the cart. It was Lévy Seignos from La Serre.

'What have you got in those two sacks?' he asked in a severe tone.

'In what sacks?' said Seignos imperturbably, without taking his pipe out of his mouth.

'The ones you're carrying, of course,' said Auzance, pointing at the cart.

'Ah! You mean those sacks? Well, it's wheat, what else would it be?'

'Exactly as I thought. And where are you taking it, eh?'

'Where do you think? To the mill, of course.'

'Very well,' said Auzance. 'Show me your papers.'

'Papers?' asked Seignos, innocently. 'I don't have my papers on me. But everyone knows me round here, and even in

Francheville.'

'Don't try it on with me,' said Auzance with a threatening smile. 'I want to see your transport permit for the wheat, and don't fob me off with anything else.'

'Oh, that's all right then,' said Seignos, looking relieved. 'You should have said so straight away! I must have it somewhere. Let me have a look.'

Muttering into his moustache, he fumbled in his pockets, turning them inside out one by one, but found nothing. Auzance eyed him sardonically. The shot had been fired, and the thrush appeared to be winged.

Suddenly the farmer cried out, 'Would you believe it? I must have lost my head! I put it in my hat. Not my head, I mean, the permit. My head too though, come to that!'

He took off the broad-brimmed beige canvas headgear for which he was known throughout the area, and extracted a crumpled scrap of paper from behind the hatband.

'Here it is, your permit! All this red tape, what a lot of bureaucracy! You never know where you are any more.'

Auzance examined the permit closely. It was a printed form, correctly filled in and carrying the official stamps. The holder, Seignos Lévy, resident at La Serre, in the commune of Saint-Boniface, was authorised to transport to Raillon's mill, on that date, between three and five in the afternoon, 120 (one hundred and twenty) kilos of wheat, in order to have it milled for private consumption. Evidently this Seignos appeared to have his papers in order. But there was still hope. The permit stated 120 kilos. Auzance knew that the farmers all had hidden stocks of wheat, so they cheated on the weight in order to get the whole quantity milled. As a result, the only valid inspection was the one carried out at the mill itself.

'Very well,' said Auzance. 'Now let's go and weigh them.'

They entered the mill, and on the gendarme's instructions the miller weighed the sacks immediately. They came to exactly 117 kilos, not even quite as much as authorised.

'I must have made a mistake,' said Seignos with a pained look. 'Now we'll have to go easy on the bread. That's a nuisance.'

There was no chance of issuing a summons. Auzance, hiding his vexation, haughtily took leave of the two men, and returned to his bicycle.

But no sooner had the sergeant gone than Lévy Seignos and Raillon winked at each other like a pair of old rogues, and burst into waves of uncontrollable laughter, slapping each other on the back and guffawing all the louder. They had indeed played a fine trick on Auzance.

In order to prevent any attempts at fraud, the permit specified not only the quantity of grain but also the date and time of transport to the mill. However, to allow for the possibility of a storm or some other major obstacle, it was the farmer himself who had to fill in the time of day on departure. Seignos had worked out how to turn this to his advantage. That morning, he had written on the form: between eight and ten o'clock. He had left for the mill, taking the first two sacks of grain on his cart. Then, by agreement with the miller, he had taken back the permit and returned to the farm with his flour. Once there, he had rubbed out the first times, which were written in pencil, and replaced them, in ink this time, with: between three and five o'clock. Then in the afternoon he had taken down another two sacks on his cart. It was no use Auzance looking for discrepancies: there were none.

The sergeant pedalled on, chewing his moustache. After passing through Denières, he reached a crossroads where a lane led off up to the Château. At the junction, he came across a woman with a big shopping bag turning out of the road from Saint-Paul. Auzance swerved to the left to avoid her, but the woman, taken by surprise, instinctively stepped back in the same direction. The cyclist had to brake sharply and steady himself with his foot.

'Can't you watch where you're going?' he shouted angrily.

The woman, pale with fright, had stopped dead.

'I am sorree,' she stammered.

Auzance pricked up his ears. She had a funny accent. Have to find out if she's one of those gypsies, making a living from petty theft! Not big game to be sure, but in the absence of thrushes, blackbirds will have to do.

'Show me your papers,' he said.

The woman trembled. All skin and bone, she had dark feverish eyes, and hair tied back in a heavy bun. From the pocket of her apron she produced a cardboard wallet, and took out a receipt for her identity card.

'Ah! You're a foreigner?' said Auzance, his face brightening.

She nodded.

'Spanish,' said Auzance, examining the paper from every angle.

It was an interesting case, for his instructions were to pay particular attention to the credentials of any Spaniards. Most of them were refugees from the civil war, and therefore suspect.

Suddenly he frowned.

'But according to this paper,' he said, hardly able to conceal his elation, 'you are a resident of Marseille. What are you doing here?'

'I am with my employers, Monsieur and Madame Martini,' she stammered. 'They are on holiday in Saint-Paul.'

She looked anxious. She knew from experience that when her papers were checked, there was likely to be trouble.

'I applied for a pass so I could come with them,' she added, taking a pink slip from her wallet and handing it to Auzance.

The latter rested his bicycle against a tree. After inspecting the paper with a sardonic expression, he assumed his chilling smile and said:

'But your pass has expired! Your papers are not in order.'

'I am sorree,' said the Spanish woman in a shaky voice. 'M and Mme Martini were only expecting to stop in Saint-Paul for a month. But two weeks ago they decided to stay the whole summer. They asked for my pass to be extended.'

And she pointed out the back of the paper, where it was written 'Request for extension received' with a signature and an official stamp.

Auzance's elation dissipated. Clearly he was jinxed that day. The woman's papers appeared to be in order. He was just about to return them when suddenly a light appeared in his eye. At last, he had his prey!

'Just a minute!' he said. 'Your pass is for Saint-Paul. But here you're at Denières, which is in the commune of Saint-Boniface. A foreigner is not allowed to change communes.'

'I am sorree,' said the woman, now quite frightened. 'I have not changed communes, but there is no baker at Saint-Paul and Madame sent me to get bread here, because it's nearer.'

'Nearer perhaps, but it's not allowed,' said Auzance.

'But it's just next door,' she said, on the verge of tears. 'Monsieur told me I could go to the next commune.'

'It's no concern of mine what your employer said,' shouted Auzance. 'I'm the one who decides whether or not you're allowed to come here. Yes, foreigners are allowed to visit neighbouring communes. But they must not leave their administrative district. Now Denières may well be next door to Saint-Paul, but it's not in the same district. That means you are not in order. It is my duty to issue a summons. Why can't you foreigners just stay where you belong?'

'I assure you, officer, I didn't know that,' she stammered. 'And it's just for bread…'

'You should get bread inside your own commune.'

'But it's seven kilometres away!' the woman mumbled,

her voice barely audible. 'That's fourteen kilometres there and back.'

'What do you expect me to do about it? Deliver your bread myself? Come on, I have no time to waste.'

He took out his pen and notebook, and promptly summonsed Dolorès Maria Mendaza, of Spanish nationality, housemaid, married, resident in Marseille, temporarily living in Saint-Paul, holding an expired pass, for breach of the law governing the movements of foreigners.

'But I haven't done anyone any harm,' said Dolorès tearfully.

Auzance was not one to let himself be won over by tears. He'd had enough of that on the demarcation line. What's more, the Spanish woman had to pay for Pinkas and for Seignos.

'Well I dare say they won't put you in prison,' he replied sarcastically. 'You'll just be expelled from the Department.'

'But that's dreadful,' she groaned. 'This is where I work.'

Auzance shrugged. That was none of his business. When you live in a foreign country, you have to obey its laws.

Completing the summons, the sergeant had it signed by the offender, and abandoned her to her despair. Mounting his bicycle, he took the road towards the Château de Rochefontaine. With the summons in his pocket, the day could no longer be considered entirely wasted.

II

George Duchêne, restyled Du Chesne on his marriage to Mlle de Laborderie, who brought him Rochefontaine Château in her dowry, was, by his own definition, an accidental landowner. Born into a bourgeois family in Lyon, his true calling was dilettantism, and it was due to some error of nature that he found himself at large in a technocratic age.

In his youth he had dabbled, one by one, in all the arts. During the death throes of the Dadaist movement, George Duchêne published, in the smaller literary journals, esoteric poems composed of words and phrases scissored at random from newspapers, and assembled into ingenious montages. He also exhibited statuettes made up using offcuts of metal sheeting, shoelaces, clumps of hair and matchsticks. He produced an avant-garde performance for full orchestra and choir, punctuated at intervals by a tramcar bell and a motor horn. He directed a 'nonconformist' dance recital; and, dressed as a peroxided poodle with a ring through its nose, he achieved a *'succès de curiosité'* for his 'Dancing Bear' set to music by Bartók. The crowning glory of his artistic career was in 1924, when he taught himself to manipulate marionettes and, with a nod to Mr Punch, invented the character of 'Kluak', whose head bristled with nails instead of hair, whose eyes were replaced by twin miniature camera lenses sticking out on bellows, and who spoke the grotesque language of a 1923 Ubu Roi. It was his marriage which decided his ultimate career.

George Duchêne had met his wife-to-be in one of the big cafés in Lyon, which the young lady had daringly agreed to visit in the company of an emancipated cousin, who had herself thrown all caution to the winds after reading *The Bachelor Girl*. Captivated by the smile of the Pre-Raphaelite madonna sitting next to him, George Duchêne, who disdained the conventional approach in love as he did in art, contrived to upset his glass of Chartreuse on her light-coloured dress. The dry cleaner successfully removed the stain and, since further progress could clearly only be achieved by means of a wedding ring, he bowed to the inevitable, with all the more alacrity in view of the young lady's considerable endowments.

Duchêne's friends expected that he would manage his wife's property in a manner which lived up to his reputation, possibly by using a rhinoceros to plough fields entirely put down to the cultivation of mandrakes. But the 'accidental landowner' had quickly shed all artistic ambition. Rochefontaine was the first sphere in which Du Chesne proved resolutely conservative. He continued the cultivation of the most banal cereals and vegetables, and raised desperately unremarkable livestock. At the same time, he abandoned the seven arts – not to mention the others – for a new one: heraldry. He even began to build up a file for a psychoanalytical study of the various symbols on coats of arms. In fact, he spent much of the year in Lyon or Paris, leaving the care of his estate to an old retainer now promoted to the rank of steward. As a result, the land, already suffering from two generations of neglect, either lay fallow or produced very little.

However, after the armistice, Du Chesne decided to take up permanent residence at the château, and make a real return to nature, since it was all the rage in any case. He took his role as a 'modern country gentleman' seriously. It was then that he dreamt up the idea of sponsoring the return to nature of a group – nay, a whole community – of intellectuals, thus combining work with pleasure. For intellectuals were not necessarily all penniless. By pursuing this initiative to return more of his fallow land to productive use, he could also entertain himself by assembling a group of like-minded people. Since he could no longer go to Montparnasse, Montparnasse would come to him.

And that was how, a few days after his arrival in Saint-Boniface, Bernard Bloch had come across the advertisement in the *Petit Dauphinois*.

The newly naturalised Haitian was some way from belonging to the class of people which the squire of Rochefontaine hoped to attract to the community. Du Chesne had drawn up a detailed statute, in a style combining early surrealism with the language of heraldic treatises. The statute included, amongst other things, an entrance examination involving a series of questions for candidates to answer:

'At what time of year should carrots be sown?' 'List some well-known Cubist still-life paintings which depict Umbelliferae.' 'Give the exact meaning of the following terms: gramineae; simultaneists; compost; pointillism; pricking out; plastic art; rake (agricultural sense).' 'Mime the three stages of milking a cow, and establish a parallel with milking a goat.' 'Recite a poem of your own choosing by André Breton.' 'Explain the cycle which determines when a ewe is on heat.' The examination ended with a final poser intended as a tie-breaker, but which put provincial candidates at something of a disadvantage: 'What is the difference between a faun frolicking amongst the flora in the field at Saint-Germain, and the fauna frolicking at the Flore in Saint-Germain-des-Prés?'

At the entrance examination, Bernard Bloch scored five out of ten, flunking every one of the arty questions but making a good stab at the others, in spite of some terminological traps. The warm welcome he received at the Rochefontaine community was not unconnected with the fact that M. Du Chesne's first six candidates, although undeniably urban intellectuals, turned out to be on the breadline, and took the squire for a benefactor offering them a life of ease at no cost to themselves. Bernard Bloch might be a common scrap merchant, not to mention a Jew, but he did not appear to be a sponger. So M. Du Chesne agreed to let him a small house situated in a part of the estate known, somewhat optimistically, as Les Ripailles. He also provided him with some old furniture from the attic, the use of a field, and half a dozen gardening tools, including a rake (agricultural sense). He gave him some words of advice, wished him luck and, in no way discouraged by the difficulties of launching his community project, decided to place a new advertisement in a different paper.

* * *

Sergeant Auzance had to ask directions several times, but eventually made his way to the spot known as Les Ripailles, and found himself looking at a rather dilapidated shack. He knocked loudly on the door, and since there was no answer he started to look around. He saw a man with his back towards him, tending a field. This, no doubt, was the Jew. Before setting off in that direction, Auzance decided to inspect the premises more closely.

At the front was a little garden, which appeared to have been recently dug and seeded. Bending down, the gendarme found a tiny shoot, enough to show that beans had been sown there. Further on, he found sowings of lettuce, cabbage and tomatoes.

From his pocket, he took the notebook in which he kept the findings of his enquiries. These were the notes which he would later manage, by the sweat of his brow, to work up into reports.

The last pages contained a draft report on a shady household in Francheville, which he suspected of black market dealings.

'Female: Lelong, Marie-Louise. Age: 33. Place of birth: Le Puy. Husband died two years ago. Consequently she describes herself as a widow. Distinguishing marks: slight moustache, considerable body hair. Male: Brely, Ernest Augustin. Age: 38. Place of birth: Francheville. Mechanic, unemployed. Claims to be destitute, but his figure is a tribute to his diet and to his concubine's cooking. Has a daughter aged five from a liaison with a woman now deceased. The above-named appear to be involved in transactions of questionable legality.'

Auzance took out his pen, drew a line under this, and wrote: 'Bloch, Bernard, Jew. Cultivates small garden. Has sown beans and planted cabbages, lettuces and tomatoes.' When Robert Auzance was on a case, he didn't want to leave anything out.

Who could know if some apparently insignificant detail might not turn out later to be of absolutely decisive importance? Then he made his way towards the man in the field who, on seeing him, came to meet him.

'I am instructed to ask you some questions,' said Auzance. 'I assume you are Bernard Bloch? Do you have your papers on you?'

'Of course,' replied Bloch, who was carrying a large bowl full of maize seeds. He pulled a thick wallet from his trouser pocket, and extracted some documents: a receipt for his identity card, his passport, a travel pass. This Bloch appeared to know exactly which papers his visitor would require.

Auzance took careful note of all the information. One detail alone puzzled him. According to the various papers, the Jew was born in Siedlce, Poland. But these same documents showed him to be of Haitian nationality. Evidently, thought Auzance, the island of Haiti must be a colony of Poland. To cover all eventualities, he wrote down: 'Nationality: Polish-Haitian'.

Having completed these preliminary formalities, Auzance decided to pursue his investigations in greater depth.

'Is this all your land?' he enquired with forced joviality. 'How did you manage to plough all that? I take it you don't have any oxen?'

'No,' said Bloch, 'but my neighbour lent me some.'

The day after his arrival, Bernard had met an obliging young farmer called Nelchet, whose land adjoined his. The latter had kindly offered to plough the fields, using his own oxen. He had refused to accept any payment. The hours spent together at the plough had made firm friends of the Jew and the farmer.

'But what about the seeds?' asked Auzance suspiciously. 'Where did you get them? Not from Haiti, I presume?'

He was probing for information because he suspected a black market deal. But you don't beat a drum to catch a hare. Bernard guessed immediately what he was up to. Actually, he had obtained the seeds through the black market; or, more precisely, an exchange deal. After some lengthy, laborious haggling, Bloch had come to an agreement with Tournier and had returned from the grocery-cum-bar-cum-seed-merchant's the poorer by a pair of new shoes, but the richer by a hundred kilos of seed potatoes and a few kilos of beans and maize. Of course these details were no business of Auzance's.

'Monsieur Du Chesne gave me some of them,' he said without batting an eyelid. 'And my neighbours lent me some. I'll give them back at harvest time.'

Suddenly, Auzance was distracted by a series of shrieks coming from the pastures on the hillside. Looking up, he saw a goat heading at full tilt towards a cabbage patch, pursued by a dark, plump, young woman with her hair streaming behind her, followed in turn by a little boy of about four wielding a stick twice as tall as himself.

'Come back, don't go down there!' the young woman was screaming. But as the goat appeared to take no notice, she changed her tune, and started to wheedle, as if charming a bird, '*Kim, koze, kim, kim…!*'

The goat was no more familiar with Yiddish than it was with French. All it recognised was patois, and even then only when it felt like it. Renée Bloch had no notion of this. But little Jeannot did his best to mimic the strange calls he had heard in the neighbouring field.

'*Bedi, bedi… Ano, ano!…*' he shouted at the top of his lungs. '*Echte, echte… Boulou, boulou!*'

But the goat was already in the distance, and the child's voice was carried away in the wind.

Excusing himself, Bernard left Auzance and rushed up the hill, just in time to avert disaster amongst Nelchet's cabbages. Then returning the goat to the care of his wife and son, he walked back to the gendarme, who had spent the intervening time scribbling furiously in his notebook.

'So what about the goat?' Auzance continued his inquisition. 'It belongs to you, I take it? Where did you get it? How much did you pay?'

It was another trap, set to find out if the Jew had come by the animal legally.

'I bought it from Monsieur Chazelas,' said Bloch circumspectly. 'He also sold me some chickens and some rabbits. I haven't paid him yet, he has to find out the going rate at the market on Thursday.'

It was a white lie. This humble assortment of livestock had cost him a fine suit and three shirts. But that wasn't any of Auzance's business either.

The sergeant pursed his lips. Not much to be got out of this Jew. He settled for asking to see the Bloch woman's papers, and copied some details into his notebook, not omitting little Jeannot, naturalised French at birth, whom he described as follows: 'Bloch, Jean. Age: 4. Jew. Nationality: naturalised (first) French; (second) Haitian.'

Let those high-ups at the Prefecture sort that one out!

Then, feeling he had carried out his duty, though somewhat disappointed at coming away empty-handed – the hare had turned out to be too nimble – he brusquely took his leave of the Jew and set off towards Les Tilleuls to seek out Rosenfeld.

III

Frank Rosenfeld's initiation into agriculture was plagued by a series of setbacks which resulted as much from his lack of experience as from boundless confidence in his all-encompassing genius.

He had decided he would make money from his farming, and that he would do so from the very first season. If all these country bumpkins could do it, why should he, Frank Rosenfeld, not be able to? For he had a plan. He intended not only to produce enough for his own consumption, but also to make a substantial profit by selling the fruits of his labour in town. In the summer, he would beaver away and put the produce into store. Then he would turn his attention to the commercial aspect. Pulses, cheese, butter and charcuterie took up little room and were easy to transport. With this sort of produce, he could apply his guiding principle of the greatest benefit from the smallest space. His fiancée, who was bankrolling the operation, did not raise any objections.

At any rate, this was the vision that the architect-turned-farmer set out with. He made a thick sowing of beans, chickpeas and lentils. At the same time, he stocked his little farmyard with hens, in full anticipation of the proverbial golden eggs. Chazelas, from the farm next door, advised him to fence off the garden before doing anything else, but in vain, as Rosenfeld preferred first to make some boxes, improved to his own design, for the rabbits. He negotiated the purchase of a few goats, and scoured the area in search of the young milk cow he – and Mme Hermelin – dreamt of.

Soon, however, M. Rosenfeld's blue sky grew overcast, and he was obliged to recognise that, sadly, he still had a few things to learn. He found that the hens, allowed to range free, had feasted merrily on the peas and beans sown in the garden. In a fit of anger, he immediately slaughtered his finest hen, roasted it, and ate it, to Mme Hermelin's horror, with a cherry sauce, according to a traditional recipe from his home country.

The goats also caused a number of worries for this pioneer of the return to nature. To begin with, they devoured his lounge suit, which Mlle Sten had taken out of mothballs to air. It may have made for rather spicy eating, but they had eclectic tastes and were none the worse for it. Furthermore, they refused to let themselves be milked by Rosenfeld's clumsy hands. Worn down by their relentless butting and charging, he asked Chazelas to look after them until he had undertaken some practical lessons in milking. As for the rabbits, housed in modern, Rosenfeld-designed hutches and fed on a synthetic diet of his own devising, they started to die, in short order, one after the other…

When Auzance arrived within sight of Les Tilleuls, M. Rosenfeld's sky had turned decidedly stormy. Lightning had passed between two highly charged temperaments: the ex-architect and Mme Hermelin. And all because of the nettles.

To save the last of his rabbits, Rosenfeld had decided to put them on an urticaceous diet. But when Mme Hermelin discovered that her tenant was tearing up the nettles around Les Tilleuls to feed them, she exploded with an anger that had been brewing against him for some time. In a torrent of invective, she accused him of disgusting wastefulness; of a suspicious delay in getting married, a delay which meant that she, daughter and mother to church ministers, was harbouring an illegitimate couple; of making free with her own bathroom; of shilly-shallying about his conversion; and above all of badly letting her down by continually putting off the purchase of a cow, when she was so desperately in need of milk!

Whereupon Rosenfeld, his nose beading with perspiration as always when under stress, launched into a vigorous counter-attack. Granted, the wedding hadn't taken place yet, but the banns had nevertheless been posted at the Mairie; if he had not yet undergone conversion, it was a matter for his own conscience; if he used Mme Hermelin's bathroom, it was only because the bathroom intended for guests was repeatedly occupied, for hours on end, by M. Hermelin (indeed, it was the only place where the poor man could escape from conjugal tyranny). And as for the cow…!

Suddenly, Rosenfeld broke off. He had just noticed Auzance, who had dismounted and was strolling towards the house. Rosenfeld muttered something and went back inside, leaving his basket of nettles behind. He preferred to leave the debating floor to Mme Hermelin rather than have to confront a gendarme.

This strategic retreat only bought him a brief respite. Moments later, a loud rapping on his door made it clear that he was indeed the object of the gendarme's visit. Rosenfeld started, but drawing on all his reserves of sang-froid, though his nose was still glistening with sweat, he went to the door and opened it.

Auzance assumed an official tone. 'Frank Rosenfeld? I am instructed to ask you some questions.'

'Entirely at your disposal,' said Rosenfeld pleasantly, though his voice shook a little. 'Please take the trouble to sit down.'

He drew up a chair, dusting it carefully with his handkerchief.

'It's to inspect your papers,' said Auzance gruffly, sitting down.

Rosenfeld breathed again. Was that all it was? What terrors had not passed through his mind in the last few seconds? He had envisioned himself searched, interned, imprisoned, crucified. By comparison, a straightforward inspection of his papers was a picnic, a mere bagatelle.

'Certainly,' he said with a broad smile. 'At your service, Officer. Please allow me to express my regrets that you have had to come all the way up here in this heat. If I had known you required my presence, I would have been pleased to come down to the Gendarmerie.'

His deference was a clear signal that he was aware of the abyss separating a miserable Jew from an upstanding Aryan gendarme.

'I have to carry out my duty,' muttered Auzance, somewhat appeased.

'Of course, of course,' said Rosenfeld, sympathetically. 'I'm just embarrassed at causing you so much trouble. It's a steep hill on a bicycle, I know from experience. You must be thirsty, Officer? It's inexcusable of me not to have offered you something to drink earlier... But I insist, I insist... You've gone to so much trouble for me, and I'm failing in the most basic good manners. Here are my papers, take your time over them, and please bear with me while I get you something.'

And he was gone. Auzance, usually able to resist temptation when on duty, could not bring himself to turn down such a gracious offer.

He applied his usual punctiliousness to the examination of the Jew Rosenfeld's papers. Meanwhile, the latter returned from the cellar with a bottle of white wine under his arm. Its seal was unbroken. At Tournier's he had paid an exorbitant price for a few bottles to lay down for special occasions. The visit of a gendarme clearly fell into this category.

'I do apologise for my simple ways,' he said, taking a couple of imitation crystal glasses from the sideboard. 'Unfortunately, my fiancée, Mademoiselle Sten, has just gone down to Francheville. She'll be sorry she missed you. She would certainly have known the right thing to do.'

He uncorked the bottle of Fontecreuse, poured a little into his own glass as he had seen others do, then filled Auzance's glass generously before topping up his own.

'Here's to your good health, Officer, and to the rebirth of France!'

There was clearly no turning down a glass of wine accompanied by such a toast. Auzance nodded his thanks and, finding the wine pleasantly cool, knocked it back in a single draught.

'I'm so pleased you have come to see me,' said Rosenfeld, putting down his glass and smiling graciously. 'These days, regrettably, inspections and identity checks are more vital than ever. I'd go so far as to say it's essential to separate the wheat from the chaff.'

M. Rosenfeld did not elaborate on this, but it went without saying that he regarded himself as belonging in the first category.

While he was speaking, Rosenfeld, anxious to spare this representative of the law any unwonted fatigue, had been considerately handing over his papers one by one. The gendarme, taking careful note of all this Jewish individual's details, found everything in order: documents, official stamps, signatures. Meanwhile, Rosenfeld had poured him another glass of Fontecreuse. Auzance would of course have turned it down if he had noticed, but since it was already poured, he had no option but to drink it.

'You are… Israelite?' he asked, trying to retain his official tone.

'Ah! I'm afraid so,' said Rosenfeld with a sigh, as if confessing to a shameful disease. 'I made all the necessary declarations when I was required to.' He produced another document.

'However,' he said insinuatingly, 'In a few days' time I am getting married to a young Aryan lady. And I'm also a veteran. In fact I served twice in the army.'

'What? You served in the Great War?'

'You could say I contributed to ending it. In the Latvian army against the Bolsheviks. Look, here are my papers. Please take a note of this, the authorities may well be interested,' he added in a profoundly deferential tone. 'And as for this war, in response to the call from a generous and hospitable French nation, I joined up again. Here's my military record.'

While Auzance was writing down all the details of M. Rosenfeld's army career, the latter filled his glass to the brim again. Then he took out his cigarette case and proffered it to the gendarme who, after another moment of uncertainty, decided he might as well be hung for a sheep as a lamb, and reached out to take one.

Politely, Rosenfeld lit it for him. Auzance, his thirst now quenched, sipped the wine more slowly. Then Rosenfeld went on, 'As you see, Officer, before the war I was an architect. Alas, France now needs bread more than it needs houses. So I resolved to devote myself to agriculture.'

He refilled Auzance's glass and continued: 'If it is of interest to you, I might add that as the country is short of fats and oils more than anything else, I intend, from next summer, to cultivate oilseed on a large scale. I'm also planning to raise two pigs, one for the rationing effort – they need them badly in the towns, and the countryside can provide so few, alas! – and the other for our own consumption. Naturally I will not forget my friends. Do you like sausages, Officer? I learnt an excellent recipe in my home country. Please do me the honour of coming by to taste them when they are ready. No, but I insist, sir, I know you suffer the same privations as anyone in the towns. Except you keep a dignified silence about it, which does you credit. What a pity it would be if we producers were not able to give some pleasure to those whose task it is to look after our personal and material security. Another cigarette?'

This time Auzance didn't hesitate. Being a Jew evidently didn't prevent this Frank Rosenfeld from having excellent manners. Nor did being a policeman prevent Auzance from being partial to sausages.

'Another drop?' said Rosenfeld, refilling Auzance's glass. 'As I was saying, your job must be very hard. You should know that some people, at least, appreciate your selfless devotion to duty. I would be the first to admit – and to regret – that certain Israelites must give you some sleepless nights. As for myself, I am about to break my last link with those whose faith I am commonly assumed to share. I won't hide from you that I intend to undergo a conversion very soon. Of course I'm telling you this as a private individual, not in your capacity as a representative of the law.'

There was only half a glass left in the bottle, but Auzance's benevolence had grown in proportion to the amount consumed. This M. Rosenfeld was right. He had lost sleep over these Jews. But in his present good mood, he only saw the funny side of his experiences. He suddenly smiled at the memory of some of the comical incidents which had occurred on the demarcation line.

'Oh yes!' he said, 'I've seen some of those crazy Israelites! You know, last year, on the line, I arrested a character who'd hidden in the forest. He knew he was trapped, and he tried to hide in a snowdrift. But he hadn't even had the wit to cover his tracks in the snow, the idiot. A sitting duck, that's what the hunters call it. And he was! A sitting duck! He was so scared he was bent double with stomach-ache. And he couldn't stop sneezing! And farting! Sneeze! Atchoo! Prrrt! And again! A sitting duck! I couldn't stop laughing, I tell you, I couldn't stop!'

Bursting with glee at the grotesque plight of the Jew, Auzance threw himself back in his chair, helpless with laughter.

'Ha! Ha! Ha! What a stomach-ache! A case of the runs, more like! A sitting duck! These Jews, I tell you!'

M. Rosenfeld listened obligingly. Now, he laughed along with the gendarme, who was clutching his heaving belly in both hands. But suddenly, Rosenfeld's laughter turned sour. Behind his screwed-up eyelids he saw the face of his grandfather, someone he hardly ever gave a thought to.

He was an old man with sidelocks, and a man of fervent faith. When Jews sacrificed their dignity in their dealings with Gentiles, he called them *shrims*. He explained to his grandson that in the olden days, certain Jews entertained their Polish overlords with comic pastiches of Hebrew liturgical chants, imitating the waddling gait and the nasal inflections of the congregation in the synagogue. These miserable jesters were nicknamed *shrims*, a deformation of the first words of the Song of Songs, and it was a name which mightily amused their lordships.

As he laughed along with Auzance at the unfortunate Jew sick with fright, Rosenfeld thought he heard the quavering voice of his grandfather murmur '*Shrim...*' but he banished the thought. Instead of boring everyone stiff with all those old stories, the old fool ought to have shaved off his sidelocks and undergone conversion!

Auzance now had everything he needed for his report. Moreover, the bottle of Fontecreuse was empty. So he rose and shook hands with his host, who thanked him for his 'kind visit' and gave him another cigarette, to smoke on his way.

Well, for sure, thought Auzance, back on the road, it hadn't been just any old hunting party. For the first time, when he was out to trap hares, he had happened upon a fatted pig. In the space of half an hour, the Jew Rosenfeld had become, in the sergeant's mind, Monsieur Frank Rosenfeld.

He was a Jew, but so what? Seeing things through a slight haze thanks to the effect of the wine, the gendarme told himself that it was he, Robert Auzance, who would decide which of the Jews of Saint-Boniface was an Israelite gentleman with impeccable credentials, and which of them was an undesirable Yid.

IV

From Les Tilleuls to La Grange took Auzance about twenty minutes, a fair part of it on foot. So his good humour had dissipated somewhat by around five o'clock, when he knocked on the door of the chalet. Nobody came to open it. But on hearing a sound behind him, he turned round and saw Philibert Vautier on his way home, carrying a mattock on his shoulder.

'Hey there!' Auzance called out. 'Nobody at home?'

Vautier sauntered towards him.

'He's not far away, the Monsieur,' he said. 'I could see him from up there. He's on his way back from Saint-Boniface. Been to the shop, I expect.'

At this he turned to go, but the Sergeant grabbed his arm.

'Tell me,' he murmured in a confidential tone, 'Who exactly is this man? What does he do?'

'Writes stuff,' said Vautier grudgingly. 'Prints things on his machine. But then what do I know?' he added, cautiously.

'We have received intelligence,' Auzance went on in an official tone, 'that he is engaged in business transactions. That he visits the farms. That he has dealings on the black market.'

It was not the most appropriate of topics. In the home of a hanged man, you don't mention rope.

Vautier looked perplexed, and scratched his head. 'Black market?' he repeated, after a short hesitation. 'I wouldn't know about that.'

'But you're his closest neighbour,' Auzance pressed him.

'Not at all. It's not me, it's La Bardette. She's right next door to him. See where her house is. But they don't get on. Had a big row just this morning.'

Auzance smiled. He knew all about La Bardette. He had summonsed the old woman just recently, regarding the fraudulent transport of six kilos of bran for her rabbits.

'A black market deal, maybe?' suggested Auzance.

'No, no. Black cat, more like,' Vautier corrected him, determined to keep clear of any shady implications. 'Monsieur Verès poisoned La Marquise, her cat. He put out poison because he had one or two rats. But the cat ate it, and that was the end of her.'

'Oh!' said Auzance, disappointed. 'But anyway, you must know if people come to trade with him, or if he visits the farms. You see him go past, don't you?'

'Well, not really,' said Vautier evasively. 'I don't see much of him. To get water he goes that way, by La Bardette's garden. She's always complaining about it.'

'You said he went shopping,' Auzance resumed, refusing to follow Vautier's meanderings. 'Does he go often?'

'Yesterday he went down to the chemist's in Francheville, for the poison. He'd have done better to stay at home. Bravo, eh, with the rat-killer! And that Bardette there is none too easy at the best of times!'

At that moment, Verès appeared at the top of the path linking La Grange to the chalet. Vautier, who was first to see him, pointed him out to Auzance and sidled prudently away. Tibor, deep in thought, had not noticed the two men. He walked on, swinging his shopping bag.

'I presume you are Verès, Tibor?' Auzance challenged him, springing out from behind the house. 'I am here to inspect your papers.'

Verès opened the chalet door, let the gendarme in, and the examination of his papers began.

Soon, the credentials of Verès, Tibor, male, Hungarian, thirty-five years of age; of his wife, maiden name Myran, Ellen, twenty-eight years of age, nationality Norwegian; and of their two children, filled a page of notes. The first problem was to classify the occupation of the subject.

Verès' identity card did indeed contain the entry: journalist; writer. That corroborated the postman Brandouille's information, as this Verès received large quantities of newspapers and letters. But to Auzance's eyes, the definition was insufficiently precise.

'Very well,' he grunted. 'But we still have to know exactly what it is that you do.'

'Well,' said Verès with an expansive gesture, 'in normal times, I write articles for newspapers. Of course, as things stand…'

'But what do you write? For which newspapers?' Auzance

pressed him. 'That's what we are interested in.'

He did not define what he meant by 'we'. Was it a royal 'we'? The Francheville Gendarmerie? The authorities at the Prefecture? The Vichy Government?

'Oh!' said Verès. 'I wrote mostly for foreign newspapers. Reports, articles on life in France, and generally anything of interest.'

'So,' Auzance summed up, 'I'll make a note: "Informs foreigners about what is going on here".'

Verès jumped up.

'But that's not right,' he protested vehemently. 'That's what spies do. I'm a journalist. Please could you note down instead: "Writes articles".'

Auzance, his surliness undiminished, scribbled a few words in his notebook.

'At present, as we're about to leave for America, because I already have a visa,' said Verès, becoming excited, 'I'm concentrating on a history book. I'm going to title it *The Paradoxes of History*. I identify a series of events, mostly little-known or misinterpreted, which I aim to present in a completely new light. For example, take Frederick the Great, King of Prussia, who is generally considered…'

His little lecture was brutally interrupted by a hoarse cry in the distance.

'Murderer! Murderer!'

Auzance jumped to his feet. Who was being killed? Where? And why? But Verès, embarrassed, begged him to sit down again.

'Please don't worry,' he pleaded. 'It's nothing. A stupid business about a cat. My neighbour is a bit excitable.'

'Hey! Hey! Murderer!' cried La Bardette who, hearing Verès' voice, had emerged from her lair. Crouched behind the closed door of her kitchen, she had not seen Auzance arrive.

'Oh, yes,' said Auzance self-importantly. 'We have received a report of this incident. You poisoned your neighbour's cat.'

Verès' jaw dropped in amazement. What a fine job the Francheville police were doing! Take that, Scotland Yard! Suddenly, a hail of gravel, thrown in through a small window which overlooked La Bardette's garden, rattled down onto the kitchen floor.

'There! Some peas for the murderer's soup!' shouted La Bardette. And she started to insult Verès in patois.

'Granda bourriqua! Viaoux pas ré! Va!'

'I beg of you, Madame, be quiet, I'm busy,' cried the journalist.

'Caliou! Alesca murlet! Granda rocha! Caliou, va!' she went on.

'Of course, if you say so,' said Verès in a conciliatory tone. 'But now, Madame, it's time to calm down.'

But appeasing this Fury would take more than that. La Bardette continued to curse him in patois.

'Lonzo braïo! Voleur d'aïgo! Achachin!'

'That's enough, Madame,' shouted Verès, losing patience. 'Hold your tongue! *Favete linguis!* Yes, Madame, *favete linguis!*'

This scholarly request for silence at least had the effect of making La Bardette drop her patois. She must have been impressed by the learned quotation.

'Poisoner! Water-thief!' yelped the old woman. 'You just try taking your can through my garden! I'll stuff your head into it! And then I'll get the police! At least that'll give those layabouts something to do!'

At these words, Auzance sprang up from his chair, and La Bardette saw the sergeant's *képi* appear framed in the little kitchen window. Dumbstruck by this supernatural vision, the old woman beat a hasty retreat and barricaded herself into her house.

'It's not my fault,' mumbled Verès, deeply embarrassed.

'Our attic is infested with rats. I've tried everything to get rid of them. I didn't know my neighbour's cat was in the habit of going there. And I still can't understand why an attic apparently frequented by a domestic feline should be so overrun with rats.'

Auzance had sat down again. After all, the murder of this Marquise was outside his remit.

'I do sympathise with the poor woman,' said Verès, 'she was very attached to the animal. But it's not very serious. She insults me in patois, I respond in Latin, and we're quits. What I find harder to understand, is how much she resents me going past her peas when…'

'We know,' Auzance finished for him, 'when you get water. You go through her garden and it leads to an argument.'

Verès could not believe his ears. This gendarme was a real Sherlock Holmes!

But he found it necessary to explain:

'I beg your pardon. On this matter, my neighbour is entirely in the wrong. The water does not belong to her.'

But already the Sherlock Holmes of Saint-Boniface, deaf to these explanations, had added to his notes: 'argumentative character'.

'So if I understand correctly,' Auzance continued, 'you are writing a textbook. Who is it for?'

Such lack of insight sapped Verès of any desire to resume his lecture. The great detectives are not of necessity learned men.

'A Swiss publisher,' he said resignedly. 'He was given the outline by Professor Ferrero, an eminent Italian historian who has been kind enough to take an interest in my work.'

To Auzance, all that was of secondary importance. He was impatient to get to grips with the heart of the matter. Which, in this case, was the black market. He pointed to the bag which Verès had placed on a chair when he came in.

'But in the meantime you're finding a few bargains, aren't you? We all have to get along somehow, eh?' he said with a knowing smile. 'What have you got in this bag?'

'Not much,' said Verès, unaware of the insidious nature of the question. 'A packet of washing powder for my wife, no coupons required; a lucky dip for my daughter; a pencil for me, and a jar of mixed pickles for all of us.'

'Mixed what?' asked Auzance, his suspicions aroused.

'Mixed pickles. It's a condiment made from a selection of preserved vegetables, an English recipe. I was delighted to find it at the grocer's in Saint-Boniface.'

'Well, well!' said Auzance, disappointed, peering into the bag. 'But what about the parcels? We are informed that you receive them regularly. Only today, the postman brought you a big one. What was in it?'

'Our stove doesn't work very well,' answered Verès, 'so I ordered a Norwegian casserole from Marseille. It's an isothermic appliance which retains the heat and extends the cooking time.'

Auzance glanced at the half-unpacked device, frowned, took up his notebook again, and wrote, in a moment of sudden inspiration:

'Foreigner, suspect. Born Hungarian, knows a Swiss publisher and an Italian Professor, holds an American visa, writes about the King of Prussia, eats English condiments, argues in Latin, possesses a Norwegian casserole...'

Then, after a moment's reflection, he added '...and a wife of the same nationality'.

That would be enough to cook this Verès' goose. But there was still something to be gained from investigating the subject's black market activities.

'We are also informed,' he said slyly, 'that you make use of a typewriter. What do you type? Accounts? Invoices? Brochures? For what sort of goods?'

This hurt Verès' pride as a historian. 'But I have just told you, sir, that I am writing a book,' he cried. 'Obviously the typewriter is for typing out my work.'

He lifted a thick file off the table and handed it to Auzance, who opened it at random. Suddenly, at the bottom of the page, his eyes fell on the following:

Equipped with a large quantity of provisions in anticipation of winter: 550 sacks of flour, 80 goatskins of oil, 90 tonnes of salted victuals…

At last he had him, the black marketeer! This Jewish idiot had mistakenly shown him his business records, instead of the so-called textbook which was a smokescreen for his wholesale transactions. Eagerly, Auzance turned the page, and continued to read:

…the Carthaginian army set out for the Alps. Even today, historians are unable to agree which of the passes Hannibal had chosen to cross the mountain chain. The author of this work tends personally to the view that it was the Argentières Pass. Whatever the case, when the Consul Publius Scipio, father of Scipio Africanus, arrived with his army…

Auzance closed the file in disappointment. As this concerned military provisions, it was a matter for the Supplies Office, not for the Gendarmerie. But in any case, he had already obtained enough incriminating evidence against Verès.

So the sergeant coldly took his leave of the Jew, put his notes in his pocket, and headed for the door. As for Verès' visits to the farms, he preferred not to mention them, for fear of putting him on his guard. But the sergeant still expected to end up with a fine summons, all the more so as, thanks to Brandouille, he knew the identity of his suspect's main supplier. The trap was set, and the hare would most certainly run into it...

V

Pushing his bicycle, Auzance reached the foot of the hill where the little cart track from La Grange joined the village road. Suddenly, he caught sight of an odd-looking figure: a tall, stooping woman dressed in beach trousers, wearing a turban with a feather. The Indian Tomb had received a telegram informing her that her new visa had arrived, and she was on the way to tell the Verès family the good news.

As he drew level, Auzance scrutinised her closely. He didn't like the look of her: neither her face nor her trousers. Obviously a foreigner. A migratory bird, eh? Already this afternoon he had downed a blackbird, that Spanish gipsy type; and this might be another. But if this was a blackbird, it was one with rare plumage. Auzance had never seen a woman got up like this, nor one with such a frightful face. But she didn't frighten Auzance, oh no.

'Your papers, Madame,' he said, blocking the foreigner's way.

The rare bird delved into a big leather handbag embossed with a sphinx surrounded by hieroglyphs, and produced two papers, one green, the other pink: her identity card and her travel pass.

Meticulously, Auzance unfolded the green concertina-style document issued by the Prefecture, and examined it from every angle. Then he turned to the pink one.

The Indian Tomb looked on with an air of supreme indifference. She was quite above all this! Anyway, her papers were perfectly in order.

But the Sergeant was not of the same opinion. His beady eye had soon spotted the chink in the armour.

'When you arrived in Saint-Boniface, where did you have your pass stamped?'

'At the Mairie, as you can see,' said Mme Clips distantly.

And she pointed out the stamp which M. Longeaud had applied above the rubric: 'Arrival visa, Mairie or Gendarmerie'.

'This stamp is not valid,' said Auzance brusquely. 'According to the new directive from the Prefecture, passes have to be stamped at the Gendarmerie, and nowhere else.'

'Oh, for goodness sake,' said the Indian Tomb, annoyed. 'All this red tape drives me mad. I feel a headache coming on. And I warn you, I have a weak heart.'

The feather on her turban swayed like the mainmast of a ship in distress.

'I am afraid, Madame, that your visa is not in order. You should have gone to the Gendarmerie.'

'How was I supposed to know?' protested the Indian Tomb. 'At the Mairie they agreed to stamp the paper. And it says here, Mairie or Gendarmerie.'

'I don't care what it says here, I have to do my job. They shouldn't have stamped it at the Mairie. And I see you arrived at Saint-Boniface after the 25th of May. From that date, any foreigner who intends to stay in the Department for more than forty-eight hours must, by law, apply for a residence permit. I can't find any sign of it here.'

'But my pass is valid for a month!' protested the Indian Tomb. 'That should be enough.'

'Well, it's not enough for us. Your papers are not in order, Madame, on two counts. It is my duty to issue a summons.'

'Do as you please,' said the Indian Tomb haughtily. 'But get on with it, because I already have a headache. Anyway, I'm leaving Saint-Boniface at the end of the week.'

And, in a tone intended to command respect, she added, 'I'm leaving for the United States.'

Auzance's nose had not let him down. Definitely a migratory bird.

'You too?' he snorted. 'You're not a Jew, by any chance?'

'Most certainly not,' said the Indian Tomb, sounding royally offended.

Auzance was not impressed. He sat down at the roadside on the bole of a big tree, and began to write: 'No arrival visa... No residence permit...'

'Don't trouble yourself,' said Mme Clips icily. 'I'm leaving here at the end of the week, and I'll be out of France in another few days. So...'

'I am afraid, Madame,' retorted Auzance, 'that you will be leaving here not at the end of the week, but on the date stated on your expulsion order. Which means tomorrow, probably.'

'But that's impossible!' cried Mme Clips. 'I sent all my clothes to the laundry yesterday. I'll never be ready tomorrow! Oh! My head!'

Auzance shrugged. These details were no concern of his.

'As you wish, Madame, but if you do not leave on the required date, I will be obliged to have you interned.'

'That's just too much!' exclaimed the Indian Tomb, her nostrils trembling. 'You are not a gentleman, sir. This is no way to treat a lady. Oh! My head! I will not forget this!'

Auzance did not appear to be listening. He had finished filling in his summons form. 'Sign here,' he said, holding it out to her.

'Oh no, Monsieur,' said the Indian Tomb with a sepulchral laugh, 'I don't give my autograph to just anyone.'

'In that case, I will have to report that you refused to sign. That's serious. Very serious.'

'Well give it here, Monsieur, you can have your signature.'

She scribbled something which resembled the hieroglyphs on her Egyptian handbag and, drawing her meagre frame up to its full height, gave the gendarme a disdainful look.

'You may go, Madame,' said Auzance, putting his papers away to signal the end of the matter.

'I shall not bid you good day,' said Mme Clips, drooping her eyelids in a macabre expression of superiority.

And with the majestic gait she had once used on screen to portray Cleopatra, she made her way to the Verès' house where, her nerves frayed to breaking point, she gave way to a violent fit of sobbing.

As for Auzance, his good mood was restored. He pedalled off in high spirits towards Francheville. The day which had begun so badly had finished with a heady double victory. Unconsciously, he found himself humming 'Oh! The policeman's lot is such a happy one…'

VI

Streaming through the shutters, the sun projected bright stripes onto the flowery bedroom wallpaper, and cast a zebra-like pattern over a woman who lay moaning quietly on a divan, a turban on her head. The Indian Tomb was no longer wearing the green headgear of happier days, but a heavy white compress fashioned out of towels. In a bowl placed on a chair beside the divan, a lump of ice was gradually melting, even though the room was relatively cool.

The headache about which Mme Clips had warned Auzance had developed into a severe migraine the night before. It had reached its peak at eleven in the morning, when a notification had been delivered to Les Tilleuls from the Gendarmerie, requiring the Indian Tomb to leave the *département* immediately.

The imminent departure of her best client, who occupied the finest room in the house, furnished with a Louis XIV chest of drawers and mirrored wardrobe, was a cause of sincere grief to

171

Mme Hermelin. For Mme Clips unwittingly paid a good ten francs more than her ordinary clients, and ate, moreover, like a sparrow. So the landlady of Les Tilleuls had offered to ask the president of the Francheville Veterans' Legion to intervene, as he was a close friend of her son Joseph.

Mme Clips, rising to the part of martyr, had turned the offer down. She would leave that very evening on the 19.25 train. She merely asked Mme Hermelin to help calm her migraine. She claimed that because of her heart condition she was not allowed to take pills, so Marguerite, the maid, had dropped everything, leaving all her work to M Hermelin, and hurried off to the butcher's in Francheville for a lump of ice.

The Indian Tomb broke off moaning long enough to count the chimes of the Empire style clock downstairs in the sitting room. One... two... three... With the help of Mme Hermelin, she had already packed her bags, and it only remained to close them once her washing was back from the laundry. But would it be ready in time? The anxiety only made her headache worse.

She tried to think about something else. M. César Fleury was coming to bid her farewell. Other visitors could be expected to follow. A pity, for she would dearly have liked to arrange more time in private with the charming musician. She already regretted not going down for lunch with the others, for that would have enabled her to say goodbye to everyone at the same time.

She sat up, took her mirror from the bedside table, and examined her face closely. Water trickled off the towel, creating rivulets in the ochre-coloured powder she had applied. With a grimace, she removed her martyr's halo, dropped it in the bowl, made herself up carefully, and hid the towel and its container behind the valance of the dressing table. César could make his entrance: Cleopatra was ready for him.

Stifling a final moan, she listened carefully. She thought she heard a noise at the bottom of the stairs. Half swooning, she closed her eyes. It was indeed the muffled sound of César's Roman sandals. A moment later there was a knock, and M. Fleury's masculine figure appeared in the doorway.

The Indian Tomb smiled dolefully and motioned the visitor to sit in the armchair placed for him beside the divan.

'I hope you will excuse me for not getting up,' she said in a weak voice. 'I am in agony.'

Every time she saw Fleury, his jet-black beard and velvety gaze had an immediate effect on her. Today he was even more carefully turned out than usual, and something virile and masterful in his bearing filled her with a languid pleasure.

'I am sorry that you are leaving,' he said as he sat down. 'The identity checks you were so unfortunately subjected to are intended for undesirable aliens, and can only be justified if they are carried out judiciously.'

'Alas!' said the Indian Tomb, 'that's not enough to protect a poor defenceless woman. I leave this evening, and not without regret, I must confess,' she added, gazing tenderly at Fleury through her false eyelashes.

'It's very distressing,' said Fleury sympathetically, 'but I might have a solution. I have just learnt the name of the new Prefect of this Department. As it happens, I know him well. We became friends a few years ago, when he was just an ordinary civil servant. I was often invited to his home, where I sometimes played chamber music with his wife, who is a violinist of great distinction and sensitivity. It would take no more than a telephone call, I would venture to hope, to secure you at least a stay of execution.'

The Indian Tomb felt a violent surge of retrospective jealousy against the sensitive violinist, and rejected the proposal out of hand.

'Thank you, sir,' she said bitterly, 'Madame Hermelin made me a similar offer, but I told her I would not be party to such a procedure. What I expect from your great nation is justice, not condescension. So I leave with a heavy heart.'

There was an awkward silence.

'The other day, you expressed a desire,' said Fleury. 'I think I can fulfil that wish today…'

The Indian Tomb revived, sat up on the divan, and gazed deeply into the dark, smouldering eyes of her visitor, her nostrils quivering, for all the world like a languorous Maharani.

'You wished to see an example of the shirt I designed,' Fleury went on.

'Oh. Yes,' said the Indian Tomb with a sigh, flopping back onto the divan, her nostrils at rest.

'Unfortunately, most of my clothes are at the laundry, and I only have the shirt I'm wearing… but maybe after all,' he added with false modesty, 'my little invention is not of such interest to you any more.'

'Oh but it is, it is,' whispered the Indian Tomb, revived again. 'I would very much like to see it.'

Fleury fingered the knot of his white piqué tie. Then: 'So, Madame, I'm a little embarrassed to ask, but may I…'

'Please do, please do,' said the Indian Tomb, her cheeks turning from ochre to dark red with emotion.

'…show you the design I drew myself.'

From the inside pocket of his corduroy jacket he drew a large yellow envelope, and unfolded the contents.

At that moment, there was a knock on the door. Mme Clips vouchsafed M. Fleury one last look, in which she tried to convey all the endearments they could have exchanged, and which must now forever remain unsaid. Then, in a weak voice, she invited her visitors in. The parade of honour to the Indian Tomb began. Bernard Bloch and André Murger appeared in the doorway, followed by Mme Hermelin. The landlady of Les Tilleuls brought good news: the laundrywoman was ironing her washing and it would all be ready in half an hour.

'Thank you, Madame,' said the Indian Tomb with a sigh of relief. 'That sets my mind at rest.'

Bloch and Murger each laid an offering before the Indian Tomb: the former a packet of cigarettes for the trip, saved from his ration, along with Renée Bloch's very first goat's cheese; the latter a parcel of Swiss newspapers, picked up in Francheville that very day.

Fleury felt he could not allow himself to be left out of this show of generosity.

'Please allow me, Madame, to give you this as a souvenir,' he said, proffering the yellow envelope. 'My shirtmaker in Lyon already has a copy.'

Completely forgetting her headache, Mme Clips lit a cigarette with voluptuous pleasure, and told everyone how touched she was by these signs of friendship.

There was another knock at the door. It was Verès, straight from Tournier's shop where, following some intensive bargaining, he had exchanged his monthly wine ration for two packets of cigarettes. Since Mme Clips was about to leave for America, it was even more important to sustain this valuable connection. Tibor placed his tribute before the Indian Tomb. In return, he received the lugubrious smile which was her sign of gracious thanks.

'So, Madame,' said Verès, 'I hear you have decided to leave us.'

'I have no choice,' said Mme Clips, with a veiled glance at Fleury. 'I am the victim of maladministration.'

'It is highly regrettable,' said Fleury, 'but if I were you I would beware of jumping to conclusions. It often happens, following a defeat, that power falls into the hands of an incompetent administration, led by military men who lack the necessary qualifications.'

'Quite right,' Verès chimed in eagerly. 'It's one of the most striking paradoxes of history. The military assert that since it is they who have lost the war, they are the only ones who can win the peace. And the whole nation goes along with them. Take Hannibal, MacMahon, or Hindenburg.'

'But in our country,' Fleury resumed, 'the era is drawing to a close when admirals could style themselves chiefs of police, and colonels of indigenous infantry regiments heads of rationing. We are at the dawn of great changes in every aspect of French life. The corporations which were dissolved by a regime of stupid, impotent, doddery old politicians are beginning to rise again. This reform alone is a tremendous step forward.'

'What!' said Murger, irritably. 'The return to a medieval institution, abandoned precisely because it was an obstacle to technical and social progress, you call that a step forward? It's a retreat! And what a retreat!'

Fleury was about to retaliate when their attention was diverted by a new arrival. Mme Hermelin, who during this conversation had been drawing up a mental inventory of the room, took the opportunity to slip out.

'So,' said M. Rosenfeld as he came in, 'I hear you are preparing to leave us. It's such a pity you didn't tell me yesterday. I've just made friends with an officer from the Francheville Gendarmerie, a most pleasant young man…'

'You have been fortunate,' said Mme Clips. 'The one who stopped me yesterday is a veritable brute.'

'If I had a word with him, we might be able to sort things out for you.'

Frank Rosenfeld liked to be seen as the magnanimous benefactor. And he was quite aware that Mme Clips had already turned down a similar offer from Mme Hermelin.

'It's very kind of you, Monsieur Rosenfeld, but it's no use. I have decided to leave. I'm leaving Saint-Boniface, in fact I'm leaving France altogether. Alas, France has let me down terribly. It's appalling to see how a poor foreign woman gets treated these days! A foreigner who, far from taking bread from the mouths of the French, has bequeathed a fortune to the country over the past ten years!'

Heads nodded politely in response to her lament.

'So you had a visit from the police?' Bloch asked Rosenfeld. 'Me too. What an honour. Bad news, these identity checks.'

'You're right,' said Verès. 'They always mean trouble.'

'Don't be such wimps,' said Rosenfeld arrogantly. 'As far as I am concerned, I'm not worried at all. Anyone who has done his duty with a clear conscience has nothing to be afraid of. Anyway, if they give you any trouble, I will protect you.'

Glancing suddenly at his wristwatch, Fleury decided it was time to leave. For he had a date in Francheville, with Génia. Apologising, he ceremoniously kissed Mme Clips' hand, which trembled with sorrow, raised his own hand in farewell to the others, and left.

Fleury's departure was the signal for the others to leave. Only Verès remained, as he was expecting his wife and had some particular requests for Mme Clips.

A few minutes later, Mme Hermelin, believing her tenant alone, reappeared carrying a basket of laundry, and holding a sheet of paper and a little paper cone.

'Here's your washing, Mme Clips,' she said, adding with contrived playfulness, 'and the little bill you asked me for.' Glancing at Verès, she went on, 'But don't trouble yourself, you can settle up with me later. Now, I was thinking about your journey. As it's the cherry season, I've brought you some. Such a short season, I'm afraid, but these are from the bottom of my heart!'

And she added her offering, fifteen or so cherries, to those already placed on the Indian Tomb's altar.

Then she slipped out. And not without good reason; as at the sight of the bill which, with all the little supplements, ran to a considerable length, Mme Clips paled. She dived down to pull the bowl from its place of concealment. The ice had not entirely melted, and she put the compress back on.

'Oh, my head!' she groaned. 'How it hurts!'

One last visitor arrived. Ellen Verès had come to wish Mme Clips *bon voyage,* bringing her latest painting, a landscape at La Barbarie.

'It's exquisite!' exclaimed the Indian Tomb with enthusiasm. 'Allow me to give you a kiss, my dear. What pure lines, and what rich colours!'

And she added, confidentially, 'My dear child, your painting will be in good company in my luggage. I'm actually taking with me a little Picasso, which I picked up for a song in Marseille, only eight thousand francs, can you believe it! I had a specialist paint over the signature, so I won't have to pay duty. When I get to the States I can have the signature restored, and I'll get at least four thousand dollars for it. That will pay for my fare on the Clipper, and I will still make a small profit. As for your painting, my dear Ellen, it will have pride of place in my sitting room. It will always remind me of you, and of Saint-Boniface, where I was having such a delightful time before this terrible thing happened to me!'

'But I hope we will meet again over there,' said Verès, skilfully seizing his opportunity. 'Especially if you are willing to carry out the little errand for me that you so kindly promised. By the way, may I ask you to do something else? I wonder if you would take the first part of my book, and post it in New York to the publisher whose address I've written at the bottom of the first page. Then, whatever happens, I'll be able to say: *non omnis moriar.*'

'Of course,' said the Indian Tomb. 'Could you put it in

my suitcase, behind the divan? I feel too weak to get up.'

Lighting another cigarette, she turned to Ellen.

'I am sure you will be a great success in New York, my dear. As an artist, and as a woman. You have such a good figure, you know. Your breasts are as firm as a fifteen-year-old's,' she said, her eyelids drooping, while her bony hand idly caressed the pale skin of the young woman's arm, which had taken on a honey-coloured glow from exposure to the sun. 'Fear not, my dear, I will help you... Not that case, Monsieur Verès, the other one, the small one,' she said, turning round suddenly.

But it was too late. Verès had already opened the larger of the two pigskin suitcases and was gazing, transfixed, at its contents. It was a complete collection of the works of the state tobacco company: fifty or more packets of *Balto, Naja, Vizir, Salammbô* and *Gauloises* displayed on a red velvet dress, as if they were jewels in a casket. Like the millionaire haunted by a fear of starving to death, the Indian Tomb, who trembled at the prospect of running out of tobacco, had built up a stock of cigarettes which she drew on only *in extremis*, relying rather on the gallantry of her companions, and scrounging mercilessly off her male entourage.

VII

That same afternoon, another woman was also packing her bags in order to take the 19.25 train.

She too was a foreigner; no longer young; tall, thin and dark. All her worldly goods fitted into a small wicker basket tied up with string. It held no cigarettes, no little gifts, no works of art with disguised signatures; merely some patched underwear, a few worn-out clothes and some photographs showing two children and a man with an emaciated face and a harsh expression.

This was her husband. A miner by profession, a corporal in the republican army, a refugee from the civil war, José Mendaza was now in a concentration camp in French Morocco.

As for the two children, the younger, adopted by a charity, had been in Mexico for the past year. The elder, aged thirteen, was still waiting in a children's home in the Creuse for a passage to America which appeared less and less likely as time went on. Their mother had not seen either of them for over a year.

This traveller – the other blackbird shot down by Sergeant Auzance in the course of his successful hunting expedition – had brought no fortune with her to spend in France. There was no doubt that she was an undesirable alien, since in holding a position as housemaid she was cynically depriving the French workforce of a job. As a result, she had received neither consolation nor comfort in the hours before her departure. Nor had anybody offered to intervene on her behalf. Only her employers could have taken such action, but they were not inclined to do so.

The Spanish woman was certainly not a bad maid. She was clean and conscientious, and generally above reproach, except that she always wore a funereal expression which displeased Mme Martini, a sensitive soul who liked to be surrounded by cheerful faces. Amongst the farm girls in Saint-Paul, Mme Martini would easily find another maid only too happy to be placed in a middle-class home, and wages in the country were considerably lower than the going rate in Marseille, which Dolores was still being paid. Why hold on to this Spanish woman at all costs, when foreigners are nothing but trouble? In short, on learning that their maid was to be expelled from the *département*, her employers did not balk at paying her a week's wages in lieu of notice, and even half her fare to Marseille. They had already forked out for the journey here, and had scarcely had time to benefit from her services. Really, she could hardly ask any more of them. On top of that, they graciously gave her a glowing letter of introduction.

'With this reference, you will easily find a good position in town,' her mistress told her kindly.

The Spanish woman thanked her, but she was pretty certain the opposite was true. With so many refugees in Marseille, there was no shortage of domestic staff. In any case, Dolorès would hardly get a chance to look for a new position: at the very first identity check they would see she had no job and no means of support, and they would pack her off to a camp immediately. Gurs, probably. That was what Dolorès feared above all else. Of course, there were thousands and thousands of people in the camps, and she knew they didn't all necessarily die, since her husband had survived in one for three years already. But it would be too much to bear if she could not send a small amount of money to her family from time to time. Oh, it would be too much to bear.

However, Dolorès fully realised that her chances of escaping internment were minimal, and as she peeled vegetables for her employers' soup for the last time, although she managed to choke back her sobs, she could not stop herself snuffling loudly.

Chapter 5
The Ship Graveyard

I

Removing the moustache net he wore for his siesta, Fleury set about grooming his beard with care.

Then, hesitating in front of the open door of the wardrobe, he decided, on mature reflection, to wear his Roman sandals. True, there was a chance of rain, and despite his principles, Fleury did not like to get his feet wet; but he would have time to change into his ordinary brown shoes before going down to Francheville.

That day, his feet had already soaked up their dose of cosmic rays. In the early morning when, as everyone knows, radiation from the earth is heightened by the radioactive effect of the dew, Fleury had taken a half-hour walk barefoot in the grass. He had finished off the treatment with an hour on the chaise longue, his feet pointing towards the sun. Fully irradiated, Fleury had returned to the dining room of Les Tilleuls where he had hungrily consumed two raw eggs, for which he paid a supplement. César expected to put his virility to the test that very evening, and was determined to rise to the occasion.

Leaving nothing to chance, he sprinkled his meal liberally with pepper. It was a low-grade version of the spice, supplied under rationing, but he hoped it might still contain some residual aphrodisiac properties.

After lunch, he went up to his room and undressed completely, even taking off his patented shirt combination, to eliminate any barrier between his epidermis and the life-giving emanations of mother earth. Then he took a siesta to regenerate his energies, and was agreeably surprised on waking to find that he was indeed in possession of his vital faculties.

He fervently hoped that he would be similarly inspired in the evening.

For it had to be admitted that for several days now, he had been haunted by a feeling not unlike fear. He had still not got over the humiliation of a few months ago which had shattered his male pride. It was all the fault of a young lady on the staff of the radio station who, after putting on a great display of reluctance, had eventually yielded to him. Unfortunately, what was evidently the right moment for her turned out not to be so for Fleury. The memory of this experience had paralysed César on each subsequent opportunity, and in the end the little minx, offended, had lashed out with words which would have rung for a long time in the head of any man. As for Madame Fleury, César had long since given up any attempt at expressing his faltering ardour.

But from the afternoon when the musician had played the *Apassionata* for Génia in the drawing room of Les Tilleuls, his daily encounters with this fascinating young Russian woman had worked a miracle. Now extremely cautious, he kept putting off the decisive moment, affecting instead a charming playfulness, just as he had in his twenties. Captivated, the young woman eagerly went along with this apparently harmless whimsicality. 'As for this one,' César kept saying to himself, 'the time will be right for her when it is right for me!' And indeed he had already fixed the time a week ago: it was to be Thursday, at 22.30. Discipline in all things.

However, as it was still only twenty past three, Fleury had plenty of time to prepare for the great test. He put on his tennis shorts, picked up the riding-crop which the Indian Tomb had left behind in the umbrella stand, and set out for a healthy walk.

Leaving Les Tilleuls, he took the lane to La Barbarie, whistling the new *Lied* he had composed, based on Rimbaud's famous poem: '*O saisons, ô châteaux!*' Twenty minutes of steady walking brought him to the first house in La Barbarie, and he knocked on the kitchen door in the hope of finding some more eggs to satisfy his appetite.

The door opened halfway, and the dishevelled head of a woman appeared, wide-eyed and covered in perspiration. La Mère Delphine was about to take her cows out to the meadow. The appearance of this stranger threw her into a panic.

'I am sorry to disturb you,' said Fleury, taken aback at the effect he had created. 'Do you have any eggs for sale?'

Trembling in alarm, Delphine could hardly even manage to repeat the only word she was able to grasp from these preliminaries.

'Eggs?' she stammered. 'Eggs?'

What did they want of her, all these strange people? That apparition in trousers the other day, and now this man with a beard and hairy legs, wearing undershorts? They had no shame, these townspeople!

She stood in the door, barring his way.

'It's just...' she said, 'eggs, at the moment... and I have to see to the cows.'

Of course nobody would dare go and bother old Crouzet, who'd brandish his pitchfork at the slightest provocation... Suddenly she noticed the stranger was carrying a riding-crop. Another one! So where was his horse? But what made the biggest impression on Delphine was his beard. All the men in Saint-Boniface were clean-shaven. This circus act looking for eggs had obviously not shaved for a month of Sundays. A beard! Ever since the old Landru affair, which Delphine had followed in newspapers borrowed from the schoolma'am who had preceded M. Longeaud, she had regarded the beard as a symbol of crime and perversion.

'I don't need many,' said Fleury, trying to reassure her. 'Say two or three...'

Delphine looked horrified. 'Two or three?' she muttered. 'At this time of year?'

But while she protested, she thought it was maybe not wise to upset a bearded man.

'I can't spare as many as that,' she said, embarrassed. 'But if four would be enough... they're freshly laid.'

'Perfect,' said Fleury, surprised. Ignorant of the nuances of local expression, he could only wonder at Delphine's answer.

'I'll get them for you,' Delphine said, reluctantly letting him in.

A moment later she came back carrying the eggs in her apron.

'But how are you going to carry them? I don't even have any paper, the times are so hard.'

'Oh, that doesn't matter,' said Fleury, who had perked up at the sight of the eggs. 'I'll have them here, right now.'

'Now?' said Delphine. 'What do you mean, now?'

'Yes, I'll eat them raw. As they're freshly laid.'

'Well it's true they're still warm. I'll just put some sticks on the fire and boil them for you.'

'No, no,' said Fleury, laughing. 'I like them just as they are, raw. When I lived in Lyon there was a farmer's wife nearby who kept fresh eggs for me because she knew I enjoyed them.'

'Well I'd like to give you something you'll enjoy,' said Dephine, determined to mollify this Landru. 'I'll put a piece of bacon on and fry the eggs with it.'

But that did not suit Fleury. Cooking considerably reduces the vital properties of fresh eggs, which are known to restore virility. So before Delphine had a chance to go one step further and offer him an *omelette aux fines herbes*, he took an egg, broke it, and gravely swallowed the white along with the yolk.

'You'll get an upset stomach,' stammered Delphine.

Obviously these townspeople were all savages! The spectre in the trousers drank cold milk, and this man in undershorts swallowed raw eggs. Wasn't that just incredible?

'Don't worry, my dear lady,' said Fleury smiling, 'I'm used to it.'

And seeing that he would get no further on the matter of eggs, he changed the subject:

'What fine weather we're having! Let's hope it lasts. That little cloud above the wood could mean rain.'

'No such luck!' groaned Delphine. 'It's not going to rain yet. Will this never end? How are we going to manage?'

But Fleury, busy with his eggs, was not listening.

'For us townspeople,' he said, 'fresh eggs are a real treat. May I come back occasionally for one or two?'

Delphine, feeling awkward, gave him the type of evasive answer which is not the preserve of diplomats alone:

'Eggs? Of course. They're always appreciated by people who like them. My daughter in Saint-Etienne wrote the other day that they can't get them for love or money. She's coming soon, to bring nails for her father, because he doesn't like to ask his clients to bring nails for their own coffins. Tournier has some in the shop, but he wants two kilos of butter for a kilo of nails. It's a disaster!'

'I will come back on Sunday,' Fleury interrupted her impatiently. 'Perhaps you could put a couple aside for me.'

'If only I could close the barn door,' wailed Delphine. 'But I can't because of the chickens. They have to lay in their nesting-box. And the Latières' dog comes and goes when it feels like it...'

'Don't you have a chicken coop?' asked Fleury.

'A house for the hens?' said Delphine, 'but they live in the barn! So the other day the Latières' dog ate all the eggs. Some people only keep animals to let them die of hunger!'

Fleury shrugged, and got out his wallet. It was too hot to breathe in the kitchen, and this conversation had begun to irritate him.

Once he had paid an appropriate sum for his whimsical snack and departed, Delphine let out a great sigh of relief. What a story! Swallowing four raw eggs just like that, like the Latières' dog! Of course you might expect anything of a man who went around in undershorts, with his legs and face covered in hair. What was more, he didn't understand a thing. He didn't know that hens lay in a barn, and he had the gall to claim that it was good weather. All the streams were dry, the fields had turned brown, the animals were dying of thirst, the cabbages were being eaten by grubs and this layabout wanted it to last! Someone who looked like the twin brother of Landru! What if he himself was also…?

Indignant and frightened, Delphine rushed over to Legras' workshop to share her emotions with him. But her husband scarcely paid any attention. He never relinquished his plane, his saw, or the chests and coffins he was making, except to sit down at table. He would let the cows die of hunger rather than mind them for half an hour. In thirty-eight years of married life, Delphine had never got him to understand anything. Not her hopes, nor her fears, nor her desires…

* * *

'What strange people these peasants are,' thought Fleury on his way back to Les Tilleuls. 'They don't even know what a chicken coop is. And an odd way of thinking. You mention eggs, and they reply with nails, coffins and dogs. They say they can't spare two or three, and then they offer you four. You say to them, "What I really enjoy is raw eggs" and they reply, "I want to give you something you'll enjoy, *therefore* I'll cook them for you." I think, therefore I am… But what do they use for thinking? That's the question.'

In fact, Fleury was entirely ignorant of how other people

thought and what they thought. Perhaps they thought like everyone else, but simply expressed themselves differently. Or perhaps, amongst themselves, they spoke good sense, and these conundrums they indulged in with strangers were just a clever system of self-defence? This enigma annoyed Fleury. They were all as French as he was. They all spoke the same tongue, patois aside, but they didn't speak the same language. A concrete wall of mutual incomprehension stood between Fleury and these anti-cartesian peasants. They inhabited the same nation, but they were different species. Bears and grasshoppers...

II

About to enter the Pharmacie Moderne in Francheville an hour later, Fleury found it packed with clients. It wasn't quite the moment to seek the pharmacist's advice on a matter of some delicacy. He fixed his attention on a corner of the window display devoted to hormonal treatments:

Firm breasts within ten days. Vigorex, for potency and vigour...

Virilor for renewed virility.

A woman of about fifty stopped next to him. Despite the heat, she wore a shawl and black cotton gloves. Since her brother, her only remaining relative, had succumbed to complications following his operation in Lyon, Amélie Martin's anxiety had reached such proportions that she was unable to sleep without pills. She walked up to the door, hesitated briefly, then resolved to go in.

Fleury was unaware that he had witnessed an act of brazen

rebellion. In purchasing medication at the Pharmacie Moderne, Mlle Martin was making a public statement of independence from Sister Félicie, from the Abbé Mignart, and from all those who would have considered it a sacrilege to buy their aspirins or their castor oil anywhere other than at the Croix Blanche.

The significance of Amélie's choice was not lost on Mme Hermelin who, having finished her shopping in town, was about to return to Saint-Boniface. The wife of the retired tax inspector was shocked to see Amélie Martin enter this shop of ill repute. The teacher from the Catholic girls' school in a dispensary run by an atheist! Scandalous! It was enough to make the landlady of Les Tilleuls completely forget about the Abbé Soury's Elixir of Youth, which she had finally decided to buy at the Croix Blanche Pharmacy, having overcome the mistrust, instinctive to someone who was the daughter and mother of church ministers, engendered by the portrait of the Catholic cleric displayed on every box.

Fleury himself, quite unaware of the pharmaceutical politics of the Francheville area, gave up on the Pharmacie Moderne and headed towards its competitor. There was only one client inside, a farmer in conversation with the white-coated pharmacist.

Grégoire Laffont, from Saint-Boniface, had already bought several items. He entrusted his health, and that of the many members of his family, to the skills of the wise M. Chameix. This chemist could make diagnoses at a distance, and his consultations had the advantage of being free. Of course, you had to pay for the medicine; but at least you got your money's worth.

'...and let me have some of the "Bronco Pastilles" like the other day,' said Laffont. 'They do my wife a world of good. And there's my mother-in-law, who hasn't been for a week. Give me some of the "Elaxtic" for her.'

M. Chameix immediately climbed up a ladder to get the

required items. He knew how the locals deformed medical terms, and this knowledge was even more useful to him than patois. Then he turned the handle on the till and held the receipt out to the farmer. Laffont took out his purse, paid for his laxatives, his bronchial pastilles and the other drugs prescribed by the highly qualified M. Chameix, and departed.

Chameix, a slightly-built young man with piercing eyes and a circumflex moustache which he cultivated to make himself look older, turned towards Fleury with a friendly smile.

'Well,' said the latter, clearing his throat in embarrassment, 'I wonder if you would have…'

At that moment, the door opened and a tall thin man with a big nose and a facial tic came into the shop. It was Pinkas, the stateless individual whom Auzance had still not managed to summons, despite following him assiduously.

'… a tube of aspirins,' Fleury finished suddenly.

'We only have boxes of a hundred left,' said the chemist, 'but that saves you three francs seventy five. Anything else, sir?'

'Oh!' said Fleury, uncertainly. 'Please serve this gentleman. I'm not in a hurry.'

'What can I do for you, Monsieur Pinkas?' said Chameix, greeting his new client with a smile.

'Three boxes of suppositories,' said Pinkas, his face contorting into a Mr Punch expression.

Chameix took three boxes from one of his shelves and placed them on the counter.

'No, not those ones,' said Pinkas, shaking his head. 'I need the proper ones, with glycerine.'

'Now, Monsieur Pinkas,' said Chameix in surprise, 'you took some of those the day before yesterday. We can only get very limited supplies of these products, you know.'

But his client insisted, and the chemist eventually gave in. Pinkas grabbed the three boxes, paid, and left, smiling broadly.

He already looked better.

'So,' said Fleury, 'what I wanted to ask you for, some sort of tonic, something fortifying, um… a stimulant, actually. Something to perk one up. Something to stimulate the private parts. It's for a friend who's suffering from exhaustion.'

Chameix had long ago guessed what his client wanted. This man with the beard belonged to a particularly profitable category of clients.

'But of course,' he said sympathetically. 'Which do you prefer: Herculine, Vigorex or Virilor?'

'Well,' said Fleury, 'Maybe you could advise me. I want something quick-acting.'

'Perfect,' said the chemist, with a serious expression. 'I'll give you a large box of Virilor. It's an almost instant stimulant, but you should complete the full course of treatment in order to prevent a relapse. It contains yohimbine, an ingredient imported from the colonies, which is in short supply now.'

'So do you really think…?' said Fleury, still unsure.

He was prevented from completing his question by the arrival of another client: short, dark, unshaven and unwashed, with bushy eyebrows and a frayed collar.

Fleury sighed. 'Do serve this gentleman,' he said.

'If you please,' said the man, with a strong foreign accent, 'I need a packet of twenty-four soup… soup… soup…'

'I beg your pardon,' said Chameix, patiently.

'Soupositorium!' the foreigner blurted out with a final effort, spluttering profusely.

'A box of suppositories,' Chameix corrected him, wiping his face discreetly. He held one out to his client.

The hirsute foreigner frowned, examined the box carefully, and grimaced.

'No good,' he said. 'I need *glytzerina*.'

'We don't have any left,' said Chameix in a tone which

brooked no argument. 'One of my clients has just bought the last three boxes.'

'Oh, he's already got them, has he?' said the man, relieved. 'Sorry, I didn't realise. Thank you. Goodbye sir, goodbye madam.' And he departed.

'Anyone would think this place was suffering from an epidemic of constipation,' said Fleury caustically.

'Particularly in certain sections of the community,' said the chemist thoughtfully. He already had his own theory, but did not feel like divulging it to his client.

'So, you recommend Virilor,' said Fleury, returning to his subject with a conspiratorial look. 'Is it really the best you have?'

A crafty gleam appeared in the chemist's eye.

'Oh! It's a reputable enough product,' he said. 'Obviously, the formula is open to improvement. Only the other day, the *patron* made some pills for himself and a couple of his friends. They were similar, but much more effective. I tried them myself,' he added with a smile full of innuendo, 'and I have to say the effect is quite extraordinary. Obviously, since they were for his own use, the *patron* didn't stint on the rationed ingredients. That's strictly between you and me, of course. I see I can trust you, sir.'

'Absolutely,' said Fleury. 'And are there any left?'

'Maybe enough for a single treatment, no more. But now I know the formula, I could make a new supply if necessary. Would you like some?'

'Yes, the whole course of treatment,' said Fleury.

The chemist disappeared into the back shop, took a large box of Virilor from the shelf, removed the pills, which he put in a plain cardboard box, and returned to the counter.

'Four pills to take *before*,' he said, scribbling something on a label which he stuck to the box. 'Then five pills every day. But may I remind you, I only sell this medication to trusted clients. I rely on your discretion.'

Fleury reassured him as well as he could, and paid 180 francs (yohimbine being such a rare commodity!). He thanked the obliging chemist and then, as it was time for his rendezvous with Génia, made his way towards the Hôtel Panorama.

However M. Chameix wrote on his sales ledger: 'Virilor, 1 box, large, 90.00 francs.' And he conscientiously turned the handle of the till.

With just a little ingenuity he had managed to double his day's pay. The *patron*, M. Astier, was entirely satisfied with the services of his dispensing chemist. Chameix owed his position to the indiscretions of his predecessor, who sometimes forgot to turn the till handle. There was no fear of that with Philippe Chameix. M. Astier, wary at first, had checked his stock frequently, and found not the slightest discrepancy. Even better, his turnover had increased, thanks to M. Chameix's graciousness and skill in providing free remote consultations. M. Astier, thus relieved of a considerable burden, could devote himself entirely to politics, and to the administration of the small town of which he was Maire.

M. Chameix, for his part, did not complain about his employer's absence. You have to get by, don't you? You have to keep up with the times, eh?

* * *

In a secluded corner of the garden at the Hôtel Panorama, reclining idly in a rattan armchair, Génia Prokoff closed her book. A history of music ending at the time of Gounod, it gave off the musty smell common to all the volumes in Francheville's municipal library. She was beginning to feel the excitement which always came over her in the moments before her encounters with Fleury. She could hardly remember ever feeling such turmoil, except perhaps as a little girl, and that was only a distant memory.

A man's step crunched on the gravel behind Génia's chair. She sat up suddenly, feeling herself blush. But no, it was only Pinkas, one of the hotel clients, getting some fresh air. He sat down at one of the tables and busied himself packing some little cardboard boxes into a larger one.

Génia leant back in her chair, letting her thoughts take her back to Paris, and a shop selling Russian antiques in the Faubourg Saint Honoré. She had come across the position in the classified advertisements of *L'Intransigeant*. She enjoyed the work, and had quickly become friendly with her employer, Tatiana. Alexandre Prokoff, still prey to his fits of *nichevo*, continued to drink and to beat his wife. But on 10th June 1940 his routine was again interrupted. Tatiana's friend and sponsor, a gentleman named Bernheim whose chauffeur had been called up, engaged Alexandre to drive his powerful Auburn down to the milder climate of the *Midi*. Génia, of course, came along too.

That was how, two days later, following some epic adventures which reminded Génia of her flight from Russia, the foursome ended up in Francheville.

A few weeks afterwards, M. Bernheim was informed that his entry visa for Brazil had arrived, and he left immediately for Marseille to make his travel arrangements. The others, who did not have such pressing reasons to leave the Old World, returned to Paris with the Auburn, which M. Bernheim had left to his lady friend as a consolatory gesture.

Upon his return to the capital, the former Russian officer underwent a curious transformation. A desire for intense activity took hold of him, clearly at the expense – who would have believed it? – of his addiction to alcohol. In the new Europe of winners and losers, anyone like him, well-educated, rich in experience and fluent in several languages, was perfectly placed to act as an intermediary between the victors and the vanquished. Count Prokoff began by driving members of the winning side around the sights of Paris. But soon, new horizons opened before him. He realised that he need not limit himself to showing his clients the delights of the city by day and by night. He applied his ingenuity to procuring for them material goods which, under new regulations, could not be traded freely. Thanks to his contacts, his nerve, his adaptability and the entrepreneurial spirit he brought to bear, Alexandre became, within a year, an important figure in the undercover economy.

Somewhat dazzled himself by this rapid rise to wealth, he established his headquarters in a hotel near the Etoile. Soon, he decided that Génia, a perfectly acceptable companion in the squalid times of the Hôtel des Terrasses, was not sufficiently 'high society'. After a few adventures over the next few months, he fixed on Tatiana, Génia's beautiful employer, who was an excellent businesswoman to boot.

When Génia found out, she did not feel too bitter. Her main resentment was towards Tatiana, for betraying her. For years now, she had suffered Alexandre as an incurable chronic affliction, no longer worth treating. Even in the days when he used to beat her in a vodka-fuelled rage, she still felt an attachment to him, mixed with pity. The new sharply dressed, self-confident Alexandre only inspired contempt. Therefore, when Alexandre sent her away to Francheville on the pretext that the fresh air would do her good, she felt no desire to return to Paris.

But it was only when Fleury came into her life that she realised how mediocre and lacking in quality her time with Alexandre had been. At last, she had met a man who, in addition to existing on a higher plane of spirituality, was a great artist. In his company she felt purer, nobler, and ashamed of her past. She would leave Francheville and the black market which was so unworthy of her, and return to the city, close to Fleury, who would find her a position in a music shop. That would allow her to earn a living 'in a rather less demeaning way', as he put it. Above all, he would teach her to look at the world anew, would draw her into the bright sphere in which he moved, and would envelop her in his tender friendship. His attention was so gentle, so different from other men's brutal sensuality. She was disarmed by the youthful timidity he sometimes showed, almost as if he was still an adolescent. Perhaps the complex feelings he had awakened in her were largely a result of this touching shyness. Occasionally, during their long walks on the empty footpaths in the woods, when he fondled her hand or brushed against her shoulder, she feared 'the beast' might emerge; but on each occasion he drew back, regained control of himself, and kissed her hand in a mark of infinite respect, as if apologising. After moments like that, returning to her room with a languid body and a disturbed mind, she slept badly, and looked forward impatiently to the next rendezvous. In the last few days she had begun to hope, to yearn even, for what she had previously feared.

There was once more a crunching noise on the gravel, near the entrance to the garden. Génia turned quickly. Fleury, smiling radiantly, stood before her. The clock on the Mairie had just struck seven.

III

An old legend, dear to the hearts of sailors, holds that the Sargasso Sea in the North Atlantic is a graveyard of ships. It is there, amongst the bladderwrack and the kelp, that vessels are believed to fetch up when they are abandoned by their crews and carried away on the current. Just like the Sargasso Sea, the Café de la Marine, on the market place in Francheville, was, that summer of 1942, a ship graveyard.

The most venerable of the hulks was a battleship – what the English call a 'man-o'-war'. Actually, George Richard Fentimore was indeed a man of war: a retired general who, after a brilliant, meteoric career, had suddenly resigned his post and taken a young actress as his second wife. He had retired to farm a nice little smallholding on the Côte d'Azur. At seventy, General Fentimore, a Colossus of a man, hardly looked even fifty. But though robust and authoritarian, he always appeared as unhappy as an abandoned child whenever his wife, a charming, slim little woman with blonde hair and pink cheeks, left his side for an instant.

Expelled from the Côte d'Azur along with all the other British residents, the General had established his quarters at Francheville, in the Hôtel Farémido. But he was often to be seen at the Café de la Marine, where the *patron* still held a stock of genuine Ceylon tea. Francheville natives only turned to it when they were seriously ill; but for this prodigal child of Albion, it was as vital as daily bread. The Café de la Marine was also the only place where the man of war and his wife – an elegant flagship of the theatre, light in tonnage – could find adequate bridge partners.

One of these partners was another distinguished hulk. A respectable ocean liner, high and dry in the ship cemetery precisely because he had taken his destiny into his own hands, and refused to cross the Atlantic while there was still time. Signor Vincente Benedetti, one of the leaders of the Italian socialist party, had declined to follow his compatriots to America for two reasons. Firstly, the Italian Armistice Commission had objected to his departure, and he had not wanted to leave in secrecy, under a false name, which would have required him to sacrifice his fine grizzled patriarchal beard. Secondly, as a dyed-in-the-wool pacifist who proclaimed that authoritarian regimes should only be overthrown from within, he did not wish to take part in the pro-interventionist meetings which would be unavoidable in America. In the circumstances and despite the risks, he preferred to wait in France until the inevitable collapse of fascism. So, storm-tossed from Marseille to Valence, then from Valence to Francheville, the ocean liner found himself quite outside the shipping lanes, and had run aground at the Café de la Marine. Signor Benedetti had occasional political differences with General Fentimore, an arch-conservative, but at the bridge table the two men were as one.

The fourth partner was Safranek, a Czech intellectual, an aesthete and a philosopher, whom the war had taken by surprise at the Bibliothèque Nationale. The lightship of the cemetery, this learned individual illuminated all around. A short, prematurely grey, frugal man who lived mainly on dry bread, which he nibbled at all times of day, Safranek had two passions: poetry and chess. Although he was certainly a good bridge player, and always willing to make up the foursome, his heart was not really in it.

His heart was elsewhere. Elsewhere meant opposite his chess partner, a little unshaven Polish Jew with hairs sprouting from his nose and ears, who spoke no single language properly, but was a genius at the chessboard. A former knitwear manufacturer, this unchartered boat bobbed ceaselessly around the lightship, as if dazzled by its radiance. Safranek had sworn a hundred times never to play against Moïse Kleinhandler again, for his breath smelt foul, he spluttered everywhere, and he insulted him in a fantasy French with random vowels, accusing the Czech of playing *trucks* on him and calling him a *bedbag*. Just as some upper-class men become enamoured of a common woman and cannot free themselves of their shameful passion, so Safranek could not cure his recidivism and extricate himself from Kleinhandler's spell.

But while Kleinhandler pitilessly exploited his power over Safranek, he was careful to toe the line with Jéroboam Pinkas. This latter, although only a mediocre chess player, had reduced the hirsute little man to a state of slavery, dispatching him at will to the chemists, the post offices in Francheville and its outlying villages, and even to the farms themselves, to take delivery of his orders. Pinkas, the trawler of the ship graveyard, liked to fish in murky waters, and therefore chose personally to give a wide berth to the coastguards: the gendarmes.

On the days when Safranek tried to throw off Kleinhandler's yoke, he chose Ernst Muller as his partner. This was an Austrian political refugee, a scrawny man in poor health, constantly racked by fits of asthma. Muller's pockets were always full of phials, tablets and pills, which he was in the habit of carrying in order to stave off or calm his attacks. The Austrian was a hospital ship. Living in poverty on meagre and irregular charity, he shunned his dingy garret to spend his days in the Café de la Marine where the *patron*, who was sympathetic to his situation, did not require him to buy drinks.

Busying itself amongst the hulks in the Café de la Marine, a tugboat could often be seen, belching thick clouds of steam. This tug was a bouncy little woman of about thirty. The daughter of a minister in the Balkans, she had known better days. A Parisian by adoption, with some skills as a seamstress, she had quickly built up a clientele amongst those inhabitants of Francheville who had some pretensions to elegance. As soon as she arrived in the café, she would throw open a little workbox, and in an instant her marble table would be covered in scraps of material, ribbons, thread, needles, thimbles, scissors and other sewing accessories. In tow, like a barge with no independent means of propulsion, would be a placid young blond athlete, a former physical education teacher and masseur, with whom she was infatuated, and who would come to sit next to her. The minister's daughter was a heavy smoker, and since the introduction of tobacco rationing she had been reduced to extreme measures. One day, devoured by a craving for tobacco, she had taken the first step towards her downfall. Entering the Café de la Marine, she had seen a virtually unsmoked cigarette left in the ashtray by General Fentimore, who had just gone. The temptation was too great. There was enough tobacco left to roll a new cigarette, albeit a slim one. Once she had tried this, she was hooked.

From that day on, the minister's daughter was always on the look-out for cigarette-ends, however small, however unappetising, which she kept in a tin. There was no going back. In the café, in a shop or at the cinema, whenever she saw a man smoking, she would approach him in the worldly manner she had learnt at her father's ministerial receptions, saying, 'Please have the kindness not to throw your cigarette-end too far away.'

Of course, it gave rise to gossip in Francheville, but the minister's daughter had long ago stopped caring what people said about her.

The submersible of the Café de la Marine was a Spaniard, Pedro Gonzalez. As his situation was not entirely legal, he would disappear prudently beneath the waves at the slightest alert. A sculptor by profession, he had been released from a concentration camp thanks to a spurious work contract provided by a monumental mason in Francheville. Unfortunately, under regulations concerning foreign labour, which was cheap for employers, the mason had to pay the government seven francs a day for his fictional employee. Obviously it was up to Gonzalez to pay this 'tax', and the former artist had to accept whatever chores came his way in order to avoid being sent back to the camp. Freedom is beyond price.

Some ships were simply passing through. Tibor Verès, for example, the packet boat who, whenever he was in

Francheville, would watch for Brandouille coming out of the post office when it opened. In addition to Tibor's own mail, the postman would give him letters to deliver in his neighbourhood. Or the decommissioned freighter Daniel Cahen, formerly a Paris sales representative for a textile firm, sacked, because of his Jewish origins, by the firm which had employed him for thirty years. At the Armistice, this neat, dignified little man had fled to Francheville in order to await the end of the war, and was resigned to the shrewishness of his wife. She, *née* Forgeron, had, in 1940, added a major reproach to the long list of matrimonial resentments she held against him: he was a Jew. After twenty-eight years of marriage, she had discovered that this hitherto unimportant trait was the root of all her problems. When, in conversation – or rather, monologue – she uttered the word 'Jew' for the third time, Cahen would pick up his hat and quietly leave. In these stormy conditions, he would take refuge in the haven of la Marine.

Sometimes a school ship would heave into sight at the café, in the shape of M. Longeaud, a vessel usually at anchor in port, attracted by a group in whose cosmopolitan company he could feel almost as if he were on the open seas. Finally, there were a few humble tramp steamers, workmen from the sawmill or the paper mill. With their gaunt, drawn faces, they would order a coffee sweetened with saccharine, or a *coup de rouge*. Most of them were not locals, having knocked around on the breadline here and there, and their employment in a Francheville factory was only a stage amongst others.

And while these coasters were docked in front of the bar, talking politics in low voices – you never know who's listening! – the waiter Marius, behind it – there was another one who didn't come from Francheville! – would be wielding his ice pick in a bucket, for the benefit of the more demanding customers seated at tables. Marius, the ice-breaker of the graveyard…

The Café de la Marine was possibly the only place in Francheville, in that summer of 1942, where the highlight of the day was not the delivery of the wine or coffee rations. There, the regulars were amongst the few inhabitants of Francheville who believed, rightly or wrongly, that the fate of their coffee ration, and indeed their personal fate, was determined on the battlefields of Russia or Africa. So they were all passionately interested in policy and strategy. Naturally General Fentimore, being a former officer of high rank, was the undisputed authority on military matters. His daily arrival in the café was eagerly awaited by those wishing to be enlightened on such-and-such a pincer movement, or on the ability of such-and-such a stronghold to resist attack. Wreathed in great puffs of smoke from his pipe, the General would expound his professional views with the discretion natural to him both as a British citizen and as a military man; views sure to be contradicted sooner or later by actual events.

Hope springs eternal and all the regulars at the Café de la Marine were optimistic concerning the outcome of the war and its implications for their own future. But they were all haunted by the same spectre: the concentration camp. Even the General himself was no exception, having been taken in a round-up when leaving the Saint-Charles station in Marseille, despite his rank, his Légion d'Honneur medal, and his papers, which were entirely in order. He might swagger, but he too trembled in fear.

To ward off this threat, the regulars sometimes offered propitiatory sacrifices, passing the hat round to make donations for those interned in the camps. Each of them had his favoured group: Benedetti had the socialists, Muller the communists, Verès the Jews. They all gave generously, and General Fentimore contributed 500 franc notes which, thanks to the devoted efforts of his wife, were quickly converted into food parcels and despatched to the camps.

The latest operation of this sort had been instigated by Jéroboam Pinkas, even though he had hitherto shown no great enthusiasm for the fundraising, and usually got away with giving a ten-franc note. But this time, he said, it really was beyond the pale, and nobody should be allowed to let it pass unnoticed. A dysentery epidemic had broken out in the Drancy camp, leaving the survivors so exhausted that their bodily functions were impaired. To add insult to injury, there were no longer any supplies in the occupied zone of genuine glycerine-based suppositories, which were the only way of treating these unfortunate people. Distraught upon hearing this report, apparently from an Aid Committee, Pinkas had offered to source a certain quantity of the precious remedy to be sent to hundreds of convalescents, and the Aid Committee had generously agreed to pay all the costs. 'For shame! How appalling!' the General had exclaimed, offering to write forthwith to his contacts on the Côte d'Azur, asking them to collect as many suppositories as possible. Everyone else had followed suit, and the result was an avalanche of suppositories in Francheville. Pinkas, evidently deeply moved, reimbursed their costs, expressed thanks on behalf of the Aid Committee, and retired with a grave expression to the garden of the Hôtel Panorama to pack the boxes.

* * *

The clock on the Mairie had just struck seven when Longeaud rolled into the Café de la Marine. As every Thursday at this hour, the school ship had taken on its full cargo of alcohol, and found itself transmogrified into a tanker. He sat down alone at a table and looked at the clock: 7.04. Four minutes late. Turning towards the door with a worried look, and tapping his foot lightly under the table, he looked like a man on a romantic assignation.

'Marius! A brandy!' he called out hoarsely, to disguise his lack of composure.

At seven minutes past seven exactly, the door opened. Philippe Chameix, the dispensing chemist from the Croix Blanche, came in, carrying under his arm an object wrapped in newspaper. Seeing Longeaud, he went over to him.

The schoolteacher's heart started to pound wildly. He guessed that the newspaper concealed the object of his infatuation: the bottle of Pernod which Chameix had promised to concoct for him a week ago. By blending the litre of fruit alcohol which Longeaud had provided with a mixture of aniseed oil, star anise and some plant extracts, the chemist had managed to produce quite a convincing Pernod.

With a conspiratorial gesture, the schoolmaster slipped Chameix two packets of cigarettes under the table, in exchange. Then he retired to the toilet, sipped the drink of his heart's desire, and smacked his lips appreciatively. He gazed in thought for a moment at the blank label on the bottle, then, in sudden inspiration, took out his pen and wrote, in capital letters:

IRRADIATED EMULSION OF VITAMIN P
FOR USE IN THE TREATMENT OF
INFANTILE RICKETS

It was a necessary precaution. Rationing inspectors might be encountered at any turn. The Vichy government was after him!

Then he wrapped the bottle up again in the old newspaper, stuffed it in the bottom of the leather attaché case he had brought for the purpose, and went back into the café. In the meantime, the chemist had gone to sit next to Pinkas, who was talking to Kleinhandler.

Longeaud shook the alchemist's hand warmly in silent tribute to his great achievement, paid for his drink and left the café to walk back up to Saint-Boniface.

It was eleven minutes past seven exactly. The chemist turned to Pinkas.

'Could I have a word with you, Monsieur Pinkas?' he said. 'An urgent matter, strictly confidential.'

Pinkas gave Kleinhandler an imperious look and the latter, understanding the implicit order, got up with a hangdog look and began to hover around Safranek. Finishing his crust and closing the volume of Valéry he was reading, Safranek called out in the voice of a man resigned to the inevitable, 'Marius, the chess set!'

'It's just this,' said Chameix, fixing his ferret-like eyes on Pinkas' worried gaze. 'I've noticed that you have used a large quantity of suppositories over the past few days. I think I know why.'

Pinkas turned bright red and lifted his hand in protest.

'It's because... I assure you...,' he stammered.

'Don't worry, I haven't come to lecture you, I've come to do you a favour. If you are using the glycerine to make soap, I have a proposal you may be interested in.'

'What gave you that idea?' Pinkas protested. 'Why soap, exactly? But anyway, what's your proposal?'

'That's more like it!' said Chameix. 'I'm in a hurry. But if you want to buy two cases of excellent medical coal tar soap, pre-war quality, tell me now. The manufacturer came to Francheville today. He sold three cases to the Pharmacie Moderne. He offered two to my *patron*, but M. Astier is a bit old-fashioned, and he turned them down. But it's an excellent deal. Just think, those bars of soap will cost you five francs twenty-five, and you can easily sell them for fourteen. I'll take thirty per cent of your profit, I don't think that's unreasonable.

But you must hurry, the manufacturer is taking the 19.25 train. We've just got time to catch him. You see, he has his own reasons for wanting to dispose of his stock quickly.'

Pinkas glanced at the sample, sniffed it, pursed his lips, spat on it and rubbed it with his index finger. His lips spread in an approving smile. The soap foamed!

'Agreed,' he said. 'I'll go along with that.'

Tossing a banknote on the table, he took off in the direction of the station, which was not far away, accompanied by Chameix.

The chemist had guessed correctly. Pinkas was concerned neither with the inadequacy of his own bowel functions nor with the dysentery epidemic in Drancy. He was putting together the raw materials for a little soap factory. Nobody at the Café de la Marine, nor in Francheville, had the faintest idea. Not even the hairy Polish Jew who ran errands for him. He already had a big enough supply of glycerine to get started. You have to get by, don't you? You have to keep up with the times, eh?

IV

The world was in flux, rent asunder by steel and fire, with bloodshed everywhere. On the plains of the Ukraine and in the sands of Libya, the German high command risked all, despatching its armoured divisions to form the jaws of a gigantic pincer movement. The fate of the globe was in the balance. On the battlefields, in the skies, in the depths of the ocean, and in the bombed-out towns, men were dying in their thousands for a cause which was rarely their own; in the prisons and the concentration camps, hundreds of thousands of human beings were left to rot in bestial squalor; in the working-class suburbs, chronic shortages were gradually deteriorating into a state of famine which showed in the haggard features of every haunted face.

Meanwhile, in Saint-Boniface and Francheville, life simply pottered along as usual. Delphine Legras' greatest concern was how to stop the Latières' dog stealing her eggs; Noémi Sobrevin was still working out how to make Brandouille bring her the overalls intended for her little Abel; and the postman, for his part, was devising a scheme to make Noémi return his bicycle pump, without having to give anything in exchange. Vautier was taken up with a clandestine operation to slaughter animals for Sarzier at the Hôtel Panorama; and La Bardette, still mourning her favourite cat, brooded on plans to take revenge on the poisoner. Mme Hermelin, expecting new guests, was obsessed with rationing problems and cost reductions. For Tournier, the world had two poles: nails and butter. M. Du Chesne de Rochefontaine was making improvements to his community project, and drafting a new advertisement. Mlle Amélie Martin, quite distraught at the death of her brother, and persecuted mercilessly by Sister Félicie, was suffering a nervous breakdown, made worse by uncertainty about the future. André Murger sometimes forgot about the drama unfolding in the East, to ponder on the enigma of Solange Fleury, which he had not been able to decipher during her brief stay at Les Tilleuls. Would she ever come back? As for César Fleury, delighted to have rediscovered his potency in the arms of Génia, he was calculating how he could devote the necessary time to his pretty mistress without awakening the suspicions of his wife. Génia herself dreamt only of love, and of the man whom she saw as its incarnation. Pinkas, who had managed to gain possession of the two cases of hospital soap, and who had talked profitably with Philippe Chameix well into the night, was revising his plans for the soap factory: the dispensing chemist was to contribute his ingenuity and skill, and become his associate. In addition to soap, he would also produce Pernod, at 500 francs a litre. This made good business sense, especially as M. Chameix could ensure a supply of surgical spirit, the main ingredient, at a tenth of that price. M. Astier, the proprietor of the Pharmacie de la Croix Blanche, would be none the wiser: Chameix would not forget to turn the handle. You have to keep up with the times, don't you? And, to conclude, the Pernod in question was what was on the mind of Camille Longeaud, the latest person to benefit from the chemist's talents.

That morning, M. Longeaud had a headache. Not exactly the hangover which followed high days and holidays, but the discomfort he usually felt after his outings on Thursdays and Sundays: thick head, furry tongue, bad breath. Pleading illness, he had left his class to his wife. They were to go on a school excursion, and she could manage perfectly well on her own. Anyway, this Friday was also the 18th of June.

The 18th of June was M. Longeaud's birthday. His fortieth birthday. How could he not feel depressed, on waking one morning to find he had suddenly completed four decades? He remembered the Alexandrine he had read in *The Counterfeiters*, in the days when he still used to read:

To be forty years old, yet not have haemorrhoids...

Well, he didn't! Revived by this reassuring thought, M. Longeaud stretched, leapt out of bed, splashed his face with water, went downstairs to the kitchen where there was still hot coffee on the stove, poured himself a large bowl, and drank it. Then he lit the first cigarette of the day. It didn't taste very good, but that was normal on a Friday morning. He didn't even have the patience to finish it. It was full of impurities, and kept going out.

Disgusting, this wartime tobacco! National tobacco, just like national coffee, national shoes, national wool. The other day, when M. Longeaud had asked Maurice Gideaux to define the word *national*, the boy had answered 'It's something that was better before the war.' The dunce! He didn't know how right he was.

But anyway, he smoked too much. Thirty cigarettes a day, on average. He should have more sense. Especially at forty. It puts a strain on your heart, it blocks your arteries, it ruins your memory. From now on, he would cut down. Ten a day, for example.

Forty years old. He had to face it: his youth was over. What on earth had he done with it?

Not a lot, he had to admit. In the last twenty years, he had chivvied a few dozen of the more able youngsters through their exams, dabbled in politics, got married, and, well, the rest of the time had been frittered away in drinking. It was not how he had imagined his career on leaving teacher-training college. Back then, his profession seemed like a religious vocation: you had to combat the benightedness of the rural areas, the lack of physical and moral hygiene, the power of the Curé. For some time, M. Longeaud had kept in touch with a few of his contemporaries, who told him of their travails. But they had been posted to less backward regions. M. Longeaud himself had also tried to fight the good fight. In his first post, he had been outspoken about hygiene – nits in the children's hair, runny noses and no handkerchiefs, unwashed ears, dirt-rimmed nails – so much so that he had put most of the mothers' backs up. Just think, their kids were demanding toothbrushes and toilet paper! He had also worked on the peasant farmers, trying to show them that they were wasting their time tending meagre flocks, individually, on tiny fragmented plots of land, often kilometres away from their house. A single shepherd would have been enough for the whole village. That was how they did things in the Jura, for example, where the pastures were held in common.

But the farmers had just shrugged, the Curé had got involved, and the whole thing had blown up so far out of proportion that he was mightily relieved when he was able to move to another post. He had learnt his lesson. It was no reason to renounce his beliefs: he kept up his subscriptions to *Le Progrès*, *La Lumière* and *Le Crapouillot*. He voted on the left, and encouraged others to. But he didn't get involved with the farmers any more. However, with a wife like his, he was done for in any case.

Done for in any case? Well, let's see about that! M. Longeaud has still not had his last word. Admittedly, he's forty; but there's life in the old dog yet. Fit as a fiddle – in all departments. And no piles! The main thing is to keep the mind and body active.

As for the body, there's nothing to beat a cold shower first thing in the morning, whatever the weather. Followed by a quarter of an hour with the dumb-bells. And he should cut down on cigarettes. Ten a day? Still too many. Eight should be enough. Three in the morning, five in the afternoon. Maybe ten on Thursdays and Sundays, because after all...

Above all, he should drink less. It's got a bit out of hand lately. Say a couple of glasses with lunch. On Thursdays, one or two more with his pals. A bit hard to start with; but where there's a will, there's a way.

So much for the body. For the mind, it's a more delicate matter. M. Longeaud hasn't read any books for years. He'll have to get back into the habit. Not turn into an ignoramus. Only the other day, he had been unable to make any retort to the Curé who, to wind him up, had quoted several writers whose work M. Longeaud had never read. Left-wingers, at that, the Curé had said in his insinuating way. So there were a few gaps to be filled. And he should learn a foreign language. A man who speaks another language is twice the man. English, for example: it's very useful, and it confers prestige. He still remembered some from his student days. Using the Assimil course he had ordered just before the war, it would be child's play. Now, at last, he knew what he wanted. What a weight off his mind!

In these matters, the hardest thing is always the decision. Now he had overcome the main difficulty! He was entitled to a reward, wasn't he? M. Longeaud took a Gauloise from the packet and lit it. The second of the day, counting the one he had not finished. After that would come the cold shower and the dumb-bells. Longeaud found this cigarette a lot better than the first. The aftertaste had almost gone.

He went out to the pump and filled a large watering can, carried it back into the kitchen, and arranged a proper shower in a tin bath. He was still in it when he noticed, through the net curtains, the figure of a man in a suit, carrying a briefcase, heading for the front door. A moment later there was a loud knock.

In his tub, the schoolteacher shuddered with cold and anxiety. Who could this man with a briefcase be? Probably a rationing inspector. The Vichy government was after him! Had they found out about the Pernod? Someone must have seen him in the café, in the toilet. That was all he needed!

'I'll be with you in a moment!' he called out in a shaky voice. 'I'm just getting dressed!'

His skin still damp, he ran barefoot in his undershorts and shirt into the Henri IV style dining room. He took three or four old medicine bottles out of a cupboard and put them in full view on the sideboard, beside his vitamin P, like bodyguards around their sovereign. Everyone knows that the more obvious an object is, the less attention it attracts.

He put his shoes on hurriedly and went to open the door. Before him stood Prosper Baudrier, the chartered surveyor, who lived in one of the bigger villages on the outskirts of Francheville.

A weight lifted from M. Longeaud's chest.

The surveyor, a short, well-fed man with an oily complexion, was there to consult the land registers in the Mairie. He had to value the estate of the late Anselme Laffont, and divide it amongst his five nephews. M. Longeaud let him in to the Mairie, which was next to the school, and before leaving him to his work he stayed to chat for a few minutes. As he spoke, he automatically held out his cigarette packet to the surveyor. The latter did not need to be asked twice. He was so used to being given things! Longeaud had already put his own cigarette to his lips before remembering the decision he had taken earlier. That was the third, and it was still only eleven o'clock. But it would be impolite to let the surveyor smoke alone.

Longeaud lit his fourth cigarette an hour later, just as automatically, after doing some exercises with the dumb-bells and eating an omelette made with bacon fat, which he cooked on a fire of pine cones. But that cigarette was already in the plan. Especially after a meal with only a couple of small glasses of wine. So now, to work.

English without Tears. The Assimil Method. '*No arduous work required. Ten minutes or more a day, on a regular basis, will be sufficient to…*' No trouble. A quarter of an hour, come to that, or even twenty minutes. No point in being stingy with his time, when he was contemplating a sort of intellectual and spiritual renaissance. '*…as there may be breaks in your work, the course will take from three to six months to complete…*' Well, there won't be any breaks. None. But anyway, let's say six months. At that rate, he could learn two foreign languages a year. Once M. Longeaud had finished the English course, he would start on Spanish, then German. Italian, even. In two years he would be a polyglot.

First (1st) Lesson (pron: feurst less'n)
My tailor is rich
Our doctor is good
Your cigarette is finished

Ah yes, the cigarette *is finished*. Such a pity. If he could smoke, he would keep up a better rate of work.

Several times, M. Longeaud read aloud the thirteen short sentences which made up the first lesson, and he even went on to the exercise *(egg'zeçaiz)*. *Our cigarettes are good… Our cigarettes are not good*. Always those cigarettes! It was designed to provoke him. Well, so what! Since the writer insists, I'll light one myself! There now! Anyway, it's only number five, so I'm entitled to it. *My cigarette is good. My cigarette is not finished*.

At the end of the lesson – it took M. Longeaud exactly eighteen minutes – the schoolteacher found to his satisfaction that he still had time ahead of him, as Mme Longeaud and the pupils were not due back until four o'clock. He leafed through La Fontaine's *Fables* and, after some hesitation, selected *The Oyster and the Litigants* as the next reading for his middle class. That reminded him that he had still not marked this group's essays from three days ago. The subject was: 'Describe any one of the features of the face.'

M. Longeaud opened Michel Vautier's exercise book. His essay was entitled: *The noz*. It was not long. This lad could never be bothered.

The noz is for breething, smelling and bloing. You can use it for spectackles, sneezing and snorring. In Maurices noz there are little brown hairs inside to catch the mike-robes. When you are cold, your noz runs.

M. Longeaud underlined the spelling mistakes heavily, and crossed out the sentence referring to Maurice Gideaux' nose, writing in the margin 'irrelevant'. He marked the passage 'Fair'. Then he took up the exercise book belonging to Dinah Sobrevin, a conscientious little girl who had chosen the theme of ears.

The ears look like snale shells. They are for hearing and wearing earrings. Aunt Rachel bought me a pair, and my mum put them away with the dolls at the top of the wardrob and she can't find them. When I'm grown up I will find them and put them on. You can also put cotton wool in your ears. Right inside there's a sort of yellow wacks. When someone pulls your ears they go all red.

Only three spelling mistakes, a good effort. 'A. Good.' The third book belonged to Maurice Gideaux. He remembered things alright, but he was too lazy. The essay consisted of two sentences.

The teeth. The teeth are like a row of soldiers, its like the tonge is the capten...

M. Longeaud shrugged and wrote in the margin: 'Why? Justify your comparison.'

...I kno three sorts of teeth: milk teeth, big teeth and fals teeth.

What a dunce this Gideaux was. M. Longeaud scribbled 'Mediocre' and considered he was being generous. He corrected another two or three pieces of homework, then began to feel something was missing. He wasn't exactly thirsty, but he had a bad taste in his mouth. A drop of something alcoholic would soon get rid of it. What was more, it would be interesting to find out how Chameix's Pernod tasted now he had the time to savour it.

He knocked it back, smacked his lips and thought for a moment. Did it really taste the same as pre-war Pernod? Hard to tell with just one small glass. Pernod requires tasting in the traditional manner. The connoisseurs are right to drink it in a large glass, with very cold water or ice.

As he mused on this, Longeaud was almost unconsciously preparing a large Pernod in the traditional manner. It was only once he had put the glass down again that he realised what he had done. Reproaching himself, and wondering how to make up for it, he felt an intense desire for a cigarette. Quickly, without giving himself a chance to change his mind, he lit up for the sixth time that day.

It was only two in the afternoon. The rest of the day stretched ahead: it made him want a drink. And now, he really was thirsty.

But what of it! It was only Friday, after all. He could begin his new life on Monday.

V

In Tartarus, the world of shadows, a man tormented by thirst thrashes about in a river whose waters recede from his lips as soon as he tries to drink. He is dying also of hunger: although there are branches laden with fruit almost down to the surface of the water, they lift out of reach as soon as he tries to grasp them.

On a sunny hillside near Saint-Boniface, amongst fairytale farms flowing with milk and honey, where bacon and sausages hung from the ceilings, where the merry clucking of the laying hens mingled all day long with the thump of the butter-churn, Tibor Verès was inclined to compare his own punishment to that of Tantalus.

Weary of the carrots and the Jerusalem artichokes which were the only products on open sale in Francheville, he had decided to devote his free time to some serious prospection in the surrounding farms. He was naively astonished to find himself shown the door on any number of pretexts, all of which sprang from a single fact: he had nothing of value to give in exchange for the products he desired.

One day, he screwed up his courage to tackle the irascible Père Crouzet. The farmer, with his pitchfork stuck into the pile of manure beside him, was engaged in sharpening a big kitchen knife. When Verès had outlined his *desiderata* – he was looking for butter that day – the man with the pitchfork fingered the blade of his knife and replied in a sinister tone, 'I haven't killed yet this year.'

Verès shuddered in fear and beat a hasty retreat, horrified by this brute's cold cynicism. The next day, Longeaud explained to him that the rather cryptic phrase simply meant that as Crouzet had not slaughtered a pig the previous winter, he had neither bacon fat nor lard, and therefore could not spare any butter.

So Verès decided to offer his services as a manual labourer. It was haymaking time, and he asked Vautier if he would like some help. Perhaps the latter would be sufficiently touched by the generous offer of his tenant, who asked for nothing in exchange, to sell him some food. Vautier gave a grunt which Verès took as a sign of agreement, and for the next three days *The Paradoxes of History* were put on hold. Equipped in turn with a pitchfork or a rake, the former journalist set about work in the scythed fields, his tall thin figure scrambling up and down slopes and stumbling over the stones. On the third day, his limbs by now so stiff he was bent double, he slid down onto a haystack, scattering the hay which the children had spent two hours piling up. Vautier conveyed to him in somewhat hermetic language that he preferred to dispense with his services. During this time he had shown gratitude for his free labour by giving him, two or three times a day, a glass of village wine, which Verès found undrinkable, and poured discreetly into the ditch. Of food, there was no mention.

To crown it all, the water dispute had entered a critical phase. Vowing eternal hate for the Verès family since the death of La Marquise, La Bardette announced one day that she would no longer allow her neighbour to cross her garden to get water. For several days, Verès had to creep through to the staunchly defended spring under cover of night. In the end, exasperated, he went to Vautier and pressed his claims. The electricity was still not installed, the stove chimney needed sweeping – Longeaud had assured him that was why it smoked – and La Bardette had cut off his water supply.

Vautier only responded to the last point. 'Well,' he growled, 'take your can and go and get some water. Don't worry, I'll be behind you. We'll see if the old hag dares to stop you on my path.'

Tibor Verès ran back to the chalet, grabbed the water can, checked that Vautier was indeed behind him, and crossed the demarcation line.

As soon as he drew level with the house, the old maid rushed out of her lair, threatening him. She began to insult Verès in patois, but Vautier quickly riposted in his rough dialect, unleashing in a spate of invective the accumulation of thirty years of disputes and vexations. La Bardette raised her voice, cackled, and spat thrice on the ground. Then they began to shout in unison, Vautier's deep baritone mingling with La Bardette's shrill soprano. In the end, Vautier, out of breath, grabbed the old woman's hoe where it lay on the path – his path – and flung it at one of his neighbour's hens, which had dared to trespass amongst his own beans.

La Bardette stopped, her mouth open in shock. Then, with a noise which sounded like the sneeze of one of the cats she lived amongst, she took refuge in her den.

'You can go on now,' said Vautier triumphantly, turning to Verès. 'She won't do that again in a hurry.'

Verès took the opportunity to fill every available container, and then went to tackle the thirty-first lesson of *English Without Tears*, which Longeaud had lent him, and which he was 'assimilating' at the rate of five lessons per day.

But La Bardette was not to be defeated. The next day, she went to the presbytery to complain to the Abbé Mignart. The priest, touched as much by the sufferings of this faithful member of his flock as by the fine rabbit she had brought for his consumption, advised her to submit the case to the district surveyor. As it happened, Prosper Baudrier was in the commune that very day. The Abbé Mignart promised to ask Vautier to accept this arbitration. It would be a mutual agreement, and the costs, which could not be very great, would be paid by the person found to be in the wrong.

M. Prosper Baudrier, chartered surveyor, who dealt with the sale of properties and businesses, had one great speciality: the division of estates. A surgeon in matters of inheritance, he enjoyed greater respect in the area than the doctor, or even the vet. Country families, who would think twice before calling the doctor when someone was ill, would not hesitate to call in the surveyor once the invalid in question had departed this world. Of course, M. Prosper did not offer his services for free. But it was a necessary evil, just like taxes, or the notary. An inevitable nuisance, like hailstorms or late frosts. An inheritance cannot be sliced up like a cheese. It would be impossible to divide an estate into equal areas without being unfair to someone. It was necessary to take into account the state of the land, its aspect and its irrigation, not to mention the buildings, whose value could be affected by a thousand considerations. The role of the chartered surveyor, therefore, was beyond price.

It had been like that in the time of M. Prosper's father, and indeed that of his grandfather – for the Baudriers were a dynasty – and no doubt it would still be so in the time of his son. Authority which has passed from generation to generation does not invite challenges. After a few score years, it seems to be a divine essence, like that of a king whom it would take a revolution to overthrow. Those who owned land in Saint-Boniface did not even dream of rebelling against M. Prosper's verdicts, nor his fees, nor his demands in kind, which increased as restrictions became more severe.

The arrival of this Solomon of Saint-Boniface was a signal for prodigious sacrifices in the respective farmyards of Vautier and La Bardette. The previous evening, Tibor Verès had already become aware of the feverish preparations which the two parties were undertaking. At La Grange, the noise of the butter churn mingled with little Michel's voice as he stumbled painfully over the words of *The Oyster and the Litigants*. M. Baudrier had arrived with an empty suitcase and a full briefcase. He took lunch at Vautier's and, to avoid ill-feeling, dined at La Bardette's. These meals were full-blown feasts, from which the chartered surveyor, red in the face, did not recover until the following day. Eventually he decided to consult the land registers, but soon discovered that the Mairie at Saint-Boniface could not provide all the information he needed. The most important document relating to this matter was a will made fifty-five years before, and lodged with a notary in Saint-Paul. He went there the next day, and twenty-four hours later, after a series of mysterious measuring operations amongst La Bardette's peas and Vautier's beans, he at last gave his verdict. It was rather unexpected. The footpath which Vautier so strenuously claimed was his, belonged in fact to La Bardette, as the result of a division of the estate over half a century ago. On the other hand, a strip of land about one metre wide, now engulfed in La Bardette's pea patch, undeniably belonged to Vautier. This meant that both parties were right and wrong at the same time. Therefore each of them had to pay half the costs.

Upon this, the surveyor partook of one more gargantuan meal at Vautier's, and this was followed by the inevitable moment, immortalised by Rabelais, when the bill must be paid; with the twist in this case that it was the guest who presented it. Then, M. Prosper went to take coffee with La Bardette, where the same procedure was repeated.

When the surveyor left early next morning, Henri, the eldest of Vautier's seven children, carried the big suitcase, stuffed with produce, on his bicycle rack.

A shared misfortune can reconcile the worst enemies. After emptying their pockets to pay M. Prosper's fees and satisfy his gluttony, the Vautiers and La Bardette felt their animosity dissolve, just as their butter had melted on the surveyor's toast. That morning, Eugénie Vautier and La Bardette had a long, friendly discussion about the demarcation line. Around one o'clock in the afternoon, wearing a new scarf, La Bardette went for coffee at La Grange. The same evening, Eugénie completed the formalities with a visit to La Bardette, bringing her, as a token of joyful reconciliation, a small bag of bran for her rabbits.

In the course of their discussions, they reached a mutual agreement to return purely and simply to the *status quo ante*. The path leading to the spring would remain in joint ownership, and Vautier would give up his claim to the narrow strip on the edge of La Bardette's patch. And as it is only human nature to seek a scapegoat for any calamity, La Bardette and the Vautiers suddenly found it was that good-for-nothing, shabby Verès who was the source of all their woes, coming all the way from Marseille just to put such good neighbours at odds with each other. There was no need for Verès to be present at this reunion to guess its conclusion. He knew as much from Vautier's sombre expression, and from the wild glare La Bardette directed at him each time he plucked up his courage to cross the international concession in search of water.

That evening, as he dejectedly passed the kitchen of La Grange, Verès heard Michel Vautier stumbling over his homework. In a sing-song voice, as if repeating a prayer, he was reciting *The Oyster and the Litigants.*

Pay all it costs to sue today
And count what's left to reimburse
Your counsel will take all away
And leave you but an empty purse.
Pay all it costs to sue today
And count what's left...

VI

The 21.13 train was running two hours late. The ancient boneshaker, which took three hours to complete the painful forty-kilometre climb from the Rhône valley up to Francheville, had jumped the rails again. Just as old nags put out to grass sometimes get the bit between their teeth again when they remember their carefree youth, so the superannuated local train had capricious moments when it left its rails and attempted to launch itself into space.

That evening, it drew in to Francheville station at exactly 23.18. About twenty passengers got off. Amongst them was a middle-aged woman wearing a felt hat, beneath which strands of greying hair protruded. The skin around her temples was finely lined. She cast an anxious look around her, waited until the last passenger had disappeared past the ticket barrier, and with a shrug of resignation dragged her suitcase to the left luggage office, keeping only a vanity bag with her.

Darkness had fallen. A sudden gust of wind blew in a few drops of rain. The woman who had travelled up from the city was reluctant to get wet. In any case, she didn't know the way. Bitterly, she reflected that the man she was to join could have taken the trouble to come to meet her. Disappointed and weary, in unfamiliar surroundings, she decided to spend the night in a hotel.

Half an hour later, Mme Blanche Fleury was making herself comfortable in room 23 at the Hôtel Panorama. She undressed, got into bed, and closed her eyes. But alas, there appeared to be a gremlin under the mattress, which plucked the divan springs as if they were the strings of a lute, whenever she made the slightest movement.

She was exhausted, however, and was beginning to drift off to sleep. Suddenly, the gremlin struck a plaintive sound on his instrument. And Blanche Fleury was sure she hadn't moved. Annoyed, she listened intently. This time she was certain. The noises didn't come from the springs of her bed. There must be another gremlin in the room next door.

And now she could hear whispering on the other side of the wall. A woman's voice gave a little moan. Then there was a muffled, staccato laugh. Blanche propped herself up on her elbow. Was it possible that two men could have an identical laugh?

She pressed her ear to the wall. No question of sleep now. Silence descended again. But she felt the proximity of two human bodies.

'Your heart is beating so fast!'

It was a woman's voice, husky, caressing. The laugh of the man who answered her made Blanche start once more. And the masculine voice she heard speaking a few muffled words left her in no doubt. Her teeth clenched, her head buzzing numbly, she jumped out of bed, put her coat on over her nightdress and fumbled in the dark to open the door.

She waited a moment at the first door to the right of her own, listened again, then, suddenly overcome with rage, rapped on the door panel. Inside, there was silence. She rapped again, bruising her hand.

'Who is it?' asked the woman in a musical voice.

'Open the door! Open it, César, I know you're in there!'

Silence fell again, followed by a muffled curse, then there was a pattering of mules on the floor.

'Who are you, Madame?' asked the voice behind the door.

'Open up now, or I'll make a scene.'

Already, in one of the other rooms, it sounded as if someone was stirring.

The key turned in the lock. Blanche, breathless with anger, pushed aside the young woman who stood in her way, and headed for the bed. The crescent moon, emerging from behind a cloud, filled the room with enough light for her to recognise the figure of her husband. With a furious gesture, she switched on the light, and stood there bolt upright, speechless, fuming with rage.

In her wrap by the door, Génia had not moved.

César Fleury pulled himself together. He wound a sheet round his body, boldly returned his wife's glare, and in spite of the ridiculous position he found himself in, felt he had this advantage over her: he was calm.

'What are you doing here?' he said sullenly. 'You might have written to say you were coming!'

Blanche could hardly breathe.

'Written? Of course I wrote. You must have got my letter this morning. And you didn't even bother to come to the station!'

Then she bit her lip. That was not the point. He was making it look as though she was in the wrong, and on the defensive. The situation was quite simply grotesque.

Fleury was already capitalising on his advantage. 'You left it too late, as usual,' he muttered. 'Your letter will probably come tomorrow. I've told you a hundred times, you shouldn't leave things till the last minute.'

Actually, that day César Fleury had left for Francheville before Brandouille had got round to Les Tilleuls.

Blanche was stupefied, dumbstruck with indignation. But César could tell from the way her hands shook that she was about to explode. He had to take the initiative.

'Come, come,' he said reproachfully, 'look what a position you've put yourself in. What on earth made you book into a hotel?'

As Blanche's eyes rolled upward and darted from César to Génia and back again, Fleury realised he had gone too far. Above all, no public scandal! Make sure Blanche could do no further damage, certainly; but he had to calm her down first. The main thing was to get her to accept a version of events which would appeal to her pride and her feminine sensibilities.

'Anyway, since you're here,' he continued, 'you could at least have waited until morning to ask me for an explanation, instead of barging in here like a character in a farce. Let's have a little dignity, shall we?'

'What do you expect? That I'd just listen quietly to your frolics through the wall?'

'Frolics! Frolics! We're still in a farce! I never thought you could be so tactless.'

Standing by the door, Génia felt her legs give way. She ought to have made herself scarce, vanished from view, but she didn't have the strength. She reached out to drag a chair towards her and collapsed into it, her face in her hands. César seemed to have entirely forgotten she was there.

With sudden determination, Fleury sprang out of bed, and drew on his shirt and trousers. Now then! He felt much more confident. He brought a chair forward for his wife and sat down on the edge of the bed.

'What a time to talk about tact,' said Blanche in a tearful voice. 'I've never heard anything like it! How can you be so callous! I get here, I find you in bed with a woman, and you… You are a selfish monster, César.'

She ground to a halt, sobbing uncontrollably. She felt how painfully inadequate her words were, but was incapacitated by the presence, at the other end of the room, of this woman who, only ten minutes earlier… She should have been speaking in a strong, clear voice, but she was afraid she could not hold back her tears. After all, maybe César was right. She shouldn't have come in. It was too late, anyway.

'And what about you?' Fleury retorted. 'As for being selfish, you're hardly blameless yourself. Do you ever think about me? Even though you know how bad my nerves are? Permanent overwork, exhaustion, lassitude. Artistic inspiration – dried up. Emotional life – completely apathetic. My poor Blanche, it's not as if you haven't had to put up with the consequences. Do you think I would have got this extended leave if my health had not been so poor? But of course, selfish as I am, I said nothing about it so as not to worry you.'

'I don't understand,' stammered Blanche, through her tears, 'what has all that got to do with it?'

'But it's obvious! If you thought about it a moment, you'd understand.'

'Understand what?'

Beside the door, Génia lifted her head and stared at Fleury in shock, the colour draining from her cheeks.

'Well, I can hardly make it clearer,' said Fleury impatiently. 'You know I had to go and see the doctor. He said that as well as boosting my diet and getting plenty of fresh air, I should undergo a sort of psychic treatment. Psycho-physical, really. You must have heard of shock therapy. Well, that's more or less what it is.'

'And that's why you've been making a fool of me with this woman?'

César's smile was that of a deeply misunderstood man.

'What a thing to say, my poor Blanche! And how you misinterpret me! You know how much you mean to me, and you know I am incapable of betraying you.'

As he said this, he glanced towards Génia, who, her eyes burning, was still staring at him, with her chin in her hands. Clearly this sentimental little lady might take things rather badly. An hour earlier, when he had promised to dedicate to her his new *Lied* to the words by Rimbaud 'O *saisons, ô châteaux*', she had told him, her voice trembling with emotion, that she had always known he would come one day, that there never had been, and never would be, another man in her life. He had replied to her in exalted tones. But so what? It's easy to talk like that in such circumstances. He would try to repair the damage when he next saw her. For the moment, it was Blanche who had to be appeased. She was his wife, and the mother of his child; in any case her little business provided him with security. His own position in radio was at the mercy of events. It would only take a change of government... anyway, he abhorred unnecessary complications. He wasn't going to let a fleeting affair change his life!

'So there. I am incapable of betraying you,' he repeated.

'As you have just proved,' sneered Blanche.

'I beg of you again, stop being so petty,' said César in a tone of exasperation. Then he continued, in a conciliating, sympathetic voice, 'Do you really think there's anything changed between us? Because of a stupid coincidence you've been witness to an incident which has little importance for a man and which, unusually for me, meant no more than what I have told you. I understand you are hurt, it makes me infinitely sad, but nothing can damage the tenderness I feel for you, don't you see that?'

'That's a lie, César,' sobbed Blanche. 'That's an outright lie! Maybe you're beginning to regret what you have done, but it's too late.'

'I see you still haven't understood,' said Fleury, with the air of a martyr. Casting a sideways look at Génia, who had still shown no reaction, he returned to the attack. 'My health, my equilibrium, my art, does none of that mean anything to you? Since I have to be blunt, the plain fact is that I needed a boost to get back into shape. For my nerves… and for my senses. An escape. An escape which would be good for me and, in the end, good for you too.'

'You're making it all up,' groaned Blanche, sticking to her guns. 'I don't know what you're talking about. Actually, I don't want to know.'

'But it's staring you in the face, Madame,' cried Génia, who had suddenly got up. 'Your husband's nerves were frayed, and to get over it he needed a little adventure. He had to sleep with a woman. Now do you understand? It just happens that I was able to provide that service, that's all.'

Fleury hardly recognised her. Eyes shining, cheeks aflame, her whole body was shaking and her voice had taken on a shrill tone.

'Come, Madame,' said Fleury, feeling his self-assurance drain away. 'Don't get so upset!'

At this appeal for calm, Génia finally lost the remains of her self-control. The world had capsized around her. There was a drumming in her temples, and beneath her robe her chest heaved fit to burst the vice in which it was clamped.

'Leave me alone!' she cried. 'I'm not talking to you.' And turning to Blanche, 'Don't be afraid, Madame, I am nothing to your husband and he is nothing to me. A little adventure with no consequences, on the doctor's orders. Nothing else, believe me. You are a mother, Madame, and you are perhaps not aware that there exist single women with no means of support, who have to earn a living. Well, I am one of them.'

She fell silent a moment, then continued in a lower tone, 'I am neither worse nor better than you. I've just not been so lucky. And now... please leave me alone. This is my room, and I need to rest.'

This time, she felt as if she had shattered the bar which was crushing her chest. It had been hell, but now she was relieved. She felt like a sick person who, to overcome an excruciating pain, had dug her nails into her own flesh until it bled. Except that relief is soon followed by nausea and dizziness, and the pain gradually returns.

Fleury stared at her, lost for words. How reasonable she was being! A little too reasonable, even. He would never have expected her to help him smooth things over with Blanche. Pretending to be a prostitute! An excellent idea. But why the devil did she seem to take things so badly at the same time? You have to beware of these sentimental little women, they're a bit naive. She might be upset by what he had been obliged to say to appease Blanche... But then again, it couldn't last for ever...

Blanche had got up. 'Come on, César,' she said quietly. 'You are right, Madame, this conversation has gone on long enough.'

She had already taken a step towards the door when she suddenly hesitated, appeared to think for a moment, and then came back towards her husband, who was hurriedly putting his shoes on. His jacket was still on the back of the chair. Blanche removed his wallet from the inside pocket, took a banknote out and, with a dignified gesture, placed it on the bedside table. Then she swept resolutely to the door, followed by César. As he passed Génia, he looked at her one last time. But the young woman was staring at the floor, her face once more inscrutable. Such a pity...

Alone in the room, Génia remained motionless for a time.

Then she absently picked up the banknote, turned it over and over in her hands, crumpled it up, then flattened it out again with a bitter little laugh.

Her gaze fell on the image. In the background, as a setting for the symbolic figures, was a château. Just like in the fairy stories. One of those castles that only exist in dreams... *O saisons, ô châteaux!*

* * *

At seven the next morning, Suzanne, the chambermaid at the Hôtel Panorama, opened her eyes wide when she saw, departing from room 23, the lady who had arrived the previous evening, along with the handsome bearded gentleman who had dined with Mme Prokoff, and whom she had seen accompanying her up to room 24. These men, really!

VII

André Murger got up to close the window. The noise of conversation outside was distracting, and he wanted to write an important letter. Since his release from captivity, he had been approached by a friend, an ex-prisoner of war like himself, escaped from Germany, who had put him in touch with a resistance organisation. André had been given the task of sticking flyers on the walls of urinals. He had spent three or four nights carrying out this mission, which he was told was urgent and important. Then he awaited further orders, but his leader appeared to have forgotten him.

When the month of June came around, André had followed his doctor's advice and left to complete his convalescence in the country. Now, after two months of silence, he had received a letter asking him if he was prepared to take up the struggle again. Well, he was more prepared than ever. But would he be given another sphere of responsibility, or would it just be back to the urinals?

In a heat wave, closing the window soon makes the bedroom airless, and noises continue to filter through from outside. So Murger leaned out to look at the group who, on this torrid afternoon, had gathered in the shade of the big lime tree behind the house.

Earlier, André had thought he heard Solange's footsteps on the stairs, but he hadn't picked out her voice amongst those which drifted up to him. However, she was there, sitting in a rattan armchair beside her mother's chaise longue. André could not see her face, which was hidden behind the magazine she was holding open, but he immediately recognised the white dress with blue polka dots he had seen her wearing at lunchtime. She remained silent, while her father held forth as usual.

Whenever there was a new guest at Les Tilleuls, César Fleury, who could never quite decide whether to be seductive or shocking, always had a theory to propound. During lunch, he had not really had a chance, because he was being so attentive to Mme Fleury, but now his time had come, and neither M. and Mme Letourneau, the new guests, nor Joseph Hermelin, were to escape his pronouncements.

Mme Hermelin had introduced M. and Mme Letourneau as 'a very good class of person'. Apparently they were one of the 'silk families' of Lyon. As it turned out, M. Letourneau was indeed in a silk firm; but he was merely employed as head of an accounts section.

Distractedly, André turned back to his letter, but the sheet of white paper appeared to be covered with blue dots. He fought the desire to go downstairs. He knew he wouldn't be able to bear Fleury's speechifying. Better to keep away.

He finished his letter, but as soon as he had sealed the envelope, the blue dots began to dance in front of his eyes again. He brushed his tousled hair, picked up a book from the table, and went out.

Mme Hermelin, having finalised the schedules for her husband and the maid in the kitchen, had just sat down in an armchair with her needlework. It was a large square of fabric on which she was embroidering a phrase which had intrigued André: 'Come to me, all ye that labour and are heavy laden.' Was it an advertisement for her guest house? Apparently not. Passing behind the landlady's armchair, he now saw the reference: Matthew 11, 28. So it was a verse from the bible. He should have known. That was why the retired tax inspector's wife hid her work so hastily when the fiancés came into view. It must be their wedding present, for the ceremony was to take place the next day, and this verse from Matthew obviously referred to M. Rosenfeld's conversion, which Mme Hermelin believed imminent. The 'surprise' which she mysteriously told her guests to expect must also have something to do with this important event.

There was no empty chair, so André sat down on the grass a short distance from Solange. Fleury was still talking.

'The so-called progress which we have turned into a sort of religion,' he was saying, 'is basically a dreadful regression. We have paid for the few inventions which improve our comfort, by physical atrophy. With each generation, we are losing the use of our arms. Why bother? We have machines! Our legs are in the process of becoming superfluous appendages, because to go anywhere we have the train, the metro, the car, the plane. We're even forgetting how to go up and down stairs, because we have lifts instead. And what about our ears and eyes? Already, we have machines which listen and look. When will we have machines to make children? It would save so much trouble!'

Blanche Fleury gave her husband an indulgent look. Mme Letourneau, a little red-haired woman of about forty, whose gaze at the world was that of a wide-eyed child, blushed deep red. Solange, behind her magazine, shrugged. Only Mme Hermelin protested vehemently.

'Oh no, Monsieur Fleury! Never! For it is written, "In sorrow thou shalt bring forth children."'

'In short,' concluded Fleury, 'it is high time we understood that in order to go forwards, we must be determined to go backwards. It's only now, when all disciplines are under strain, that we begin to recognise the benefits of authority. Whereas the great minds of the middle ages knew long before we did that mankind is fundamentally bad. Human beings are a band of wolves who would tear each other to pieces, if it wasn't for fear of the whip or the revolver.'

'But isn't it rather the regime which is bad?' remarked Murger. But nobody noticed.

M. Letourneau's placid face, the shape and colour of a cider apple, exhibited profound stupefaction. Since the rout of France, he had not known which horse to back. Fleury's theories plunged him into total bewilderment.

'In any case,' said Joseph, 'the good thing about the middle ages is that the Jews were banished from society.'

'Long live the ghetto!' Murger muttered, as if to himself.

Fleury rounded on him. 'Why not? It was an elegant and sensible solution. It meant Jews could be eliminated from the community. All those belonging to that accursed race which poisons, withers and destroys everything it touches, could be left to live amongst themselves.'

'According to you,' said André, forgetting the wisdom of his earlier resolution, 'if a Jew bakes bread, the bread is bound to be bad.'

'Exactly. I hold that if a Jew were to make bread, it would

be intrinsically bad, even if it didn't immediately give stomachache to anyone who ate it. I'm using the conditional, because do you know any Jewish bakers? I don't. That's one of the main aspects of the problem. Jews are averse to productive work, because they prefer to be intermediaries, parasites. And even if, by some chance, they manage to produce something, a building, say, or a book, it's always fundamentally bad.'

'But people often say that Jews are highly intelligent,' ventured Letourneau.

'Alas,' Joseph interjected, 'the more intelligent they are, the more harm they do.'

Mme Hermelin's younger son, rather overweight for his thirty years, was sweating profusely. In spite of the heat, however, he thought it would not be seemly to remove his dark jacket. Of average height, he had black brilliantined hair and a pallid face punctuated by a Chaplinesque moustache.

'That's not the point,' Fleury protested. 'You obviously think Jewish intelligence is dangerous. As for me, I'm not afraid of it, I despise it. All their intelligence is directed towards destruction. In fact it just boils down to an overdeveloped business sense, and a taste for shady deals. Their excessive cerebrality is a poor match for the common sense and equilibrium which are the privilege of healthy races. The Jews are rootless, they have nothing like the ancestral wisdom, the result of centuries of tradition, which is the inheritance of even the humblest Frenchman, and the only measure of true strength.'

'But the Jews also have traditions, and a long history, so they should not lack ancestral wisdom, to use your expression,' said André insinuatingly.

Fleury gave him a contemptuous smile.

'They lost it centuries ago. A cut of meat which is top-notch today will smell bad tomorrow and be completely rotten the day after. The Jewish people have made the mistake of uselessly prolonging their existence, to become agents of decay. When you look closely, you always find the Jew at the origin of the great ills of civilisation. Take this war, for example…'

'The freemasonry of the Elders of Zion,' interrupted Joseph, 'aims to take over the world. That's the danger. And anyway, there's something slimy, something clammy about the Jew, which personally I find repulsive. It's always that feeling of repugnance and irritation which tells me they're Jews, and I'm never mistaken. It only takes me five minutes to know if a man standing beside me is Jewish. There must be an objective reason for that.'

'Of course,' opined Mme Hermelin. 'They have not yet embraced Jesus.'

'If I understand you correctly, Monsieur Fleury,' said André, 'it's the Jews who bear the responsibility for this war.' He had to force himself to speak calmly, for the musician inspired in him the same, almost physical, abhorrence that Joseph had described. 'For people with an overdeveloped business sense, they're getting a bad deal. Because they're more hunted and persecuted than ever.'

'They've just miscalculated, that's all,' retorted Fleury.

'Come on!' said André. 'It's easy to blame the Jews for all our ills. It's so convenient that if the Jews didn't exist, you'd have to invent them. But when this war is over, the whole of humanity will blush in shame at this collective Jew-hating madness. Never again will we see a return to the pogroms and the anti-Jewish massacres. Anti-Semitism will disappear, along with the Hitler regime.'

M. Letourneau, who always instinctively sought a compromise when there were acute differences, tried to smooth things over.

'Basically, gentlemen, we're all agreed. There are too many things wrong in our country. Changes will have to be made!'

'Exactly,' said Mme Hermelin, folding her embroidery. 'Changes do have to be made, and they will come about when mankind returns to the Lord. M. Rosenfeld has understood that, and he's undergoing conversion. We are sincerely happy for him, so I have a surprise in store, for the grand occasion of his marriage.' She got up as she said this, shaded her eyes with her hand and peered at the horizon. Seeing nothing, she made an impatient gesture.

'Please excuse me,' she said with a mysterious air, 'I have to go and see if the surprise has arrived.'

When she returned, somewhat disappointed, and dived straight into the kitchen, the Letourneaus had already gone up to their room, Joseph had left, and Mme Fleury had got up from her chaise longue.

'I'm going up to change,' she said. 'We'll go for a little walk, shall we, César?'

He kissed her hand ceremoniously. 'As you wish, my dear. I'll wait for you in the drawing room.'

Fleury's newfound tenderness towards his wife had taken on added intensity since the previous evening, when he had tried in vain to see Génia again. Suzanne, the chambermaid, had told him that Mme Prokoff had not come down from her room for twenty-four hours, that she was 'tired' and that she had hardly eaten. Fleury had asked Suzanne to persuade her to receive him, but she had come back shaking her head. 'Madame Prokoff does not want to see anybody,' she said. 'And as soon as she feels better she's going to leave.'

A pity, of course, but César could do nothing about it.

In the shade of the lime tree, Solange was still leafing through her magazine. A short distance away, Murger was pretending to read. But in fact he was gazing at what he could see of Solange: her bare arms, the hem of her dress, and her long sun-tanned legs. Did she even realise he was there? Did she share her father's opinions? For that matter, did she have any opinions? What could she be thinking about at the moment? André was tempted to ask her outright, but he remembered, just in time, the surprised, cold look she had given him on their first encounter, when he had offered to carry her bag to the house. What was behind this impenetrable, distant princess air? Maybe nothing. Maybe an awful lot. What might it mean to be Fleury's daughter?

André got up from the grass and sat in an armchair, without taking his eyes off the magazine which hid Solange's face from view. If only she would just glance at him! He would like to see her smile, to find out if she had dimples.

Meanwhile, in the drawing room of Les Tilleuls, Fleury struck a few chords. Then he launched into Bach's *Well-Tempered Clavier*. Whenever Solange's father was at the piano, André felt better disposed towards him.

'You must be musical too,' he said in an effort to initiate a conversation. 'You should give us a little concert one day.'

Even a travelling salesman might have found a better ploy, but he had to say something.

The magazine was lowered slightly, Solange's face emerged, and – a miracle! – two pretty dimples appeared in her cheeks, transforming the distant princess into a smiling child.

'Not at all! My father never wanted me to learn music. I don't even know my scales.' In spite of the smile still playing on her lips, her voice was tinged with regret, perhaps even resentment.

'That's strange,' murmured André, 'for such a passionate musician… But he does put forward some unusual theories,' he added.

'For those who find his ideas shocking,' said Solange brusquely, her expression becoming impassive once more, 'he offers the compensation of his music. Not everyone can do that.'

She stood up and headed for the house, without glancing at André.

Stung by this, André was going back to his book when he saw Mme Hermelin come out of the kitchen and go towards her chair. But instead of sitting down in it, she climbed onto the seat and, shielding her eyes with her hand, peered towards the footpath which was a shortcut from Francheville to Les Tilleuls.

'The surprise,' she whispered confidentially to André.

Suddenly, with a little cry, she swayed, and would have fallen backwards if the young man had not held out his arm to steady her. 'Well, really!' she muttered, pointing towards the footpath.

André, looking at the lane which followed the line of chestnuts, saw two figures making their way towards Les Tilleuls.

'I don't understand,' stammered Mme Hermelin. 'I can see it's my son, Jérémie, the Minister, but he's not alone… that other man… it's just not possible!'

André squinted to make out the vision which had so upset the landlady of Les Tilleuls. It was a man dressed in black like his companion, but instead of a pastor's suit, he was wearing a priest's cassock.

'A Curé! And it isn't the Abbé Mignart!' croaked Mme Hermelin. 'But I'm being silly. He's probably not coming here,' she added hopefully.

Her hope was to be shattered. They were indeed coming to Les Tilleuls, these two clergymen, and although at present they were chatting amicably, each was determined to convert, to his own faith, the still-vacillating soul of Frank Rosenfeld.

Chapter 6
Towards the Unknown

I

For three days now, the Sobrevins' dog Lion has been roaming the countryside in search of home, the farm at Les Mottes.

He is terribly scrawny. His dirty grey coat has lost the last of its sheen, and mud clings to the tawny-coloured tufts that remain. Round his neck is a wide strip, rubbed smooth, where his collar once was. On one flank is a livid roundel of flesh, inflicted by a pan of boiling water thrown at him by a peasant woman, when he got too near her kitchen. Tail drooping, ears pinned back, with bloodshot eyes and his muzzle close to the ground, Lion continues to roam and search.

Three days spent combing the woods, the ravines, the drought-stricken fields, his skin scratched by brambles and his fur clogged with thistles, three days without shelter, without food, without master, chased off everywhere with sticks or snarling fangs: it is enough to turn the most respectable of dogs into a tramp.

Lion does not understand. He senses vaguely that a dreadful catastrophe has overtaken him, a disaster which has obliterated the whole of his earlier existence. He is desperately unhappy, although without a trace of revolt. It is simply a feeling of immense distress, a poignant, almost human nostalgia for a paradise lost: the big house full of children, the shed, the great red cooking-pot redolent of bacon, the fields, the cows, the goats. He had been brutally torn away from all that. Crammed into a basket by his master, Elie Sobrevin, he had spent two long hours in the dark being thrown from side to side in this prison cell, while the scents of woods and fields reached his nose in turn. At length he was dragged from the basket, and found himself beside his master in a house he did not know, along with an old woman who sometimes visited Les Mottes. Then his master tied him up in an unfamiliar barn, and immediately vanished. Lion's despair was complete.

The most terrible misfortunes, horrors beyond our understanding, sometimes have surprisingly simple causes. What has befallen Lion is in fact an everyday occurrence.

Lion is ten years old. That is, like a working man over fifty, while not exactly senile, he has reached an age where his faculties are no longer so acute, his reflexes begin to slow down, his legs become stiff, and physical decline is just around the corner. Sometimes he is discovered dozing in the field. He is not quite so quick and eager in rounding up the cows and goats when they stray into forbidden pastures. In short, he is getting past it.

Elie Sobrevin had been dissatisfied with Lion's services for some months. From a neighbour, he had acquired a young bitch, Friquette, which he had begun to train. There's a lot to be said for bitches. They are more loyal, they don't stray into the other farms; in short, they give you less trouble. Of course, they do have litters, but the stream isn't far away… And anyway, in a few months, a year at the most, Lion will have to be replaced because he won't be good for anything.

Unfortunately, Lion's presence did not help with Friquette's training. Whenever Elie gave her a command, Lion, unwilling to see his own position usurped, would rush off first, bark at his rival, and sometimes, in uncharacteristic outbreaks of bad temper, go as far as nipping the cows' heels. In short, he was too eager to please.

But this occasional zeal did not fool his master. Elie could see that Lion made up for these bouts of frenzied activity with long periods of apathy, and that the dog's strength was waning. To crown it all, Lion did not get on at all with Friquette. He would snarl viciously at her in the pastures and beside the cooking pot put out for them to lick, and display sudden irrational outbursts of anger, even biting her at times. Being jealous, he was determined to give Friquette a hard time. Obviously it could not go on. One solution might have been to tie the semi-retired worker up in the barn while his successor was being trained; another might have been to feed the two rivals separately in order to avoid fights; but there was no point going to all that trouble to feed a worker no longer earning his keep.

Elie Sobrevin was the first to break the taboo and voice what the whole family was secretly thinking: they had to get rid of Lion. But of course you can't give a week's notice to a dog. In vain would you explain that you no longer require their services, that the position is taken, that they should apply elsewhere. Granted, dogs are not stupid; but there are certain things they will never understand.

As it happened, Elie's mother, who lived in an isolated house on the edge of a hamlet about thirty kilometres from Les Mottes, had just lost her own dog. The old woman only had three goats and two ewes, but she was no longer very agile and she needed a dog to guard the little flock as well as to keep her company. Maybe she and Lion would get on together: after all, they were both old. So Elie had removed the collar which bore the address of Les Mottes and, to symbolise the transfer of power, fastened it around Friquette's neck. That's how it goes!

So for three days now, Lion had been roaming the country-side. On several occasions he thought he had found the way to Les Mottes, but the scents soon mingled and got confused, the trails criss-crossed each other, and he kept finding himself in unfamiliar territory, with dogs he didn't recognise and men he didn't know threatening him with sticks, or throwing stones at him.

Twice, the trail led him to a fast-flowing, seething river. Lion stopped, barking at his own reflection in the water which glinted in the sunshine. No chance of swimming across: his master had seen to that. There was only one bridge in a twenty-kilometre stretch, and to find it he had first to turn away from Les Mottes, as there was a great bend in the river here. Elie had thought it would be a miracle if the dog found the footbridge.

The miracle came about nevertheless. And on the afternoon of the fourth day Lion, a mud-bespattered shadow of his former self, his tongue hanging limp, his coat matted like that of a starving wolf, came into view of Les Mottes. As soon as he realised that, this time, he was on the right track, the desperate rage which had pressed him on for four days subsided. The nearer he got to Les Mottes, the more timid he felt. He would have liked to gallop joyfully back to the rediscovered paradise, but it was as if his limbs were paralysed. Did he somehow sense that in returning he was defying his master?

Reaching the vine-clad pump, about thirty metres from the house, he stops. That is where he always went to lie when his master was displeased with him. The familiar smell of soup wafts out from the kitchen. Lion snuggles into his nook, happy, but wiped out with exhaustion, hunger and fear.

All of a sudden, he pricks his ears up. At the top of the lane, he can hear the steel tip of a walking-stick striking the stones. Lion knows this sound: he has heard it every day for years. It's one of those noises that automatically sets him off barking. Lion nurtures a deep hatred of Brandouille, the postman, of the pungent odour of wine which precedes and follows him, and particularly of the steel-tipped stick which he waves under his muzzle to provoke him. One day the sharp tip even stuck into his side, and Lion bit the man carrying the bag. Now, every time he sees him, he feels like doing it again.

But today Lion is too tired, too distressed by everything that has happened to him. He doesn't bark at Brandouille. He watches in silence as the enemy with the steel-tipped stick approaches.

A few paces short of the shed, Brandouille stops. This is where Elie Sobrevin keeps his tools. Brandouille's gaze has fallen on something interesting. The door is ajar, and he has caught sight of a bicycle pump – his own bicycle pump, the one Noémi has confiscated in order to make him bring the child's overalls he owes her. He has a unique opportunity to retrieve it.

Lion does not know what Brandouille's motives are. All he can see is that the enemy is trying to gain access to a building which forms part of his paradise, while the masters are absent. Suddenly, his training as a guard dog overcomes his fear, remorse, hunger and exhaustion. Barking furiously and baring his teeth, he lunges at the postman. The latter brandishes his stick, but Noémi is already on the kitchen step. Brandouille thrusts a letter at her, his eyes turned shiftily away, and retreats hurriedly, muttering threats. He is determined to get his pump back without delivering the overalls in exchange. He paid the official price for the rabbit, so that's enough of that!

'Look! It's Lion!' cries Noémi.

Above all, she's astonished. But she is also rather moved. You have to hand it to him! How on earth did he do it? Dogs have been known to return from afar, but given all the precautions they took: shut into a basket on a bicycle carrier, taken thirty kilometres away, and the bridge so difficult to find! Yet he still made his way back.

Lion has been part of the household for ten years. He was a present to Noémi from her cousin, when Noémi was newly married. She trained him. When he was a puppy, she let him sleep in the kitchen, and wrapped him in straw because he shivered with cold. When he needed worming, she pressed the pills into little balls of bread, and when he got distemper she gave him black coffee. She had saved his life, just as she was convinced she had saved her son Abel from diphtheria by smearing paraffin on his throat when he was choking. Lion is really one of her children, the eldest of eight, as he has seen all the others born. Good old Lion!

The children arrive back from school, singing at the tops of their voices. At the sight of Lion, they throw themselves on him, patting him and jostling him. He puts up with them as they climb on his back, and pull his tail and ears. Lion licks them all in turn, yelping in delight. What joy it is to be back in the bosom of the family!

'I told you so,' says little Abel triumphantly. 'Now, we won't let him go.'

'Just look how thin he's got,' says Noémi. 'That's incredible, in just four days. He must be starving, the poor thing!'

She throws a chunk of bread which Lion catches in the air and swallows greedily. His paws tremble with pleasure, exhaustion and emotion. They take pity on him. Noémi brings a wooden bowl of whey and pushes it under his nose.

'Here you are, Lion, you poor old boy, drink this, you've earned it.'

'We still have to get rid of him,' declares Elie when he gets home for tea, a few minutes later. 'We can't afford to go on feeding him like that.'

But it's not as if Lion has a big appetite. And he isn't a fussy eater. It's only in books that dogs are carnivores. Those in Saint-Boniface are pretty much vegetarian. Vegetarian and occasionally coprophagous. They are content with a little soup, or some leftovers. As for meat, they only know what it tastes like from the well-gnawed bones thrown to them by their masters, or the rabbit tripe on feast days.

Elie Sobrevin is annoyed. For some time now, the dog has only been trouble. He can't afford to feed him when he isn't earning his keep, just so that he can die a natural death. He's seen some of these animals live to sixteen. It's Lion's hard luck, he should have stayed with the old woman.

'May as well have it over and done with straight away,' he says. And he goes into the cellar to find an old sack.

Noémi feels a bit uncomfortable at this. Poor old Lion! Elie does seem to be in rather a hurry. But anyway, sooner or later...

She cuts another slice of bread and throws it to the dog. He has always liked bread, and only gets to eat it on special occasions. She pours a little coffee, made from grilled rye, into an old saucepan for him. The condemned man's glass of rum.

Elie comes back from the cellar with the sack. He whistles to Lion, as he used to when he was needed in the pasture. The children are excited in anticipation. Lion is their entertainment, he is theirs to taunt.

Only Abel stays in the kitchen with his mother. He has never liked raiding birds' nests, or transfixing butterflies and pinning them to sheets of paper. Nor does he like to see rabbits or baby goats slaughtered, or hens bled. He's not like the other children.

'Come on Abel, come and watch us drown Lion!'

Abel turns his back on them. He doesn't want to see. He feels sad.

'Go on, you silly thing,' says his mother. 'Don't look so miserable, it's only a dog. What does a dog matter, especially now that so many people are being killed by bombs?'

'Yes,' says Abel thoughtfully. 'But I don't know them. I know Lion.'

Elie Sobrevin has reached the stream at the end of the pasture. Lion follows willingly. He has stopped trembling. His master isn't angry with him. He called him like he did in the good old days. His recent terrible experience has just been a nightmare.

Elie stands beside the rushing water. He picks up a boulder and places it in the bottom of the sack. Then he whistles to Lion again, and the dog comes up to him, trusting, wagging his tail.

Then something incomprehensible happens. Incomprehensible, and terrifying. The master seizes Lion as he did on the day he put him in the basket, crams him into the sack, and once again it is pitch dark. Lion barks in desperation. Are they returning him to the old woman? Well, he'll come back again!

Meanwhile Elie ties the sack with one end of a long rope. The children gather round him, their eyes shining. The show has begun.

'Papa, are you going to leave the sack in the water?' asks Dina.

Elie shrugs. These children! Leave it in the water? It's still a perfectly good sack. Why not order a wooden coffin for the old dog while we're at it!

Gradually, he lifts the sack, while Lion struggles furiously inside, barking himself hoarse. He grasps the other end of the rope and drops the sack in the water. The weight of the boulder drags it to the bottom. Lion has fallen silent. This time, he won't find his way back.

A few minutes pass. Eventually, Elie pulls up the sack, with the animal's corpse inside. It is quite a weight. Already the children are making preparations for Lion's great burial ceremony. What fun that will be! Lion will have entertained them unto death. For them, the show goes on. Only for Lion has it come to an end. Ten years of loyal service. For better and for worse. A dog's life.

II

It's a long way to Tipperary,
It's a long way to go…

Joseph stopped, suddenly realising he was singing an English marching tune. How could he, after everything that had happened at Mers-el-Kébir and in Syria! But he liked to keep up a rhythm when he was walking, so he switched to the first song which came into his head:

Maréchal, nous voilà!
Tu nous as redonné l'espérance!

He had just passed the last houses in Francheville and embarked on the road to Saint-Boniface. As a state employee he was entitled to a few days' leave, and his mother had already taken advantage of this to dispatch him into town on a number of errands. Joseph was bent almost double under the burden of an enormous rucksack.

On leaving active service with the rank of lieutenant, he had found himself a post as Head of Rationing in a small town about fifty kilometres from Francheville but in the same *département*. It was a stop-gap until he found something better. Believing the war would be over in a few months, Joseph thought there was no future in the post. But as he climbed the hill, he smiled at his earlier misjudgement. Two years had passed, and his job now seemed considerably more secure than at the time of his appointment.

What bothered Joseph now was the moral aspect, the ideological side of things. Granted, France had at last got rid of the bunch of Freemasons and Jewish vermin who used to run the country. The country was going to change for the better: even in servitude, the newfound discipline was preferable to a freedom where anything goes. But even so, things were not quite right.

First of all, there were general matters to be seen to. Although the bastards had been taught a lesson, they still popped up everywhere, opposing a passive resistance to the orders they were given. The scum wouldn't lie down and die. They would only be completely wiped out when a new Europe was built, shielded by Germany to the East. But was it quite certain that Germany would prevail? It seemed to him that after each victory, the conquering hero performed a little pirouette, like an acrobat completing a tour de force, acknowledging the applause, and moving on to even greater feats. But now the performer seemed to be getting short of breath. He was bathed in sweat during his turn, and at the end of it, as he wiped his brow, you could see his knees were shaking. Doubts filtered insidiously into Joseph's mind. There were, of course, fixed rules to hold on to: follow the orders, apply the principles. But in practice, it was not always as easy as that. Take, for example, his own sphere. Joseph remembered the turnips in brine.

In ordinary times, you would have to be certifiably mad to dream up the grotesque idea of taking a sturdy vegetable like this, one which required no special treatment for its preservation in good condition from one harvest to the next, and pickle it. But this was not the scheme of a madman. Although all fresh vegetables were sold at a fixed price, processed foods were not subject to official controls, and could be sold for exorbitant sums. For this reason, in March 1942, retailers preferred to sell turnips in brine rather than in their natural state. A shopkeeper in town had ordered a shipment of half a dozen barrels of this novel delicacy, from Algeria. Unfortunately, his customers proved to be decidedly unenthusiastic about this overpriced, unappetising fare, and the turnips began to go off. Rather than write off the loss, the shopkeeper chose to take the supplier of the goods to court. It seemed to Joseph that the Rationing Department should have had the means to force the merchant to put the turnips on sale at a reasonable price, rather than let them spoil. At the moment, everyone was short of vegetables! But this merchant was an influential member of the Veterans'

Legion, and he had already had enough trouble during the Republic. By now, the turnips were reduced to a stinking mush, and the salt, an inadequate preservative, had begun to eat into the barrels themselves.

Joseph left the main road and took the lane to La Barbarie. Mme Hermelin had been promised a dozen eggs by Delphine Legras, and her son was under strict instructions to pick them up on his way back from Francheville.

Outside Les Mottes, Joseph became aware of the acrid smell of roasted grain. The kitchen door was wide open, and he could see Noémi shaking a smoking pan. She was obviously making coffee from rye. This modern alchemy was strictly forbidden by the rationing authorities, and Joseph even knew the number of the relevant decree. But nobody really believed this prohibition was observed in the farming communities. Had not Mme Hermelin herself served coffee made from roasted barley at breakfast that very morning?

With a shrug, Joseph continued on his way. Behind the house, Elie Sobrevin was on the threshing floor, brandishing a flail. He acknowledged Joseph and continued his work without a break. He was threshing wheat. Now all the wheat from Les Mottes was supposed to have gone through the mechanical thresher the previous week. Elie Sobrevin was certainly not the only farmer to keep back a few sacks in order to thresh them in secret. That too was strictly forbidden. But Joseph was on leave, not on duty.

Deep in thought about the lack of discipline and the selfishness of the peasant farmers, Joseph took a footpath through the pine woods and came out in front of the first house at La Barbarie. A distant noise floated to his ears, which he instantly recognised as the distinctive sound of a butter churn. So Delphine Legras was making butter, was she? In spite of the fact that farms supplying milk to the rationing authorities were expressly forbidden to make butter for themselves!

Joseph rapped on the door. The noise stopped, and Delphine's dishevelled head appeared in the doorway. Seeing Joseph, her eyes widened in fright. She came out and shut the door carefully behind her. Once she had found out what brought Mme Hermelin's son to her house, she relaxed somewhat, disappeared into the barn, and re-emerged with a little basket and a handful of straw. A moment later, the eggs were bedded safely into Joseph's bag.

'Your mother can pay me later,' she said when Joseph offered payment. He thus remained unaware that yet another regulation was being flouted, this time on the price of eggs. Mme Hermelin might be tight with her money, but she certainly paid more than the official rate.

Continuing on his way, Joseph went past old Crouzet's garden. A large square was devoted to plants with very recognisable leaves. Tobacco. Tobacco planted in defiance of the strictest prohibition. Sixty plants at the very least. Almost all the farmers in Saint-Boniface did the same.

'Chick, chick, chick!' Félicie Latière, carrying an old saucepan, was feeding her hens. She was clearly scattering grains of wheat for them. Had all these peasants got up a plot to show him their contempt for the law of the land?

As he passed Laffont's house, he saw the Francheville butcher emerge, the one who usually supplied Les Tilleuls. He jumped on the bicycle he had left at the gate and pedalled rapidly off, down towards the town. There was no doubt about it: the butcher had been talking to the farmer about slaughtering a pig for the black market.

The black market, that was the real enemy. In a field behind Seignos' barn, three piglets were playing in the grass. Unless he supplied them to the rationing authorities, the owner of La Serre was only allowed to fatten one each year. But nobody in the village, or even in the whole *département*, supplied pigs to rationing. Pig farming was dead! On the markets, you only saw young pigs, whose price was not fixed, and which therefore sold at five times the price per kilo, compared with a fattened pig. Under these rules, you would be crazy to fatten a pig, given the large quantities of potatoes, cabbages and bran required.

Yes, it was a vicious circle. The more you fix the price of goods, the rarer they become. The economic machine of the National Revolution could only operate with the active support of its citizens, and they would have to be prepared to make sacrifices. In principle, it was not impossible. No revolution takes place without citizens committing themselves to actions which are apparently not in their immediate interests. They turn themselves into cannon fodder, or renounce their privileges, like those idiots on the night of 4th of August. But Joseph knew of nobody who had given up any of his rights to further the National Revolution.

He adjusted his haversack and continued on his way. This took him past the farm at Les Chirolles. A delicious smell of fresh bread reached his nostrils. Old Chirolles was baking. In this period before the harvests, breadmaking at home was temporarily forbidden throughout the *département*. 'White bread on the farm, black despair in the town!' cried the radio and the newspapers. Obviously the country people didn't care about that any more than they did about all the rest.

Joseph chose a shortcut which took him past Vautier's house. Stuck on top of a pile of waste and rubbish of all descriptions was a banner whose colours had washed out in the rain, but where you could still make out 'Saint-Boniface 1937. Work, Family, Fatherland!' No doubt a pennant belonging to the local section of the Croix de Feu, as its slogan indicated – a slogan subsequently adopted by the National Revolution. At the time, Vautier, a sworn enemy of the Popular Front, was a committed member of the Croix de Feu. Nowadays he was only a half-hearted warrior.

Joseph sighed. Before Vichy, everyone had thought the National Revolution was a cracking idea!

III

Mme Hermelin had a surprise in store for M. Rosenfeld: she had invited her minister son, Jérémie, to his wedding. But her tenant, for his part, had one in store for her: he had asked the Abbé Paroli, a valuable contact he had courted in town, to spend a few days in Saint-Boniface.

The chestnut-lined track leading to Les Tilleuls from the main road was unsuitable for motor vehicles, and when the Abbé Paroli got out of his car at the junction to proceed on foot, the first person he met was the minister Jérémie Hermelin, who had arrived at Francheville on the midday train. It was this chance encounter which had caused Mme Hermelin one of the worst upsets of her life. The short distance spent walking together had made firm friends of the two clergymen. As firm, at least, as is possible between representatives of rival ecclesiastical establishments.

Clearly the minister and the Abbé were unaware that in addition to this rivalry of a general nature, there was another, rather more personal, issue which was to divide them during their short stay at Saint-Boniface. To which of them would fall the privilege of ensuring the eternal salvation of Frank Rosenfeld's vacillating soul? Every time she wrote to her son, Mme Hermelin had assured him that thanks to the influence she had gained over her tenant, his conversion was virtually a *fait accompli*, and required only the supreme blessing which, in her opinion, should be delivered on the occasion of his marriage.

Mlle Sten was already a Protestant, so after the ceremony in the Mairie, the couple could be united before God in accordance with the doctrines of the Reformed Church. But the Abbé Paroli, for his part, had reason to expect he would soon welcome M. Rosenfeld to his own flock, and he even entertained secret hopes of attracting his fiancée to the fold too.

The prospective novice himself was somewhat perturbed by this simultaneous attack on two fronts. For M. Rosenfeld had not yet made up his mind how best to save his soul.

However, for some time he had been inclined to think that he would find a safe haven, the security he so craved, in the bosom of the Apostolic Roman Church. In France, the protection afforded by the Catholics appeared vastly more reliable than that offered by the Protestants. The latter were only a small, marginal minority, whilst the Catholics were everywhere, from the humblest public servant to the highest offices of state.

International movements, he knew, were of varying hues. He was terrified of the Reds. He had nothing but disdain for those he regarded as Pinks – the ones in exile in London. As for those designated by a yellow star – the Jews – he was well-placed to be of the opinion that they had already drawn quite enough attention to themselves. But he was positively mesmerised by the international movement whose members dressed in black: the priests.

While on the horns of this dilemma, M. Rosenfeld nevertheless felt flattered by the attention it brought him. At a time when any Jew without resources was more impure than an Untouchable in India, two eminent Aryan public figures, a minister and an Abbé, no less, were actually competing for his favour. In all sincerity he would have liked to choose both religions at once, and thus ensure satisfaction all round.

Yet another option had come his way. Chazelas, his neighbour, was a devout member of the Salvation Army. He had already taken him to two Sunday meetings. Captain Chaudeval, their President, had welcomed him with open arms. For a moment Frank Rosenfeld, seeking the most efficient prayer-to-salvation ratio, had been strongly tempted to join. But while General Booth's army was a force to be reckoned with in the Anglo-Saxon world, its influence in France was minimal.

With three religions thus seeking his favour, M. Rosenfeld, on the quiet hillock where Les Tilleuls stood, felt rather like Paris on Mount Ida, required by three goddesses to declare which of them was the fairest.

But words are transient, whereas scriptures endure. In order to enlighten her protégé's soul, Mme Hermelin had opened wide the doors of her bookcase, which contained an honourable number of pious works. Once, finding a fine Bible on his bed-side table, he had shrugged, thinking it was a gift from his fiancée, Mlle Sten. In fact, it was a gesture from the lady whose ambition was to be his sponsor in the Church. That day, when none of her tenants was about, she had entered his rooms through the French window. It wasn't the first time, either. But on this occasion she had not contented herself with inspecting his wardrobe and his food-safe – where on earth did he get those goat's cheeses? – but had also daintily placed a copy of the Holy Scriptures beside his bed.

The Abbé Paroli was also an experienced practitioner of religious propaganda. He had sent M. Rosenfeld a number of works he deemed appropriate, including a little book bearing the title: *Beautiful Conversions*. The former architect had read it with interest. The conversion of Henri IV in particular had given him food for thought, and convinced him that there was always something to be gained by playing for time.

So when the day of his marriage came, Frank Rosenfeld was still undecided. The ceremony took place in the Mairie on the day following the arrival of the two clergymen, and in strict privacy, according to the wishes of the bride. Apart from M. le Maire, M. Longeaud, and the betrothed, the only people present were M. Hermelin, as witness for Mlle Sten, and Ferdinand Gideaux, a wealthy farmer from Saint-Boniface and President of the local section of the Veterans' Legion, as witness for M. Rosenfeld. For even in the strictest privacy, the former architect liked to associate with influential people.

No religious ceremony took place, however; whether Catholic, Protestant, Salvationist, or even – in spite of Bloch's straight-faced suggestion the previous evening – Jewish. Bloch had offered to scour Francheville to get together a *minyan* – that is, a group of ten male Jewish witnesses – and even to rig up the traditional canopy, using an old blanket of Mme Hermelin's; thus fulfilling the two requirements for the ritual to be recognised under Mosaic Law. Bloch, who appeared to be very keen on his little scheme, had even gone as far as offering to perform the function of Rabbi. When Rosenfeld brusquely rejected the whole idea out of hand, Bernard Bloch seemed inconsolable.

* * *

This solemn day, which she had been looking forward to for weeks, brought Mme Hermelin only distress and disappointment. First, there was the arrival of the Abbé Paroli. Never before had Mme Hermelin allowed a cassock under her roof. But as Jérémie, the minister, had insisted that the Abbé should be accommodated not in the annexe where M. Rosenfeld was staying, but in one of the more comfortable guest rooms in the main house, she had been obliged to put up with the man in black. Worse, she could not stop him eating at her table, which included partaking of the magnificent wedding cake she had made, sparing neither eggs nor sugar, and which in her mind was also intended to celebrate a happy conversion. But of conversion there was no mention. As far as Mme Hermelin was concerned, it was all the doing of this accursed Abbé, who had come to carry out a diabolical task: the seduction of a man's soul.

Had the Abbé turned out to be the very devil himself, Mme Hermelin would scarcely have been surprised. Especially since M. Rosenfeld had told her that Paroli was the leader not just of a parish, like the lowly Abbé Mignart, but also of a number of highly important missions. What could these be? Satanic missions, without a doubt. Indeed, there was something diabolical in the insidious way he proclaimed the virtues of camping, of athletics, and even, God forbid, of dancing.

'Quite apart from sport,' said the Abbé, whose modernist tendencies made Mme Hermelin's flesh creep, 'there's another form of exercise which we should encourage amongst the young. I'm talking about dancing.'

'Really?' responded Mme Hermelin, pursing her lips.

'Can there be any more appropriate way to let off steam, calm the senses, and prevent young people from misdirecting their energy?' continued the Abbé. 'Of course, I'm not advocating the gyrations of Isadora Duncan, and certainly not the *Biguine* or the *Lambeth Walk*, or any of those horrors which spring from the basest forms of sensuality.'

'And that's an understatement,' said Mme Hermelin poisonously.

'I am referring,' the priest resumed, 'to the harmless traditional dances which are performed without men and women touching each other. That's the important point! The *Bourrée* in the Auvergne, for example. Or the *Branle*. Our new régime, which has done so much to revive fine local traditions, should restore these dances to their rightful place! What comfort it would give us to see our village squares, on a Sunday, filled with young and old, parents and children, engaging in such healthy, aesthetic pursuits!'

The Abbé was as persuasive as he was clever. But it would take more than that to convince Mme Hermelin. Despite all his provisos, despite all the subtlety of his argument, the fact remained that this fisher of souls was singing the praises of dance, which was the work of the devil. Mme Hermelin had known immediately. And it was brought home to her in the clearest possible fashion when, after lunch, emotionally exhausted, she retired to the empty dining room, where she liked to take her siesta stretched out on a chaise longue. She had a strange, incoherent dream. She was in the Pharmacie de la Croix Blanche, asking M. Chameix for a bottle of the Abbé Soury's Elixir of Youth. As she turned it in her hand, the label came to life, the face winked at her and turned into that of the Abbé Paroli, who met her gaze with his piercing grey eyes, then whisked her away into a primitive dance, a *Branle* maybe, or more likely the *Biguine*, as the two of them were definitely obliged to enter into very close contact in order to perform its complicated figures.

Suddenly, there was a terrific crash of broken glass. Whirling about while her cassocked partner held her tightly around the waist, Mme Hermelin had swept all the bottles of Elixir off the shelves. She woke with a start, to find M. Hermelin standing before her, ruefully gazing at the shattered remains of an imitation crystal bowl which he had been putting away in the sideboard after finishing the washing up. Once she had got over the shock and severely reprimanded her husband, Mme Hermelin remembered her dream and trembled in horror. The fact that, far from feeling revulsion for her dancing partner, she had willingly submitted to his embrace, was proof, were any needed, of the diabolical nature of the Abbé's propaganda.

The door of his hotel room locked with a double turn, Moïse Kleinhandler is sitting *shivah*. He is not on a low stool, bare-foot, in accordance with the customs of his religion; but mentally he is observing the ritual required following a family bereavement.

He is mourning the deaths of his father, his mother, his two sons and his daughter. On the table, amongst several days' worth of left-over food and greasy wrappers, beside a chess-board with its pieces knocked over, there still lies a postcard from Poland, forwarded from Paris.

'Your parents and your children have died in hospital of a contagious disease. Condolences. Benjamin.'

The sender's name and address are clearly fictitious. But one thing is obvious: it must come from a friend or a family member who knew Kleinhandler's address in Paris.

Tired of pacing the long narrow room where he keeps bumping into the crates and rolls of paper for Pinkas' illicit enterprises, Kleinhandler throws himself onto an unmade bed. The sheets, which haven't been changed for weeks, smell of sweat, and from splits in the quilt woollen entrails spill out, which have tangled with a stray sock in the bedding. In a fit of exasperation, Kleinhandler grabs the sock and flings it onto the lid of the commode. He stretches out on his back and gazes at the ceiling where the ever-patient spiders, untroubled by any broom, apply themselves to spinning their webs.

* * *

In 1931, Kleinhandler had taken advantage of the special arrangements put in place for the Colonial Exhibition, to obtain a visa for France. As an involuntary tourist, instead of going to see the replica of the Angkor Temple, he chose to visit the Carreau du Temple, along with the little synagogues in that part of the city. This was not to pray to God, but in the hope of making some useful contacts. And indeed, just a few days later this textile worker from Lodz, long unemployed, found a job in a knitwear factory just by the rue des Rosiers. His employer, another Polish Jew, had come to Paris in 1925 with a tourist visa, when the decorative arts exhibition was on.

His boss was not too fussy about work permits, but unfortunately the police were. It took them fourteen months to discover that Kleinhandler was working without papers. Once they found out, his accommodating employer got away with a fine, whereas Kleinhandler was given to understand he must leave France forthwith.

But this undesirable alien had not entirely wasted his fourteen months in Paris. He had managed to earn a few thousand francs, and although unversed in the niceties of the French language, he had made up for it by gaining some useful experience. He knew that the variously coloured edicts which the Préfecture de Police rained down on people like him were only definitive and irrevocable for those poor beggars who had been caught before they had a chance to put some savings together. By paying a thousand francs to a *macher*, an intermediary with contacts at the Préfecture, he got the order suspended for long enough to let him find a job with one of his former boss's competitors, and despite his terror that they might catch him a second time, he arranged for his wife and his son Maurice, aged two, to come from Poland to join him. A year later, in return for a further payment, even more substantial this time, the *macher* got him an official craftsman's permit.

Then came the years of plenty. Lying on the damp sheets and the disembowelled quilt, recalling those splendid times, he does not recognise the man he was then. He would do anything to earn his *parnose*, his daily bread – or meat, in the prosperous times! It was a ceaseless, frantic, clawing struggle. He had left his boss, set up his own workshop, bought machines on credit, taken on as workers two Polish Jews (of which the second had just arrived thanks to Expo-37), built up a customer base and added two new Kleinhandlers to his family. Admittedly, there was still a whiff of misery hovering over all this magnificence. The kids, naked from the waist down, would be screaming in the room next to the workshop because their mother, who spent her days mending knitwear that came off the machines faulty, didn't have time for them; their apartment was hardly less covered in wool dust and bits of thread than the workshop itself; they ate what they could, when they could, between receiving the orders and making the deliveries; and it was a feverish, soul-destroying life. Ah! The good old days! With the endless games of chess on Sunday, in the gloomy back room of a café in the Faubourg du Temple, which made Kleinhandler forget dinner time and earned him tears and recriminations from his wife.

All that was a period of happiness, and the domestic rows were an integral part of it. Then, one day, everything fell apart. Sarah Kleinhandler, her eyes worn out by a lifetime of picking up stitches, was out at the market when she was knocked down by a truck. She died two hours later at the Hôtel-Dieu. What to do with the three children, two of them infants? The simplest solution was to send them back to their grandmother in Poland. Helped by a neighbour, Kleinhandler filled two battered suitcases with their Uniprix toys and other belongings, bundled the whole lot up together, kids as well as luggage, with lavish use of straps and safety pins, and had himself driven to the Gare du Nord.

When he sent his children to Poland, he was condemning them to death. Even in the first year of the war he'd had a premonition of this. Now, his crime has been perpetrated. His children died in hospital of a contagious disease. Contagious, or hereditary?

Moïse Kleinhandler gives himself a shake, gets up, and starts to pace the room again. He can't breathe. Even though the window is open, the permanently sunless room smells putrid. Everything in it stinks.

Suddenly choking with nausea, he puts on his jacket and shoes and goes out. What does it matter whether he sits *shivah* by walking up and down in his room or pacing the streets of Francheville? In any case Kleinhandler has not practised his religion for twenty-five years. But now he finds himself mechanically muttering the words of the *Kaddish*, a prayer the eldest son must recite for his father's soul to rest in peace, which has come back to him from the depths of his memory. Stupid, but he can't help it. *Yit'gadal v'yit'kadash sh'mei raba...* How ridiculous he must look, tears streaming down his face despite himself. He seems to be walking through a fog, with street children laughing and pointing at him. Well let them laugh, the little *shkutzim*, and all the *goyim* too for that matter! They should try being Jews! That would teach them!

Yit'gadal v'yit'kadash sh'mei raba... the words spring unbidden to his lips. Odd that he has not forgotten this prayer. When he, Moïse Kleinhandler, is no longer, there will be nobody to say *Kaddish*. His two sons have died in hospital, victims of an epidemic.

He passes the Pharmacie Moderne, crowded as always after the market. He sees his face reflected in the narrow strips of mirror glass around the window. What were those brats laughing at just now? His hairy sticking-out ears? The three-day stubble smudging his cheeks? The flies of his threadbare trousers gape open, and his jacket, frayed at the cuffs and spattered with grease stains, has a big tear beneath the sleeve where the lining pokes through. There's dandruff on his collar and cigarette ash on his lapels. But so what? Are not ashes and torn garments signs of mourning?

He comes upon a bench, its back turned to the Hôtel Farémido, under the plane trees which line the avenue de la Gare. Kleinhandler suddenly feels overcome by weariness. He no longer has the strength to walk, let alone to continue the struggle. Anyway, how could he continue? Armed with what? There isn't much choice. When he'd had to renew his foreign resident's permit in Marseilles, they had taken away his knit-wear craftsman's card, replaced it with an unemployed person's card, and entered 'of no profession'. No chance of getting a job with that. The last resort was the black market. They say that the laws are designed to force people like Kleinhandler into illicit trade. But he's not a natural. Two out of three of his deals fall through. A right *schlimmazl*, that's what he is now. In the black market, you have to be able to brazen it out, like Pinkas; it's a job for the cunning ones. So he prefers to run errands in return for tips. From time to time, Pinkas slips him a ten or twenty franc note to get suppositories from the chemists', or butter from his regular suppliers in the remote hill-farms. This supplements the meagre income he gets at irregular intervals from the Jewish Union, which is his main source of funds. Anyway, why continue the struggle? Nothing is worth it any more... except maybe chess. Chess! What a marvellous game! At the chess board, Kleinhandler is another man altogether. Reality fades away entirely, and he himself becomes powerful, feared, magnificent... He feels a tide of admiration rising towards him. He captures queens, destroys castles, displaces bishops, is victorious in battle. When playing chess, to his own amazement, he is sometimes overcome by great waves of daring, insolence and disdain, as he taunts and insults his opponents. Yet they are the very same men he has to kowtow to in real life. Chess, for him, represents poetry, dreams, escape...

It's three years since he left his children. Maurice was already a big lad when he was sent back to Poland. He wasn't a particularly good-looking child. His ears were too big and stuck out like his father's, his nose was a bit hooked, and he was covered in freckles – a redhead, too, like his mother, poor woman. Not that he was stupid, far from it. At seven, he could see a chess game right through to the end. And what a rascal he was! A *yidische kepele*! A good little Jewish head on him! For months on end, Kleinhandler felt his chest tighten when he thought the Germans might have recruited his little Maurice for the SS. They say that's why they pick up Jewish children. Or maybe to turn him into a Maurice Scharf, who was made to accuse his father of a ritualistic crime. All things considered, maybe it was better that he died in hospital. As for the other two, Kleinhandler hardly knew them. What did that really mean, 'in hospital'? Maybe they did die of a contagious disease. Typhoid fever, dysentery, typhus? But the expression could signify a ghetto, or a concentration camp... Pinkas assures him that according to London, the Germans are exterminating the Jews, adults and children. But surely that's propaganda. You don't kill children, even Jewish children. Maurice, Aron and Rachel must have died in some accident, along with their grandparents. A bomb, most likely. But one thing is for sure: his little Maurice will never be a chess master.

Kleinhandler hears voices behind him in the garden of the Hôtel Farémido. Three people are taking tea round a wicker table. Turning, Kleinhandler can see them through the sparse hedge. He knows two of the clients: M and Mme Wolff, who are Jews from Alsace. As for the grey-suited man with them, he's never seen him before. The Wolffs are looked up to in Francheville. Money, jewellery, fine clothes. Before the war, they too were in the knitwear business. But Kleinhandler was in luxury knitwear, and they were in ready-to-wear. A more profitable business.

'Please don't worry yourself, Madame,' said the man in the grey suit, 'Your family has been French for generations, so nobody's going to confuse you with these aliens the country cannot absorb.'

M. Wolff sounded pained. 'Unfortunately,' he said, 'we do suffer from their presence. We're the ones who have to pay the price for their unscrupulousness, their bad manners, and their aggressive business practices.'

'Well in any case, I am officially informed that they alone are the object of the measures being discussed at the Prefecture.'

A big truck rattles out of the Garage de la Gare next door to the hotel. The conversation behind the hedge continues, but Kleinhandler can no longer hear. New measures being talked about? So what? For months now, there have been new measures every week. Prohibited to be resident in the cities… Prohibited to travel to any departments other than those designated to receive you…Prohibited to undertake any employment not mentioned on your identity card… No end to it, if you had to worry about all these prohibitions. Kleinhandler would never have been able to stay in France if he had played by the book all those years ago.

Clearly none of that bothers M. Wolff. Even if he is a fellow Jew. Being a fellow Jew doesn't make him a brother. A brother, him? This well-fed, well-turned-out gentleman, with his signet ring and his French affectations? M. Wolff isn't a Jew, he's an Israelite. Kleinhandler, for his part, is sure he is not M. Wolff's brother. At the most he might be a distant cousin, a poor relative. Even if he were to meet him at the synagogue, intoning the same prayer… but what a ridiculous idea. In Paris, M. Wolff doubtless worships at the fine synagogue on the rue de la Victoire, whereas he, Kleinhandler, would attend some evil-smelling *schoule* in the rue des Rosiers. But it's been years since Kleinhandler last set foot in a place of worship.

The truck has disappeared down the road to Saint-Paul, and he can hear the voices behind the hedge again.

'The gendarmes are going to pick them all up tomorrow morning and send them home. But as I said, you don't need to worry. Your home is in France.'

It was all said in a very even tone, like a conversation between men of the world, and the words themselves had an everyday banality. On his bench, the little unshaven fellow has remained motionless. But behind his furrowed brow, the thoughts and the words clash and tumble like pieces in some diabolical game of chess. The gendarmes... being picked up... the great round-up... the Last Judgement...

The contagious disease has reached Francheville.

Behind the hedge, the three voices continue to hum in his ears, changing in register, pitch and intensity. For Kleinhandler it is now no more than a meaningless background noise of which he is barely aware, like the pianist at the cinema.

'Send them all home!' What a joke! Nobody believes that, not even the grey-suited stranger. Once the machine has claimed you, it's all over. You're thrown into one of the Jewish camps where, even if you don't die straight away, you end up catching some fatal illness. A new Egypt, where you're cudgelled into building pyramids. Except the pyramids are in the salt mines or the rotting marshes. And this time, no Moses. Suddenly, through the mists of time, the Prophet's words surface in Kleinhandler's memory.

'Prepare yourselves to flee, ye children of Benjamin, away from the midst of Jerusalem, for evil looketh forth from the north, and a great destruction.'

His inner voice falters, leaving the psalm unfinished. Kleinhandler can't remember the rest. He was never very good at Bible Studies. He tries to force his memory, but from its scattered remnants he only manages to dredge up a lament, a refrain from his long-ago childhood in Poland: *Ay veh, Yiden, Ay veh!*

Still on the bench! What is he thinking of? Quick, quick! The pogrom is tomorrow! And yet, no. The pogrom will not take place. He, Kleinhandler, appointed by fate, will not allow it to happen.

* * *

At two o'clock in the morning, his flat feet killing him, his shirt soaked with sweat, his empty stomach rumbling, and with a bitter taste in his mouth, he gets back to his hotel room, which smells of rotting matter and lice. But he is happy. Eternal peace is within him. He has warned all the Jews around of the danger facing them, and begged them to take flight. He has seen Pinkas, Verès, Bloch and three other families, one of them at Manvin, twelve kilometres away in the hills. Breathlessly, he told them the news, asked if there were other Jews nearby, and without even sitting down to rest, left to pursue his mission as harbinger of doom. He had no time to notice that most of them didn't believe him. The Ehrlichs, at Manvin, had almost thrown him out. 'Some people take pleasure in frightening people,' says the woman, as soon as he has turned to go.

But Kleinhandler didn't care. Nothing could stop him from doing his duty. Nothing, that is, apart from the gendarmes. All the way, he was gripped with fear at the thought that Auzance, or one of his colleagues, could ambush him at a turning and demand to know where he was heading in such haste.

Suddenly he realises what a mess his room is in. He must clear it up. Pick up the litter. Empty the commode, stagnant since yesterday evening. Make the bed, pack his belongings. He knows they won't be prepared to wait for him. Best remove the spiders' webs too. When you go, you have to leave the place clean. How simple it all is! Why bother to go on living when there is no hope left? Salvation is for others. He himself is only just about good enough to be the *kapore*, to sacrifice himself in order to redeem the Jews of Saint-Boniface.

At about seven in the morning, when the adjutant from the Gendarmerie, followed by a young trainee, comes to knock at the door of the Hôtel Michel and goes up to room number seven to pick up the Jew, he finds Kleinhandler a little pale, his eyes puffy from lack of sleep, but perfectly calm. Placed on a chair is a bundle containing some clothing and a chess set.

For the first time in his life, Kleinhandler isn't afraid of the gendarmes.

* * *

The same morning, at the end of M. Rosenfeld's wedding night, two uniformed men on bicycles arrived at Les Tilleuls. The former architect was awoken by a heavy knock on the door and a ringing call, 'Open up, in the name of the law!' Running to the door in his nightshirt, he found himself face to face with Auzance, accompanied by a young colleague. Rosenfeld rubbed his eyes. Secure in the immunity that his friendship with Auzance conferred on him, he had only smiled distractedly last night when Bloch slipped him a warning note. The latter, sent by Kleinhandler, had advised him to make himself scarce for a few days while the storm passed. That's what Bloch was going to do. Nelchet had offered him an old shack deep in the forest.

'Maybe you're right to take cover,' Rosenfeld had told him. 'Myself, I have nothing to fear.'

His friend Auzance turned out to be in strictly official mode. He was under orders to conduct the Jew Rosenfeld, Frank, to Francheville, where a vehicle was waiting to take him, along with other Jews, to the concentration camp at Vénissieux. M. Rosenfeld was allowed neither the time nor the opportunity to proffer hospitality or to exercise his diplomatic skills.

In the same sombre conveyance were four other foreign Jews who had been picked up locally; those who had not heeded Kleinhandler's warning. Neither Verès nor Bloch were yet included in the category of Jews destined for deportation, as they both had children who were entitled to French nationality. Pinkas should have been taken, but at the Prefecture someone had forgotten to put him on the list. On the other hand, the hapless Muller, the hospital ship of the Café de la Marine, even though he was not a Jew and could prove it, was taken on board despite his vehement protestations.

V

Three days after leaving Nelchet's shed, where he had remained hidden during the round-up, Bernard came home from hoeing his potatoes to find two letters waiting for him, forwarded from his previous address in Cassis. One envelope was marked 'Bouches-du-Rhône Prefecture'. The other read 'Quaker Charities, Marseille'. Bloch, who had a keen sense of protocol, opened the letter from the Prefecture first.

It was a circular, addressed to him. It required him, in severe administrative tones, to report 'forthwith' to collect the exit visa which had been granted him.

Bernard Bloch burst out laughing. He had applied for this visa six months ago, when he still hoped to be able to leave for Haiti. Now that the bureaucrats in Vichy had finally decided to approve it, it was of no use to him.

The letter from the Quakers informed him that two suitcases of personal belongings, sent by friends in Paris via the good offices of the Quakers in the capital, had reached Marseille. The addressee was requested to check the contents and take delivery of them.

'Drat!' cried Bloch. 'I have to go and get them, and I wouldn't put it past those idiots at the Gendarmerie to refuse me a pass, just because I'm assigned to residence here.'

'But look,' said Renée, 'you're summoned forthwith to the Prefecture at Marseille. What more do you need? For all they know at the Gendarmerie, we're still leaving for Haiti!'

Bloch went down to Francheville at ten the next morning, fully prepared to catch the train to Marseille in the event the Gendarmerie issued his pass with immediate effect. Approaching the drinking trough exactly halfway between Saint-Boniface and Francheville, he saw a woman sitting on the bank at the side of the road, with her back to him. From her shawl he could tell it was Amélie Martin, the teacher from the convent, whom he had seen a few times in the village. He had always thought her a little strange, and she had been behaving even more oddly of late.

She must have heard his footsteps, for she turned round suddenly and sat up. Greeting her, Bloch was struck by her expression. Her gaze was blank, and the dark circles under her eyes made her look ill. Bloch would not have been able to explain why, but he felt sorry for this lonely woman. In some inexplicable way, she reminded him of Kleinhandler.

In the Gendarmerie, Bloch explained his request to the Sergeant, who stared at him in incredulity and attempted to dismiss him on the basis that any foreigner wishing to travel to the Bouches-du-Rhône department had first to obtain permission from the Prefecture of that department. But on seeing the document which unequivocally required Bloch's presence in the Bouches-du-Rhône, and 'forthwith' at that, he scratched his head, went to consult his superior in the adjoining office, returned, rummaged in a cupboard, produced a pink form, and declared to Bloch, in the tone of a good fairy granting a wish to someone particularly favoured, 'You may have an 8C, a pass for exceptional circumstances. Come back at three o'clock.'

The Café de la Marine, which had suffered the full force of the round-up, was almost deserted. No one knew what had happened to Rosenfeld, to Muller, or to Kleinhandler. By the window, Daniel Cahen was reading a newspaper, a glass of beer beside him; his wife must have been in a bad mood that morning. Alone and despondent, as if widowed, Safranek gazed absently around, a poetry anthology open in front of him. If only he could have played one more game of chess with the little Jew! He could have called him what he pleased – a *truckster* or a *bedbag* – he would have submitted to it with pleasure!

It depressed Bloch to see such devastation in the ship cemetery. He spoke briefly to Safranek, went out to buy some Swiss newspapers for the journey, and set off towards the Hôtel Panorama.

Although it was only 11.30, a number of people were already seated in the restaurant, waiting for lunch. On some of the tables, creased napkins indicated the places reserved for residents. Bloch carefully chose a table which, judging from the pristine tablecloth and the vase of flowers, appeared to be free. He took a seat, opened his copy of the Journal de Genève, placed the other papers on the windowsill, and addressed himself to René Payot's weekly commentary on international affairs.

Suddenly, there appeared before him a stocky man with a heavily freckled face, a great mop of red hair, and a white napkin draped over his arm. It was the *patron* of the hotel.

'Excuse me, sir,' said Sarzier, politely but firmly, 'this table is reserved.'

Bloch was about to get up, when another man appeared

behind the proprietor. Aged about forty, he was tall, poised, and very elegantly dressed. He was freshly shaven and lightly powdered. His appearance and his gestures all exuded distinction.

'Don't worry, Sarzier,' he said, 'there's no need to trouble the gentleman. The table is big enough for two.'

He spoke good French, with a slight foreign accent.

'As you wish,' said Sarzier, obsequiously. 'Only I didn't want you to be inconvenienced.'

The hotelier retreated, bowing. 'How about that? Lunch with a prince!' thought Bloch, intrigued.

Sarzier, still over-attentive, bustled back with an apéritif for his distinguished client, who then turned towards Bloch.

'May I have a look at your newspaper?' he asked, gesturing towards the pile on the windowsill.

'My pleasure,' said Bloch, handing one to his companion.

The latter flicked absently through the headlines, then quickly immersed himself in the financial reports on the back page. Bloch, behind his own paper, did not miss a single movement. 'Must be a banker,' he thought. 'Why else would he be reading the Zurich stock exchange figures?'

The banker quickly wrote down a few figures, handed the paper back to Bloch with a friendly smile, and sipped his glass of port. When Sarzier reappeared with the wine list, he asked him for the train timetables.

'At your service, Monsieur Beer,' said Sarzier, turning with a pirouette.

A moment later, M. Beer's wish was granted. The manner in which he began to consult the Chaix timetable betrayed an intimate knowledge of this somewhat esoteric work. 'Must be a great traveller too, this banker,' concluded Bloch.

M. Beer appeared to be interested only in long-distance trains, especially connections to the Spanish border. He turned to the international section in order to check something.

'Lucky chap!' thought Bloch. 'He's going to Spain, and then he can get out of Europe.'

The stranger was about to summon Sarzier to give him the Chaix back, but Bloch stopped him. 'Do you mind if I have a look? I'm leaving for Marseille this afternoon.'

When he closed the book in his turn, he was surprised to be addressed by his companion.

'So you're leaving for Marseille?'

Thus began a conversation whose consequences were to change the course of Bloch's life. Within the space of a few minutes, the stranger knew everything about the vehicle dismantler's return to nature – which he congratulated him upon – and the reason for his trip to Marseille. For his part, Bloch had the satisfaction of confirming his hypothesis about his companion's line of business. M. Beer, originally from Czechoslovakia, was indeed a banker, and was now planning to leave Europe for a South American republic. He was in Francheville awaiting the date of his ship's departure.

'Since everything is ready and I've got all my visas,' he added, 'I was thinking of going directly to the Spanish border from Francheville, instead of travelling via Marseille again, as I hate the place. But unfortunately, HICEM, the organisation I have asked to take care of the arrangements, tell me that the ticket can only be picked up at their offices, by me or by my representative. I've just telephoned them to ask them to send it by post, but they say they can't. What bureaucracy!'

Bloch suggested diffidently that maybe he could do the errand, on condition, of course, that his companion found him sufficiently trustworthy.

'Come, come,' said the banker with a smile. 'I can see perfectly well what sort of fellow you are. Since you are kind enough to offer, I am delighted to accept. I will make sure the agency is informed this very afternoon by telephone.'

At this moment the waitress brought Bloch his starter, a meagre salad of cucumbers and tomatoes, while M. Beer was served a plate overflowing with *hors d'oeuvre variés.*

'It would give me great pleasure,' said the banker, 'if you would allow me to take care of this. Mademoiselle,' he went on, 'please tell Monsieur Sarzier that this gentleman is my guest.' And he offered the plate of *hors d'oeuvres* to Bloch.

The meal of which Bloch partook that day, incompatible on several counts with the strictures of the Ministry of Rationing, was certainly the best he had enjoyed since the beginning of the war. So much so, that he made no effort to conceal his astonishment to M. Beer. But the latter pursed his lips.

'Second-rate cuisine,' he said, with the aplomb of a connoisseur. 'It would benefit from less in the way of quantity, and more in the way of care. In the French provinces, restaurants are either very good or frankly mediocre.'

Bloch was inclined to protest, but said nothing. This man must be a regular client at restaurants like the Ritz and the Savoy, through whose doors he, Bernard Bloch, had never penetrated, and so it was entirely natural for him to find mediocre what he, Bloch, found absolutely extraordinary.

'Of course,' the banker went on, 'I should have booked in to the Hôtel Farémido, where the cuisine is quite good, but when I arrived there was no apartment available. And if I went there now, it would hurt poor Sarzier's feelings, because I know he has bent over backwards to satisfy me. Anyway...' and shrugging in resignation, he poured a glass of Burgundy for his companion.

In the course of the meal he let slip a few more confidences.

'I had the choice between North America and South America. The formalities would have been quite easy in the United States, as my family is related to the Morgenthaus. Our office in Prague looked after their interests in Bohemia for two generations. But in the end I decided on a new country.'

Bloch's admiration for his host was growing by leaps and bounds. M. Beer was not just any old banker, he was the patrician head of some venerable Jewish financial institution, belonging to a family like the Rothschilds. He had not been far off the mark in taking him for an aristocrat. What was more, he had an established pedigree in the world of finance.

A young woman with dark hair and slightly almond-shaped eyes, accompanied by a very well-dressed man, had just sat down at the next table.

Although he was highly interested in what the banker was saying, Bloch couldn't help glancing at her for a moment. Where had he seen her before? At Les Tilleuls, dammit! He had passed her once at the front door, and he had seen her later with Fleury! She seemed to be enjoying herself with her escort, at whom she kept smiling rather provocatively.

'Actually,' the banker went on, while coffee was being served, 'I wonder if I could ask you to do me another favour at the same time. Only I wouldn't like to take advantage of your kindness.'

'Not at all,' Bloch protested. 'What is it?'

'Well,' said M. Beer, offering his guest a cigar, 'I still have some cash left in francs, and I need to dispose of it before I leave. Oh, not a large amount, less than a million. The rest of my wealth has already been transferred. But for the trip I would prefer to carry it in dollars. I was thinking of getting an exchange agent to come here for the transaction. But I don't want to send him a letter, because of the censors. I don't deal with him very often, and we don't have an agreed code to write in. If you had time in Marseille, perhaps you could take him my card and explain. He knows me by my reputation, I'm sure of that, and I think he would agree to come.'

Bloch assured the banker that he would be delighted to oblige, and upon this M. Beer took two visiting cards from his wallet, one for the travel agency and one for the exchange agent. He scribbled a few words on each of them, slipped them into little envelopes, and handed them to his guest.

With an anxious expression, the restaurant owner came up to the table and asked the banker if he had enjoyed his meal.

'Very much so, thank you,' said Beer affably. 'By the way, Monsieur Sarzier, I see Rio Tinto has fallen three more points on the Zurich stock exchange. I think I forecast that the other day.'

'Indeed you did,' said Sarzier in admiration. 'You obviously know a thing or two!'

'Oh!' said the banker, 'it wasn't hard to forecast, given everything that's happened. And it's just a profession like any other.'

But it was clear from his tone that only the chosen few were privy to the secrets of the gods.

Upon this the banker stood up, shook Bloch's hand, took his leave benevolently of Sarzier, who executed a few bows, and went upstairs to his apartment.

Bloch left the restaurant in his turn. The world had taken on a golden glow, and all his distressing problems seemed easy to resolve. Was this only due to the feeling of euphoria after a good meal? Surely not. There was also his exchange with a member of the élite who, far from being corrupted by money, was made more scrupulous by it. During his childhood as the son of a country coachman, Bloch had felt a sort of admiration mixed with envy for the children of rich families who had their own bedrooms, with fine carpets, mechanical toys and governesses who taught them French. This feeling had still not entirely left him. Those who had benefited from such a childhood easily grew up to be men like M. Beer, with his assured manners and his natural distinction. Bloch felt delighted and flattered to have chanced upon such an encounter.

It was still too early to report to the Gendarmerie. Without thinking, Bloch made his way to the Café de la Marine. It was more or less empty at this time of day, and Bloch only found Jéroboam Pinkas, who had also just come out of hiding, and was somewhat reassured to find that the gendarmes had not even come to look for him. His face twitching, he was writing down a column of figures in his pocketbook. With a little friendly gesture, he invited Bloch to sit at his table.

'I've just heard from M. Safranek that you're going to Marseille,' he said. 'How about doing something to cover your expenses?'

Bloch sat down beside Pinkas and looked at him questioningly.

'You could take something with you,' said Pinkas in a confidential tone. 'A little consignment of the best *savon de Marseille*. They don't make it like this any more. You can easily sell it at a fifty per cent mark-up.'

From his bag he took a piece of fresh soap, still soft, and proudly showed it to Bloch.

'No, thank you,' said Bloch with a smile. 'I promised myself I wouldn't take part in trade. I intend to remain a farmer until the end of the war. But tell me, do you have any news of Kleinhandler and the others?'

'Well,' said Pinkas, 'I hear they're to be taken to Drancy. After that, who knows? But anyway,' he insisted, 'for the soap, do you really mean it? You're passing up a good deal, a certain profit, no risks attached.'

Bloch shook his head, stood up, took his leave of the soap dealer, and left the café. After an hour spent in the company of such an aristocrat of finance as M. Beer, he could only feel sorry for the ridiculous little black marketeer. Nevertheless, Pinkas' proposal had a certain piquancy. Supplying Marseille with *savon de Marseille*! In this topsy-turvy world, even business was done backwards. There were probably crafty devils 'exporting' silk to Lyon, claret to Bordeaux, and who knows, maybe even cigars to Havana.

VI

When Renée Bloch and her son got back to Les Ripailles, with the goat in tow, they found a large yellow envelope slipped under the door. It was addressed in a woman's hand which Renée did not recognise. Inside were two more envelopes, of normal size, each bearing her name in Bernard Bloch's writing. Scribbled in haste in the corner of each was 'Letter no. 1' and 'Letter no. 2. Do not open before the first one!'

Curious, she put aside envelope no. 2 and opened the first. The letter was in Yiddish, the only language Bernard could write more or less correctly. In translation, it read roughly as follows:

Marseille, 18th August 1942

My dearest wife

I have an opportunity to write to you without being intercepted by the censor. I have just met a lady called Mme Prokoff, a refugee from Francheville, who has kindly offered to take this and post it on her return.

I must tell you straight away that this letter contains no good news. Quite the opposite! I curse the moment I decided to go to Marseille. I wish I had broken my leg on the way to the station.

My thoughts are in such a whirl that I hardly know where to begin. You know what it's like when bad luck strikes out of the blue.

I told you in my last letter how I had met M. Beer, the rich banker who asked me to run a couple of errands. I have to remind you of this, so you understand what I'm going to tell you.

I spent the night in Cassis in our old room on the avenue Victor-Hugo, and took the bus for Marseille at six in the morning. Of course it was too early to go to the Quakers, so I went to the Café Noailles, just like we used to, for a hot drink. That's where my troubles started.

About half past eight I saw Jacob Schlesinger come in. You remember him, don't you, he's the man who had the leather business on the rue de la Roquette. I knew him in Poland, and we met him once in Marseille, near the Stock Exchange. He came to sit at my table and started to moan, as usual. 'Aie aie,' he said, 'just listen to my bad luck! My cousin in New York has finally sent our visas, for me and my family!' 'Is that what you call bad luck?' I said. 'A shame I don't have the same bad luck as you!' 'Oh, you don't understand,' he said. 'I've got all the visas, I've reserved the boat ticket, but even so I can't leave. All I have is a gold ingot, and I can't hope to get that through three customs inspections. I have to change it into dollars. But – just my luck – last week there was a big round-up in Marseille, and all the exchange agents have gone to ground. And I'm stuck here with my gold! What bad luck, aie, aie! What bad luck!'

I know what you're going to say. Of course I didn't need to listen to any of Schlesinger's business. I've been a kochleffel, stirring up trouble again, I admit it, and, believe me, I am full of remorse.

'Well,' I said, 'I can put you in touch with a businessman who turns dollars over by the shovelful!' And he is so keen that I take him straight to the Hôtel Splendid, to the broker, a M. Angelotti, whom I was to see on M. Beer's behalf.

This M. Angelotti, a Corsican, turns out very friendly when I show him M. Beer's card, and he says he is ready to help Schlesinger. There's not much haggling, and five minutes later they agree on a deal at an exchange rate which I have to admit is pretty favourable to Schlesinger. I was pleased for him and I even thought that if he had any manners he would invite me to the restaurant on the Cours Belzunce where I heard they serve an excellent stuffed carp. That would have been a change from the disgusting bouillabaisse made with salted sardines they serve up at the station buffet in Marseille. But wait, there's more.

Angelotti counts out the dollars to Schlesinger, who has handed over his gold bar to the Corsican. Then Schlesinger goes to the window to hold the dollars up to the light, and the other weighs the ingot and makes sure it rings true. I don't think they quite trust each other. So as I want the deal concluded to the satisfaction of both parties, I suggest they have the goods inspected by a valuer.

Angelotti agrees immediately. He says he just has to cancel an appointment, and he will be with us. He makes a phone call there and then, just a few words in Corsican, and we set off.

So now we're walking down the Canebière to take the ingot to the valuer, in the Quatre-Chemins district, when suddenly, beside the Eglise des Réformés, two men grab hold of the Corsican and say, 'Police', showing the backs of their lapels. Angelotti protests and tries to fight them off, but the policemen push him into a car, shouting, 'To the police station, for questioning' which doesn't sound too good.

All that takes only a few seconds. Schlesinger, who's been hiding in one of the church entrances, comes out white as a sheet, trembling in fear.

'What a fright!' he groans. 'That was close! Lucky I've still got the dollars on me! Poor M. Angelotti! Now I'm sorry I tricked him out of two thousand francs. He didn't know the rate for the dollar has gone up three points since yesterday evening!'

And he starts to laugh in between his groans. But a quarter

of an hour later, at American Express, he isn't laughing any more. The clerk has told him all the banknotes are forgeries, complete forgeries. Now that is something to wail about, and Schlesinger surpasses himself.

'I'm a lost man,' he keeps saying, tearing his hair out. 'Now we're no better than beggars. What am I going to do in America without a penny, and with three children to feed? I'll never dare to tell my wife the truth!'

I have to say I felt responsible for the whole sorry mess. But Schlesinger was so overcome that he forgot to blame me. I felt really sorry for him, even though I'm used to him complaining. So we both tried to find Angelotti, though without much hope. We found out from an insider at the police station that nobody of that name was taken in this morning. Now, I'm convinced Angelotti is a crook, and he stage-managed his own arrest, to give us the slip. He set it up on the phone, right in front of our eyes, and we fell for it like idiots. I thought I was smart, but I'm certainly not up to the tricks of these Marseille gangsters. The worst of it is, there's no way you can take legal action in such a shady matter involving ingots and dollar notes. It's not exactly kosher. However, there's one silver lining: Angelotti won't be able to take M. Beer for a ride. So that's something!

In any case, don't expect me at Saint-Boniface tomorrow or the day after. I am going to move heaven and earth to find that Corsican bandit. If I don't manage to, I don't know how I'm going to compensate poor Schlesinger. Believe me, it's a funny feeling, contributing to the ruin of a man you have nothing against. And when I think of the reproaches you will heap on me when I get home, I lose what courage I still have.

Your wretched Bernard

Bernard Bloch's second letter read as follows:

Marseille, 19th August 1942

My dearest wife

I have had a fantastic stroke of luck. First of all, I have met Mme Prokoff again, at the Café du Mont Ventoux. She has put off her trip until this evening, and she can take this second letter along with the first. So you can be reassured immediately.

You must think I am crazy to speak of good fortune, after everything you read in my letter no. 1. But in fact this is an extraordinary, unbelievable stroke of luck, so extraordinary that I can hardly believe it even now. I have to feel my pocket every five minutes, and even look in my wallet to check I'm not dreaming: the sixty thousand-franc notes there, not forgeries this time, dispel my doubts. From this morning, I am the owner of three hundred thousand francs, and what's more, an official promise of a visa. If all goes well, we can soon leave for South America! What do you say to that, eh?

But I have to tell you everything in the right order. I spent a dreadful night in Cassis, blaming myself for this business with the forged dollars. I got up at five o'clock to catch the bus to Marseille, because I had phoned yesterday to make an appointment for M. Beer's boat ticket. So at nine o'clock I went to the HICEM office in rue Paradis. It wasn't as crowded with emigrants as last year, but even so there were about forty people in the hall. After a quarter of an hour, the official called out 'Monsieur Bloch!' And as two of us stood up – these days, you meet Blochs in all the emigration offices – he added 'Monsieur Bloch from Cassis'. Then this chap jumps up from his seat and rushes towards me, very agitated. He says he has to speak to me, and he'll wait for me to come back out. I wondered what he could possibly want, as I had certainly never seen him before.

M. Beer's business only took a few minutes. The tickets were ready, and as the clerk knew I would be coming, he gave them to me straight away when I showed him M. Beer's business card.

Back in the hall, the man's sitting on a bench waiting for me. He takes me outside, and asks me, mysterious like, if I really am M. Bloch from Cassis. I'm pretty surprised, and I ask him, what's it to him? 'You'll see,' says he. 'But you have to tell me your exact address in Cassis.' 27A, avenue Victor-Hugo, I say. 'Now I understand!' he cries, 'I can explain everything! But to be on the safe side, I have to ask you to give me proof of your identity.' Since I'm paying for the hotel on a daily basis, I show him the receipt the landlord gave me yesterday, and my summons to the Prefecture into the bargain. Now, he's convinced. He looks me in the eye and says, 'Monsieur Bloch, are you expecting money from someone?'

Then I twig. This chap's got money for me. And who could it be from, except Uncle Isidore? One of my seven letters to New York! It got through!

'Yes,' says I. 'From my uncle in New York. It's so long ago, I'd almost given up hope.'

'You're a fine one,' he says, shrugging. 'Do you think it's easy to send money from New York to Marseille these days? But anyway, you're in luck. Your uncle found a way to do it. I have three hundred thousand francs for you.'

I was dumbstruck. I had to ask him to repeat the amount, to be sure I had heard him right. Then he explained how he had come to be my banker. As he had to leave for New York, he had asked a business colleague to send him a list of people who needed to pay money to people in France. He made these payments, obtained receipts, and would be repaid in dollars once he got to America. A clearing system which is *quite common at the moment. This was the last amount he had to pay out, and he had been looking for me in the Cassis-Marseille area for five days, but without this extraordinary coincidence he would never have found me. I have to say the telegram he had got about me was full of mistakes. No forename; incorrect address: 7 rue Victor-Hugo, instead of 27 avenue Victor-Hugo; and so on. Luckily, there was no mistaking the amount of money.*

You kept telling me we would never hear from Uncle Isidore. Well, now we have! How about that then! Davke! Who says the word 'family' has lost its meaning? Only thing is, I don't know which of the Isidores I have to thank.

He wanted to give me the three hundred thousand francs on the spot, in return for a receipt which read, 'Love and kisses to Cécile. Signed: Bernard Bloch.' C's the third letter of the alphabet, meaning three hundred thousand francs. It's obvious when you think about it.

So then he went off, full of beans.

Coming out of the HICEM office my head was spinning, as if I'd had one too many. Not so much because of the money – though I've never had such a fat wallet – but because I could already see us getting out of Europe. It's not good being a Jew in the Old World. Rosenfeld and Kleinhandler and the others being arrested reminded me how much I want to get out.

But I haven't finished yet. I went back to the Café Noailles where I'd arranged to meet Schlesinger. He hadn't arrived, but I ran into José Vagaria. Remember him? The Spanish go-between who used his contacts to help people get away to South America. I told him I'd received a little money from my family, and that I felt like going to see what life was like on the other side of the pond. He told me it was virtually impossible these days, because they weren't issuing visas any more. 'What! No more visas?' I cried. 'In my pocket I have tickets for one of my friends, who has just got a visa for four hundred thousand francs!' Because M. Beer told me how much he had paid for it. Vagaria didn't believe me at first, but when I showed him the tickets to prove it, he turned bright red. He thought the reason he couldn't do deals with the consul who issued M. Beer's visa was that he was incorruptible, when in fact he was simply too expensive. 'Wait here,' he said. 'I'll be back shortly.'

He came back an hour later, even redder than when he left, but pleased as punch. 'I've just been to see the consul,' he said, 'and we've had a little talk. This is a one-off opportunity, I've got you the visa for a song: a hundred thousand francs all in, for you, your wife, and the little one. I told the consul you're a farmer, that's why he gave me such a good price. Apparently they don't have enough people over there who know how to grow stuff.'

Know what I think, my dearest Renée? I suspect Vagaria dropped a friendly word in his ear – I don't like to use the word blackmail. The visas he got us can't have cost him more than three hundred and seventy five francs, the official rate. He's a crafty one, our Spanish pal. Anyway, he took me straight to the visa office where they greeted me very politely, and promised to get all the papers ready for tomorrow.

As my late grandfather used to say, 'Az es geit, loift es'. Events take on their own momentum! In fact so much so, that we'll have our tickets tomorrow. I went straight from the consulate to the HICEM office, to find out when we might be able to leave. As you know, people usually have to wait for months, but we're still in luck. There's a boat leaving Europe for South America at the end of the month, and there are two places available because someone has been waiting so long she has given birth to a baby in Marseille. The doctor *says she has to stay put for the time being, and her husband is staying with her. So what's unlucky for some ...*

Coming back to poor Schlesinger, he spent all day with a privately hired police inspector looking for the Corsican bandit. Naturally, he wasted his time and his money. But thanks to Uncle Isidore's generosity, once we have paid all our expenses we will still have a tidy sum left, so I will compensate Schlesinger as far as I can. When I told him I would take on part of his loss myself, he threw his arms around my neck and kissed me – though I could have done without that, his breath smells terrible. But it didn't stop him moaning as usual, and stuffing the forged dollar notes into my pockets to get rid of them.

Tomorrow I will try to complete the last formalities and I'll pay Vagaria's commission, as he seems to be in a hurry. He's somebody who goes straight to the takhles: business is business. I'll be back to you with the visas, the tickets and the rest of the money. I can't wait to get out of Marseille, away from the consuls, the heavies, the crooked go-betweens, the ersatz bouillabaisse and the watery ratatouille, which is just about all they serve in the restaurants which are not in the black market.

I hope Jeannot is helping you look after the goat, and you have made some good cheeses. Have you remembered to water the tomatoes?

With my tender thoughts

Bernard

PS To think I owe the whole of this wonderful adventure to the Quakers! If they hadn't taken care of my belongings, it would never have occurred to me to go to Marseille, and so I would never have met Uncle Isidore's messenger.

André Murger quickened his stride. The drizzle, which had taken him by surprise as he left the outskirts of Francheville, had begun to seep through his clothes, and he couldn't wait to change into something dry.

This time, the die was cast. He would take the midday train to Lyon tomorrow, as he had just confirmed by telegram to his friend. It was straightforward, really. Even so, until this morning, he had still lacked the strength to take a decision. Staying on certainly made no sense. But leaving while she was still here, didn't that make even less sense? But then his friend's letter had arrived, settling matters once and for all. They needed him. This time, it wouldn't just be decorating the urinals in Lyon.

The rain began to fall more insistently, penetrating the canopies of the chestnut trees along the roadside. Only another ten minutes' walk. He was already within sight of the bend with the tumbledown shed where Mme Hermelin's farmer sometimes stored his crops.

The rain began to fall in earnest, and André broke into a run to take shelter in the old shack. Inside, he felt a presence. Shuddering, he stood still, holding his breath, and trying to peer through the darkness.

'My word, anybody would think I frightened you,' said a voice from the depths of the building.

It was Solange, sitting on a log, looking at him mockingly.

Murger stammered unintelligibly, and pushed back his dripping hair.

'Poor thing, you're soaked to the skin!' she said, in a tone of false solicitude.

Hurt, he made no reply, but continued to try to shake the water off, while she went on, laughing, 'You look like a weeping willow! Even more than usual, if that were possible!'

Annoyed, André went up to Solange and seized her by the arm.

'Ouch! That hurts!'

'Well, it's my turn. You've hurt me enough the past few days. You never miss an opportunity. Even when you say nothing, you make sure you hurt me by showing you're ignoring me!'

He knew these admissions would make him appear ridiculous to Solange. But so be it! Since he would be leaving tomorrow anyway...

'I don't understand you,' she said. 'And I don't think you know what you're saying.'

She had got up and, turning her back on the young man, she made for the door.

'It's almost stopped raining. Goodbye!'

And she was off, hurrying towards Les Tilleuls.

Murger suddenly felt his anger dissolve. This young woman walking away from him, so distant and inscrutable, would he never know what she really thought? He had fallen for an enigma. Solange Fleury! What a strange girl! He ran to catch her up.

'I'm sorry I was so rough,' he said hoarsely. 'I didn't want to annoy you, believe me. But I'm leaving tomorrow, and we may never have another chance to talk.'

'So?' said Solange, without turning her head. 'What of it?'

'What of it?' echoed André. 'You're right. I'm leaving, that's all. Say farewell, rather than goodbye... but there's so much I wanted to say...' he muttered in a low voice.

She pretended she had not heard the last few words.

'Well, that's ok then. Farewell!'

And without favouring him with the slightest glance, she went into the house and quickly climbed the stairs.

'My poor Monsieur Murger!' cried Mme Hermelin, coming out of the kitchen carrying a little basket of peaches. 'You're completely soaked! You'll catch your death! I'll make you an infusion straight away.'

'Thank you, Madame, but please don't trouble yourself. I'm going to change. Just bring me dinner in my room later, if you wouldn't mind. I have to pack my bags, and I'm a little tired.'

He had made up his mind not to see Solange again, even at dinner.

'Certainly, Monsieur Murger. I'll get Marguerite to bring you a good bowlful of nettle soup – you're lucky, it's the last of the season, as the nettles are getting a bit tough now – a fried egg, and – she took on a gracious air – a peach from my garden. The tree isn't in full fruit yet, and we shouldn't pick more than we need. But our health comes first, doesn't it?'

At half past ten, André was busy transferring the contents of his wardrobe into his open suitcase on the table, when he was startled by a vigorous knocking at the door.

'Come in,' he responded mechanically.

Solange stood in the doorway. She was wearing a nightgown which came down to her ankles, making her look taller than usual. She had a strange look in her eyes, and her lips were trembling. André felt that he was seeing her properly for the first time.

'I can come in, can't I?' she said with a contrived air of assurance, and without waiting for an answer she closed the door behind her. 'Apparently you have things to tell me. Well, I'm listening.'

André stood there in silence, a pile of clothes in his arms. She went to the window, saying, 'Don't you close the shutters at night? I know there's nobody opposite, but I don't like being woken up too early by the sun.'

André couldn't believe his ears. Was it really Solange Fleury, his 'distant princess', speaking like this?

'Why don't you say something?' she asked anxiously. 'You wanted to speak to me. Have you changed your mind?'

Her lips were trembling, like a child about to burst into tears.

'Do you still not understand?' she went on, forcing herself to smile. 'I want to spend the night here... with you... Now do you understand?'

Murger put the pile of clothes down, stepped towards Solange, took her hand, and looked straight into her eyes. Articulating each syllable separately, he said, 'I understand nothing, absolutely nothing. I hope you'll explain all this tomorrow. Now, you look very tired. Go back to your room, and go to bed.'

For the first time, he felt something like pity for her. She seemed at the end of her tether, and her voice was not her own. Neither her voice nor her words. What had happened in the last few hours? Despite the clothes which made her look taller, she seemed as lost and miserable as a child who has been beaten.

'No! Don't send me back!' she cried through her tears. 'I can stay here if I want... if you want. Today I'm twenty-one, I'm not a minor any more.'

'That's no reason to act on impulse. Now calm down and think things over,' he said gently, seeing that she was shaking with silent sobs.

'It's not an impulse. I've thought about it. I'm not a minor any more,' she repeated stubbornly. 'I guessed what you wanted to say to me. And because I... I like you a lot, I thought...'

André took her by the arm and led her to the armchair.

'There – sit down, let's talk as friends.' He drew up a chair, sat down, and took Solange's hands in his.

'You're worried, and you need someone to talk to. Consider me your friend. It's trite, I know, but I mean it. The first day I met you, when you had *War and Peace* in your pocket, I felt friendly towards you. Maybe more than that,' he added under his breath.

Solange lay back, rested her head on the chair, and closed her eyes. Her lips had stopped trembling.

'Me too...' she said. 'I'm sorry I hurt you. I couldn't help it. This dreadful contrariness! I get it from my father. A lot of other things too. If you only knew how afraid I am of being like him! Tell me honestly, am I really like him?'

'Not in the least,' said André vehemently.

'You don't know how dreadful he is! Sometimes I hate him... I've had enough! Enough! I've waited years for this day... It's been sheer slavery! Now I don't have to live according to his theories, his inhuman principles! His tyranny, his idea of discipline, it's been a nightmare! But now it's all over! He's told me often enough that I'd only be free when I reached the age of majority! Well, this is it! I'm twenty-one now. You said you're leaving tomorrow, you'll take me with you, won't you? Don't worry, I won't be a burden, you won't have any obligations towards me... I have a little money of my own. Tell me, you will take me, won't you?'

'Are you sure you haven't gone quite mad?' he murmured.

This improbable situation was rather disconcerting. Only a few moments ago, in his despair, he could have sworn that he would never get a smile or even the slightest sign of interest out of Solange. Now, there she was right in front of him, ready to throw herself into his arms, begging him to accept her, while for his part he was giving her advice like an elderly uncle. It was a rather thankless role; but he felt he had no right to take advantage of her evident confusion. His instinct had not failed him: there was indeed an enigma locked inside Solange, but it was an enigma to which he now had the key.

'Gone quite mad?' repeated Solange thoughtfully. 'Maybe. But anyway, I've made my mind up.'

She rose from the chair, and gave André a hard stare. For a moment she really did look like her father.

'If you refuse to take me,' she said, 'I will go alone. But I am determined to go.'

'Solange, my dear,' he said, sitting her down again, 'that would really put the cat among the pigeons. A dreadful scandal. Unnecessary, too. What would your parents say?'

'Oh, my parents...' she said. 'My father, well, now you know what I think of him. My mother is a decent woman, but she only sees things through his eyes. I hardly count for her. Really, I'm alone in the world. As for scandal, the sooner the better! Then they certainly won't be able to stop me leaving.'

André hesitated, avoiding Solange's eyes in order to think clearly. He felt that any moment now, the elderly uncle might disappear down a trapdoor.

'If you've really thought about what you're doing... to be completely fair to you, I also have to tell you a secret. From tomorrow, my life will not be entirely my own. There are times when you have to take a stand. That's what I've just done. I've made my choice.'

She gazed at him for a long time in silence. Then: 'I know what your views are. I know there are situations where personal considerations have to take second place. I accept your conditions.'

'Very good,' said André, gravely.

He took her in his arms and kissed her.

'And now,' he said at length, recovering his composure with an effort, 'you are going to bed. I'll make it for you. I'll sleep in the armchair, with a chair to put my feet on. It'll be perfectly comfortable.'

She took his hand and pressed it against her cheek.

'Thank you,' she said. 'You're a decent sort.' Then, suddenly changing her tone, 'But I want a scandal. It'll save having to explain. I want to show once and for all that I'm independent now.'

Quickly, she pulled off her white espadrilles, picked up André's shoes from beside his suitcase, opened the door, and placed the two pairs side by side in the passage.

* * *

The scandal at Les Tilleuls took its course as planned. At seven in the morning, following his daily routine, M. Hermelin collected all the shoes left at the guests' doors, attended to them with trembling hands, and returned them to their place half an hour later. Mme Hermelin happened upon him as he was leaving Solange's espadrilles outside Murger's door, and began to reproach him bitterly. 'Have you gone completely senile? What do you think you are you doing with Mademoiselle Fleury's shoes? That's not her room!' The ex-tax inspector protested with all the energy he could muster. That door was exactly where he had picked them up. Just then, the door opened and Solange appeared, dressed in a man's pyjamas.

Mme Hermelin felt herself turn a shade of green. She couldn't breathe. How could he do that to her! Under her own roof! That really was too much! Who would have believed that this M. Murger, for all his apparent innocence, was a seducer, a pervert, a brute, a lecher! And Solange no better than a common whore! The devil was everywhere!

In the meantime Solange, smiling nonchalantly, picked up both pairs of shoes, thanked M. Hermelin graciously, and closed the door.

Mme Hermelin, rooted to the spot, was still staring at the door panel behind which the orgies of eternal damnation had been taking place, when Fleury, dressed in his patent shirt combination and a sheet draped in the style of an improvised toga, emerged from Solange's room, his beard bristling and his eyebrows furrowed into a frown.

'What does all this mean?' he asked, turning to Mme Hermelin. 'My daughter is not in her room and the bed hasn't been slept in. Do you happen to know where she is?'

Like a silent, avenging archangel, Mme Hermelin gestured dramatically towards Murger's bedroom door.

That was the moment when the scandal broke, bringing an unprecedented storm crashing down on Les Tilleuls, and throwing the life of the guest house into complete disarray. A series of violent scenes took place. César Fleury cursed all and sundry in tempestuous fits of anger; his wife kept bursting into tears; Mme Hermelin's lamentations continued in the background. But they were faced with a *fait accompli*. Solange and André took the 11.45 train.

During the afternoon, the storm returned with a vengeance. Mme Hermelin having dared to make a barely disguised allusion to the evils of a non-religious education, Fleury burst into a paroxysm of rage, claiming the landlady of Les Tilleuls was complicit in his daughter's impulsiveness, and accusing her of proxenetism. Mme Hermelin was not sure exactly what the word meant, but she associated it with visions of debauch and apocalyptic lust. 'Proxenetism!' Had she obeyed the commandments of the Lord for sixty-one years in order to be insulted thus? It was so grotesquely unjust that she did not have the strength to retaliate. She simply told Fleury that his family had brought dishonour upon her house, and that he must leave immediately. César did not demur. He caught the train that evening, taking his wife with him.

It was Joseph who had the last word.

'Shall I tell you something? Well, your Fleury, in fact, is probably called Blum,' he said to his mother. 'I smelt a Jewish whiff about him from the start. His vanity, his bad faith – there's no mistaking signs like that. Disgusting! And he thought he could fool me just by changing his name and ranting against people of his own religion!'

Joseph's universe was singularly populated with phantom Jews.

Chapter 7
The Potato Revolt

I

At the Hôtel Panorama, the kitchen was a hive of activity. It was ten in the morning on market day, and Sarzier and his staff were up to their eyes in work. Behind them, the great range was laden with simmering pans, and all the maids were busy round a long table, peeling vegetables.

By the window, Sarzier, who had not yet donned the tall white hat which usually covered his leonine mane of hair, was settling up with Tournier for his latest delivery: sardines, sugar, coffee; all sourced from the stock which the grocer-tobacconist, reluctant as ever to kowtow to the authorities, had laid in before rationing.

Suddenly, through the open door, he caught sight of Vautier waiting, fidgeting with his hat. Sarzier cut things short and dismissed the grocer. He wanted to know if the owner of La Grange had brought him the rabbits and the sausages he had ordered. As usual on a Thursday, the restaurant was fully booked: the regulars of course, plus some of the market traders, three travelling salesmen, and then Chameix, and Longeaud and his friends. But he had to speak to Vautier behind closed doors.

There followed an energetic dispute about the price of sausages, and Sarzier had only just finished settling up with Vautier when his attention was caught by a petrol-fuelled car drawing up at the door. He hadn't seen many of those in the past couple of years. Sarzier left his ovens and hurried to greet his client, who had already got out and slammed the car door. Sarzier stared at him in disbelief. Was it really possible?

M. Prokoff himself, Mme Génia's husband!

It was indeed M. Prokoff, no doubt about it, but what a transformation! Sarzier had first met him, in June 1940, as the rather disreputable-looking chauffeur who had driven that elegant lady back to Paris, along with his wife.

Sarzier prided himself on knowing quality when he saw it. Now, Prokoff was clearly a gentleman. And what a gentleman! A grey suit in the latest style, a gabardine raincoat of a quality you could never get these days, and especially this splendid car! To cap it all, he had the natural assurance of someone who doesn't have to worry about money. Sarzier could recognise people like this a mile off. At lunchtime he would bring a bottle of *Hermitage* up from the cellar. He would serve liqueurs. There was money to be made.

When he found out that his wife was away, Alexandre made no attempt to hide his displeasure. This was a blow he had not anticipated. It meant he would have to write to her, instead of getting things over and done with face-to-face.

However, as he was tired after the journey, he decided to take a bath, shave, and stay at the Panorama until his departure that evening. Sarzier hurriedly prepared Génia's room, which he considered was now free. Génia herself, having abandoned all trace of her former reserve, had gone off for a week with a travelling salesman from Marseille. Sarzier himself supervised the transfer of all her belongings to the attic, as he wished to leave nothing to chance. 'Well! For all her airs and graces, she was just as randy as all the rest of them!' he thought, as he put aside a particularly compromising item.

At a quarter past ten, M. Beer appeared in the restaurant for his breakfast. Sarzier hurried to wait on him personally. He knew how to take care of his best clients. He brought him real coffee, courtesy of Tournier; milk from Vautier; butter and honey from Laffont. It wasn't as if Sarzier had any particular fondness for the Jews. In fact he resented them, for they tended to favour the Hôtel Farémido. But even though he was a multimillionaire, M. Beer did not put on airs. And it was a real pleasure to listen to him talking about the Stock Exchange.

Sarzier's admiration was not entirely disinterested. He had some money to invest, and he was counting on M. Beer for a sure-fire tip.

As the banker ate his breakfast, Sarzier resolved to seek his words of wisdom. M. Beer listened intently, then, with a concerned expression, said, 'In the present circumstances, with paralysis on the Stock Exchanges, I only see one safe invest-ment: the dollar. Particularly because at the moment it is slightly undervalued. We can expect it to go up. Also, as devaluation is just around the corner, it is only the blue-chip investments, in dollars or Swiss francs, which offer real guarantees.'

Sarzier drank all this in eagerly. He would have liked to ask more questions, but as a new arrival was making his way towards M. Beer's table, he had reluctantly to withdraw.

Bernard Bloch, exhausted by the night he had spent standing in the crammed train corridor, shook M. Beer's hand and, at his invitation, collapsed into an armchair.

'Well, what news from Marseille?' asked the banker, pushing aside his coffee cup. 'Have you carried out my errand?'

Bloch handed him the envelope with his tickets inside, let out a long sigh, and launched into a complicated account of his adventures in Marseille. To illustrate his story, he took out of his pocket the bundle of counterfeit notes which the Corsican middleman had palmed off on his friend Schlesinger.

M. Beer was alarmed and indignant by turns. Ah! What a gang of thieves! What are things coming to! Is it not appalling that men of business are at the mercy of such bandits! However he was delighted to learn that everything had turned out well for Bloch, and congratulated him on offering to compensate the victim of the scam.

'The gesture does you great credit, but please allow me to pay you back. I feel rather responsible because I gave you his address as an intermediary. I should have checked his references. I can't forgive myself for this.'

And brushing aside Bloch's protests, he wrote him a cheque for 50,000 francs.

'My dear friend, you are in no position to be so generous,' he said cordially. 'And as for that Corsican bandit, leave him to me. I will not let it go at that. If the police can't find him, I will track him down myself. I'll hold on to these notes, they're such obvious fakes. They will serve as evidence.'

Bloch's admiration for the banker reached a new peak. Not only was M. Beer a gentleman of distinction and integrity, he was also capable of empathy. And to think that so many people claim Jews are constitutionally unable to be generous where money is concerned! One Jew like M. Beer made up for a lot of stinginess.

Bloch thanked the financier profusely, took his leave, and made for the post office. In his bag he had seven thank-you letters, addressed to the seven Isidore Blochs in New York, which he had not had time to post in Marseille. Obviously, six of them would be completely nonplussed at this gesture; but the seventh would know that his nephew, Bernard, was not ungrateful.

Bloch had no idea of the truth. In fact, none of the seven Isidores would have the faintest idea what his letter was about. The money which had come to him completely out of the blue, right there in the HICEM office, was not from his uncle, and furthermore was not intended for him at all. In New York, as elsewhere, Bloch is not an uncommon name, and it happened that the Haitian Pole had a homonym even amongst the refugees living in the avenue Victor-Hugo in Cassis. This latter, who had also applied to emigrate, had been more fortunate than Bernard in contacting his family in America. But he had had the ill luck to be arrested by the police in Marseille before the money for his ticket had arrived. Unaware of any of this, and misled by the fact that the street number had been copied down wrongly, the stranger at the HICEM office had given to Bernard Bloch, of Cassis, the sum of money which his contact had received in America. Bernard Bloch would never know that his good fortune was due not to the generosity of an uncle, but rather to mistaken identity and the fate of one of his unlucky brethren.

* * *

Half an hour later, Alexandre Prokoff, freshly shaven, sauntered on to the terrace of the Panorama and ordered an apéritif. Since the lowly guide had transformed himself into a successful businessman, profoundly committed to bringing Europeans together for mutual economic benefit, he had decided to dump Génia. A man who climbs the ladder rarely keeps the woman who helped him on to the first rung. Alexandre had decided it was time to replace his wife officially with Tatiana, her former employer. Why the devil had Génia chosen this moment to leave? In taking her by surprise at her retreat in Francheville, Alexandre had hoped to get off lightly. Presence of mind had never been one of her virtues.

'So, Monsieur Prokoff, did you have a nice bath?' asked Sarzier, who had come in person to serve this new distinguished client. 'I had some soap taken up to you, it isn't bad, is it?'

'Excellent,' said Alexandre, 'my compliments. You can't get that quality in the shops any more.'

'Well, if you would like to take some with you, it's easy to arrange. The young man who manufactures it is a client of mine. In confidence, naturally.'

And so it was that towards the end of lunch, Sarzier brought Chameix to Alexandre's table. They took coffee together, chatting about this and that. Alexandre, continually on the lookout for a business opportunity, asked the pharmacist about his little enterprise. Chameix, flattered, and graciously accepting compliments which in truth were mostly due to Pinkas, expounded his commercial proposition. Alexandre became more and more interested. He was curious to know the price of the raw materials. Could one get enough suppositories? How much did they cost? What about other types of fat? Glycerine was too scarce, what could it be replaced by? How much did lard cost? Oil? Beef dripping? Butter? In the Francheville area, butter was clearly the easiest to source, even if it was a bit pricey. Alexandre thought for a moment.

'Let's just work out a few figures,' he said.

He ordered two Armagnacs and took a notebook out of his pocket.

When they took leave of each other half an hour later, they already had an outline agreement. Chameix and Pinkas, in their workshop, would now produce soap based on butter, which would allow them to increase their turnover tenfold. Alexandre Prokoff would provide the capital investment and take care of transport. Once a week, a consignment of Francheville soap would leave for Marseille, in a truck belonging to the Armistice Commission, where Alexandre had cronies. You have to keep up with the times, don't you?

II

Longeaud put down his pen and looked at the clock. It was 9.20 p.m. Pleased with himself, he reread the lines he had just written in a thick exercise book which was adorned in flowing script with the title 'Books I Have Read', in red and blue ink.

25th August. Flaubert: *Madame Bovary – Provincial Lives*. A powerful masterpiece, full of drama. The scene in which the author shows us the heroine's visit to the Abbé Bournisien (Part II, chapter 6) is a particularly good example. Emma, in the grip of profound internal conflict, has come in search of comfort from the priest. Total incomprehension on his part. Preoccupied with his own petty concerns, and entirely absorbed in the chores of everyday life, the Abbé lets her leave without realising that he has failed in his duty as a 'physician of the soul'.

Two things are to be noted:

No.1. At critical moments in life, the need for confession is inherent in human nature. Throughout history, the Church has exploited this tendency in order to increase its power. *Cf*: the role of Jesuit confessors amongst the ruling classes.

No. 2. The need to replace those who professionally exploit the human soul with secular confessors, who would be true guides of the conscience.

It was day two of Longeaud's new course of study. It included readings in literature, history, and sociology; works by Durkheim, Marx, Seignobos and Mathiez, and a collection of novels, ranging from Flaubert to Proust. He had worked out the details of his programme with care, and highlighted them in coloured pencil: red, blue and green.

The schoolmaster of Saint-Boniface had given up studying English. Foreign languages were after all only a matter of secondary importance, hardly the way to enrich the mind. History and literature, on the other hand, were full of valuable insights.

According to his schedule, at 9.30 p.m. he was to turn to Durkheim. He had ten minutes to spare: enough for a cigarette and a glass of wine.

At length he opened the book, but then he was distracted by dogs barking in the village. Going to the door, he opened it and looked out, but seeing nothing untoward he closed it again and returned to his seat. Durkheim is after all rather dry reading. The dogs had stopped barking, but Longeaud now thought he heard noises in the schoolyard. He got up, went over to the window, and looked out.

For the last half hour, Amélie Martin had been walking up and down outside the school. First she had waited for Mme Longeaud to go out, and after watching her leave she decided to wait a little longer. She counted to a thousand. Then she went towards the door, but when she was about to ring the bell she hesitated again. She retraced her steps as far as the electrical transformer, then came back into the covered part of the playground ten minutes later. Even now, she might not have plucked up the courage if she had not sensed that Longeaud, standing at the window, had seen her.

Now there was no going back; she had to take the plunge. In any case, if she did not voice her anguish this evening, she would never find the strength.

Longeaud, delighted at the excuse to interrupt his work, pressed her to come inside.

Feeling shy and awkward, Amélie came into the room and loosened her shawl slightly.

'Do have a seat, Mademoiselle,' said the schoolmaster with unaccustomed cordiality. 'What a day, eh? This heat wave, it knocks the stuffing out of you. It's a relief to be able to breathe a little in the evening. I suppose you came to see Madame Longeaud?'

Amélie did not answer. She took her gloves off, then nervously put them back on again.

'She's gone out to see Noémi Sobrevin, who's just had her baby. She seems to have to be present at all the births these days, I suppose it gives her something to do!'

Longeaud's pleasure at receiving an unexpected visitor began to give way to a slight feeling of boredom.

'No, it's not to see Mme Longeaud,' said Amélie with an effort. 'But I'm interrupting you. I see you are working,' she added, gesturing with her gloved hand towards the book open on the table.

It doesn't look as if she's going to leave, thought Longeaud. Well, we'll just have to make conversation.

'Ah, yes, I devote my life to work. I believe we have a duty to continually learn and enrich our minds. So I'm doing a little reading,' he continued with affected detachment. 'There's nothing like literature to open up new horizons...'

He fell silent for a moment. Amélie, her eyes cast down, said nothing.

'But I'm forgetting,' he said, 'I hear you're leaving us. Between ourselves, I think it was bad form on their part to wait until August to tell you your contract wasn't being renewed. But what do you expect of the Catholic schools? As soon as they can dispense with your services, you're shown the door. They don't care. They just expect you to find another school!'

'Oh, that doesn't matter. Other things have changed...'

'Obviously, if you have to find a job in town, you'll find it very different from the country. Especially as rationing is so strict in the towns.'

'Rationing,' she said under her breath. 'If that was the only problem... but there are worse things in life...'

'Oh, but I beg to disagree! Don't underestimate the effects of rationing. It was Marx who proved how essential material factors are in our lives. That reminds me, I mustn't forget to tune in to Lyon at ten o'clock. They're supposed to be announcing an additional wine ration for grape pickers. I'm interested, because I've got a little idea. A friend of mine is a wine grower near Tain. I can get him to take me on as a grape picker, because the secretary at the Mairie is an old acquaintance of mine from the Ecole Normale. Actually I'll switch on now to make sure I don't miss it. Fifty litres of wine, just think! It's not to be sniffed at!'

The wireless came on at full volume, and an explosion of jazz filled the room. Quickly, he turned it down.

Amélie, very pale, waited patiently while he fiddled with the set. It was obvious that he had no idea what she expected of this conversation. But he was about to find out. As long as she could find the words. It would be her last attempt to come to terms with the world.

'It's true they haven't been fair to me,' she said in as composed a manner as she could summon, 'but that's not important. Obviously, it's a nuisance to have to leave the countryside and move into town. But since I came back to live in France, I haven't really been able to settle down anywhere. For me, home was abroad. There, I represented France, I meant something. Here, I'm less than nothing. When I came to Saint-Boniface, I gave up a lot.' She had taken her gloves off again, and stared at her hands, with their damaged skin and broken nails. 'But I thought this would be a place of safety, here in the country... warm... pure... spiritually uplifting, the sort of thing I've always associated with the church... I'm not expressing myself very well... but there's so much pettiness, people whose duty it is to convey moral strength can be so disappointing... when you think how many people put their faith in them!'

'Oh, not as many as all that,' said Longeaud, with a sideways glance at his wireless. 'How many pupils do you have? Thirty, at the most? How do you expect them to keep you on? You were replacing Sister Thérèse, weren't you, and she's coming back, now she's better. And that's even if they all turn up to class! You don't need me to tell you half of them are always away. We're in the back of beyond out here, and even my wife and I have trouble showing there's enough work for the two of us. I had to put six town children on the register, who are only staying in the farms for the summer holidays. Every year when the inspector comes it so happens they are off sick, of course. Just between ourselves, that is. It's my way of making up the numbers. You know how they did it in Louis XIV's time? They invented soldiers' names on the roll to increase the size of the regiment…'

He gave a malicious laugh, pleased with himself.

There was a brief silence.

'If only you knew what I've had to put up with,' said Amélie. 'That stupid woman, that evil Sister Félicie, treated me like her servant. And as for the Abbé Mignart, for all his fine moral principles…'

'The Abbé Mignart is no different from any other priest,' said Longeaud, carefully avoiding the issue. The woman was not going to get him involved in parochial disputes! 'It's high time,' he continued nevertheless, 'that we replaced those who professionally exploit the human soul with secular confessors, who would be true guides of the conscience.'

Amélie's face lit up.

'You are so right, Monsieur Longeaud,' she said enthusiastically. 'I'm a believer myself, but why should we not be able to call on anyone with an open, generous mind, regardless of their religious conviction, when we are assailed by doubt…' Her voice tailed away… 'and losing faith in life…'

'As you say… as you say…' said Longeaud, drumming his fingers on the table. 'The clergy are so narrow-minded! Excuse me, I think the broadcast is starting.'

He lunged towards the wireless and turned up the volume. The voice of the presenter reverberated round the room.

'Now, from Berlin, a report from the headquarters of the Führer. Fighting around Stalingrad intensified yesterday evening…'

'No, that's not it yet… what were you saying… oh, the clergy, well you know…'

'But they are the ones who should be mediating between God and the conscience of Christian people… do they always understand their vocation, do they not take advantage?'

In desperation, Amélie realised that her words were running away from her. Like clumsy toads, they tumbled over each other and fell into a bottomless pool.

'But of course they take advantage! Of course they do!' Longeaud said. 'Look at Abbé Mignart, he knows which side his bread is buttered. As he's secretary of the Farmers' Cooperative, he can make sure Delphine Legras brings him two dozen eggs every week. She doesn't raise any objections, even though she's not even a Catholic. And I'm the one who loses out, because she used to keep the eggs for me. But dammit, it's ten past ten, haven't they finished with their dratted reports yet?'

He turned the knob and looked at the wireless with a worried expression.

'Despite terrorist attacks, production in German munitions factories has increased by…'

'No, that's not it either,' he said, drumming on the table again. 'So anyway, if you want to see Madame Longeaud, I'm afraid you're in for a wait, she'll be some time yet. A new baby in Saint-Boniface, that's quite something!'

'Yes, births… deaths…' murmured Amélie. 'And some deaths are more…'

'If you really want to see her this evening, you could always call round at the Sobrevins'. It's only a quarter of an hour away. And the moon will be up soon. Ah! The local news! Now we'll find out. People think wine is just a luxury, but they're wrong.

It's good for you, it's an essential form of nutrition. Since wine has been in short supply, I've been losing weight! Five kilos in the last year, it's no joke!'

Amélie got up. Her gaze was expressionless. She wanted to say something more, but her words stayed knotted in her throat. Longeaud stood up too, intending to see her out; but distracted by the news broadcast, he stood still, and she found her way to the door alone. She did not look back. She opened the door and went out into the night. The moon was not yet up.

Longeaud listened until the presenter had finished, then looked at the clock. 10.25p.m. Too late to go back to work. He poured himself a glass of wine. No need to go easy, since he was soon going to get an extra fifty litres. He closed the Durkheim book. Definitely too late to go on this evening. And tomorrow he had to give out the new rationing cards, so he wouldn't have much time for anything else. Never mind! His course of study could wait a day or two. His new life would begin on Monday.

III

Noémi Sobrevin was at long last enjoying a sensation of complete euphoria. She had given birth the previous evening and was now resting on her freshly made bed, in the alcove which was separated from the kitchen by a curtain. As it was not drawn, she could amuse herself by watching people coming and going in the house. By the wall, the baby – another boy! – carefully wrapped up in his cot by a neighbour, was sound asleep.

Noémi gave herself up self-indulgently to this delicious state. For the next three days at least, she was on holiday. She could do some reading. Beside her on the pillow lay a popular novel with a garish cover, along with the latest issue of her paper *Arise!* a protestant publication. Well, she had earned a rest!

At four in the afternoon the day before, Noémi – who was never mistaken in these matters – realised that she would be going into labour in an hour or two. She sent the youngest children outside to join Abel and Dina who were looking after the cows in the pasture. Alone with David, who was asleep, she washed her feet and put herself to bed. Shortly afterwards, Elie came back from Tournier's, where he had been to telephone. The news was that they shouldn't count on the midwife, as she had a delivery in town and did not have enough petrol to call in at Les Mottes in the meantime. But in any case, Noémi was no longer a novice.

Between contractions, she remembered that she would need scissors. She asked Elie to look in the drawers, but as he couldn't find them she sent him to borrow a pair from Delphine or the Latières. When he came back, it was all over. And that was exactly when she needed the scissors.

Noémi stretched voluptuously and picked up her paper. In the cowshed, she heard the calf mooing plaintively. It had not been fed since this morning. Never mind, it would wait until Elie came back from the fields! She also heard a chicken clucking in its nest. She should be going to get the egg it had just laid, but so what? Noémi had decided nothing was going to disturb her. It was a day of rest!

There were two knocks on the door, and the tall figure of Tibor Verès appeared on the threshold.

'Come in, Monsieur Verès, come in! Come and look at my new little one. He's a darling, isn't he? He's the image of my Abel when he was born. When Madame Longeaud came to see him yesterday, she said he was a strong little chap.'

'Please allow me, Madame, to express my warmest congratulations on the birth of this strapping lad, and my best wishes for your speedy recovery.'

Noémi blushed with embarrassment and pleasure. Although

this was her ninth child, she had never yet been the recipient of such elegant compliments.

'You must have come for your litre of milk,' she said, in an attempt to find a way of expressing her gratitude. 'But my husband isn't here to get it for you.'

'Oh, no,' said the journalist, 'Please don't worry today, I wouldn't be disturbing you if you hadn't asked me to come.'

Noémi suddenly remembered that it was she who had asked him to call in.

'Oh good heavens,' she cried, 'that's right!'

'But what was it about? I'm all mixed up, since yesterday! Oh yes, that's right, silly me! Of course! I have something for you. Would you believe it, I found a letter addressed to you, inside my newspaper. It must have been Brandouille, the imbecile, who put it there by accident. He'd probably had one too many that day. I'm sorry you had to come over for such a small thing, but I wanted to explain to you myself. I must have had it for two or three days. But I hardly get a chance to read unless I'm lying in. I found it when I opened the paper this morning.'

Seeing the heading on the envelope, the journalist turned pale and sat down, feeling faint. It was the letter he had been waiting months for. 'United States Consulate. Marseille.'

With shaking hands and anguish in his heart, he tore open the envelope and extracted the letter, which read as follows:

Monsieur
Your visa has arrived and your presence is requested urgently at the Consulate Offices, Place Seinos, Marseille.
Signed: Illegible.

Feverishly, Verès read the date at the top of the letter: 17th July 1942. It was now 25th August. In fact, Verès had known for two days that even if his visa did eventually arrive, he no longer had any hope of emigrating. On 21st August the Marseille police had closed the offices of the Emergency Rescue Committee, which had agreed to pay for the Verès' trip. And even the finest visa in the world can only do so much: though it provides right of entry into a country, it cannot come up with the boat fare. Tibor Verès himself could hardly even finance the family's journey as far as the border, which was merely the first stage of the trip.

'As I was saying,' Noémi went on, 'Madame Longeaud came in yesterday. It was very kind of her. I asked her to fill in the form to claim maternity benefit, as I haven't had time to take it to the Mairie…'

As she chattered on, Tibor Verès worked out what must have happened. The letter had arrived in Francheville on 19th July. Brandouille must have brought it up to Saint-Boniface on the 20th. If he had received it in time, say on the 25th at the latest, he would have gone straight to Marseille with his family. They would have had time to complete the formalities and get on their way well before the Emergency Rescue Committee was closed down. By now, they might already be in the United States. His god, Brandouille, had betrayed him. At that moment, the fervent postalist felt his faith desert him.

Tibor Verès was not to know that in fact it was the epic dispute involving the rabbit, the overalls and the bicycle pump, which had resulted in the gates of the New World being closed to him. A few days after the death of Lion, Brandouille had come to Les Mottes determined to get his pump back. Unlike the other day, the filthy mongrel was no longer there to warn that shrew Noémi of his arrival. Screwing up his courage, he had crept round to the barn and had just opened the door when – horrors! – he heard a sound. It was Noémi coming out of the house. Brandouille panicked. He was still carrying the rest of the post for Saint-Boniface: Noémi's paper and a letter for that Jew who made sure that someone sent him something every single day. In haste, he slid one inside the other, and tossed *Arise!* through the open window of the farm, over the dirty nappies which were draped on the sash.

Noémi had not had a chance to read anything until the day after she gave birth. As a result, the summons from the Consulate had slumbered between those inspirational pages for almost six weeks, on the kitchen sideboard at Les Mottes.

* * *

Out in the field, Bernard Bloch, sweating profusely, set down his spray. He had been working all day, and he was shattered. In the morning, he had repaired the cowshed roof which was threatening to fall in, and in order to clean the shed out he had carried all the manure up to the field. In the afternoon he had applied a sulphate spray, using equipment borrowed from Nelchet. He would not benefit from the harvest himself, but what did that matter? He was proud of his potato crop. To the best of his ability, he had fought the drought which had afflicted Saint-Boniface. Having absorbed the country lore that one hoeing is worth three waterings, he had hoed often and his efforts had turned out not to be in vain.

Renée had been scolding him all day for wasting his time on the shed and the field, instead of helping her to pack. For they were leaving the day after tomorrow. But Bernard had not wanted to listen. He believed in finishing a job once he started. Especially one he loved. Working the land was on another plane, more authentic than reducing old bangers to a pile of scrap metal. Long ago, during his year at agricultural school in Poland, he had learnt to love the land. But life does not always turn out as you want it to. Especially when you are Jewish. He had wanted to go to Palestine and be a farmer on a kibbutz, but they wouldn't let him in.

And was he not now being forced to emigrate for the second time? Obviously it was better not to become too attached to the land. Now, for example, if he insisted on staying in Saint-Boniface, the police would come sooner or later to take him off to a concentration camp. It's hard for a Jew to play the farmer. Even with hands like his. Although all might seem well for the time being, a Jew had to be ready at any moment to dispose of all his belongings.

Despite repeating these mantras to himself, he found it hard to leave behind his potato fields, the garden, his animals. He was sorry too to leave this harsh, beautiful countryside, the wild hills topped with ragged clumps of broom and zigzagged around by tracks, the mysterious ravines, the countless little streams which criss-crossed the fields, the woods of pine and chestnut where – he could almost smell them – mushrooms would soon be appearing. He would even miss the taciturn peasant farmers, Nelchet, Seignos, Chazelas, in whose company, for the first time in his life, he had forgotten he was a Jew. Could it be, as Verès said, that these peasants were 'not sufficiently socially evolved' to fall prey to anti-Semitism?

He was woken from these thoughts by the sight of Verès, climbing the slope breathlessly, and clutching a bundle of newspapers.

'Ah! I've found you at last!' shouted the journalist. 'Have you heard the news?' and once beside Bloch, 'Oh, you should see the fuss in town! Everybody's talking about it!'

Bloch stared at him in astonishment. No sensational news had reached Les Ripailles.

By way of explanation, Verès pushed the latest edition of a Swiss newspaper under his eyes. On the back page, a short news item was circled in blue pencil.

SWINDLER INTENDED TO EMIGRATE TO AMERICA
Barcelona, 31st August, from our special correspondent
(I.N.S.)

The Spanish police have arrested an audacious swindler as
he was attempting to board a ship bound for Argentina. A
Czech national named Svoboda, he passed for a wealthy
banker under the name of Beer. He had many victims in
the French Unoccupied Zone, particularly in Marseille. His
arrest took place at the request of the French authorities,
following a number of charges made against him. In order
to inspire the confidence of his victims, which included many
Israelites, he claimed to be a Jew, and it was this claim that
enabled him to benefit from the emigration services. (I.N.S.)

'One of the guests at the Panorama found this in the paper,' said
Verès. 'Sarzier went straight to the bank to check a wad of
dollars Beer had sold him. They were fakes, of course.'

Bloch was thunderstruck. 'Were they indeed,' he said, recovering himself. 'I bet those were the dollars I brought back from
Marseille myself! The scum!'

What a blow! To think he had taken Beer for a nobleman, an
aristocrat of the financial world, an artist in matters of business!
Idiot that he was, he had carried out the swindler's errands in
Marseille when the bogus banker couldn't show his face there,
because he knew he had been found out. No use trying to cash
his cheque: it had no more value than the counterfeit dollars.

But there was one thing above all which Bloch could not
forgive himself for: he had taken the so-called Beer for a Jew.
True, he could recognise Polish and Russian Jews at first sight;
but he lacked the necessary instincts when it came to his co-reli-
gionists from Central Europe: Czechs, Hungarians, Austrians,
Romanians. They didn't speak, behave or often even look like

the Jews he knew. So, he had been royally had. Oh my poor Bernard, you ought to have noticed there was something not very catholic going on, or rather not Yiddish enough. It's cost you 50,000 francs to learn that little lesson, you're lucky it wasn't more!'

They discussed the whole story at length, then eventually turned to the subject of Bloch's departure.

'You must be pretty pleased,' said the ex-journalist, concealing his envy with difficulty. 'When I think I should have been leaving before you!'

'Yes, fate is blind,' said Bloch philosophically. 'But I admit that I'm sorry to be leaving. Things aren't so bad here, I don't mind telling you. I'd have had a good harvest, you know,' he added melancholically. 'I was thinking of leaving it all to you, if you feel up to carrying on.'

'Oh, me!' said Verès, shrugging. 'Agriculture has never been my strong point. I wasn't made for the plough. Whether it's because I'm Jewish, I don't know.'

'Not at all!' said Bloch meditatively. 'Jew or not, you love the land or you don't. To come back to my harvest, I will ask Nelchet to do the work and to share it with you. But if you want my opinion, even if you don't want to farm, you should do a bit of gardening. Put your name down at the Cooperative straight away to get next year's seeds. Anyone can tend a garden, there's nothing to it, and there's so much satisfaction in it! Not to mention that you'll need the food.'

'I'll see,' said Verès doubtfully. 'Obviously, the big problem here in the country is the rationing authorities. I don't know how you manage, but I can't get anything out of them. So the other day I had an idea. I asked my wife to establish some useful contacts by offering to paint people's portraits. Not oils, we don't have the materials, but pastels. As Delphine up at La Barbarie often has butter, my wife went to paint a little portrait.

Nothing too modern, naturally, that would frighten her off. *Ad usum Delphinae*, as it were.'

'So what happened?' asked Bloch, amused.

'Well she didn't have much success, I'm afraid. Delphine and her husband thought the photographer in Francheville made "a better likeness", and didn't ask people to sit for half an hour without moving. For her fee, my wife got six eggs, and that was all.'

'And they probably still think you owe them a favour,' said Bloch. 'If I were you I wouldn't try to swap art for food, and I'd speak to them in a simpler way. You speak French so well that nobody understands you. I speak it badly, but nobody notices.'

'Maybe you're right,' said Verès, a little taken aback. 'I can't expect these good people to follow every meander of my thoughts. But in fact I'm not sorry to be staying here among them. Who knows, maybe it's Providence? At least if I stay in Europe I can keep up with events which will provide me with many more chapters for my *Paradoxes of History*.'

* * *

Never, since Francheville was Francheville, had it been the scene of so many sensational events in the space of twenty-four hours.

Hardly had the inhabitants got over the news of the bogus banker's arrest, than two other dramatic events occurred to upset their mundane daily lives. That very evening, it was reported that Mme Rosenfeld (whom everyone continued to call Mlle Sten) had disappeared. In the afternoon, a 'strange-looking' foreigner with a big leather briefcase had come to visit her at Les Tilleuls, and they had had a long conversation. At dusk, 'Mlle Sten' had packed her bags in apparent agitation and asked Chazelas to drive her down to the station. Leaving the house, she promised to send news soon to Mme Hermelin. In

Saint-Boniface, and even in Francheville, there was much gossip about the reasons for her departure, which looked suspiciously as if she was running away. Joseph Hermelin proposed a plausible hypothesis which everyone ended up agreeing with. He thought that Mlle Sten, although a foreigner, had worked throughout the world as a French spy, both before and during the war. Her visitor must be a messenger from the intelligence services to tell her that the Germans were on her tail. No doubt it was to give herself an alibi that she had taken refuge in the country and agreed to become Mme Rosenfeld.

Finally, the third drama. At dawn the next day, the mutilated body of Mlle Amélie Martin, the teacher from the Catholic School, was found on the railway rack between Denières and Saint-Boniface, where she had thrown herself in front of the train that night. Although it might only be a silly little provincial train, it could kill just as efficiently as a mainline express. Several hypotheses were rumoured immediately, but none of them gained general acceptance. Even those who thought they knew Amélie were unable to account satisfactorily for her desperate act. Not Sister Félicie, nor Rosalie Tournier, nor even M. Longeaud.

Naturally, the Abbé Mignart refused to give her a Christian burial.

IV

In the last few days, Chameix had started to feel anti-Semitic. He had hardly met any Jews prior to the war, and he had no fixed opinion about them. Since then, he had met a few, and Pinkas in particular. Pinkas had come to represent all Jews. And the pharmacist was less and less enamoured of this cunning man with a face like Mr Punch.

Chameix had started to wonder why he still needed the services of this yid. Since his encounter with Alexandre Prokoff, everything had changed. The manufacturer of Pernod and bath soap had found occasional local suppliers of butter, plus a butcher who delivered beef dripping on a regular basis. Business had taken off, and the workshop had turned into a factory, at least in Chameix's eyes. In the courtyard of the house where he lived, in the Francheville suburbs, there were empty buildings next to his room, and no close neighbours. Along with his fiancée and her brother, Chameix could devote himself to his alchemy on the pretext of preparing medicines. M. Astier, the owner of the pharmacy and Maire of Francheville, was absorbed in the affairs of the town, and had blind faith in his pharmacist. He left the entire running of the Croix Blanche to him, and had no reason to complain since turnover continued to grow. It would not have occurred to him to visit his employee at home.

As agreed, Prokoff had provided capital investment, and undertaken the transport and distribution of the product. The Armistice Commission truck, shuttling weekly between Lyon and Marseille, called at Francheville to load up the week's production before resuming its journey. M. Chameix had taken all the precautions necessary to ensure secrecy of manufacture and delivery. Once the goods were in this official vehicle, no inspections were to be feared.

M. Prokoff received 50% of the profit. That was only fair. What was intolerable, was how the rest was distributed: 20% for Chameix and 30% for Pinkas. The same proportion as in the beginning. But what was Pinkas doing to earn it? It was like paying him a pension! Chameix had read one day in the *Signal* that the Jews were all parasites. How true it was! Pinkas was a good example. He put on airs as if he was a big businessman, on the basis that he was more or less the origin-ator of the scheme. Chameix had had enough of this.

The pharmacist, tidying the jars on his shelves, was mulling over all this resentment when the shop doorbell rang. It was Sergeant Auzance coming in.

'Monsieur Chameix, what can you give me for this dratted thing in my eye?'

The sergeant had a stye. Chameix quickly made up a lotion and gave it to him in a bottle, along with copious professional advice.

The till handle turned with a grating sound, and Auzance was about to leave when he had a sudden idea.

'By the way, Monsieur Chameix, since I'm here, maybe you could give me some information. That Pinkas, what does he do exactly? I've seen you together a couple of times?'

For the past few weeks Pinkas had not been among those sending parcels at the post office, and Auzance wanted to get to the bottom of it. He was certainly involved in the black market; but in what way, and how could he be caught? This time Auzance was determined to take no risks.

'Pinkas?' said Chameix, embarrassed. 'What does he do? I'm afraid I don't know.'

'But what sort of fellow is he, really?' insisted Auzance.

'What do I know? He's a Jew.'

'Of course he's a Jew. I wonder why he wasn't on the list from the Prefecture the other day, to be picked up with the others. He should have been on it. Of course in these cases we can only carry out orders... but I wonder whether he's in the black market.'

Chameix was becoming uncomfortable.

'Well, I... maybe he is, maybe he isn't. How am I supposed to know?'

If Auzance pursued this interest in Pinkas, he might uncover their little secret, and he, Chameix, would be the one in trouble. He would end up paying the price for this parasite! That would be the last straw. There was no doubt it was time to get rid of Pinkas. The sooner the better.

'Anyway, if you want my opinion,' he said, 'I don't think he's engaged in the black market. But as for the rest,' he said insinuatingly, 'I wouldn't be so sure.'

Auzance pricked up his ears.

'Ah! I get you! Politics!' he said with a knowing air.

'I wouldn't necessarily call it politics, that might be going too far,' said Chameix. 'But he talks a lot of rubbish. He goes on about what he's heard on the radio. He listens to London all day, like most Jews. Then they all meet up to discuss things. They all get on like a house on fire. He's got friends…'

'Ah! Has he really?' said Auzance. 'Do you know them, too?'

Chameix had let his words run away with him. Since Kleinhandler and the other foreign Jews had been deported, he did not know who Pinkas was in the habit of seeing. But he could not go back on what he had said. He remembered that he had once seen Pinkas in the Café de la Marine at the same table as the old Jew from Paris, the one with the wife who was always making a commotion.

'He's not short of cronies. There's Cahen, in particular. The one with the little grey moustache.'

'Good, good,' said the gendarme thoughtfully. 'So I have to bathe my eye twice a day?'

Despite his stye, Auzaunce was now on good form. His daily summons was on the way.

* * *

Daniel Cahen shrugged in exasperation.

'But I really don't understand why you're asking me about Pinkas. I hardly know him, and we haven't spoken for at least three weeks.'

For the past quarter of an hour, and with all the skill he could muster, Auzance had been grilling the former Parisian sales representative, now a refugee in Francheville. He had come to the little ground floor flat near the Mairie, without warning, at dinnertime, to give himself an advantage. But this insignificant little man was proving a tough nut.

'He's been spouting anti-French propaganda right in front of you!' insisted Auzance. 'Why don't you admit it!'

But Cahen shook his head obstinately.

'And you've been complicit in listening to him, instead of reacting as a Frenchman should.'

'I don't need any lessons from you,' said Cahen.

Since Mme Cahen had gone away two days earlier, following a particularly stormy scene, he had enjoyed a little rest. And now this moron in uniform had come to poison the holiday his Xantippe had granted him. It was ridiculous, as he hardly knew the refugee in question. It would be a good idea to warn him as soon as possible, though.

'That's enough, Monsieur,' he said to Auzance. 'If this is all you have come for, I think we have exhausted the topic.'

Auzance took this badly. When he was engaged in his enquiries, he did not allow the other party to take initiatives. He was there to ask the questions, and the other was there to answer them.

'I have to point out that you are lacking in respect. This could cost you dearly. Be careful!'

'And I am telling you to get lost,' said Cahen with poise, taking a cigarette out of his pocket.

Auzance's bloodshot face turned brick red.

'So that's your tone, is it?' he spluttered. 'Well, we'll see about that. The charge is a simple one: insulting a police officer. But I'll give you one last chance: tell me everything and I will pretend this hasn't happened. If you don't, I can summons you and escort you to the police station.'

'I am at your disposal,' said Cahen, drawing on his cigarette. 'Don't trouble yourself. I hope your chief is there. The more the merrier.'

'You're doing it again!' thundered Auzance. 'Insubordination!'

Auzance's raised voice concealed the fact that he was in a tight spot. This Jew seemed to be taking him at his word. He had no desire to escort him to the police station. He had embarked on this little inquiry on his own initiative, as an amateur, and was by no means sure his superior would approve. He began to have cold feet.

But Cahen already had his coat on. He picked his wallet up from the side table, took out a few banknotes which he placed in the drawer, checked he had his papers, and was calmly making his way out when he seemed to remember something, and picked up a small metal case.

'Right,' he said, 'I'm ready!'

Auzance raised an eyebrow. What was the object the Jew was trying to take surreptitiously? An explosive? It could be. They can make these things very small now. Something the size of a fountain pen stuffed with explosive materials could do an awful lot of damage. The more he thought about it, the more it seemed a plausible explanation. Pinkas and Cahen were in league to manufacture engines of destruction, for anti-French purposes.

'What's that?' he asked in a severe tone.

'Oh just a personal object. A little souvenir.'

'Really? A souvenir? Open it straight away, if you are brave enough!'

'No! Not here. We'll see about it at the police station.'

'We'll see about nothing at all. You'll be banged up for insulting behaviour, along with your souvenirs.'

'Not with my souvenir, I'm afraid. I'd like to see you put that in prison!'

'That's enough!' cried Auzance. 'Give me that thing straight away, otherwise…'

If he brought his chief an engine of destruction which he had discovered, he might be in line for a promotion. For the moment there was no risk, as it wasn't primed. He tried to grab the object. But Cahen sidestepped him, and in a sudden fit of rage hurled the box out of the open window.

Auzance threw himself down on his stomach. He waited motionless for several seconds, anticipating the explosion. Then, slowly, he lifted his head. Cahen was looking at him stupefied; but now he burst out laughing. The gendarme leapt up, put his leg over the windowsill and jumped outside.

The box was there on the grass in front of him. It looked inoffensive enough. On second thoughts, maybe it was not an engine of destruction after all.

Auzance picked it up and opened it. His mouth fell open. Inside the case was a war decoration. Who would have thought it! This rat had the Military Medal!

The scoundrel was right when he said that his souvenir could not be put behind bars. Auzance knew the regulation in question, which specifies that the Military Medal can under no circumstances be allowed inside a prison. If its owner is ever incarcerated, the honour of this most prestigious decoration must be preserved by attaching it to the outside of the cell door.

* * *

At 9.15p.m. Auzance, who had given up on Cahen without even taking him to the station, stood at the door of Pinkas' house. He was accompanied by a colleague; for this time he intended to play it by the book.

He pressed his ear to the door for a moment, then suddenly his expression brightened. The London 'pips' rang out behind the panel – three pips, then a fourth. The broadcaster's voice could be heard clearly over the jamming: 'This is London calling. Here are some personal messages.'

And while certain French people conveyed to others the information that the concierge had a black eye, Auzance turned the key in the lock, entered, and summarily arrested the Jew Pinkas, charged with listening to a prohibited broadcast.

Pinkas protested in vain that everyone in Francheville tuned in to London, but Auzance would have none of it. Listening to Allied broadcasts was strictly forbidden, and he was simply carrying out his duty. Caught in the act, the Jew was escorted straight to the police station.

The next day Pinkas was transferred to Lyon. A few months later, when the postal service was reinstated between the two zones, Chameix received a letter from Pinkas pleading for a food parcel. The stateless individual was interned in the Drancy concentration camp and had just got over a serious bout of dysentery. He asked Chameix to enclose in the package a box of glycerine suppositories.

V

At a quarter to one, M. Longeaud tuned out of Vichy and in to Sottens. In a trice, he was transported to neutral territory. In nasal Swiss tones, the broadcaster announced the latest news of the arrival of Anglo-American forces on the shores of Africa. It was 10th November, and for the past two days M. Longeaud had been following events more attentively than usual. In the playground, the children were letting off steam, shouting at the tops of their voices. Mme Longeaud had gone out straight after lunch to get supplies at Tournier's grocery.

Halfway though the broadcast there was a sharp knock on

the door. M. Longeaud leapt back to the dial of his wireless set and re-tuned to Vichy. Usually he locked the door carefully before listening to 'dissident' stations, so he wouldn't be taken by surprise – inspectors and informers were everywhere. 'Come in!' he cried, putting on an assured voice. Slowly, the door opened. It was Philibert Vautier.

He stood on the step, clearly embarrassed, fidgeting with his cap and nodding his head.

'It's about the potato crop,' he began, taking a step forward.

M. Longeaud gestured towards a chair. The owner of La Grange might be a bigot, but year in, year out, he slaughtered a good few pigs. The supply of bacon and sausages was a factor to be taken into consideration. From Vautier's muddled explanation, Longeaud deduced that matters stood as follows:

In spite of a disastrous potato harvest due to the drought, Saint-Boniface had been required to supply a large quantity to the rationing authorities. More, in fact, than the farmers could deliver. Longeaud knew from his own experience that on this occasion the peasants were not complaining just for the sake of it; for he had been obliged to go to tremendous lengths to scrape together the paltry 400 kilos his household needed for the year.

Rationing had required the farmers to begin delivering the previous week, at the latest. With few exceptions, however, they had actually supplied nothing at all, in the hope that the cooperative's managing official could intervene to obtain a significant reduction. But the newly appointed Director of General Rationing in Francheville happened to favour more expeditious methods than his predecessor, and as a result, Brandouille had that day delivered warnings to five of the farmers, which informed them that they had three days not only to pay a sizeable fine, but also to deliver the whole of their allotted amount, on pain of severe penalties.

Vautier was apologetic. He was very sorry to trouble M. Longeaud, especially at this time of day, but he had decided he must appeal immediately and he did not know how to go about it. Time was short, and M. le Curé was away.

Even if Longeaud had not known that the Abbé Mignart was away, he would have guessed as much when he saw the names of the farmers who were being made examples of. Four of the five were members of the Veterans' Legion, and three of them were devout Catholics. The new Director of General Rationing, who knew nothing of local people, opinions or customs, had not chosen his victims wisely.

'You could appeal,' said Longeaud, scratching his head. 'Unfortunately, it might not work.'

Vautier paled. 'But that's dreadful,' he groaned. 'If I give them everything they want, we won't have enough to get through the winter. What am I going to feed the pigs with? And what am I going to sow next spring, if they take everything? The other four are in exactly the same position.'

Longeaud, for all his worried expression, was privately delighted. Let the regime do its worst with these bigots! They had got away with too much already. It pleased him to see Vautier hanging on his words like a patient waiting for the doctor's verdict. Suddenly, he had an idea.

'Well,' he said, 'since you're all in the same situation, you'll have to take action together. United, you stand!'

'That's what people say,' said Vautier. 'But how?'

Longeaud lit a cigarette, taking his time, and watched the farmer sweat profusely as his mood swung between hope and despair.

'There might be a way,' he said finally. 'Last year, Rationing wanted too many eggs and dairy products from the farms up at Manvin. As they didn't deliver, the same thing happened as now: some of them got fined in order to frighten the others. But they all agreed not to deliver anything until the quantities were revised. When the police and the inspectors turned up to deliver the summonses, they found that Rationing was demanding eggs from farmers who didn't have hens, and milk from those who had calves to raise. That stirred things up badly. The Director of Rationing got hauled over the coals by the Prefecture, and they ended up revising the quantities required. You might like to think about that.'

M. Longeaud's story was true. Moreover, it provided an excellent opportunity both to annoy the Curé and to play a trick on the inspectors.

Vautier's eyes opened wide. 'So we don't have to pay the fine?'

Longeaud made a gesture which indicated 'What do you think?' but he did not express assent.

'I'm not giving you any advice,' he said. 'In my position it's too risky. You will have to decide for yourself. I'm simply telling you how others have managed in the same situation. They got together and said, "Today, it's my turn; tomorrow, it'll be yours." But if you don't want to do the same as them, I can write a letter for you.'

Now Vautier understood. To avoid the fine and reduce the quantity to be delivered, the best way for him, Philibert Vautier, was to persuade the others to back him. He would tell them what M. Longeaud had explained to him: 'Today it's my turn, tomorrow it'll be yours.' The farms up at Manvin…

'Up at Manvin,' said Longeaud, reading his thoughts, 'they all went straight to the Mairie. They got themselves organised, and signed a protest letter to the Préfet. Even the President of the Veterans' Legion branch signed it.'

'Maybe we could that too,' said Vautier, regaining confidence. 'I'll go and get the other four now, and we'll go round the farms. I'll arrange a meeting tomorrow at the Mairie and try to get the

President of the Legion branch to come. Thank you, Monsieur Longeaud, for your good advice.'

Longeaud protested. 'Easy now! I didn't give you any advice. You decide together what you have to do. Above all, nobody is to know that you have spoken to me about this.'

'I understand,' said Vautier, with a knowing look. 'You can count on me. Oh, and I thought you might like this.'

He produced a packet of tobacco and put it on the table.

'You are most kind,' said Longeaud, graciously accepting this token of homage to his wisdom.

After Vautier left, Longeaud felt like shaking hands with himself in congratulation. Wasn't that a masterstroke, pressing Vautier forward for such a venture? One of the left-wing farmers, or even one of the Protestants, wouldn't have a chance. Whilst Vautier on the other hand...

The schoolmaster felt he had discovered a Machiavellian streak in his nature. Carefully concealed in the wings, he could pull political strings in Saint-Boniface, and why not in the surrounding area too? Great things were possible. There is a potato story at the basis of every revolution. Admitted, he was already forty years old, but that is exactly the age at which statesmen begin to make their mark. Now there was action, real action! Not just sterile studies in English, or literature!

He realised it was time to begin his class. He had missed the broadcast from London. Never mind! He had tuned in to the local community instead.

* * *

News of the next day's meeting spread quickly in the village, and even out to the farthest hamlets. Vautier and his comrades in misfortune crisscrossed the countryside tirelessly, haranguing all the farmers over a glass of sharp local wine. 'United, we stand,' Vautier told everyone. 'Today it's my turn, tomorrow it'll be yours.' The peasant farmers, their indignation aroused, agreed to support him.

In late afternoon, when Verès went out to wait for the milk delivery at La Barbarie, he found three of the farmers engaged in animated discussion. The locals were not in the habit of tarrying by the roadside for a lengthy chat, and it was certainly unusual for them to get so heated. But Verès already knew about the potato business, and recognising Ferdinand Blache, the cooperative official, he guessed immediately what all the fuss was about.

Ferdinand Blache, on his way back from Francheville, had been set upon by Jean Nelchet and Lévy Seignos.

'You idiot!' cried Nelchet, 'you shouldn't have let them rope you in!'

'And since you were stupid enough to get involved, you should have just told them to get lost when you saw what kind of dirty work they were getting you to do,' added Seignos.

The official angrily defended his position. Because of his reputation as a socialist, he had been recruited into the local Cooperative as a matter of course. Once there, however, he had soon found himself rendered powerless by the secretary, the Abbé Mignart, and the latter's cronies.

'Told them to get lost?' he growled. 'A lot of good that would have done you!'

'And what good are you doing us now?' retorted Nelchet. 'It was you and the Curé who drew up the list of what everybody's got to supply. You've saddled me with one thousand two hundred kilos of potatoes to deliver, and you know perfectly well I haven't got that much.'

'You have no idea!' protested the official. 'I've even landed myself with more than I can supply. They gave me no choice. There was a fixed amount required from the whole village. The best I could do was to divide it up equally. Proportionally, it's fair. If I'd let the Curé and his pals have their way, the big farms would have had less to deliver, and the small ones a lot more than on my list. As for you, you'd have been stuck with at least two thousand kilos. I had to choose between resigning, which would have pleased the Curé's lot, or staying and saving what little I could. I chose the lesser evil.'

'So now see what you've done,' said Seignos.

'The whole village has to appeal and demand a review,' Blache went on. 'I'm all in favour of that. But in the meantime, I've obtained an official promise that we'll get all the seed potatoes we asked for. I'd like to see what you'd have done in my shoes.'

Seeing Verès pacing up and down about twenty metres away, he took the opportunity to change the subject.

'Ah, Monsieur Verès!' he shouted. 'I've put you on the list for seed potatoes. You'll get fifty kilos for your plot.'

Verès came up to them.

'Thank you, Monsieur Blache,' he said. 'That is very kind of you indeed. So is it true there's a meeting tomorrow at the Mairie about the potato business?'

'Yes, nine in the morning,' said Nelchet.

'So are you all going to support M. Vautier? He's in a very difficult position.'

'It's not about Vautier,' said the official. 'He can afford the fine, with everything he sells on the black market. It's every man for himself. He's right when he says "Today it's my turn, tomorrow it'll be yours."'

'*Hodie mihi…*' began Verès, but he broke off when he remembered Bloch's advice.

'Actually,' said the official, 'that makes you a member of the cooperative, so you can come to the meeting if you're interested.'

Blache had no idea how much pleasure this gave to the foreigner. At last, the locals were letting him in to their secrets! It reminded him of his past achievements as a journalist. What a scoop he would have made of this!

The official took advantage of the interruption to put an end to the discussion. He continued on his way, leaving Verès with the two others.

'So,' said Seignos with a smile, 'you're taking up farming?'

Verès had not met the owner of La Serre before. But he took an instant liking to him, with his honest smile, his direct gaze and his jaunty hat.

'Not exactly,' said the journalist, 'I'm not so wildly ambitious. Just a bit of gardening. You see, when people in future ask me what I did in the war, I'd like to be able to say "I survived." Like the politician who went through just the same sort of troubled period as we are in, and came safely out the other side.'

'Ah, yes, Sieyès,' said Seignos.

Verès stared at him in astonishment.

'You know about the Abbé Sieyès?'

'Of course,' said Seignos, drawing on his pipe. 'The one who said, "What is the Third Estate? Everything."' The journalist's jaw dropped. How could he know that old Seignos was an avid reader, with a bee in his bonnet about the French Revolution? At La Serre, Seignos had a dozen books on the period, which he had read so often he knew them by heart.

Long after he had taken his leave of the two farmers, Verès was still shaking his head in wonderment. These men of the soil! One moment they're talking to you about the ''lectric' and the next moment they're quoting Sieyès. Verès, for all his education, could make neither head nor tail of it.

VI

Just before nine the next morning, Verès left the chalet to go to the Mairie. Passing the Chirolles' farm, where he sometimes went to listen to the radio, he met the farmer's wife.

'Any news?' asked the journalist, as usual.

'You must know already,' the old woman said, 'all the men are down at the Mairie. About the potato crop. My husband's there too. He was going to sow onions for next year, but he's had to drop that. So he's going to be late again, he's waited too long already. He should have done it last month, but with all the chestnuts, you know...'

'But on the radio, nothing of interest?' Verès interrupted her.

'It's always the same,' she said. 'One lot's advancing, the other lot's retreating. They say the fighting's almost finished in Algeria. Oh, and the Germans are everywhere.'

'What do you mean, everywhere?' asked Verès anxiously.

'Well, Vichy, Lyon, Marseille, everywhere. They've occupied the Free Zone.'

Tibor Vères suddenly felt weak at the knees. That was news indeed. The war was entering a new phase. And it wasn't just the war...

'But that's not going to help us with the potatoes,' she continued. 'We've got a three thousand franc fine to pay. Can you believe it! I don't know how we're going to manage.'

Verès left her and walked on, in turmoil at what he had just heard. The Chirolles woman was ridiculous. Concerned only about potatoes and seeds at a time like this!

'But after all,' he thought in a moment or two, 'maybe she's right. However bad things get, you still have to look after yourself. The French do say you have to look after your onions... and your potatoes too, I suppose.'

The meeting had not yet started when he arrived at the Mairie. The big room was packed with peasant farmers on benches, on chairs, and leaning against the wall, which was covered with administrative notices. 'Plenty here for a quorum,' reflected Tibor, thinking of the many occasions when he had attended parliamentary sittings at the Palais Bourbon. At the far end, behind a plain committee table, he saw Longeaud with three members of the town council beside him. Some seats were still empty. Nobody paid attention to the former journalist. Nelchet alone noticed him, and with a friendly gesture beckoned him to a nearby seat.

Suddenly, a door opened behind Longeaud. It was the Maire, accompanied by the Curé and two other town councillors. Everyone shuffled around to make space for them at the table.

'The Government!' quipped Verès, leaning towards his neighbour.

Then the cooperative official appeared. A murmur of disapproval was heard, along with some booing. The potato affair appeared to have seriously damaged the popularity ratings of the Agriculture Minister.

The Maire, a clear-eyed man of about fifty with a rather formal manner, was respected for his wisdom, and never got personally involved in the disputes brought to him. He invited Vautier to present his case.

The owner of La Grange needed no further encouragement. He began to speak rapidly in patois. Verès's face fell. He could not understand a word. But it was not hard to see that although Vautier stumbled dreadfully when speaking French, he was perfectly at ease in patois, and people seemed to be listening to him. He peppered his explanation with a few words in French and ended, adeptly, with two phrases also in French: 'United we stand' and 'Today it's my turn; tomorrow it'll be yours.'

A ripple of appreciation greeted his words. Longeaud was careful to appear indifferent; but inwardly he was rejoicing.

Immediately, Ferdinand Gideaux, the President of the local branch of the Veterans' Legion, took the floor. A burly man with the moustache of a Gaul, Gideaux was a practised speaker and spoke eloquently in French. He addressed his words to the Curé, who had displayed signs of impatience while listening to Vautier but looked at the new speaker approvingly.

'The situation Vautier describes is certainly awkward,' Gideaux began. 'The quantities required are too great, and I myself am having the utmost difficulty in meeting them. But that hasn't stopped me making the first delivery, and I am determined to see it all through. Times have changed. We can't argue with the authorities any more. We have a duty to show we are worthy of the trust our government places in us.

'Remember what this is all about. We are required to supply potatoes for those who are starving in our cities. Some people here today prefer to keep these potatoes for their pigs. I understand them, because these days it's very hard to raise livestock. But that doesn't mean I agree with them. When you think about it, the real question is, do we feed the pigs, or those unfortunate children in the cities? How can any true Frenchman be in doubt? We can feed the pigs anyway, with vegetable peelings and chestnuts. So I'm going to deliver the whole volume required of me.'

'You can talk about volume!' shouted Nelchet. 'You've got plenty of it! We're not all as loud as you are!'

This was greeted with general hilarity. But the President did not rise to the personal allusion, and continued, 'It would be foolish to oppose the government. We would be powerless. What would we do if they retaliated by withholding our ration cards or even our bread rations? Or if they requisitioned our livestock? As for potatoes, we should be glad we're getting the seed potatoes at the official price! Let us deliver what's required, it's a matter of give and take. Let us not duck our duty. We are the conquered nation, everyone has to make sacrifices.'

Some of the farmers clustering around Gideaux showed muted approval, but the remainder of the audience maintained a cold silence. In Nelchet's corner there were mutterings of protest; but the Maire raised his hand to quell them. Verès observed that, as in all parliaments, the farmers of Saint-Boniface had a left wing and a right wing. It seemed to be a law of nature.

It was Blache himself, the cooperative official, who took on Gideaux. He spoke in patois, and Verès could only follow with Nelchet's help. It wasn't a question of choosing between the pigs and the children in the cities, he said. The cities were not short of potatoes this year, because the harvest had been a good one overall, especially in the North. The Francheville area had been particularly unlucky.

'These requirements are unfair, and we want fairness. We have limited resources and we would be mad to waste them. We have to protest to the Prefecture, explain our situation, and request an official review. Let them come and inspect our cellars, we have nothing to hide!'

Tournier, the grocer, fidgeted awkwardly on his bench. This last suggestion did not appear to please him.

In conclusion, the official read out a draft statement of collective protest, drawn up earlier with the assistance of M. Longeaud, and requested that after it was voted on, it should be signed by all those present.

This speech, in which Blache hammered his points home energetically, dissolved the mistrust with which he had been received earlier, and was greeted with shouts of 'Bravo!' Longeaud scanned the reactions of the assembled audience with a broad smile. The Curé looked worried; the President of the

Legion was red-faced with anger. M. Du Chesne, the Master of Rochefontaine, seated near Gideaux, shook his head sceptically. This business did not concern him directly: his land was well irrigated and he could supply the necessary quantities without too much trouble. He would not even have come to the meeting if he had not been personally invited by the Curé.

The success of Blache's proposal already seemed assured, when Lévy Seignos raised his hand to call for silence. His gravelly voice raised to drown out the remaining mutterings, he began to speak in patois; then, after uttering a sentence in French, he gave up the local idiom.

'We came here to take action,' he said, 'not to sign a letter. Send a protest to the Prefecture? Very well. But does our problem come from the Prefecture? Not at all. It comes from Francheville, from the Head of Rationing. This gentleman is being over-zealous; he thinks it will bring him promotion. He doesn't care about us; he thinks he can get away with anything. Well, we have to show him he's wrong, and he can't take us for a bunch of pillocks.' There was a storm of applause. 'We mustn't be afraid to shout, it's the only way these gentlemen will understand. Too bad for the Head of Rationing, if it causes him problems.'

'Stop beating about the bush, what do you want us to do?' shouted old Crouzet, brusque as always. He was one of the five who had received fines, and this made him more irascible than ever.

'Well, here's the plan. Tomorrow, as it's market day in Francheville, we all take our carts down at the same time. We block all the roads, stop the traffic, and then go together to find the Head of Rationing, to demand the immediate lifting of the fines and a reduction of the quantities. If he raises objections, we'll jostle him a little. He's been making fun of us, it'll be our turn to have a laugh at his expense.'

This met with general enthusiasm. That Seignos! No one could beat him when it came to getting his own back on people who put a spoke in his wheel. Go down with the carts, all at the same time, block the streets, stop the traffic, now there was a good wheeze! That would teach him a lesson, that little jumped-up official!

The temperature was rising in the room. Now it's up to the mountain farmers, thought Verès. The schoolteacher and the cooperative official had wanted to obtain redress through due process; but they had been brushed aside.

When the uproar died down a little, M. Du Chesne turned towards Seignos and said, in an ironic tone of voice, 'Yes, gentlemen, let's go. Take the carts? Why not? But why not do something really new while we're about it?'

Amidst a murmur of varied reactions, M. Du Chesne continued, 'I propose that we have schoolchildren with rattles leading the procession. We'll bring cows, with wreaths of chrysanthemums round their necks. We'll get the Salvation Army band to play a fanfare. That'll get their attention. And why not hoist a bull onto the roof of the Mairie, and bring it down with a parachute? We shouldn't be content with half measures.'

M. Du Chesne's cold irony, which bore the imprint of his surrealist past, barely concealed his annoyance. The Master of Rochefontaine didn't like to see the peasants rising up in this fashion. Although he was an atheist, he was in full agreement with the Curé, who had just been listening to him with an indulgent smile. On certain matters, the Château and the altar were in complete agreement.

Seignos stood up.

'That, Monsieur Du Chesne, is a carnival. What we want is a demonstration. It won't be the first time, round here. Sometimes it's gone a bit too far, as well. You should know that, because from your window you can see the ruins of the Château de Beauregard, which the peasants burnt to the ground in the Revolution. The peasants said that the landowners were laughing at them.'

'Is that supposed to be a threat?' asked Du Chesne, cut to the quick.

'I wouldn't dare,' answered Seignos. 'Just a little historical reminder.'

Very unsettled, the Abbé Mignart tried to redress the situation. He only had to be away for twenty-four hours for madness to prevail in Saint-Boniface. If he had been able to talk to Vautier the evening before, none of this would have happened. You can never take too much care of your flock.

'Calm down, my friends,' he said. 'Let us be reasonable. You don't think the gendarmes would turn a blind eye, do you? M. Seignos didn't really mean it. Everyone knows he has a sense of humour. Let's see the funny side, but let's not forget our duty. Pride is a bad counsellor! It's not by some sort of uprising against authority that you can hope to lighten your burden. It is said, "Render unto Caesar the things which are Caesar's." We have to give the authorities what they are due. Pay the fines, deliver the first load of potatoes, even if it seems too much, and then respectfully request a review of the quantities required. That's the best way, believe me.'

But these words, which were intended to appease, had the opposite effect. Pay, deliver, what do you take us for? We'd never get our money back! Nor our potatoes!

Then, in the midst of the hubbub, Nelchet raised his powerful voice.

'Render unto Caesar the things which are Caesar's, Monsieur le Curé? That's what they taught us at catechism. Well, we have to give the Head of Rationing what he deserves, which is a kick up the backside. Not only will we not deliver our potatoes, but we will suspend delivery of everything else too: milk, butter, cheese and all the rest. What do we have to fear? In Francheville there are five gendarmes in total. There'll be a hundred and fifty of us – and that's not counting the cows.'

'And we'll have pitchforks,' shouted old Crouzet.

'And there will be more of us than that,' continued Nelchet. 'The farmers in the other villages are in the same situation as us. They also have fines to pay. So much the better! The more of us there are, the safer we will be. So I propose we alert the other villages straight away. As Vautier says, united we stand. Tomorrow we take our carts down to Francheville. The whole area will be with us.'

By the time Nelchet had finished, everyone in the hall was stamping their feet. 'A born leader,' thought Verès, gazing at his neighbour in admiration. The opposition had been routed. The Curé raised his arms to heaven. The President of the Legion was purple in the face. Longeaud and the cooperative official exchanged distress signals. The movement they had initiated had overtaken them. The schoolmaster felt as if he was sitting on burning coals. That was all they needed, a peasant demonstration, maybe even with physical violence. The authorities would see it as political agitation. And if Vautier was careless enough to tell anyone about their conversation the previous evening, Longeaud would look like one of the main agitators. He wiped his brow. He exchanged a few words with the Curé, left his place at the presidium, descended into the arena, and plunged into the seething crowd to do his best to calm things down.

Verès, watching him, reflected that it was characteristic of all revolutions that their instigators quickly become overwhelmed. Once violence breaks out, the leaders, unable to control events, are usually swept aside in their turn. Saturn devouring his own children. A historical cliché. Indeed, nobody was listening to the schoolmaster's objections. They only had eyes and ears for the promoters of direct action: Nelchet and Seignos. And it was not without difficulty that the latter had managed to calm down old Crouzet, who had worked himself into a frenzy, proposing they head for Francheville without delay, complete with carts, pitchforks and scythes. 'We have to strike while the iron is hot,' he kept repeating stubbornly. At last, after a few minutes of debate, the Nelchet-Seignos plan was adopted almost unanimously, with only a few abstentions. The Crouzet amendment was thrown out by a large majority. 'United we stand!' shouted Vautier, drunk with glory, believing himself the hero of the hour. Indeed, everyone's blood was up, to the point of intoxication. A wind of revolt gusted through the room.

*　*　*

But the potato revolution never took place. In the early afternoon, the Abbé Mignart went to see Vautier, and had a long conversation with him. A father of seven, a well-respected farmer, a good Catholic to boot – could he afford to risk all that on a whim? The reprisals would be terrible. The house and livestock would be sold off, he'd be put in prison. Not only that, but his soul would be in danger. The sin of pride, the spirit of revolt – it was a poor excuse that he was only following the advice of a non-believer. Fortunately it was not too late. Vautier could repent, and deliver what was required. In that case, and in that case only, the Abbé Mignart would intervene in person to obtain a review.

The Curé of Saint-Boniface was used to getting his own way. Contrite and repentant, Vautier hastened to heap the blame on M. Longeaud. The Abbé gave a pinched smile, he had thought as much. Vautier hurried down to Francheville to pay his fine. The three other faithful, carpeted in the same way by the Abbé Mignart, followed his example. Only one remained defiant: old

Crouzet. But one swallow, even armed with a pitchfork, does not a summer make.

The news that the united front had collapsed spread quickly. The next day, most of the carts on their way down to the market in Francheville carried potatoes for General Rationing. The mountain of Saint-Boniface had brought forth a mouse.

VII

Stopping to take a vast man's handkerchief from her bag, Mme Hermelin wiped her steel-rimmed spectacles and blew her nose vigorously.

It was the sixteenth day of November, and according to the cracked sundial on Rochefontaine Château it was three o'clock in the afternoon. Despite this, all the clocks and watches in the village showed five o'clock.

The landlady of Les Tilleuls had just left Delphine Legras' house. She had spent the whole afternoon visiting the main farms around Saint-Boniface. It was for potatoes again; but this time Mme Hermelin didn't want to buy them, she wanted to sell them. Having inherited Frank Rosenfeld's crop, she had sixteen sackfuls to dispose of. This was an inheritance without a will, as Rosenfeld had sent no news since his arrest on his wedding night. And in spite of her promise, his wife had not written either. Admittedly, following her sudden departure after the arrival of the mysterious stranger, the rent had been paid up to the end of the month; but the landlady of Les Tilleuls considered that she was entitled to at least three months' notice.

From time to time she wondered what had become of M. Rosenfeld. He could get a bit carried away, but he didn't really mean any harm. Although he had let her down over the cow. And she had still not forgiven him for using her private bathroom.

Nevertheless, Mme Hermelin hoped nothing serious had happened to him. Maybe Joseph was right, and he had been repatriated to his native country. Mme Hermelin prayed that the Lord might continue to protect him, even though he had put his conversion off for too long. As a good Christian, she wished him well. However, if he had returned to Saint-Boniface unexpectedly, she would have found herself in an awkward position. Partly because of the chickens and rabbits he had left behind, but mainly because of the potatoes. He had planted a lot, and his crop had been pretty good in spite of the drought. But once they had been sold, or bartered, he could hardly hold her to account; especially as at the official price they were worth just about the same as what he owed her, plus the days of harvesting she had had to pay for.

In short, the landlady of Les Tilleuls had decided to dispose of the potatoes. But the Saint-Boniface bumpkins were not easy to do business with. When she had offered them to Noémi, the silly goose had thought she was offering her charity. As for Vautier, it was impossible to tell if he was saying yes or no. He might make her wait for weeks. Seignos was just about prepared to take the lot, at the official price, but Mme Hermelin wanted bacon and sausages as a bonus. From Delphine, she wanted regular deliveries of milk and butter, but the butter was already promised months ahead to the daughter in Saint-Etienne.

Leaving the track from La Barbarie to join the road, Mme Hermelin made a big resolution. The very next morning, she would go down to Francheville to make a proposal to Sarzier. Obviously, it was repugnant to have to do business with this dishevelled, red-haired Antichrist; but you have to make allowances in life, don't you? At the same time she would call in at the Croix Blanche to buy that bottle of the Abbé Soury's Elixir of Youth which she had yearned so long for.

Suddenly she came to a halt, and looked around with a frown. She was on the point of squatting down when she saw a wheelbarrow appear at the bend, followed by a tall young man pushing it. It was Verès, accompanied by Zette, and his wife, who was herself pushing a pram. The wheelbarrow was piled high with suitcases, and perched regally on top of them were an easel and a Norwegian casserole.

'My goodness, Monsieur Verès, are you moving house?' asked Mme Hermelin curiously.

Verès stopped, wiping his brow.

'My respects, Madame,' he said, with a ceremonious bow. 'Yes, we are moving. We're going to live in Bloch's old house, at Les Ripailles.'

'Really? Will you be more comfortable there?' asked Mme Hermelin.

'Definitely. Even though it's further from town, and from the post office in particular,' said the journalist. 'Anyway, M. Vautier wants his chalet back.'

It was true. Vautier had come to the conclusion that the Verès family, being increasingly short of cash, were no longer a viable proposition. What was more, the dispute with La Bardette had cost Vautier almost a year's rent in legal fees, and he blamed the tenant, whom he held mainly responsible. He calculated that it would be more cost-effective to use the chalet to house the billy-goat he had raised that summer; so the building would revert to its former use. With the increase in prices, he could get ten francs for every kid. And there was another benefit: he had just bought a small hand mill, which he could set up secretly in the upper floor to grind his wheat, as well as that of his neighbours. In exchange he would keep a portion of the flour and all the bran. As the two mills in Francheville were now under very close official scrutiny, he would certainly find plenty of clients. All in all, he would be able to raise two more pigs at no extra cost to himself, and considering the price of bacon…

'At Les Ripailles,' Verès said, 'we'll be right beside the forest and we'll be able to collect as much firewood as we want. In the winter, that's quite a saving. Monsieur Du Chesne is a real gentleman, and he gives sound advice. So I've decided to take up gardening. It's so easy, and it provides such satisfaction! Really I'm only following in the footsteps of Candide.'

'That's if they let you,' said Ellen, disconsolately. 'I'm afraid you're letting your optimism run away with you again.'

'I'll come to visit you in your garden one day,' said Mme Hermelin mincingly. 'But I must leave you now, I'm late.'

She set off again, jangling her keys. Suddenly, she heard the racket of a motorcycle, which quickly passed her on the road. It must be the new electricity meter reader – she just had time to see his leather jacket.

The motorcyclist disappeared into the distance and Mme Hermelin looked round her once more. Nobody in sight. There was a bend in the road a hundred paces away, but what of it? She'd have time! But just as she was rearranging her skirt she was startled by a cracking noise coming from the bushes at the side of the ditch. A moment later M. Longeaud appeared, his hair dishevelled, his cheeks scratched by the brambles and his clothes soaked up to the waist.

Looking around furtively, he pointed in the direction of Francheville, where the motorcyclist was no longer to be seen, and asked hoarsely, 'Who was that?'

In his discomfiture he had forgotten to greet the retired tax inspector's wife.

'The new electricity meter reader. Do you not know him?'

'Oh, only him,' said the schoolmaster.

He was relieved, but also somewhat ashamed of having taken fright. Earlier, at school, while he was holding forth on the perils of alcoholism, he had heard the sound of an engine. Looking out of the window, he had seen a man in a leather jacket. This form of dress was very unusual in Francheville. It could only be an inspector from the Vichy special branch. He was there to arrest him, no doubt about it. This was where that damned potato business had got him!

With no time to waste, he broke off his lesson in mid-sentence and, to the astonishment of his pupils, jumped out of the window into the garden. As if the devil was on his heels, he plunged through the clump of broom and tumbled down the slope at high speed.

At the bottom of the hill he had stopped to catch his breath. But hearing the motorcycle, he realised he was not yet out of danger. The man had not found him at the school, so he had set off on the road after him. He only just had time to dive into the ditch to escape him.

But it was only the new employee of the Vercors Electricity Company. M. Longeaud hadn't seen him before.

'Well,' he said, to change the subject, but a few months behind current events, 'I suppose you're looking for potatoes for your guests.'

'No, no,' said Mme Hermelin, 'they've all gone now. My last client left a fortnight ago. And I can't tell you how glad I am! What a lot of trouble they've been this summer, and what ingratitude!'

'But you were not unhappy to have your tenants. Like Monsieur Fleury...'

'Oh! I don't want to hear that name ever again, I beg you. I'd rather deal with the Jews. They're not all bad, whatever people say. But what I don't understand is that they are never completely in order with the authorities. Strange, isn't it? But anyway, all's well that ends well. Everyone is back where they belong, and that's best for us all. There are no foreigners left in Saint-Boniface, apart from poor Monsieur Verès who's going to live up at Monsieur Du Chesne's. But it's a bit far away, so we won't see much of him. At last we are left to ourselves!'

In the distance, a faint roar of engines could be heard coming from Francheville. It increased quickly in volume, and a minute later two open-backed trucks packed with German soldiers – the first to be seen there – hurtled past Mme Hermelin and the schoolmaster, heading at top speed for the Mairie at Saint-Boniface.

Biographies of Ladislas and Nathalie Gara

The Garas in Paris and the Free Zone

Having emigrated from their countries of origin in the 1930s because of restrictions on the number of Jews allowed into the universities, Ladislas Gara and Nathalie Rabinowicz met at the Sorbonne in Paris, as students of French and Philology. On completion of their studies, he scraped a living as a journalist and she translated romantic novels. Their combined language skills included German, English, Hungarian, Polish, Czech, Russian and Hebrew. Nathalie and Ladislas belonged to a cosmopolitan left-wing intellectual group which included the writer Arthur Koestler and the economist Raymond Aron. Ladislas began to devote much of his time to the translation of Hungarian poetry into French. At the outbreak of war he attempted to join the French army – possibly the Foreign Legion, as he was not naturalised French – but was turned down. Then, as the Germans advanced, he decided that the family would have to leave Paris. Eventually, they reached Oradour-sur-Vayres, where they were taken in as guests by a pharmacist friend.

The family then made plans to leave for America, to join other members of the Gara-Goldmann and Rabinowicz-Levinski families. For this, they first had to move to Marseille in order to follow the necessary, tortuous, administrative procedure. Ladislas and Nathalie picked up many anecdotes and stories from fellow-supplicants queuing in front of a variety of institutions, and it was at this time that they began to conceive the book that would later become *Saint-Boniface et ses Juifs*. The tale of the Seven Isidores for example, however fantastic it may seem, is based on real stories from this period. Their efforts to emigrate, however, were in vain.

From 1941, Jews became subject to increasingly systematic persecution. Seeking greater safety, Nathalie took her daughter to live for a time in a children's home in the department of the Creuse, which was sheltering a number of young German Jews. Shortly after the Garas left, the entire colony at the children's home was arrested and deported by the Nazis. With the help of a young Dutch woman, the family then moved from the south of France to a small village in the Ardèche, which is still a very isolated, rural part of France.

But it was not enough. After the great round-up of August 1942, which echoed the round-up of the Vélodrome d'Hiver in July of that year, it was clear they would have to go into complete hiding. With a guide, and under cover of darkness, they eventually found themselves in a supposedly uninhabited house in the tiny village of Balaron, in the care of brave but wary country people, on condition that they would not go out in daylight and not allow telltale smoke to escape from the chimney. Their daughter was looked after in a farm a few kilometres away, did not go to school and, when not reading the only book in the farmhouse, the Bible (for the farmers were Protestants), tended the goats. For some time Ladislas and Nathalie were entirely cut off from the world; but they began to think more and more that the experience was worth recording in a novel.

From the middle of 1943, the family lived in a little house in the centre of the village. Ladislas joined the resistance movement, which was particularly active in the Ardèche.

At the end of the war, they returned to Paris, but with nowhere to live. As there was a severe lack of housing, they stayed for months in shabby hotels. But Ladislas and Nathalie found work at the International News Service, run by an old friend, Paul Winckler. They were also commissioned by Les Editions du Bateau Ivre to translate one of the earliest first-hand accounts of Auschwitz, written by Olga Lengyel. This appeared in French as *Souvenirs de l'Au-Delà*. However it was many years before the importance of accounts of this sort was fully recognised.

Publication of *Saint-Boniface et ses Juifs*

Now Ladislas and Nathalie returned with renewed enthusiasm to the novel which they had sketched out during their enforced stay in the Ardèche. Their aim was to counter the heroic tone of contemporary media coverage, and portray the ephemeral phenomenon of the 'Free Zone' in a humorous light. At the same time, they wanted to break the taboo of silence surrounding organisations and individuals who had played unwonted or ambiguous roles during these complex events. Although it was a brave project, perhaps even a foolhardy one in this immediate post-war period, Les Editions du Bateau Ivre supported it.

They started by writing a synopsis, as if it were a film script, bouncing ideas off each other and noting the best ones. Ladislas contributed the overall shape, situations, and characters; Nathalie reviewed the structure of the book, eliminated contradictions and proposed new links and poignant details. It was truly a book written in partnership.

On publication, it was widely reviewed in France and abroad. Ladislas had a knack for amusing publicity, including a (somewhat exaggerated) story of the manuscript being eaten by a goat, and these anecdotes published in the press contributed to sales, leading to the book being submitted for the Grand Prix de l'Humour, a prestigious award at the time.

However, not everyone – even those with good intentions – understood the book. Some thought it was a purely comic work, with harmless puppets as characters. It was not really published at the right time: in one sense it was too late because in 1946, after years of stress, the French wanted to open a new chapter in their history, and consign the recent past to silence. In another sense, it was too early: more complex historical analysis was to come only later.

The first edition quickly sold out; but as paper was in short supply a reprint was postponed. The Garas' proposed sequel,

L'Apocalypse à Saint-Boniface was also postponed as Ladislas began to turn his attention back towards his native country. Although a draft of this sequel was written in the end, the manuscript has been lost.

After the War

Ladislas Gara then worked for two years as a journalist in France, and was on the point of being appointed the official French correspondent for Hungary, when he became involved in a series of cruel and absurd political developments in his native country, and a victim of Stalin's paranoia. Recalled to Budapest in 1952, he was prevented from leaving until 1955. At the time, all everyday family matters – travel, schooling, bank accounts – required the husband's authorisation, and in order to become legal head of household, Nathalie was obliged to divorce him. It was an irony worthy of *Welcome to the Free Zone*. After these three years of semi-arrest, Ladislas returned to Paris and to his family, a changed man.

Ladislas was still determined to play a role in the literary links between Hungary and France. He threw himself into an ambitious project to produce an anthology of Hungarian poetry in French; developing, in the process, a new approach to translation. This involved, first, delivering to well-known French poets (many of whom were involved in this huge work) a rough literal translation from Hungarian into French; secondly, a repeated recitation of the poem to 'train the ear' of the poet; and thirdly a more sophisticated version in French, produced by the French poet himself. The method, known as 'Garaism' in Hungary, was controversial; but this anthology set the tone for others to follow. However the cost of paying the poets and a number of secretaries ruined Ladislas. The project had brought him more in the way of trouble than financial gain, as he no doubt knew it would.

At the age of sixty-two, Ladislas, evidently considering that he had fulfilled his mission, and in full possession of his faculties, chose to end his life. On the evening of 9th May 1966, he put Mozart's 40th Symphony on the record player, and took an overdose of sleeping pills. A letter written beforehand, explaining his reasons, was given to the police and appears to have been lost. A large number of the French and Hungarian literary intelligentsia – including some who should perhaps have come to his aid earlier – attended his burial at Bagneux cemetery. A rabbi mysteriously appeared and made a short speech.

Nathalie was greatly distressed at her husband's death and sought comfort in her family. Retired from the International Chamber of Commerce, she received a pension from Germany for persecution suffered during the war – a pension which Ladislas himself obstinately refused to accept, even though it would have helped him greatly. She continued her translation work, chiefly from English to French, and died at her daughter's house, eighteen years after her husband, beside whom she is buried.

Ladislas Gara and his work have recently undergone a remarkable revival, especially in the ex-Soviet countries. With much effort, his personal archives have been repatriated to Hungary and are now recognised by researchers as providing invaluable information on intellectual life in Eastern Europe. This novel, sadly the only one, written with his wife Nathalie, was reprinted in France in 1999, with a preface by the renowned novelist Georges-Emmanuel Clancier. This translation into English, with its accompanying notes, is proof that there is indeed life after death.

Translation by Bill Reed from notes supplied by Claire Gara-Meljac

Ladislas (Laszlo) Gara: b. Budapest 1904 – d. Paris 1966
(original family name Goldmann)

Nathalie Rabinowicz-Gara: b. Warsaw 1905 – d. Paris 1984
(original Hebrew name Tauba Nechuma)

Translator's notes

Acknowledgements
I would like to thank Kate Webb and Markus Stückelberger for introducing me to the book and its background, and for their many suggestions for narrative and dialogue; Claire Meljac for her enthusiasm; Martha Pooley of Hesperus Press for her understanding, reactivity and pragmatism; and Sharon Nolan for her support and patience.

Welcome to the Free Zone
In translating this book, which falls between fiction and non-fiction, I have discovered a cornucopia of references and allusions which it would be too distracting to include as footnotes. The interested reader will be able to follow up biblical, historical and literary references; but here are a few quirky items it would be a pity to miss.

The Names
It is clear that the Garas had fun with names. In 2, III Rosenfeld suggests that Mme Hermelin should call him simply 'Rose'. The writers must have had *Romeo and Juliet* in mind: 'What's in a name? That which we call a rose / By any other name would smell as sweet.' The character Robert Auzance was inspired by an officious gendarme who interrogated the Gara family in the village of Auzances, in the Creuse. His name contrasts ironically with *aisance* – comfort. The postman Brandouille's name suggests *bredouille* – coming away empty-handed, as he does in the bicycle pump incident – and *bredouiller* – the stumbling speech of the drunkard he is. Verès has truth and honesty. La Bardette suggests *ça va barder* – 'there's going to be trouble'. The name of Chameix – who has never met a Jew before – is a term for a rabbi's assistant.

Other allusions are also not as random as they might seem. In 1, 1 Mme Hermelin puts an advertisement in *Le Nouvelliste*. Using what appears to be an invented name, the Garas have actually chosen Haiti's oldest-established newspaper. It comes up again, appropriately in association with Bloch, in 2, IV. Bloch moves to *Les Ripailles* which sounds like a random place name, but is an expression meaning 'feast' or 'blow-out'. In 3, VII Mme Hermelin is given a choice of bottled spring water from four commercial sources: Vichy, Pestrin, Vals and Moïse. The last three of these are local to her in the Ardèche; Vichy, ironically, is the odd man out.

The song *Gloomy Sunday* merits a mention. It is quite possible that Ladislas himself had published an article about it, as it was composed in Paris by his compatriot Rezsö Seress in 1932. Billie Holiday's version, released in 1941, was nicknamed *The Hungarian Suicide Song*. Amazingly, it remained banned by the BBC until 2002. The singer Björk performed a version of it at Alexander McQueen's funeral in St Paul's Cathedral in 2010.

The Lambeth Walk, mentioned in 6, III, was also in the news at the time. In 1939, the Nazi Party described it as 'Jewish mischief and animalistic hopping'. In 1942, Charles Ridley of the British Ministry of Information made a propaganda film, *Lambeth Walk – Nazi Style*, which featured footage of Hitler and German soldiers edited to look as if they were dancing to the music. Joseph Goebbels was apparently enraged.

Visual References

In 4, VI Verès accidentally discovers Mme Clips' stash of cigarettes: 'Fifty or more packets of Balto, Naja, Vizir, Salammbô and Gauloises displayed on a red velvet dress, as if they were jewels in a casket.' These were real brands, and readers would have seen, in their mind's eye, that the images on the packets symbolised Mme Clips' background, current location and future destination. *Naja* are 'goût oriental' and have Cleopatra and the asp on the design. *Gauloises* are French. *Balto* are 'goût américain' and the picture on the packet depicts the cigarettes as Manhattan skyscrapers. With *Salammbô*, the Garas manage to connect Flaubert, Carthage and Hannibal with Saint-Boniface.

In 5, VI Blanche Fleury pays off Génia with a banknote which symbolises Génia's romantic dreams: 'In the background, as a setting for the symbolic figures, was a château. Just like in the fairy stories...' The early 1940's 100 Franc 'Sully' design shows an idealised – inaccurate – picture of the Château de Sully in the background of a bucolic scene. The reader would therefore have known what Blanche considered the appropriate amount – enough to get rid of her, while still expressing disdain. The château theme is also an ironic link to Fleury's setting of Rimbaud's poem '*O saisons, ô châteaux*' which is about male seduction and abandonment.

Saint-Boniface?

Finally – and to return to the beginning – why Saint-Boniface? For a start, it's a welcoming sort of name – as Bloch remarks. It begins with a B, as does its likely model, Saint-Basile near Lamastre (Lamastre itself has a lot in common with Francheville). Saint Boniface himself, though born in Britain, is a patron saint of Germany, which is irony enough. One of the symbols associated with him is a book and pen; another is a sword piercing a heart (he was put to death by a band of pagans). There is no Saint-Boniface in the Michelin gazetteer of France.

Bibliography

Callil, Carmen, *Bad Faith: A Forgotten History of Family and Fatherland*, Jonathan Cape, 2006

Gildea, Robert, *Marianne in Chains: In Search of the German Occupation 1940–1945*, Macmillan, 2002

Horne, Alistair, *Seven Ages of Paris: Portrait of a City*, Macmillan, 2002

Jackson, Julian, *France: The Dark Years 1940–1944*, OUP, 2001

The Fall of France: The Nazi Invasion of 1940, OUP, 2003

Judt, Tony, *Postwar: A History of Europe since 1945*, Pimlico, 2005

Vinen, Richard, *The Unfree French: Life under the Occupation*, Penguin, 2007

HESPERUS PRESS

Hesperus Press is committed to bringing near what is far –
far both in space and time. Works written by the greatest
authors, and unjustly neglected or simply little known in
the English-speaking world, are made accessible through
new translations and a completely fresh editorial approach.
Through these classic works, the reader is introduced to the
greatest writers from all times and all cultures.

For more information on Hesperus Press, please visit our
website: **www.hesperuspress.com**